SCORING
THE *Princess*

SIENA TRAP

Foreword

A comprehensive list of trigger warnings for those who need them can be found on my website: www.sienatrapbooks.com

This one is for all the girls who thought they found the one, only to discover they were wrong.

Mr. Right is waiting for you just around the corner, I promise.

Andy, thank you for waiting around the corner for me.

CHAPTER 1

Natalie

It was done. The papers that would legally set me free from a ten-year marriage were officially signed. The truth was I would never be free; I'd only been granted a slightly larger cage. The choices I'd made at eighteen years old would define the rest of my life, as well as my children's.

The course of my life changed when I had been swept off my feet by a real-life prince at sixteen years old. Prince Leopold Arthur George Remington—of the tiny European nation of Belleston, nestled in the Alps between Italy, Switzerland, and Austria—had charmed the pants off me during a summer vacation in the Caribbean, and I hadn't known what hit me. Leo, as he was known, was second in line for the throne—behind his father—and would someday become the King of Belleston.

Marrying a prince was every teenage girl's dream and, for a while, it had been the fairytale the world expected it to be. Without warning, it had turned into a nightmare, and I'd found myself fleeing the country with our three young children in the dead of night, back to my hometown of Hartford, Connecticut.

A voice cut through the haze to my left. "Ma'am?"

Lost in thought, I pondered the consequences of closing this chapter of my life when someone on my right gently touched my arm, causing me to flinch. That was my auto-response when touched without warning—another souvenir of my marriage to Leo.

Brought back to the present, I remembered where I was.

Private conference room.

Lawyers.

Divorce papers.

Feeling the heat creep into my cheeks, the words rushed out of my mouth. "I'm sorry."

My lawyer smiled a sad smile. I couldn't imagine doing his job, watching as families fell apart and assets divided. It was hard enough experiencing it this once.

Gathering the papers in front of him on the conference room table, he stood. "I'll have these filed and send copies for your records."

Nodding, numb from everything that got us to this point, I replied, "Thank you."

Stonecrest Palace, located in the capital city of Remhorn, had been my home for the past decade. The richly appointed walls surrounding us had borne witness to hundreds of years of Bellestonian history. My failures were now a black mark on the illustrious legacy that was the House of Remington.

Leo would now be the first monarch to take the throne after a divorce. I wasn't naive enough to believe every marriage in this family's centuries-long history was perfect, but they found ways to stay together. Whether that meant living separate lives or finding new companions, I didn't know, but I couldn't stay here one minute longer. Life with Leo made me fear for my safety, and protecting my children was well worth the cost of leaving.

I remained seated as the lawyers filed out, leaving my now ex-husband and me alone in the room. I went to great lengths over the past few years to avoid situations such as this one. Without witnesses, Leo was at his most dangerous.

Neither of us was the same person we were when we had gotten married.

Entering our marriage, I had been young—too young—idealistic, and enthusiastic at the prospect of making a difference in the world. My whole future had been in front of me. That future suddenly changed when I was dealt not just one, but two teenage pregnancies, thus ending any hopes I might've had of continuing my education. Falling instantly in love with my babies, I hadn't mourned the loss of that path.

What I hadn't realized was that my wings had been clipped long before then.

Leo had been so charismatic, instantly drawing me in with his personality and blond good looks. He'd been groomed for public life and was an expert at putting on a public show. Appearances were of the utmost importance. He had demanded perfection of me, requiring I be the ultimate accessory by his side for the rest of our lives. When I had buckled under the pressure, he turned on me, letting me know exactly who was in charge of my life.

Spoiler alert—it wasn't me.

Leo folded his hands on the table, his demeanor as calm and calculated as ever, as he addressed me for the first time since we entered the room. "Are you happy now, Natalie?"

Could he have asked a more loaded question?

Was I happy that my children had become an inconvenience to their father?

Was I happy that when I'd left two years ago, I had spent countless nights awake, scared he'd come and demand that his children be returned to their rightful home?

Was I happy that my life had crumbled around me to the point where I no longer recognized myself?

Leo had spent years breaking my spirit, my sense of self-worth, and any semblance of my identity. I wasn't sure if I would ever feel *happy* again.

Leveling him a glare from across the table, sarcasm dripped from my words. "Fucking thrilled, Leo. What do you want me to say?"

He shrugged, appearing bored in his three-thousand-dollar navy suit. "You got everything you wanted." When I merely scoffed in response, he got slightly more aggressive. "What more do you want from me? You have full custody of the children, and you've taken enough money from me that you'll never have to work a day in your life."

Of course, he would mention money like that had been my only objective in obtaining this divorce. I didn't want his money, didn't want him thinking I owed him anything. I had a trust fund from my parents and could have taken care of the kids comfortably with those funds, but my in-laws insisted on a lump sum as part of the settlement. My children were their future, after all.

The only thing I cared about was my kids—nothing else mattered. Leo gave me custody of them so easily that it almost felt like a trap. That's how it worked with Leo. He made you believe you were in control until he flipped the script, showing you he'd been pulling the strings all along. The last ten years under his thumb would leave me wary for the rest of my life.

Deciding to poke him a little bit to confirm that he never really cared about me—or our children—I responded, "What more could I want? Let's see . . . A father—or *husband,* for that matter—who cared enough to find out why we left and tried to make it right. To fight for us."

"You were acting like a child, Natalie. I was not going to indulge you in the costly game of hide-and-seek you were playing."

This was what I came to expect from Leo after ten years together. Every single issue was turned around on me. I wasn't allowed to have emotions or even an opinion on matters in my own life.

How many times had he told me that I chose to live this life? That I should be grateful to be at his side, a princess and future queen?

When I didn't respond immediately, he continued, "I have responsibilities here. I can't just abandon them when my wife decides to be dramatic. You've always known that. I don't get to do what I want to, like Liam."

Ah, Liam.

I was wondering how long it would be before he threw that in my face. His younger brother, Liam, took a liking to me very early in our marriage. He was much closer to my age, being only two years my senior compared to Leo's five, and immediately took me under his wing, protecting me in any way he could. He granted me the same protections as their own little sister, Lucy. When I left, he not only supported me, but dropped everything in his life to move in and help me with the kids, becoming the most stable male presence in their lives.

Leo and Liam were polar opposites in every way.

Leo thrived when working a crowd with a smile on his face, but darkness lurked behind that polished façade—he was not the same man in private that he was in public. Liam was stoic, almost to the point of looking angry all the time, but was fiercely loyal, going above and beyond to protect those he loved.

They were as different on the inside as they were on the outside. Leo stood out in his family, with his blond hair and brown eyes, while Liam resembled the majority of the Remingtons, with his pitch-black hair and striking blue eyes—famously called "Remington blue".

Leo always resented that Liam seemingly had more freedom because he wasn't in the direct line for the throne as the second son—the spare, if you will. But even that was a farce, a public show to make him look less entitled. He craved the attention that came with being the heir. Leo chased the high he felt when controlling others. I shuddered to think of the kind of ruler he would become with five million people under his reign.

Trying to steer the conversation back on track, I countered, "It doesn't matter anymore. We can't change the past. It's time to move forward with our lives."

It was clear that he wasn't ready to move forward as he continued to bait me. "You know what *they* say about him moving in with you, right?"

The *they* he was referring to were the press or, more accurately, the paparazzi. *They* were part of why I ran away with my children, but it didn't matter. We were followed across the ocean; we would never be able to outrun who we were. Every move I'd made since I was sixteen was closely watched and scrutinized. Privacy no longer existed. The toll that took on my mental and physical health became borderline dangerous, and I'd reached a breaking point.

Liam had accompanied us when we fled Belleston, going so far as to buy a house in my hometown, in hopes that Leo couldn't track us. My best friend, Amy, had also moved in, creating a "blended family sitcom" vibe. They provided the support I desperately needed, but it created an open season with the press. Stories went wild about how I was having an affair with my husband's brother, which was the furthest thing from the truth. Sex sells, so a new picture of us together or him with the kids every few weeks led to a new story about our "forbidden romance".

I wasn't going to let Leo goad me. I'd been down that road too many times, and it never ended well. "If I were you, I would care less about what *they* have to say and more about what Beau is saying."

Our marriage produced three children. Amelia and Jameson were Irish twins, only ten months apart, and Beau was our baby. He was currently just shy of three years old, but he'd been only ten months old when we'd left. He barely knew Leo.

Leo took the bait. "What is Beau saying?"

Knowing by now that words could hurt as much as a physical strike, I used my words to throw what I thought was the ultimate jab. "Half the time, he calls Liam his daddy."

Narrowing his eyes, Leo's voice was so cold that I shivered as he asked, "Is he?"

I stood. "I'm done here."

It wasn't the first time Leo had questioned Beau's paternity, and while I may not have been perfect, I wasn't an adulteress. Beau was, without a doubt, Leo's son—much as I was loathe to admit. All three of my children deserved a better father, and I couldn't help feeling like I was to blame. I could have chosen a better life partner, but I chose Leo. Now, we all paid the price.

He taunted me as I began to walk out of the room. "You always were too weak to stand up and fight."

Yeah, and whose fault is that?

Pausing, I closed my eyes for a second, taking a deep breath before I turned around. Reminding myself that he could no longer hurt me, I stood tall. "We've made our choices. You chose your job. I chose our children."

Leo smirked, and I mentally braced for impact. He always got this look right before he tore me apart with his words.

Leaning back in his chair, he fired, "You're never going to find what you're looking for. You're not particularly lovable, Natalie."

That wasn't news to me. It had taken me years to figure it out, but I learned he never loved me—he loved controlling me.

Not willing to give him the satisfaction, I counted to ten in my head as I stared him down. Then, I turned on my heel and walked out of the room, not stopping until I reached the sleek black sedan that would take me to the airport so I could go home.

Watching the palace disappear in the rearview mirror, I knew I would never return. This place was my past. My future awaited in Connecticut.

It was time to start over with my kids and hope that someday we could find peace.

Back in my safe haven, I had a heartbreaking conversation with my nine-year-old daughter and eight-year-old son, letting them know the divorce was final. They understood that the only real change was a piece of paper. They would continue to live with me, and their father would be mostly absent.

Amelia was sad, but primarily for me. She was old enough to remember how nasty it got behind the closed doors of our apartment inside the palace. She was protective of me and her younger brothers, something I was sure she'd learned from years of watching her uncle, Liam, do the same.

Jameson was angry. He was a daddy's boy, and it hurt that his dad didn't reciprocate the same intense feelings of love and loyalty.

Needing an escape from our real lives, I took the kids on vacation to try and forget, but the emotional wounds were deep. The scars left behind would always serve as a reminder of our past with Leo.

Amelia and Jameson seemed much older than their age because of all they were forced to witness. Their lives would never be truly normal due to their royal status, but I wanted them to have an opportunity to be carefree children. Two weeks in the Caribbean, letting them run and play seemed to help a bit, but there was still an underlying sadness.

While my children tried to enjoy the tropical paradise, I sat in my chair daily, evaluating how I'd gotten here.

My life had changed without warning one summer when I was sixteen years old. Summer growing up meant weeks spent in the Caribbean, and one day I happened to meet an incredibly charming young man.

Leo had drawn me in with his surfer-boy good looks—shaggy blond hair and a toned, not overly muscular body. We'd spent many summer nights sneaking around the resort as we shared stolen, intimate moments. He was five years older than me—twenty-one at the time—and seemed so worldly. I was no match for his charm and charisma.

I didn't find out who he really was until I'd made it home. It was thrilling at first, the idea of dating a prince. He was handsome, and he wanted *me*.

When he'd proposed a year later, I'd initially turned him down. I was seventeen years old, a senior in high school, and in no way ready to be a wife, especially in what promised to be a very public marriage. When my parents found out, they'd pushed me hard to reconsider. My father was a self-made man in the technology sector—the epitome of *new money*—and he saw my marriage as an opportunity to climb into higher social circles by virtue of his only daughter marrying into royalty. I cut ties with them a few years into my marriage, when I realized they'd sacrificed my well-being for their ambitions. It was their job as parents to protect me, and they had failed miserably.

I should have listened to my gut.

I was the product of a generation of girls who idolized cartoon teenage princesses. Now I was jaded, wondering where the hell their parents were while they were wandering off with much older men. Their parents seemed about as invested as mine in protecting their young daughters.

The one thing those cartoon stories didn't showcase was what life was like after that fairytale "I do". Men in a position of power felt like they were untouchable, and Leo was no exception. I could only hope those made-up princesses fared better than I had.

The only regret I didn't have about my marriage was my three beautiful children. They were my shining light in the darkness, and I was willing to give up everything to protect them. They were also the only reason I couldn't completely shut the door on this chapter of my life. I would forever be tied to my former life because, like it or not, my oldest son was the future of my ex-husband's family—the future of his country, someday being required to take on the title of King.

My job now was to raise Jameson to be grounded, compassionate, and kind. To foster his sweet nature so that he wasn't just putting on a show in public. I wanted to ensure that he was the same person in the spotlight as he was when no one else was looking.

Liam would take care of the rest with his intricate knowledge of the monarchy. He was my rock. I don't think I could have made it this far without him.

Speaking of Liam, he'd dropped everything to support me when I'd fled the country, stepping up for my kids. Even now, he was out on the lawn playing catch with Jameson. We'd learned that throwing the baseball was Jameson's coping mechanism, and Liam was ready to throw with him whenever he asked. Today, Beau had his soft, squishy ball, and Liam was throwing to each of them in turn.

The scene seemed so normal. Only, Liam wasn't their dad. He tried to fill the role the best he could, but it was never the same. It made me think about Leo's dig after we signed the papers. What if Liam had been their father? Would things have been different if I had met Liam instead of Leo on that fateful summer vacation?

I was shaken from my stream of what-ifs by Liam's cry. "Whoa!"

Instantly on alert, I stood from my chair. "What?"

Beau answered first, jumping and chanting, "Ball! Ball! Ball!"

Liam laughed, setting me slightly at ease. "Our boy, Jameson, threw the ball clear over the fence."

Shaking my head, I sighed. "Well, I guess we're done for the day."

Jameson whined, "Aw, come on, Mom. I can hop the fence and go get it."

I looked to which side of the fence it had gone over before answering, "Let's not add trespassing to today's activities. It's on Jaxon's side. We'll be able to get it back if we ask, but you've got to get ready for dinner right now."

"Fine." He made a show of sighing with his whole body. "Make sure to get it back before Saturday. I've got practice!"

"Of course. Now, go inside and wash up. Take your little brother with you."

They headed inside, and Liam joined me on the deck, taking a seat on the chaise and patting the spot next to him in invitation.

Sinking onto the padded seat, I closed my eyes in a rare moment of silence. My eyes still closed, I asked, "Do you think he will ever let go of his anger? Have my choices damaged him permanently?"

Liam paused, so I opened my eyes to look at him.

He rubbed his jaw. "With time, the pain will fade. For all of you."

"What if I'm not enough?" Years of being torn down by Leo would always have me asking that question.

"You sell yourself short. You always have. They will grow up secure, knowing you've given them everything," he promised.

"I hope you're right." I sighed.

"If all else fails, he's gaining quite the arm. Shocked the hell out of me, clearing the fence. I couldn't even see it through the trees. I can go get him a few extra balls tomorrow."

I shook my head. "It's fine. I'd consider it a loss if it had gone in any other direction. Jaxon's a good guy. He'll give it back."

A strange look crossed his face. "Let me go over there and get it right now. No one will ever know."

"I told Jameson no already. I can't let you go and do it. I'll get it back."

Liam looked unsure, which made zero sense.

Jaxon Slate had only been our neighbor for as long as we'd lived in this house, but I'd known him for years. He was one of the best professional hockey players in the league—the star of the hometown team, the Connecticut Comets.

Ace Moreau was the team's head coach, and I was best friends with his daughter, Hannah, who was my age. They'd moved to Hartford when we were teenagers, and we made our debut together. Our close relationship led to my unofficial adoption into the Comets family. I had passing interactions with Jaxon for years as a result of that connection.

Shrugging it off, I patted Liam's leg as I stood. "Don't stress over it. Let's go in and save Amy from the hungry mob."

As we walked into the house to the chaotic chatter of my children being herded by Amy to the table, the ball over the fence was quickly forgotten.

CHAPTER 2

Jaxon

SWEAT RAN INTO MY eyes as I raced to the puck in the corner. Cal was on defense and closing in quickly. Beating him there, I gathered the puck and shot it to Benji, who was parked in front of the net. Benji hit the one-timer past the goalie for the score. I raced over for a quick fist bump as the whistle blew at center ice.

"Bring it in!" Coach Ace Moreau called out.

The handful of us participating in the friendly pickup game gathered at center ice, taking a knee.

Coach continued, "Great workout today, guys. You all look like you took your summer training seriously, so I expect you to challenge the new recruits coming to training camp in a few weeks. Show them what being a Comet looks like, on and off the ice."

He dismissed us to enjoy our weekend. Next month would start my tenth year playing professional hockey, and all eyes were on me. I was the hottest recruit out of juniors at eighteen years old, but so far, I'd failed to reach the top of the mountain. All I wanted was my name engraved on that holy grail we called a championship trophy.

This year had to be our year.

We filed into the locker room, and I sat at my stall, removing my upper gear before untying my skates. Cal and Benji flanked me on either side. We entered the league at different times, in different ways, but they were my best friends on and off the ice.

Cal bent over to untie his skates but looked over his shoulder. "So, are we going out tonight? Last bender before the season? Wheel some bunnies?"

Benji nodded. "You know it! Jaxon, you in?"

I sighed. "I'm in. For the drinks, that is. I'll be your wingman."

"You've gotta let loose, man." Cal groaned.

"Just because I'm not interested in being the most promiscuous Comet, it doesn't mean I don't let loose. Ever heard of discretion?"

"Borrrrrrrrring," Benji chimed in.

I shrugged. "You want me to come or not? I'm just as happy to chill at home."

Benji put his hands up. "All right, all right. Please come. Break all the beautiful ladies' hearts when you turn them down, then let us pick up the pieces. I don't care if I'm second choice. Your name is quickly forgotten once I get them alone."

"Nice." I rolled my eyes.

Cal clapped me on the shoulder. "Don't worry. Your name might be forgotten, but they never bother to learn his."

Benji called out his objection, but I laughed.

That was what I loved about being a part of a team. We became like brothers, spending every single day together for nine months of the year. We knew everything about each other and always had each other's backs. But that didn't mean we didn't mercilessly tease each other every chance we got. That's what brothers were for.

Of the three of us, I was the first one on the team. I'd been drafted at eighteen and thrown right into the deep end as one of the hottest prospects in a decade. It was sink or swim with all the hype surrounding my entry into the league.

Next came Callum Berg—or Cal, as we called him. He was a few years older than me but went to college after his draft, then had a stint in the minors before getting called up. He'd been granted the time to grow into his massive adult frame—not an exaggeration; he was six-five, two hundred and forty pounds—and develop his offensive-minded defensive game before being thrown onto the professional stage.

Last was Benjamin Mills, our Benji boy. He'd worked hard as an un-drafted free agent to get his contract with the Comets. He was on the smaller side but made up for his size with his speed and skill—something he used on and off the ice as the Comets' resident playboy. Benji's only type was female; he wasn't picky beyond that.

I finished removing my gear, tucking it into my locker for the equipment crew. Grabbing a towel, I headed for the showers, pausing before going in. "Where are we going, and what time?"

"10:30 at Spades," Cal called over.

"Do you need a nap first, grandpa?" Benji joked.

I scoffed but fired back, "I'd be more worried about obtaining a fake ID to get in if I were you, little boy."

Walking into the shower, I could tell that tonight was going to be a long night.

Benji was right. I was getting too old for the nightlife. It had its appeal when I was younger—as a way to blow off steam and meet women—but it all seemed so meaningless now. Women merely wanted a night with *the* Jaxon Slate. They didn't care about what was under the surface, only what I could produce on the ice. I was just a story to tell their friends.

Even though I was done with the random hookups, I wasn't in the market for a relationship either. The team was on the road almost one hundred days a year. Hockey took the place of a significant other in my life. Maybe someday, I'd have the time to commit to settling down and starting a family, but for now, hockey was my focus.

Ding dong.

The sound of the doorbell piqued my interest. The front gate hadn't buzzed with a delivery or visitor, so it had to be someone within the community. Some of my favorite visitors were the neighborhood kids, who would drop by to tell me about an exciting game of their own or how they tried a move they'd seen me make.

Youth hockey was growing in America, leading to Americans taking a larger chunk of the formerly Canadian-dominated presence in the professional league. The growth was primarily due to players like me, who were American-born, being visible and promoting the youth aspect of the game. I loved being a role model for any kid who wanted to try hockey, and I craved hearing their stories—seeing a fresh love for the game through their eyes.

Reaching the door, I opened it with a smile, expecting an excited child. The face that greeted me on the other side had me closing my eyes and reopening them to make sure I wasn't dreaming.

Standing there, staring up at me with her chocolate brown eyes, was the woman who'd held the permanent starring role in my every fantasy.

Once the air returned to my lungs, I breathed out, "Natalie."

Natalie flashed her dazzling smile, and I could have sworn my heart stopped beating.

"Hi, Jaxon. I'm sorry to bother you, but my son threw his baseball over your fence earlier this week. He's got practice tomorrow, and I promised him I'd try to get it back. Think you could help me out?"

Chuckling, I drank in the woman before me. Natalie Remington, the girl—now woman—who had been off-limits since Day 1. Not that her untouchable status kept her from my mind. As if being infatuated with a married woman—a princess, no less—wasn't enough, Coach kept her under his protection as an honorary daughter.

To add insult to injury, the universe gave me the ultimate middle finger when she'd moved in next door a couple of years ago.

She was so close, but she could never be mine.

Now, here she stood, stunning as ever in a simple white sundress, her skin tanned to perfection. My fingers itched to reach out and see if her skin was as soft as it looked. Her face, framed by long blonde hair, was free of makeup, yet she was still the most beautiful woman I'd ever laid eyes on. Beyond that, she was one of the most genuinely kind people I had ever met.

Natalie was perfect, but I could never have her. She was in a very high-profile marriage, with three children, I reminded myself.

She's not for you, Jaxon.

Realizing I was staring, my eyes snapped back to hers. "He could have hopped the fence. I wouldn't have minded."

Natalie rolled her eyes, and damn, if that wasn't adorable. "Oh, not you, too."

I smirked. "Guessing that was a 'mom said no' kind of deal?"

"Something like that." She flashed me another small smile.

"Forget I said it. It can be our little secret." I held a finger to my lips conspiratorially.

She mouthed, "Thank you."

God, I could picture that mouth on me. Or better yet, screaming my name.

Get a grip, Jaxon!

Taking a step back from the doorway, I made room for her to enter. "Well, come on in. Let's go find that ball." Natalie stepped inside, and I closed the door behind her. Pointing towards the glass doors through the vaulted living room, I added, "We can head out this way."

She nodded and walked ahead of me. The sway of her backside in that dress had me reminding my cock to calm down. It couldn't be embarrassing me in front of the girl that I liked.

Jesus, the girl that I liked? How old am I? Thirteen?

As Natalie surveyed the room, I found myself caring whether she liked my place or not.

It was modest compared to some players' homes, and I made enough to afford someplace bigger or more flashy, but it was just me here. I spent most of my time at the rink or on the road, so it was a place to crash most days. Modest or not, it was still a decent house for a single guy. Set in a gated community, the four-bedroom house featured an open floor plan, a basement I turned into my man cave, a pool, and a private backyard.

Plus, moving meant not living next to her anymore.

Natalie looked back and smiled, throwing over her shoulder, "Love all the white walls. Just move in?" Then, she winked.

That had me stumbling down the step onto the patio. Was Natalie Remington *flirting* with me? I shook my head to clear it.

No.

I was imagining things.

She was married.

With a capital M.

Not for you, Jaxon.

Joining her outside, Natalie looked around and spotted the microscopic view I had of her house. Well, her roof, if we were being technical. She began heading in that direction, muttering to herself, "Gotta be somewhere this way."

She peeled off to the right side of the fence on our shared property line, so I opted for the left, calling out, "I'll check over here!"

Finding the white ball amongst the green grass and tree trunks didn't take long, but I wasn't ready to say goodbye yet. Stuffing it into my shorts pocket, I leaned against the nearest tree and watched her continue searching from afar.

I could still remember the day I met her with crystal clarity. That day had changed my life.

I heard her before I saw her. The sound of her laughter caught my attention. It was real and unfiltered, rising above the music of the pre-game picnic at the country club. Like a moth to a flame, I followed the sound until I reached its source.

Sitting with Coach's youngest daughter, Hannah, was this smiling, laughing beauty bouncing a baby in her arms.

Dressed casually in a plain white T-shirt and jeans shorts, was the most classically beautiful girl I'd ever seen, giving off a total girl-next-door vibe. Her hair was the color of champagne, and her warm brown eyes were the perfect compliment. Her pure joy was so infectious that I found myself smiling, drawing ever closer.

I had no idea who she was, but I knew I would never be the same.

Hannah noticed me and called out, "Jaxon! Over here!"

Perfect. Now, I could find out who her companion was.

Turning on the charm, I addressed them, "Hello, ladies."

Hannah turned to her friend. "Natalie, this is Jaxon Slate. We just picked him up in the draft."

The girl, Natalie, turned her brilliant smile on me, continuing to bounce the baby, whose raven black hair was a stark contrast to her own golden mane. "So nice to meet you, Jaxon."

I was so drawn to her that I couldn't stop myself from coming closer, tickling the baby's toes. "And who do we have here?"

That's when her smile went to the next level. She positively beamed. "This is Amelia."

Looking into her eyes, I could tell she was young. Easily close to my age, and I had just turned eighteen. Silently, I prayed, "Please, be the nanny."

Hoping to get the answer I'd prayed for, I asked, "Which player does she belong to?"

She laughed again, and I had to bite back a groan at the sound. "Oh, no! She's mine."

My heart sank, and that's when I caught the flash of the diamond on her finger. She not only had a baby, but she was either engaged or married. Some lucky bastard had gotten to this beautiful girl first. Of course, they had. That was just my luck. For years, my days were spent in cold ice rinks as I chased the ultimate reward of a professional hockey contract. That meant I didn't have any spare time for girls.

Hannah was oblivious to my internal distress and added, "Natalie and I went to school together."

The wheels started turning in my head. That meant she was nineteen or twenty at the oldest, and she already had a man and a baby. She seemed so damn happy, and it killed me.

"So, where do you come to us from, Jaxon?" Natalie asked.

I snapped my attention to her. "Minnesota, ma'am."

She giggled. "I think that's my first 'ma'am'. Not quite ready for that."

"My apologies. Force of habit."

"Well, you can tell your mama that you have good manners. So, Minnesota. American-born then?" she asked.

"State of Hockey, born and raised," I confirmed.

Natalie smiled again. I'd say just about anything to keep her smiling. "It must be hard to be so far from home. If you're just drafted, that would make you . . ."

"Eighteen," I finished for her.

Hannah leaned over. "Too bad you're going home soon, Nat. We could have some fun with a player younger than us. I'm so over being the Comets' unofficial little sister."

Snapping to attention, I asked, "And where is home?"

Natalie stroked the baby's soft hair and tucked her into her shoulder. "Home will always be Hartford, but these days I live in Europe."

She was very young and already married, so I ventured a guess, "Military?"

Natalie bit her lip, and damn, if that didn't do things to my insides. "Not exactly."

"Jaxon!" I heard the call over my shoulder and glanced back to find a group of older players gathered by the pool, beckoning me over.

Turning back to the ladies, I excused myself. "I guess that's my cue. It was nice to meet you, Natalie. Safe travels back home if I don't see you again."

Natalie smiled again, and I took my leave, heading toward the group of players likely ready to haze the new guy at his first team party.

Ty Stephens, our captain, greeted me. "Can I get you a Shirley Temple, rookie?"

The guys all laughed, so I decided to roll with it. "Extra cherries. Thanks, Ty."

That earned me a few back claps from some of the other guys.

Grabbing a seat at the high-top table, my eyes continued to stray across the patio to where I'd left Natalie and Hannah. I felt my blood pressure rising as an average-height, blond, preppy-looking man walked up to the girls, taking baby Amelia into his arms. I didn't know this guy, but I already hated him.

This guy—who looked like the poster boy for those frat boy assholes spending their summers in the Hamptons or at the Cape—was way too old for her. He looked like he was coasting on a career his daddy built, never having seen a hard day's work in his life. Looking at that seemingly perfect blond couple, the black hair on the baby seemed out of place, like she couldn't be theirs.

She looked like she could be mine.

Holy shit, where did that thought come from?

I was eighteen and barely knew how to do my own laundry. Maybe I'd been hit in the head too many times. I'd better get my head checked because these thoughts were not *normal.*

Ty set my drink on the table and took the seat next to me. Following the direction of my gaze, he noted, "I see you've met our resident princess."

My head whipped around so fast to stare at him that I swear I heard a pop. "What?"

He nodded to the small group's canopy. "Natalie."

My eyes bugged out of my head. "She's a princess?"

"Yep."

"But she's so normal." I was stunned.

"She married into it."

"She's so young." Now, I was in denial.

"She's the same age as Hannah, so she might as well still be a kid. Coach treats her like his fourth daughter. Can't stand her husband, though. Total douchebag, but I guess it doesn't matter when someday you'll be a king."

I felt my heart twist inside my chest. Of course, the most amazing girls always ended up with jerks.

The voice that had captivated me almost ten years ago broke me out of my mental flashback. "He's going to be so upset if I don't find it."

Pushing off the tree, I pulled the ball from my pocket. Thankfully, her back was turned so she wouldn't realize I'd had it the whole time as I called out, "Found it!"

Spinning around, Natalie flashed me that dazzling smile that still had the same impact on me after all these years. "Thank goodness! I owe you one."

"He must have a great arm to make it this far over the fence." I tossed it up and down, catching it easily as I spoke.

A shadow passed over her eyes. "He's been throwing quite a lot lately. He's still upset about the divorce."

And just like that, my world stopped.

CHAPTER 3

Jaxon

DIVORCE.

There's no way I'd heard that right. I reached out to hand the ball over in an attempt to get a better look at her left hand.

No ring.

My heart was soaring, but I tried to throw on a sympathetic face. "I'm sorry."

"I'm not," she countered.

There were rumblings that her situation hadn't been good for a while, and then she'd come back home, where she'd stayed for the past couple of years—her husband notably absent. Living next door, I would've been a fool not to notice, but I never imagined she'd ever become available. Guys like her ex were the type that didn't let go without a fight.

Natalie certainly didn't seem broken up about it. So, without thinking, I blurted out, "Can I get you a drink?"

A slight smile graced her lips. "You know, a drink sounds amazing."

Heading back toward the house, she fell into step beside me. It was almost as if she belonged there, right by my side.

Once inside, I walked to the kitchen, opened the fridge, and threw over my shoulder, "What can I get you?"

Natalie walked up right behind me, so close that I could feel her breath on my ear. "Something strong, please."

I closed my eyes and swallowed. She was *killing* me. Turning around, I found us practically nose to nose. Natalie smelled like the beach, the scents of coconut and pineapple wafting off her exposed skin. We'd never been this close, and I would have given anything to wrap my arms around her right now.

My voice was low and raspy, sounding strange to my own ears, as I offered, "I think I have some scotch around here somewhere."

Natalie stepped back, and I shivered as cool air rushed between us. Heading for the couch, she didn't wait for an invitation before sitting and replying, "Scotch would be great."

Grabbing two lowball glasses, I threw a few ice cubes in each before pouring two fingers of scotch. Walking over to where she sat, handing her one, I chose to sit in the lounge chair perpendicular to the couch she occupied.

Getting too close to her was dangerous. Something was changing. I could feel it.

Raising the glass to her lips and taking a sip, Natalie moaned. "Oh, God."

If that wasn't enough to get me hard, the way her tongue darted out to catch an errant drop on her lips did the trick.

Shifting in my seat, my voice was strained as I raised my glass. "Cheers."

Her eyes met mine, then she flushed. "Ohmigosh, I'm so rude. I got lost in the fact that I haven't had a real drink like this in so long."

Not wanting to push, I simply asked, "Oh?"

She sighed. "You don't want to hear my sob story. I don't get to complain."

"We've known each other a long time. If you need to vent, I'm here."

That got a small smile from Natalie. "I'm fine. Really. I just wasn't allowed to *imbibe* beyond the occasional glass of wine or champagne."

"Allowed . . ." I repeated. What kind of prison was she living in?

"It's fine." She shrugged.

"Really?" How could she be all right with what sounded like a controlling situation?

Her eyes snapped to mine. "No, not really, but it's over now."

"How do you feel about that?" I was genuinely curious.

Setting her glass on the coffee table, Natalie stood and moved to the end of the couch next to my chair. Looking up at me with those big brown eyes, she asked, "Between friends?" I nodded, so she continued, "When things got bad, I shut down. I refused to feel anything in order to protect myself. I've been living in a state of numbness for years."

As she quickly looked away after that admission, I couldn't help but stare at how her long black lashes fanned against her cheeks. Someone had stolen the spark that drew me to her all those years ago. It hurt my heart to know her spirit had been broken, and her only defense mechanism was to shut herself off from all emotion to survive.

When I couldn't stand the silence a moment longer, I started, "Natalie—"

Looking back at me, she smirked right before she reached over and placed her hand on my thigh. I could feel the heat from her palm seeping through my khaki shorts, and my cock began to swell in response. This was the first time we'd ever touched, and she was mere inches away from the undeniable proof of how desperately I wanted her.

Rationally, I knew I had to put a stop to this, so I started to pull away, but she gripped my thigh, and I couldn't hold back the groan that slipped past my lips.

Licking her lips, Natalie uttered words so low that I had to lean closer to hear them. "Jaxon. I want to feel something again, but I'm not sure how."

I swallowed. Hard. Was she coming on to me?

Giving myself a minute to process what was unfolding before me, I broke my silence. "Tell me what you want, Natalie."

The air around us was charged. I could feel something was going to happen, but I wasn't sure what. Nervously, she twisted her hair in one hand. "I want you to do me a favor."

Against my better judgment, I said, "I'm listening."

Natalie bit her lower lip, and I was tempted to use it as my own personal chew toy. Her eyes flared mere seconds before she whispered, "Take me to bed?"

Even if it felt like this was where the conversation was headed, I would never be fully prepared to hear those words—words I'd only ever heard in my fantasies.

As I struggled to process the clash between reality and fantasy, she must have taken my silence for an answer, because her entire demeanor changed.

Letting go of my leg, Natalie stood, flushing from head to toe as she backed away. Then the rambling began. "Oh, God. Please forget I said that. I don't know what came over me. I'm so sorry. I did *not* come here for this, I swear. I've got to go."

Panic set in. She was leaving?

Bolting out of my chair, I stepped toward her, gently gripping her wrist as she was about to flee. Turning back, her dark eyes pleaded with me. As she opened her mouth to speak again, I put a finger to her lips, silencing her.

I searched her eyes before daring to ask, "Why me?"

Shut up, Jaxon. Who cares why you? This is everything you've always wanted.

Removing my finger from her lips, she swallowed before responding, "I don't know if this is even going to work. Maybe I'm broken forever. But I thought—" She took a deep breath, her chest expanding, drawing my attention to her pert breasts. "I thought you might be the only person who wouldn't tell anyone. I know I'm asking too much. We're friends, and this is crossing a major line. I'm not looking for anything other than just once. To see if it can jump-start me back into the land of the living." Natalie took a shaky breath before asking, "Will you help me?"

Moving my free hand into her hair, I cupped her head gently. "Are you sure? Maybe it hasn't been long enough. You might need more time."

Natalie leaned into my hand, begging on a whisper, "Please?"

"Just once?" I searched her eyes for any sign of hesitation. If I saw a single trace, I would walk away—it would kill me, but I'd do it.

She nodded. "Just once. No strings."

How could I say no to the woman I'd dreamt of for a decade? She was here, begging me to take her, to make her *feel*. This might be my only chance. I couldn't dare tell her how I felt about her—she would spook for sure—so I had to take this opportunity to show her. Even if it was only this once.

"One condition," I stated. Natalie stared up at me, her brown eyes seemingly staring into my soul. "If at any point you want to stop, say the word."

She ran a hand up my chest, and I closed my eyes at the contact. When the light brush of her lips grazed against mine, my eyes popped open.

A shy smile graced her kissable lips. "All right."

Running a thumb over her lower lip, I held her stare. "You are so beautiful."

Blushing, she broke my gaze. "No."

"No?" Was this night over before it even began?

I saw the shift when she met my eye, a devilish gleam sparkling in hers. "I don't want you to make love to me, Jaxon. I want you to fuck me. Or do I need to go somewhere else?"

Growling, moments before gripping her hips, I brought her body flush against mine. She gasped, feeling my erection pressed against her, as I whispered in her ear, "Say the word 'fuck' again, and I won't be held responsible for what happens next."

"I was wondering when the sexy Jaxon was going to show up," she teased as I felt her breasts brush against my chest with each rapid breath she took.

"You think I'm sexy?" A corner of my lips quirked up.

Her eyes darkened with lust. "Just shut up and kiss me."

How could I resist?

Giving in to everything I'd ever dreamed, I slowly lowered my head to hers, savoring the taste of her lips against mine. My brain was working overtime, trying to memorize every single moment. If this was going to happen once, I needed to be able to replay it over and over in my mind for the rest of my life.

Going slowly went out the window the second she ran her hands into my hair, gripped two handfuls, and took complete control of the kiss, demanding entry. Opening for her, I let her tongue sweep into my mouth before I began to battle back with my own, deepening the kiss. Holding her in my arms and kissing her rocked me to the core.

Natalie rubbed her body against mine, trying to get closer. Using my hands on her hips, I pushed her back a step, putting space between us. Breaking the kiss, she batted her eyelashes at me.

I nipped at her lower lip. "I'm trying really hard to control myself here, Natalie. Keep rubbing against me like that, and I won't be able to."

That wicked gleam was back in her eyes, and she closed the distance between us, grabbing my ass to bring us even closer. "I don't want you controlled. I want you to fuck me. Hard."

She was egging me on. If that's how she wanted to play, that's how we'd play.

My hands moved six inches from her hips to her ass, gripping as I lifted her, feeling her heels digging into my lower back as she wrapped her legs around me. With her dress fanned around her thighs in this position, I could feel the heat coming from her center as she ground against my rock-hard dick.

"Fuck yes," she whispered against my mouth.

Taking her mouth hungrily, I gave in to her demands as she rocked against my pelvis. Her hands were still tangled in my hair, gripping hard, the bite of pain heightening the pleasure coursing through my veins. Moving my mouth, I peppered hot, open-mouthed kisses down her throat to her collarbone. Her moans were barely permeating the haze of lust gripping my body.

Taking two steps backward, the back of my knees hit the couch, and I sat, allowing her to straddle me. With my hands now free, they roamed her body, up her hips, to the indent of her waist until I reached her breasts. She arched into the touch as I gently tested their weight, just enough to fill my palms. I groaned when I realized she wasn't wearing a bra beneath the thin white cotton, her nipples pebbling beneath my hands.

Lowering my head, I sucked a nipple into my mouth through the thin material, using the friction to drive her wild. Natalie held onto my shoulders, nails digging in hard as her head lolled back. I tugged a nipple between my teeth, and she ground down even harder, calling out, "Oh, God!"

Torn between living here forever, feasting on her irresistible breasts, and getting her upstairs before I embarrassed myself like a teenager dry-humping on the couch, I slowly drew on the nipple before releasing it, causing her to whimper at the loss of contact. Leaning her forehead against mine, the puffs of air from her labored breathing fanned my face. Her hair curtained us, so I reached up, tucking the golden locks behind her ears to stare at her face. Her chocolate brown eyes had changed from milk chocolate to dark, shadowed with lust. The wetness between her thighs soaked through her panties and onto my shorts.

Wanting more, and needing to know that she did too, I dared to ask, "Upstairs?"

Natalie nodded, her eyes flaring. Afraid that one or both of us would wake up from this dream if I broke body contact, I stood, keeping her in my arms as I carried her up the stairs. The second we hit the top landing, I pinned her against the wall.

The taste of her mouth was intoxicating, traces of mint mixed with the scotch still lingering. Sucking her tongue into my mouth, I moved one hand between our bodies, under her skirt, and shoved her panties aside. My fingers found her drenched beneath, and I nearly growled, knowing I did this to her. She wanted this as much as I did.

Lightly circling her clit, her hips began searching for firmer contact. I held back, teasing.

She tore her mouth from mine, breathlessly begging, "Please, Jaxon."

My mouth moved along her jaw. "Tell me what you want, Natalie."

She squirmed against my hand. "You."

I smiled against her skin. "No, Natalie. Tell me exactly what you want."

She made a frustrated sound, and I looked up at her, noting her flushed neck and face. Was she really embarrassed when I had her this vulnerable? Withdrawing my hand enough for her to realize I meant business, I pressed again, "I need you to tell me what you want."

Closing her eyes, Natalie groaned. "I want you to make me come."

Pure pleasure shot straight down my dick. I would be replaying those words on repeat for the rest of my life. Flashing her a wolfish smile, my hand returned to her slickness. "With pleasure."

As a reward for how obviously hard it was for her to tell me what she wanted, I didn't tease her. I rubbed her clit with my thumb, slipping one finger inside her. As she writhed against me, I added a second finger, pumping in and out, fucking her hard with my hand.

She threw her head back against the wall, breathing, "Yes, Jaxon!"

A few more pumps, and I felt her thighs begin to shake. She was close. It wasn't enough to just feel her come apart. I wanted all of her. I stilled my hand right as she was on the edge.

Her eyes snapped open to look at me, silently begging, as she whimpered, "Please."

"Eyes on me. I want to watch you come for me."

Natalie swallowed but nodded, never breaking my gaze as I went back to work. Curling my fingers inside her, I pressed down on her clit with my thumb, allowing her the perfect pressure to shatter as she bucked her hips against my hand. I watched her mouth open in a silent scream as she convulsed around my fingers, flooding them with her release.

Holding her against the wall, I waited until her breathing slowed before removing my hand and carrying her limp form the rest of the way to my bedroom.

Setting her down gently on the floor, I made sure that her shaking legs were stable enough to hold her up before reaching for the hem of her dress and pulling it off over her head. She was laid almost completely bare for me, so I took a minute to drink her in fully.

Her rose-colored nipples stood out against the tan of her skin, causing me to groan, realizing she'd only achieve a tan there topless—the mental image was enough to drive me wild. Continuing my perusal down her body, I frowned when I realized I could count each of her ribs as I scanned down to the nude bikini panties covering the last bit of her that was hidden from my view.

Seeing the self-consciousness enter her eyes, I realized she'd misunderstood my frown.

Wrapping both arms around her midsection, she rushed to explain, "I know I don't look like other girls you've been with. There are changes that come with becoming a mom."

Gently prying her hands away, I shook my head. "You're stunning just as you are."

To emphasize my point, I ran my hands down her sides before tracing with my fingertips the almost invisible silver lines scattered across her hips and lower abdomen. There was the tiniest hint of loose skin above the waistband of her panties and cellulite on her thighs—proof that she'd carried life inside her body.

None of that mattered to me. Natalie was beautiful inside and out—a few imperfections only made her more endearing. She was human like the rest of us, no matter how much I'd built her up in my mind.

Flushing again, she reached out to the hem of my T-shirt, but I stopped her hands. She looked up, confused, so I shook my head. "I'm not done with you yet."

Natalie's eyes widened. "I'm good. It's your turn."

"This is about you, not me." Holding firm, I had every intention of worshiping her body fully before I allowed myself release.

Shyly she replied, "I want to see you."

How could I say no to that?

Licking my lips, I nodded, hissing as her small hands brushed against my abs as she raised the shirt up and over my chest. Dropping it on the floor, she stared at me for a minute before reaching out and skimming her fingers down my chest to the waistband of my shorts.

"Wow, you grew up," Natalie breathed out.

I couldn't contain the chuckle that escaped past my lips. I'd put on about thirty pounds of muscle since I was drafted. If I'd known that Natalie would appreciate it so much, I would have doubled my efforts.

Closing the distance between us, I walked her backward until her knees bumped into the mattress. Sitting, she scooched back, centering herself in the middle of my massive king-sized bed. Kicking off my shoes, I joined her, taking her mouth and lowering her to her back as I hovered over her body.

It didn't take long before she was worked into a frenzy again from my deep kisses, straining against me. Leaving her mouth, I moved down her body, giving attention to both of her breasts in turn, before moving lower, pausing to kiss each rib I found protruding. It pained me to know that something drove her to this extreme. She hadn't always been this painfully thin, but I pushed those thoughts aside when she breathed my name, bringing me back to the present.

Lower I went until I reached the elastic waistband of her panties. Hooking my thumbs inside, I took my time in dragging them down her legs. When she kicked them off, I allowed myself a moment to appreciate the fully naked dream laid before me.

She was gorgeous, and for tonight, she was all mine. Raking my gaze from the top of her head to the tips of her toes, I noted the thatch of dark hair at the juncture of her thighs, exposing the secret that she wasn't a natural blonde.

A rush of possession flowed through me, knowing I now held this intimate knowledge of her. Starting at her knee, I teased kisses up her thighs until I was situated between them. Her pretty pussy was still soaked from her earlier orgasm, pink and glistening, and my cock was throbbing at the prospect of tasting her. Spreading her thighs wide for greater access, Natalie raised up on her elbows.

Smiling against her flesh, it pleased me that she liked to watch.

That was, until I heard her call out, panicked, "Wait!"

Closing my eyes, I mentally prepared for the cold shower that would be required to walk away from her now. Daring to look up at her, I kept my voice calm. "Do you want to stop?"

Natalie was wide-eyed. "What are you doing?"

Looking at her waiting pussy, then back up to her face, I teased, "I made a bet with myself that you'd taste sweeter here than anywhere else I've already sampled." She looked concerned, so I dropped the act, asking seriously, "Is this not all right?"

Biting her lip, she blushed yet again.

Damn, I'd do just about anything to keep her blushing. It was the most arousing thing I had ever seen on a woman. I was used to women acting in the bedroom to make me feel like a man, but her reactions were so authentic. It was sexy as hell.

She paused. "I just . . . I mean . . . I've never . . ."

Holy shit.

"Never?" I asked, almost in disbelief. When she shook her head, I was filled with an emotion I'd never felt before in bed—anger.

Selfish bastard.

He'd had the woman of my dreams all these years and never worshiped her properly? What kind of man didn't take care of his woman before seeing to his own needs?

No. He didn't belong here.

A primal sense of satisfaction filled me when I realized I'd be the first to put my mouth on her—claiming her in a way never done before.

Mine.

I looked up at her. "May I?"

Covering her face with both hands, she nodded.

Taking my time, I lowered my head and breathed in her scent. I could hear the hitch in her breathing as she waited, unsure of what I'd do next. Having her completely at my mercy, I took a slow, long lick, ending with a little flick on her clit.

Her hips bucked against my face, and she let out a little squeal. Humming against her in response, the vibrations against her sensitive flesh elicited a moan from her lips. If I was going to be the first to love her with my mouth, I was going to take my time. I wanted her to feel me here for days, to flush from head to toe at the memory.

Teasing little circles around her clit, I smiled against her when she raised her hips, trying desperately to force my mouth where she needed it. The tangy taste of her flooded my mouth, and I was instantly addicted. I began alternating quick flicks with slow long strokes, getting her right on the edge before slowing down again. Natalie was actively riding my face, seeking release, so I reached under her ass, lifting her hips to get a better angle.

Natalie was writhing against the bed, against my face, begging, "Jaxon, I need . . . I want . . ."

Knowing what she wanted, I gave it to her as I began my relentless assault, back and forth, faster and faster, until I felt her thighs lock tightly against my head before she came all over my tongue, screaming my name. My cock was throbbing, begging for its turn as it strained against the fly of my shorts.

Kissing my way up her body, slowly trailing my fingers along her skin, she arched into each touch. She was so responsive, her reactions so unfiltered, that all I wanted to do was bring her to climax again and again. Reaching her mouth, I kissed her deeply, allowing her to taste herself on my tongue. She moaned as she pressed her body against mine.

Pulling back, I gazed down at the goddess in my bed.

Her eyes were heavy, pupils dilated with desire. Dazed, she asked, "What was that?"

Smiling, I teased, "I was in the mood for dessert."

Natalie's eyes went wide—I'd shocked her. Stammering, she asked, "Th-that's what they call it?"

I drew little circles on her collarbone with my fingers, raising goosebumps along the way. "With a pussy as sweet as yours? Absolutely. I think I won that bet."

Her breath hitched, and I found myself smirking. Clearly, no one had ever talked to her like this. Judging from the way her eyes darkened and her pulse beat faster at the base of her throat, it was turning her on. The way that she tiptoed around asking for what she wanted in bed was adorable. I now took it as a personal challenge to get her to express herself freely.

"Tell me what you want, Natalie," I growled in her ear.

She groaned, frustrated. "Why do you keep asking me that?"

Pushing the hair away from her face, I cupped her cheek. "I need you to say the words. I will give you anything you want, so long as you ask me. *Anything*."

I prayed she heard how I poured meaning into the emphasis on that statement. I would give this woman the world if she asked me for it.

Withdrawing slightly, Natalie searched my face. "I want to feel you inside me."

Thank God.

Reaching over to my nightstand to pull out a condom, I had one in my grasp when I felt her hand on my arm. Looking back at her, there was an unreadable emotion on her face.

Timidly, she asked, "Do you have an unopened box?"

There was something there, but I couldn't figure out what. Maybe a hint of fear, but not of me. Willing to do anything to erase whatever was scaring her, I nodded. "Yeah."

Natalie held her hand out. "Can I have it?"

Raising an eyebrow, I got up, grabbing a fresh, unopened box from a bathroom drawer before returning and handing it to her. Inspecting it, she broke the seal before ripping off one packet and passing it to me. "Thank you."

I rolled that around in my brain for half a second. She was thanking me for letting her open a new box of condoms?

There was way too much to unpack with this woman, and I wondered if I'd ever get the chance to see what made her tick. Before I could ponder what happened to her to create this extreme level of distrust, my brain short-circuited when she undid my shorts, reaching inside and gripping my dick firmly.

Groaning, I lowered my forehead to hers. "Natalie, I'm going to need you to stop."

Pulling away, she stared at me, that hint of fear creeping back into her eyes. "I'm so sorry. Do you not like it?"

She seemed spooked, so I rushed, "Baby, no. I like it way too much. I want to come buried deep inside you, and if you keep touching me like that, I can't promise I'll make it."

That was the moment she realized the effect she had on me. I could sense the change in her—the boldness that overtook the shyness holding her back to this point.

Natalie got on her knees between my legs, tugging my shorts down my legs, leaving me only in my boxer briefs, which she removed next. As she took a moment to stare now that she had me fully naked, I was thankful for every sweaty day in the gym and on the ice carving my muscles.

Natalie licked her lips, and I could see what she was thinking, so I sat up, flipping her so that she was beneath me, growling, "Don't even think about it."

Reaching over to grab her hand-selected choice of condom, I ripped it open before rolling it on. Her eyes flared as I settled back between her thighs, the tip of me sliding through her slick and swollen flesh before teasing her entrance.

She arched, trying to take me inside. I kissed her hot and hungrily before she begged breathlessly, "Now, Jaxon."

White-hot pleasure hit me full force as I slowly sank into her tight heat. The sensation was heightened by watching her close her eyes, head back, mouth open, lost in her own pleasure at our joining. Kissing a path down her throat, I prayed I'd be able to last more than a minute with how amazing it felt to be inside her. I knew I was a goner as soon as I started to move.

Raising her hips, Natalie desperately tried to gain friction. Taking both her wrists in one hand, I raised them above her head, holding them there as I began with slow, hard thrusts. She strained against me, her moaning only serving to spur me on. I could tell she wanted it hard and fast, but I wanted this to last forever, so I held back, keeping a steady pace, drawing out our mutual pleasure.

Her legs linked around my hips, trying to urge me to change pace. My control began to fray, and I wanted to throw her over the edge once more before I sought my release. Rising up on my knees, I wanted a full view of her while I fucked her to remind myself that this was real.

Gripping her hips, I pumped harder as she keened against me, shamelessly seeking her release. The sight of her writhing before me threatened to throw me over the edge as I began to feel the intense pleasure building in my balls, tightening. If I wanted her to come first, it had to be soon, so I reached between our bodies, rubbing her clit furiously as I maintained my punishing pace between her thighs.

Natalie came apart beneath me, screaming, her release so unfiltered that no matter how hard I tried to stave it off, I was lost to the orgasm ripped from my body. Losing myself in her, I groaned as I came, pumping harder, trying to draw this moment out forever, not wanting this to end. Collapsing next to her, I pulled her close as our erratic breathing filled the room.

Looking at her, I found her eyes closed as she was peacefully tucked into my side. If I wasn't already obsessed with her, the sight of her sated by my hand would have done it. Getting a real taste of her only cemented what I'd always known—she belonged here, with me.

As my mind raced, desperately trying to work out how to get more than one night, her eyes opened, a soft smile gracing her lips. I would never understand how she was always able to steal the breath from my lungs with a single look.

Her breathing was still ragged as she spoke in choppy fragments. "Three. Orgasms. Really?"

I teased her. "You said you wanted to feel."

She laughed in short bursts. "Touché."

Her eyes closed again, so I stroked her hair until I heard her breathing deepen. There was something so comforting about holding her close that I fell asleep right alongside her, falling into dreams of what it would be like to have her here every day.

CHAPTER 4

Natalie

Buzzzzzzz. Buzz buzzzzzzz.

Slowly, breaking out of the haze of a deep sleep, I stretched, reaching over to stop the alarm on my phone. When I met nothing but the mattress, I realized I wasn't in my own bed. Sitting bolt upright, taking in the darkened room, I felt movement next to me. Jumping, I realized I was as naked as the man in bed next to me.

Oh my God. What have I done?

Memories flooded back.

Jaxon's mouth on me intimately, in a way I'd only ever read about before.

His body, hard where I was soft, straining against mine.

Three different orgasms in three different ways.

Easing my way out of bed, I felt the pleasant soreness between my thighs. I had no idea what came over me earlier when I'd practically begged Jaxon to sleep with me. Dropping to the floor, I crawled around, searching for my clothes. Instead, I found Jaxon's phone buzzing with texts coming in and repeated missed calls, the lock screen lighting up the floor. I knew I shouldn't, but I was too curious not to look.

Cal: *Where are you?*

Benji: *Don't tell me you bailed on us! You're supposed to be our chick bait.*

Heat flooded my cheeks. I knew his teammates, and it was obvious from their messages that I was just another conquest. That's what professional athletes did. They slept around.

You came on to him, Natalie.

I knew he had experience. That's why I made the snap decision to proposition him. It had felt different, special even, but that must have been all in my head. God, he probably had women throwing themselves at him all the time, and I was no better than the puck bunnies who trolled the rink.

I am such an idiot.

Grabbing my dress and panties, I threw them on and fled the room. Tiptoeing down the stairs, afraid of waking Jaxon, I snatched Jameson's baseball off the coffee table before leaving the house, silently latching the door behind me.

Walking back to my house, I could feel him with every step I took.

I would never be able to face him again, having made a total fool of myself. What was I thinking asking an acquaintance I saw regularly for a one-night stand? Of course it was going to end in disaster.

Mentally, I berated myself. As a mother of three, I couldn't be casually sleeping around. I didn't have the luxury of making mistakes like this, so I swore to myself that I would take this secret to my grave. Only the two people involved could ever know.

How long had I been asleep? I hadn't bothered to bring my phone next door—expecting a quick trip—so I had no idea what time it was. I knew it was dark, which meant my absence was likely noted by everyone at home. I'd been home alone when I'd ventured out, so no one would know where I'd gone, unable to reach me by phone.

Making it back to the house, I took a moment to check my appearance. Running fingers through my hair, I smoothed my dress, rumpled from hours on the floor. Taking a deep breath, I turned the knob of the front door. There was no chance that Amy and Liam weren't waiting for me on the other side.

As expected, Liam was camped out in the formal living room off the foyer. Closing the door, I mentally braced for the lecture as he stood, almost shouting, "Where the hell have you been?!"

Amy's voice floated down the hall. "Is she back?"

By the time she made it to where we stood, I managed to force out, "I'm so sorry. I lost track of time."

That wasn't enough for Liam—the scowl he used on everyone except the kids was present on his face. "No. I had to put your children to bed tonight. They didn't know where you were, and I couldn't tell them. Because you left your phone here!"

He used his words to hit me where it hurt, knowing full well that I would die before upsetting my children.

If Liam was the bad cop, Amy came in as the good cop. You'd never expect a redhead to be so rational, but Amy was always calm and in control.

She stepped in, her tone understanding. "Nat, we were just worried about you. Where did you go?"

Suddenly remembering half of my alibi, I presented the ball. "Got the ball back."

"That took hours?" Liam wasn't convinced. Why should he be?

Sighing, I responded, "No. I decided to take a long walk. There isn't much space to clear my head around here. I needed a minute."

Liam raked his fingers through his jet-black hair. "You're dealing with a lot right now—I get it. Next time, let us know where you are. Or at least take your phone, okay?"

Nodding, I gave the appearance of being sufficiently chastised. "I'm sorry. It won't happen again."

"If that's settled, I'm going to go for a swim," he said.

"Go. I'm going to go to bed. Thank you for looking out for me."

A corner of his lips quirked up, the closest thing he ever did to a smile. "Always, little sis."

As he left, I walked to the kitchen for some water. Apparently, mind-blowing sex made you dehydrated. Who knew?

Amy trailed behind me, taking a seat at the kitchen island as I opened the fridge. Taking a long pull from a bottle of water, I turned around. She was eyeing me closely, and I could tell she was measuring her words carefully. We'd been friends our whole lives. If anyone could see right through me, it was her.

Finally, she spoke, "You know I love you, right?"

I swallowed. "Yeah . . ."

"Liam may have bought that story, but can I add some advice?" She took my shaky nod as enough of an answer, so she continued, "Next time, take a shower before coming home. I can smell the sex and cologne from over here."

Heat flooded my face, and I gripped the edge of the counter, needing support as my knees buckled. "Oh my God."

Lowering her voice, she added, "I'm not here to judge. Your life is none of my business. I don't want to know where you were or who you were with, but you need to be careful. You know the press is waiting for you to make a wrong move."

"I made a mistake," I whispered. "I don't how it happened, but I know it can never happen again. Please don't tell Liam."

There was compassion in Amy's emerald green eyes—we'd been friends for over twenty years, been through every major life milestone together—but it was mixed with pity. "I'm not going to say anything. You know I'm on your side, and so is Liam, or we wouldn't be here. Life hasn't been fair to you."

Like my life wasn't already a mess. "Who says I'm entitled to fair?"

"Nat, you didn't do anything to deserve what he did to you. It's not your fault, but I know how hard it is to see that when you're in an abusive relationship. Whatever happened tonight, if it made you happy, fine. *You* are in control of your life from now on."

Shaking my head, I was so ashamed. "Nothing about tonight was about happiness. I thought maybe it could fix me, help me move on."

"It's healthy to try and move on. You can't live stuck in the past, especially one as dark as yours. I just want to see you happy again."

"Baby steps. It took years to break me down and will probably take years to put me back together."

"I'll still be here." She winked.

I blew her a kiss. "And that's why I love you."

There wasn't much time to ponder my first and only one-night stand. The news finally broke about the divorce. My phone was constantly blowing up with notifications every time my name or the kids' were mentioned in the press, along with calls from news outlets looking for a statement.

The kids went back to school, leaving me alone at home, watching the news all day, every day. Amy and Liam begged me to turn it off, but I couldn't. I'd been trained to know what was being said about me—both the truth and the lies. It affected me mentally and physically.

Withdrawing into myself, I spent most days in bed, repeating the words that Leo had drilled into me for years.

You're not good enough. If you tried harder, they would leave you alone.

I was nauseous watching the twisted version of my reality that they spun—stories that I stole my children from their homeland, denying them their birthright. Worst of all, Leo was eating up the attention, using any and all sympathy to look like the injured party, playing the doting father who was lost without his children. Controlling the narrative; that's what he did best.

My reputation was ruined, but I didn't care. What mattered was keeping the vultures away from my children. I was given a second chance to keep them an ocean away, but they still needed protection. When the paparazzi began staking out their school, the security team deemed it too risky to continue sending them, so I kept them at home, hiring a nanny and a tutor.

Eventually, the heat would die down, and they could go back. At least, I hoped.

Weeks went by and the coverage dwindled, but the thought of it still made me physically sick. It reached the point where I couldn't hold down even the few things I managed to eat. I was letting this mental block keep me from my kids, and I hated myself for it.

Amy had finally had enough and sought to intervene. It was safe for the kids to return to school, and as soon as they were gone, she entered my room, not bothering to knock.

Sitting on the edge of the bed where I was curled up, she sighed. "Nat, you have to get out of bed. They win—*he* wins—if you can't move on. I can't sit here and watch you waste away. If not for me, do it for the kids. They need you."

Groaning, I replied, "Do you think I want to feel like death?"

"I think you're punishing yourself. It's not your fault that Leo is a walking nightmare."

"I married him." I would never forgive myself for falling for the villain. My kids deserved so much better.

"You did, but you had no idea what you were getting into."

I closed my eyes, swallowing against the nausea churning in my gut. "There were red flags. I knew something was off."

"You couldn't have known he would flip a switch like he did." Amy was trying to bring rational thought to my pity party.

"Maybe I asked for it." That was another mantra Leo had drilled into me. Everything was *my* fault.

She was stern. "No. I won't have it. You did *nothing* wrong. Do you hear me? No one asks for what he did to you. That's him in your head. He doesn't belong here."

Opening my mouth to respond, I quickly shut it, bolting toward the master bathroom and hugging the toilet before losing the contents of my stomach for the second time that day. Amy followed me, holding my hair back and flushing for me when I slumped against the wall.

"I hate seeing you like this."

Wryly, I replied, "It's no picnic for me either, Ames."

"I'll get you a cool washcloth." She sighed, heading for the linen closet. Eyes closed, I heard her pause once she opened it. "Hmm."

"Hmm, what?"

"How many boxes of tampons do you need? This closet shelf is full."

Frowning, I opened my eyes, breathing deeply to calm myself. "They keep coming on auto delivery."

Amy knew that I was underweight, and my periods were sporadic as a result. "Shouldn't at least some of these be open?" she mused.

I tried to think back to the last time I'd had a period. Maybe May? Or was it April? I was lost in my thoughts when Amy asked, "There's no chance, right?"

Feeling horrible, my temper was short, so I snapped. "No chance of what, Amy? Spit it out."

"You couldn't be pregnant, right?"

My mind raced, my heart beating so loud that I swore I could hear it pounding in my ears. "No. I mean . . . I made sure."

She gave me a knowing look. "You can never be sure."

"No! I was!" I protested, panic starting to set in.

"Natalie, there's no harm in ruling it out. You're probably right, but I can't ignore how sick you've been. It's been years since Leo, but . . ."

"I hate you so much," I whined.

She finally made good on her promise of the cool washcloth, helping me to my feet and tucking me into bed. Squeezing my hand, she added, "I'll be back later."

Dozing off for a bit, I awoke to a home pregnancy test on my nightstand. There was no way I could face the possibility alone, so I texted her to come upstairs for moral support. She was always there for me when I needed her most. I didn't know what I'd done right in my life to have my live-in support system, but I silently sent up a prayer of thanks.

When she re-entered the room, Amy found me sitting up with the box in my hands. My best friend sat by my side, and I leaned my head on her shoulder. She grasped my hand, promising, "I'm here for you, no matter what."

Nodding, I stood, heading for the bathroom yet again. I could barely breathe, the reality of this situation sitting like a two-ton elephant on my chest. There was no way. I'd paid my dues. With four unplanned pregnancies already under my belt, I couldn't do this again.

I peed on the stick and capped it, getting up to wash my hands, placing it on the bathroom counter. Still drying my hands, I caught the lines in the mirror's reflection. It had barely been a minute, and it was already showing positive. Collapsing on the bathroom floor, I began hyperventilating.

This wasn't happening.

It couldn't be happening.

Unsure of how much time had passed, I heard Amy knock on the door before entering, finding me on the floor. Pity colored her words. "Oh no."

Numbness was my emotion of choice by now, even if my body's reaction was telling a different story. "What am I going to do?"

Joining me on the floor, my best friend was steadfast, taking my hand. "I will support you no matter what you decide."

The implications hit me in full force.

I could make it all go away.

But how could I look at the three little faces of my children, knowing there should be one more, and I had made a choice to change that? No, I couldn't go down that path. On the other hand, things were finally settling for our little family. This baby would throw our lives back into chaos. My summer indiscretion would be revealed, changing our family dynamic and giving ammunition to the paparazzi when they were finally leaving us alone.

Tears burned behind my eyes, and I squeezed Amy's hand. "I have to tell you something."

She squeezed back. "Nothing you tell me right now will leave this room. You know that."

Closing my eyes, I swallowed before whispering, "I slept with Jaxon Slate."

My declaration was met with silence. Daring to open my eyes, I found Amy staring at me, eyes wide, mouth hanging open.

"Say something!" I demanded, unable to bear the silence a moment longer.

I could see her collecting her thoughts before she responded, "Okay . . ."

"Okay, what? None of this is okay!" I shouted.

"Sorry, I needed a minute to process. I have so many questions."

I buried my head in my hands, muffling a frustrated scream. Resigned, I sighed. "Fire away."

Seriously, she asked, "First things first. Which one of you went backpacking in Western Europe?"

Only Amy could get me to laugh when all I wanted to do was cry, citing a scenario from our all-time favorite sitcom. I put my head on her shoulder. She'd been by my side through thick and thin. It strengthened me to know that no matter what happened with my current situation, she would be there, as steadfast as ever.

Wiping away tears from laughing instead of crying—for once—I answered honestly, "Sadly, it was me. I came on to him. Only God knows why. I went over for Jameson's ball, and then he offered me a drink. I know I should have said no, but something inside me snapped, and I wanted to forget my life for one night."

There was a smile in her voice as she teased, "Can't say I blame you. That man is sex on a stick. That's going to be one good-looking baby."

Somehow, Amy always helped me find the light in any situation. Even on my darkest days, she'd helped me find the silver lining. I only hoped that her optimism would carry me through this impossible situation.

CHAPTER 5

Natalie

THE SKY WAS STILL dark before dawn as Amy drove us to my OB's office to confirm that the positive test had resulted in a viable pregnancy. There was still a tiny part of my mind in denial, but I'd been down this road too many times. I could pretend it wasn't happening, but like it or not, a helpless new life depended solely on me to get my act together.

Amy never left my side as they took all my vitals and ran preliminary tests. I couldn't bear to look at the scale when they checked my weight, and embarrassment flooded me when I couldn't pinpoint the date of my last period.

Coming to my rescue, as she so often did, Amy prompted, "Maybe that's not important? You know the date of conception, right?"

I closed my eyes. Yeah, I knew that. "Um, it was August third." That seemed to satisfy the nurse checking me in, and she left us alone for a few minutes while we waited for the doctor. I couldn't stop myself from asking Amy, "How bad was it?"

She knew instantly what I wanted to know. "Which side of the scale is deemed 'bad' these days?"

Leo had made me believe that the press was fixated on my weight for years, saying my size six body was fat. He'd even gone so far as to suggest a tummy tuck after Beau was born. I'd learned later that he had been the one feeding those stories and pictures to the gossip rags. He'd wanted to see how far he could push me. To break me mentally, asserting complete control.

The years of mental torture took their toll, resulting in extreme body dysmorphia, which then led to my anorexia. Breaking free and putting an ocean between us still wasn't enough to shake the conditioning that I would never be thin enough.

I *knew* I'd taken it too far, but I couldn't stop. Looking in the mirror, I couldn't see what my family saw when they begged me to take better care of myself. Liam and Amy became desperate, showing me pictures of myself on the tabloid websites, and I remembered how shocked I was. I couldn't believe I was the same person depicted in those photographs, going so far as to claim that they'd been photoshopped because that skeleton-thin woman couldn't be me—I didn't want to believe that it was me. They'd confirmed that was what they saw when they looked at me, and I had an emotional breakdown.

I wanted to do better and be healthier for my kids, but eating the proper amount changed from a mental block into a physical one. I got sick if I ate more than a light portion of a meal. Doctors explained that my stomach shrank because of the low volume of food I'd consumed over the course of the previous years. The only solution was to keep eating, and eventually, it would expand back to its original size. They warned me it would be uncomfortable, but try as I might, I couldn't force myself to eat more frequently. This disease had me firmly in its grasp, and I feared I would never break free.

Smoothing the paper gown over my lap, I couldn't meet Amy's eyes. "How underweight?"

I heard her sigh. "Nat." When she didn't continue right away, my eyes raised to meet hers—full of compassion but laced with concern. "It's bad. If I'm being honest, I don't know how you're still standing here. I could *kill* him for what he's done to you."

Don't cry. Don't cry.

As I was blinking back the tears, I felt her hand grab mine. She whispered, "He can't hurt you anymore."

Nodding, knowing that wasn't true, I managed the only words I could. "I love you, Ames."

Squeezing my hand, she replied, "Love you always, Nat."

A knock at the door shook me out of my thoughts. I watched as the doctor's mouth moved, barely hearing her as she began going through the motions to check on a baby that would change all our lives. What finally snapped me out of my fog was when the monitor turned in my direction, showing a tiny, squirming, gummy-bear-looking shape on the screen.

There it is. This is real.

She had my attention now, and I heard the doctor for the first time as she declared, "Looks healthy and right on track for the dates you gave. Right around eight weeks, maybe a couple of days past."

Finishing the ultrasound, she removed her gloves and rolled away on the stool. Briefly, she glanced at Amy before addressing the elephant in the room. "Do we need to discuss options?"

"No. I'm keeping it." That decision was made before we made this appointment.

She nodded. "In that case, I have some concerns."

Panicked, I grabbed for Amy's hand again. "You said it was healthy."

The doctor's lips turned down. "Yes, the baby is healthy. For now. I'm sure you're well aware that your health must remain the top priority. In your current state, I don't know that your body will be able to handle carrying a baby to term. I can see from your chart that's been an issue in the past."

Pushing that to the back of my mind, I explained, "I've tried. I can't even eat a child-sized portion before my stomach rebels."

"I can prescribe some anti-nausea meds to help with the morning sickness you're experiencing. There are some high-calorie shakes you can sip on throughout the day, which may be helpful in putting on weight without upsetting your stomach like solid food. If that fails, your only option may be a feeding tube, which I would not recommend. At that point, I would urge you to reconsider your options regarding the pregnancy."

Shaking my head, knowing the alternative, I promised, "I'll make it work. I *have* to."

Nodding, she stood. "All right. I'll see you in four weeks, barring any issues. Please take care of yourself so that you can take care of this baby."

"I will."

Once back in the car, I let all the information wash over me. By the end of April, I'd be the mother of four. Maybe. There were so many variables—some I had control over, but so many others that I didn't.

Amy had remained silent but decided I'd stewed long enough. "Are you going to tell him?"

A flat laugh left my lips. "Which him?"

"Are we playing that game?" She knew I was deflecting. When I didn't respond, she continued, "Guess so. Fine. It's none of Leo's business. Liam will figure it out eventually, considering he lives with us, so that leaves Jaxon. You know, the father."

"I know I should . . ."

It was the right thing to do, but the thought of telling Jaxon terrified me. Chalk it up to past trauma; the memories I had of telling a man I was pregnant were filled with images of Leo's disgust, disdain, and blame. I'd always been made to feel guilty for falling pregnant, regardless of the fact I'd been firmly in a committed relationship—a married woman. This time I didn't even have that to back me up.

Amy sighed, knowing my history. "Nat. He lives next door. What do you think is going to happen? He won't notice you have a new baby? One that has a high chance of looking like him? That he won't realize the dates line up? Keep dreaming."

"You don't understand. The night I slept with him, I found his phone while searching for my clothes."

She made a show of an exaggerated gasp. "Oh dear lord, he has a phone? How *dare* he!"

Rolling my eyes, I explained, "It was blowing up with messages from his boys about how they were waiting for him so they could pick up women. I'm probably not even the only woman he slept with that night!"

"Didn't you say you came on to him?"

"Yes," I groaned.

"Then how can you hold it against him for having a life?"

Chewing on that for a minute, a lightbulb went off. Maybe I could turn this to my advantage. Jaxon hadn't planned on me walking in that day and begging him to sleep with me. He certainly hadn't planned on creating a baby that night.

What if I played to the playboy side of it? I could offer him zero responsibility. Let him off the hook, and in return, he'd have no interference in my life, the baby's, or the rest of the kids'.

That was it! It would solve everything.

Returning home, the kids were already off to school for the day, and I found Liam enjoying his coffee out on the deck while the weather was still mild. For how much he'd given me these past few years, it was only right that I tell him before I told Jaxon. He'd always supported me, but I knew he would be so disappointed in me. Everyone was going to be.

Reminding myself that I'd made the choices that led to my current situation, I opened the sliding glass door and walked toward where Liam was sitting. The smell of his coffee hit me, and I gagged before I could stop myself. On a normal day, I didn't like the smell of coffee, but my sense of smell—and my gag reflex, for that matter—were in overdrive now.

Thanks, gummy bear.

Liam's senses were honed during his years of mandated military service, so he instantly heard the almost silent noise, standing on high alert. "Whoa, are you all right?"

Waving my hand dismissively, I responded, "Sorry, you know I'm not a big fan of the coffee smell."

Walking past me, he took the cup inside before returning. "Better?"

"Much, thank you." I smiled weakly.

"Come, sit down." He guided me to the chair next to the one he'd just vacated. "I know you haven't been feeling well lately."

Heat rushed to my cheeks. "Yeah, about that."

"Nat, I know it's hard, but you have to put your blinders on. You're safe here. I will never let anything happen to you."

Oh, the irony. "Too late."

His whole body tensed, and he forced out through gritted teeth, "What did he do?"

Reaching over, I touched his arm. "No, it's nothing like that."

"You scared me," he breathed out, his body relaxing in visible relief.

"Liam, I'm pregnant." That was the first time I'd said the words out loud. It still didn't feel real.

The color drained from his face as his eyes darted, his brain working on overdrive. "Preg—How?"

Well, Liam, when a man and woman find each other attractive, blood rushes—"

He held a hand up, cutting me off. "*Not* what I meant." He dragged a hand down his face. "I'm aware of the mechanics involved," he muttered dryly.

Continuing to use humor as a deflection technique, I pressed, "Are you sure? I can explain the birds and the bees. It's not that complex."

"Natalie . . ." I sat up straighter at the warning tone in his voice.

Ashamed, I looked down, avoiding his ever-present scowl. "I didn't mean for this to happen."

Instantly, his tone softened. "Who is the father? Oh God, do you even know who the father is?"

My eyes snapped up. "Jesus, Liam! You live here. How often have you seen me go out? Of course I know who the father is."

Sufficiently chastised, he took my hand in apology. "I'm sorry. I'm trying to process this. You're divorced and never go out. Who could possibly be—" I knew the exact moment he figured it out as his eyes went wide. "No, Nat. Please tell me it isn't who I think it is."

Play dumb. No way he knows.

"I don't know what you're talking about." The way my voice wavered, I couldn't even convince myself of that lie.

"That night you came home late. No phone, no car." I winced, but he kept going. "It was him, wasn't it? I've seen the way he looks at you."

"Excuse me?" I had no idea what he was talking about.

"You can't be that naïve." Liam scoffed.

"There's no way we are thinking about the same person. I don't know what you think you saw."

"Jameson's ball. You went next door to get it." Then he muttered under his breath, "I *knew* I should have hopped the fence."

I whispered his name, confirming, "Jaxon."

Liam stood, pacing, his tone deadly. "Fucking Jaxon Slate. He's had his eye on you for *years*. I'm going to kill him for taking advantage of you like this." He moved toward the door to the house like he was headed to Jaxon's this minute.

Jumping to my feet, I yelled, "No!" That startled him enough that he paused long enough for me to explain. "Sorry to break it to you, big brother, but *I* was the one who begged him to sleep with me. Yes, you heard that right. I *begged* him."

This whole conversation was cringe-worthy. If it was this hard to tell Liam, how was I going to tell Jaxon? How was I going to tell my kids?

I gave Liam a few minutes to pace the deck. He looked like he was going to tear his hair out the way he kept reaching into the midnight-black tresses and yanking.

He was a large man, both in height and build. At six-two and over two hundred pounds of muscle, he used his size as an intimidation factor, but I'd never been afraid of him. It might be useful in scaring Jaxon off, and that would certainly solve some of my problems, but I needed to do this my way. Liam couldn't protect me forever. I needed to stand on my own two feet. I was twenty-eight years old, for crying out loud—if not now, then when?

My heart hammered against my chest, so I took a calming breath. "Did I break your brain?" He paused his movements, so I added, "I can't do this without you, Liam."

Just like that, my rock was back, taking two steps and wrapping me in his arms. Leaning into him, the tears threatening for days finally fell. Liam stroked my hair, allowing me to cry as he whispered, "I'm sorry, Nat. This isn't about me." I simply nodded into his shoulder, and he asked, "Does he know?"

Looking up at him, I shook my head. "Not yet."

"Maybe he doesn't have to. We didn't tell Leo when—"

I cut him off before he could continue. "This isn't the same. *He* isn't the same."

"We could move." He was dead serious and had the resources to make it happen. He'd done it once before.

I shook my head. "I'm done running. But I do have a plan."

He raised an eyebrow. "Care to share?"

"I need to wait a few weeks and see if this one sticks. They're not sure it will if I can't put on weight."

"Oh, Nat." He pulled me close again.

I needed to figure out how to get past my mental challenges, but there was no greater motivator than my children. All four of them now.

I could do this. Then, I would take the steps to keep control in my hands for possibly the first time in my adult life.

"Please! You have to come!" Hannah whined.

Opening Night for the Comets was tonight, and it was tradition for Hannah and me to go together since we were fourteen, and her dad first became the coach. Even when I was living in Belleston, I had made the trip to attend the home opener as often as I could. Not wanting to run into Jaxon, I'd purposely skipped the pre-season barbeque this year. My poker face was not strong enough for that.

Turning down Hannah twice in two weeks wasn't an easy task. The third part of our best-friends trio, Hannah was the feisty one. Growing up around hockey as the daughter of first a player and then a coach, she was like one of the guys. That meant most women didn't like her, feeling threatened by her familiarity with the men they hoped to snag.

I knew I liked her the first day she walked into our school freshman year in high school. She'd seemed fun and outgoing—everything I'd wished I was. Without a thought, I'd approached her, inviting her to sit with Amy and me at lunch, and the rest was history. The three of us have been best friends ever since, each bringing a different element to our unique friendship.

I sighed. "Hannah, you know that I love going to games with you, but the kids need me right now."

Sympathy shone in her blue eyes. "I know that they do. It's been a hard year for them. But sometimes, you need to get out and do things for yourself. It makes you a better mom."

If only she knew that getting out and *doing* a certain hockey player was going to make me a mom. Again.

As much as I wanted to trust her with possibly the biggest secret of my life, I couldn't. Not yet, at least. I had to keep this one close to the vest. I wasn't even sure how it was going to pan out once I let Jaxon know.

"Pleeeeeeeeeeeeease, Nat," she begged, clasping her hands together.

Hannah wasn't going to let it go, so I gave in. "Fine. I'll come. No promises on staying for the whole game, though."

She was jumping up and down, excited that she'd won the battle. "Deal!" Transferring the ticket to my phone, she practically skipped out of the house, calling over her shoulder, "See you tonight!"

So, there I found myself, in the family box, watching the players skate during warmups. I couldn't help it as my gaze immediately went to Jaxon. He was hard to miss, with his effortless, long strides on the ice. With that raw power and agility on display, my mind began flashing back to our night together.

His strong arms carrying me, pinning me to the wall. The hard planes of his body flexing as he moved over me. The way he played my body like an instrument, knowing exactly what I needed and when.

Completely lost in my thoughts, I nearly jumped out of my skin when a hand touched my shoulder. Spinning around revealed a shocked Hannah, and I blushed—my thoughts were beyond inappropriate for such a public setting.

Hannah rushed out, "I'm so sorry! I didn't mean to scare you."

Patting the seat next to me, silently inviting her to sit, I apologized in turn. "No, it's not you."

Taking the offered seat, she gave me a side hug. "I'm so glad you came."

"You were right. It's tradition, and I needed to get out."

The game started, and I got lost in it. Not in the game itself, but mesmerized in tracking the one player who stood out amongst the rest. He threw a hit, crunching an opposing player against the boards. Usually, that impact would have me flinching, but there was something different about him. He was in control of his actions, adjusting to the situation and using force only when needed. He could be strong and domineering on the ice, but he'd handled me with such care. I had no idea it could be that gentle with a man.

He's going to hate me. I'm about to ruin his perfect bachelor life.

"Earth to Natalie." Hannah's words jarred me from my daze.

"What's that?" I forced myself to tear my eyes away from the man on the ice.

"We scored, and you didn't even react. Are you okay? Usually, you're leading the screaming section up here." Concern etched her features.

She was right. Leo had deemed hockey a distasteful blood sport and had flat-out refused to accompany me to games. That meant it was one of the only places where I'd felt comfortable enough to be myself without fear of repercussions. Hockey was fast-paced, exciting, and always got my blood pumping.

Are you describing hockey or Jaxon?

"Sorry, I was somewhere else." It was a lame excuse but vague enough to fly under the radar.

Her look softened to one of pity—God, I hated the pity. "I shouldn't have pushed you. I know things haven't been easy. What we really need is a girls' night—just you, me, and Amy. We don't even need to go out. We can stay in. Whatever is best for you right now. Just us girls and some margs."

Now, I felt even worse about my secret. Between the three of us, no two relationships were stronger than the others, but sometimes Hannah felt left out because Amy and I lived together. Amy already knowing wouldn't help with those feelings, especially given who the father was. Hannah was much closer to Jaxon than Amy.

I'd tell her, I promised myself. Just not today.

Smiling weakly, I nodded. "Yeah, we'll have to do that soon."

"Tell me about your trip."

What trip?

Sticking with the vague answers, not having a clue what she was talking about, I replied, "It was good."

"When you told me you planned a trip the same weekend as the barbeque, I couldn't believe it. We always have the most fun at that event."

Get a grip, Natalie. You're losing it. You lied to one of your best friends. Remember?

Tracing the lettering on my upper back, she added, "This one asked about you."

"Who?"

Hannah looked at me like I had three heads. "Um, Jaxon? You know, the player whose jersey you're wearing?"

Duh.

You couldn't have worn any other jersey in your closet? You might as well have a neon sign pointing at you, saying, "I slept with Jaxon".

Be cool.

"He did?"

Smiling, she nudged me. "He's always asked about you. I think he has a crush on you."

Unable to stop the blush that crept up my neck, I nudged back. "Stop it. No, he doesn't."

"You know. You're single, he's single. He's hot, you're hot. It makes sense. You know Dad has that whole no-dating-my-daughters rule, so I have to live vicariously through you."

She was getting too close for comfort, so I deflected, "Yeah, the hot hockey player and the single mom of three. Unlikely." I threw in a scoff at the end for good measure.

Shrugging, she mused, "It could happen."

Oh, it definitely happened.

We fell back into our companionable silence, and like a magnet, my eyes went right back to Jaxon on the ice. The first period ended, and I watched him leave the ice.

I knew I had to tell him, and soon. Time was not on my side. It wouldn't be long before this baby made its presence known.

As soon as I tied up the last of the loose ends, I'd tell him the truth.

CHAPTER 6

Jaxon

LEFT. RIGHT. LEFT. RIGHT.

The ice carved beneath my skates as I pushed myself harder and faster, my thighs screaming as a result of the intense effort. I'd stayed behind after practice, needing some peace in the only place I could turn off my brain.

Or at least, it used to be.

Now, *she* had crept into my sanctuary, consuming my thoughts. After I'd woken up alone in my bed, Natalie had effectively ghosted me. I shouldn't have been surprised. I'd given her what she'd asked for—one night. Clearly, that was enough for her, but now that I had gotten a taste, I wanted another.

It became clear she was avoiding me on purpose when she skipped out on the pre-season barbeque. Hannah had told me she was out of town, but I knew the truth. She'd said no strings, but I knew better. I began to wonder if I would ever get to lay eyes on her again. Was I so obsessed that I'd be pulling out binoculars to try and catch glimpses of her through the trees?

Snap out of it, Jaxon!

My legs begged to be done for the day, and I finally gave in, heading toward the locker room. Cal and Benji were showered and dressed, the only ones left after practice. They stopped whatever conversation they were having as soon as I entered.

"Don't stop on my account, boys," I offered, moving toward my stall.

Cal was clearly nominated to go first. "What are you trying to do out there?"

"Endurance training?" I brushed him off.

Shaking his head, he continued, "No, there's something off about you."

Benji chimed in, "Yeah. You've been weird since that night you ditched us at Spades. Now, we can't even get you to agree to go out."

"Maybe you need to get laid," Cal offered.

That's exactly what I need.

The problem was that the only woman I wanted had vanished. For ten years, I'd stayed away from blondes, not wanting to sleep with anyone who could remind me of her. Natalie was one of a kind, and I didn't want a cheap knockoff. Now, the thought of being with another woman was enough to turn my stomach.

Every night, Natalie invaded my dreams. Every morning, I woke up alone, with her scent still on my pillowcase—a reminder that she had been real. Once.

Even months later, I could still taste her on my tongue, craving her more than ever. I began to question whether I'd made the right decision. Was sleeping with Natalie once worth the possibility of never seeing her again?

Cal's words snapped me out of it. "You know who I heard is divorced now? Natalie."

Brushing him off, I countered, "I heard she skipped town."

"That's weird. I could have sworn I saw her with Hannah last week at the opener."

He had my attention now.

She'd been there? Was she there for me?

Stop fooling yourself. She left you alone in bed, remember?

Benji couldn't help but tease, "You looooove her. Now that she's finally single, you should give it a go. If I had a tasty little piece of ass like that living next door, I wouldn't hesitate to make a move."

Rolling my eyes, I punched his arm. "She's a mom, Benji. What kind of animal do you think I am?"

"Yeah, a mom I'd like to—"

Standing, I yelled, "Enough!"

Both of them were shocked into silence, as I didn't often lose my cool. I couldn't bear the thought of them thinking about her like that. Rubbing my jaw, I broke the silence. "I'm sorry, guys. You know how important she is to Coach. What if he heard you talking about her like that?"

Eyes wide, Benji nodded. "You're right. I was over the line."

Cal clapped me on the back. "Sorry, man. I shouldn't have brought her up. Whatever is eating you, you need to deal with it. We can't afford to get a slow start on the season."

I shrugged. "It's not an issue. I'm fine."

He looked doubtful. "If you say so."

Ding dong.

I was expecting a dinner delivery—planning on turning in early tonight before our matinee game tomorrow—but was busy switching the laundry when the doorbell rang. I called out from the back of the house, "Go ahead and leave it! Thanks!"

Knock knock knock. Knock knock knock.

Frustrated, running toward the door, I threw it open. "I said you can leave it!"

Not food delivery.

Standing wide-eyed on my front porch was the one woman I couldn't get out of my head.

Startled, Natalie took a step back. "I'm sorry. I came at a bad time."

I started to reach out to stop her, but halfway there, I caught myself and dropped my hand. After two months, here she was, looking better than ever. Light makeup only highlighted her natural features, and her golden hair fell in loose curls over her shoulders. Her tan had faded, but there was a different kind of glow about her skin. Her tight black leggings showed off that she'd filled out since the last time I'd seen her. My fingers itched to grab a handful of that now-rounded ass.

Having been silent too long, she took another step back, turning to leave. "I can come back later."

"No!" I called out before I could stop myself, and she flinched. "Sorry, it's a good time. I thought you were my dinner delivery."

Natalie blushed, looking down before asking, "Can I come in?"

Hell yes.

Nodding in response, I stepped aside to allow her to walk past me into the house. Her signature scent infiltrated my nostrils as she passed, and boom, I was half hard.

Down, boy. Don't spook her.

Closing the door, I turned and realized how different she seemed from the last time she was here. Instead of acting like she owned the place,

Natalie stood just inside the entryway, twisting her hands and biting her lip.

Motioning to the living room, I offered, "Would you like to sit down? Can I get you a drink?"

There was something about her, something uneasy, and it was unsettling.

She nodded. "Nothing to drink, but I will sit. I won't take up much of your time."

Taking the lead when she didn't move, I headed for the couch. Following, she chose the chair, placing her purse on the ground beside her. Something was off. She kept looking around the room, smoothing her shirt down.

Deciding to break the ice, I said, "I heard you made it to the opener. Did you have a good time?"

Her eyes snapped to mine before she shrugged, explaining, "You know Hannah."

I laughed. Hannah was a force, the most spirited of Coach's daughters. I didn't want to talk about Hannah, though, so I started, "Natalie, I—"

Cutting me off, she blurted out, "I'm pregnant."

I felt myself stand, but my body went numb.

Did she say *pregnant*? No, I'd heard that wrong. What rhymes with pregnant that she probably said? Repugnant? Indignant? I was racking my brain trying to think of what she'd actually said because there was simply no way she had said the word *pregnant*.

While my mind raced, grasping at straws, I watched her as her mouth moved, hands gesturing. The words that finally reached my ears through the fog were, "You don't have to do anything. I've already taken care—"

Oh, God. Did that mean what I thought it meant?

Air rushed into my lungs. Had I stopped breathing?

I forced the words out, "Did you—I mean are you going to—?" The thought was so unimaginable that I couldn't bring myself to say it out loud.

Understanding dawned in her eyes, and she rushed, "Oh, no. I didn't mean it like that." Reaching into her purse, she pulled out a manila envelope, placing it on the coffee table, explaining, "Once the paternity test is completed—"

"Paternity test," I repeated.

Blushing, she added, "For legality. You're the only man I've been with in years."

"*Years?*" I was definitely hearing things. Maybe an MRI was in order. I'd have to make a call to the team doc after this.

"That's not important. What is important is that once the test confirms paternity, you can sign the termination of parental rights papers I have here."

Testing the words on my tongue, I managed, "Termination—what?"

"I know how much the game demands of you—the time commitment, the travel. Plus, this was completely unplanned. I've been a single mom for years and have lots of help, so I can handle this. It's all right."

She wanted me to walk away from my baby? *My baby.*

Oh God, this was really happening. Did she expect me to sit next door while she was raising our child? Did she think that little of me that I wouldn't want to take responsibility? Or worse, did she want me out of her life, too?

"You want me to walk." Saying the words out loud caused me to flinch visibly.

"It would make everything easier," she confirmed.

"Easier?"

"You didn't sign on for this. This way, you can move on with your life like nothing ever happened."

Ding dong.

Natalie's eyes went wide, her body went rigid, and before I could blink, she bolted for the kitchen. Dazed, I headed for the door, opening it to the delivery driver with my food. Tipping him quickly, I shut the door, making my way into the kitchen.

The sight of her, white as a sheet, gripping the kitchen island and physically shaking, did me in. I had to wrap my brain around this quickly because she was visibly struggling. There was no way I was letting her handle this all on her own.

Placing the takeout bag on the counter, I asked quietly, "Are you okay?"

Her voice shook. "I—I can't have this getting out. The kids couldn't even go to school when news broke about the divorce. Can you imagine what would happen if the press found out you and I were having a baby together?"

Rubbing a hand over my face, I countered, "So, no father is better than me? What happens when this kid grows up and finds out I've been next door this whole time? Did you even think about that?"

She collapsed onto a kitchen stool, her voice breaking as she asked, "What do you want?"

I want you.

This was it. My one chance to get close enough to show her how much I'd always cared about her. A baby meant we were tied together for life. Maybe it was dumb luck, or perhaps it was fate, but whatever it was, I had to grab ahold of this opportunity with both hands. There was no chance in hell I was signing papers that would give her permission to disappear again.

"I want to be involved. I want to be there for you in any way you'll let me. I can't sign those papers, Natalie. I'm sorry."

"I understand." She nodded, unable to meet my eye.

"I can keep it quiet," I promised. "We don't have to tell anyone, not until you're ready. I know it will take time for you to trust me, but I want to help."

"It's not just me. My kids don't know." It broke my heart to hear her voice so small, so defeated.

"I want a chance to know my kid."

Tears rolled down her cheeks as she looked up, trying to blink back more that threatened to fall. It killed me to see her like this. All I wanted to do was scoop her into my arms and hold her, but I respected that she needed space.

"I'm sorry," she whimpered.

"You have nothing to be sorry about."

Shaking her head, she continued, "No, I do. I have three kids with a father who doesn't give a shit about them, and here I am trying to force you to do the same. I've been out of control of my life for so long, and I thought . . ."

"Thought what?" I truly wanted to understand.

Natalie took a deep breath. "I thought if I asked you to sign away your rights, it would make it so that you could never take this baby away from me. I wouldn't survive it. My kids are all I have."

Jesus, what kind of monster did she think I was to take away her child? Did she know me at all?

"I would *never* do that," I vowed. "You said it yourself. I'm constantly at practice, games, or on the road, so my time is limited. I wouldn't even be able to devote whole days to taking care of a baby. It doesn't make sense to ask for custody only to hire help when their mother and siblings are right next door. I trust you. Let me be there when I can, and I won't ever ask for a formal custody arrangement."

Eyes wide, she asked, "You trust me enough to do that?"

"Let me be a part of this. That's all I ask."

"Okay." She stood, and I mirrored her actions, following as she walked back into the living room. Taking the folder off the coffee table, she placed it back inside her purse. Retrieving her cell phone, she held it out to me. When I didn't take it, she prompted, "Your phone number?"

I took the phone. "Oh, yeah. Of course." I plugged in my number and handed it back.

She inspected it before adding, "I'll send over the details of the lab for the paternity testing."

"Thanks."

"I should go." As we headed toward the door, there was an awkward silence. It was like neither one of us knew what else to say.

Opening the door, I managed, "Please let me know if there's anything that I can do for you."

Natalie nodded. "Sure."

I watched her walk across the driveway until she disappeared down the stone path that ran between our two houses. Closing the door, I leaned up against it, running my hands through my hair.

I knocked up Natalie Remington.

I was going to be a father.

Holy shit.

CHAPTER 7

Jaxon

THE PATERNITY TEST RESULTS came back after a couple of weeks, confirming what I already knew—I was the father of Natalie's baby. I was on the road, but she texted me with the news, including an attachment of the official lab report. Keeping my promise, I hadn't told anyone, but she agreed that it would be appropriate to tell my parents and Coach in case any family obligation interfered with my schedule.

My little brother, Braxton, had followed me to Connecticut and was playing college hockey at Hartford State University. Early November meant the start of his season, and my parents were coming to town to see some of his games and mine. Their visit was my chance to tell them they were about to become grandparents.

Setting up a dinner at my house, I invited Coach and my parents. Coach became my mentor when I'd been drafted young, so we had a closer-than-average relationship. He wouldn't think twice about being asked to have dinner with my parents.

My parents I could handle, but Coach? He'd made it clear early on that Natalie wasn't only off-limits because she was married—she was off-limits because he viewed her like a daughter. I would be lucky if my legs survived the on-ice punishment he would dish out if I even saw the ice again after he found out what I'd done.

"Knock knock! Anyone home!" my mom called out as she let herself and my dad in.

Rushing to the door, I placed an obligatory kiss on her cheek before hugging her. "Hi, Mom."

She pulled back, assessing me from head to toe. "You look tired, Jaxon. Are you tired?"

"Leave him alone, Shannon. He looks fine." Dad had entered the chat, a man of few words as it was hard to get any in around Mom.

I nodded to my dad in gratitude. "Thanks."

Shoving a platter in my face, Mom announced, "I brought dessert!"

Chuckling, I took the platter. "Of course you did. Looks great. I'll take it to the kitchen. Make yourselves at home."

By the time I returned, Coach had arrived and was exchanging the usual pleasantries with my parents. They became close early in my career as Coach was the one to look out for me. I'd been lucky that so many people had my back. Not everyone entering the league so young had a support system to keep them on track. Too much money combined with a lack of supervision was often catastrophic for young players.

Coach caught sight of me as I entered the room. "Hey, there he is!" Turning to my parents, he added, "I can't tell you how impressed I've been with Jaxon this season. He's been pushing hard outside of practice. Not many guys in year ten are putting in that amount of extra time. His ability to lead by example makes him an excellent captain."

Mom beamed. "We are always so proud of our Jaxon."

Not making this any easier, Mom.

Clearing my throat, I asked, "So, do we want to sit for drinks first? Or go straight to dinner?"

Waving her hand, Mom proclaimed, "Drinks! Let's chat for a bit before we eat."

Grabbing drinks from the kitchen, I tried to gather my courage. Carrying a loaded tray, I made my way back into the living room before setting it down and taking a seat.

Patting my knee, Mom prompted, "Tell us what's new with you, dear."

Well, it's now or never, Jaxon. Time to man up. Just rip off the bandage.

"Actually, I do have some news."

Lighting up, she bounced in her seat. "Oooh! You never have news!"

Breathe, man. You can do this.

"I'm going to be a dad this spring." The silence was deafening as three sets of eyes stared at me. When I couldn't take it anymore, I asked, "Anyone have anything to say about that?"

Dad went first, lecturing, "Son, what did I tell you when you left home at fifteen?"

The words had been drilled into me. "Always wrap it up."

"So, what were you thinking? Was it worth it? Now, you'll have some woman coming for all you've worked for. Plus, a child on top of it? You're not ready for any of that."

Some woman?

Nobody had the right to talk about Natalie that way, and my temper flared. "For your information, Dad, I did use protection. It apparently wasn't enough. And what do you know about what I'm ready for? I'm twenty-seven years old!"

Scoffing, he remarked, "This is something I might expect from Braxton, but not you, Jaxon. You're better than this."

Standing, I threw my arms wide. "Why? Because I'm expected to be perfect all the time? I'm sick and tired of living up to the golden boy image of me you have built up in your mind."

Ignoring my outburst, he continued, "How do you even know she's telling the truth that the child is yours?"

"Goddammit, Dad! Would you like a copy of the paternity test?"

Clearly uncomfortable, Coach asked, "Why am I here for this?"

Time to drop the bomb.

Taking a breath, I dropped into my seat before responding, "Natalie is the mother."

I watched the shift in his demeanor. He'd been my coach for ten years, so I knew what he looked like when he was about to blow.

Explosion incoming.

"*Natalie?*" he boomed. "What did I tell you? How long has this been going on?"

"Coach, it's not what you think—"

Dad interrupted, "Well, of course, you're going to have to marry her."

Coach countered, "No way in hell can he marry her!"

"He has to take responsibility," Dad argued.

"Michael, *enough!*" Mom yelled. Once again, silence descended as all the men turned to Mom. Calmly she asked, "Jaxon, how do you feel about all of this?"

I had never loved her as much as I did in this moment. Trust Mom to focus amidst the chaos. Sighing, I said, "I've had a little time to let it sink in. I'm dealing with it."

Mom smiled. "I don't know Natalie, but how do you feel about her?"

Before I could respond, Coach blurted, "Anyone with eyes knows how he feels about Natalie. He's been looking at her like a lovesick puppy dog for years!"

Not backing down, Mom addressed Coach, "I was asking my *son*, Ace." Turning back to me, she prompted, "Jaxon?"

Rubbing a hand over my jaw, I was honest, "I have feelings for her. Coach is right. I've always had feelings for her."

"And how is she doing?"

"She's scared." The mental image of Natalie terrified in my kitchen weeks ago had my heart twisting inside my chest.

"Poor thing." She was in full-on mom mode, and I could tell she was yearning to mother Natalie.

"She's terrified of what will happen if anyone finds out. Especially the press. She wants to protect her children."

"She has older children?" I could hear the slight shock in her voice. No one anyone outside of Coach or my teammates could picture me picking up a single mom.

Nodding, I confirmed, "Three of them. She's only been divorced for a few months. This would be a difficult time for her regardless of the pregnancy."

"How can we help?" This was what Mom did. She took care of everyone selflessly. Her kindness knew no bounds.

"What she really needs is privacy. I promised to keep things quiet. That means, this information doesn't leave this room. You can't even tell Braxton."

Turning to Dad and Coach, she asked, "Gentlemen? Think you can do that?" They both nodded—she'd sufficiently scared them into silence. "All right, done. Now, next things next."

Confused, I asked, "What's next?"

"If you care about this girl, it falls on you to take care of her. I don't think a marriage of obligation is a good idea." She threw a pointed look at Dad. "But that doesn't mean you can't build a relationship. You might be doing things a little bit backwards, but nothing can be done about that now. Be there for her, and the rest will follow. *If* she's what you want."

Nodding, I whispered, "She's everything I've ever wanted."

She smiled. "Then go get her. Take care of your family."

My family.

Damn, that had a nice ring to it. I knew that with Mom on board, she'd whip Dad into shape eventually. He needed time. Hell, I needed time, but that was a luxury I couldn't afford.

Coach stood. "If you'll excuse me, I don't think I'll stay for dinner." I stood, mirroring him as he added, "And don't worry, I won't tell anyone. Not for your sake, but for Natalie's. She's been through enough."

Willing to take what I could get, I knew he would be pissed for a while.

Once he left, Dad stood. "I've lost my appetite."

Mom chastised, "Michael . . . We came here to spend time with Jaxon."

"You stay. I can come and pick you up later."

I touched her arm. "It's all right, Mom. Want some food to go?"

Pulling me into a hug, she whispered, "Think about what I said?"

Hugging her tighter, my words were muffled in her hair. "I will."

Pulling back, she smiled. "Just be you. You've got this."

Kissing her cheek, I was grateful for her support. "Thanks, Mom."

Heading toward the door, she called back, "Call if you need anything. *Anything*, you hear me?"

"Yes, ma'am."

As they headed out the door, I could hear Mom chastising Dad, "You need to lighten up, Michael. We're going to be grandparents. Find the silver lining. If our son is happy, you need to be happy for him."

Their voices floated further away, but I heard Dad respond, "I need time, Shannon. It's a lot to process."

I moved forward to shut the door, just in time to hear Mom close out her argument, "This isn't about you. Get over yourself."

Thanks, Mom.

She was right as she so often was. I needed to step up and take care of Natalie. She had to come first. It wasn't going to be easy to earn her trust. I knew it was going to take time. Luckily, we had plenty of that—eighteen years, to be exact.

Hopefully, it wouldn't take quite that long.

Ding dong.

My parents had only been gone roughly fifteen minutes, so I hustled to the door, throwing it open, saying, "What did you forget?" When I finally looked up, I was met with the striking blue eyes of Liam Remington.

Liam was Natalie's guard dog, but he also happened to be the brother of her ex-husband. It always struck me as odd that he took her side when things went south, moving in with her and the kids when they'd relocated.

Was there something more going on there? The press had always speculated there was something going on between them, but with how timid Natalie had been during our one night together, it didn't seem like she was very experienced.

The man made it no secret that he didn't like me, and now I'd given him a reason.

I breathed out, "Oh, it's you."

Narrowing those piercing eyes on me, he crossed both arms over his massive chest. Liam was a large man, but I wasn't scared of him. He might be only a couple of inches taller than me, but easily had thirty more pounds of muscle. The size difference between us wouldn't matter if he tried to get between me and my family.

Not mincing words, he stated matter-of-factly, "I saw your company leave. We need to talk."

Rolling my eyes in response, I made my annoyance clear. "Stalking me now?"

"You're one to talk."

"Did you come here to insult me? Or did you want to talk?" I narrowed my eyes.

"Fine. Can I come in?" Liam grunted in annoyance. You'd think a prince would have better manners.

Stepping aside, I allowed him access. "Sure." Closing the door, I leaned against it, not formally inviting him in. "What do you want?"

He huffed, repeating my question, "What do I want? I want you to leave my sister alone."

If he wanted to play the alpha male, then fine, we'd play. "Not going to happen."

"She doesn't need you. She has me, and she has Amy."

Glaring at him, I wasn't budging. "I think you're forgetting something. That's my baby she's carrying."

"Why couldn't you just walk away? She gave you the chance. Take it. It's not too late." Was it *his* idea, those papers? I clenched my fists, anger coursing through my veins at the thought.

"Could you walk away? If it was your baby?"

He broke my gaze. "No."

"I'm not going anywhere."

Liam's eyes snapped to mine, sharp and menacing. "You have no idea what she's been through."

"I have some idea." I shrugged.

"You have no fucking clue. My brother is a monster."

His admission set me on edge. "So, let me get this straight. You're trying to protect her from me, but you couldn't protect her from your own brother?"

A shadow passed over his eyes. "There were a lot of things that happened behind closed doors that I didn't find out about until it was too late."

Intrigued, I asked, "Like what?"

Liam shook his head. "No. That's not my story to tell. I might not have been able to protect her from the things I didn't know about, but I sure as hell helped get her out. I dropped everything in my life to bring her home and take care of her. And you know what? She was worth it."

"You think I don't know that? She deserves my support right now. *My baby* deserves a father."

He scoffed. "You have no idea what it means to be a father."

Crossing my arms, I challenged, "And you do?"

"I'm the closest thing those kids have had to a father in years."

"I'm glad you've been there for them. I'm not trying to force you out. I'm only trying to support her in any way I can right now." Pushing off of the door, I headed for the kitchen. "Speaking of which, could you take some of this lasagna back with you for her?"

Following me in, he laughed humorlessly. "You really are clueless."

Scooping some lasagna into a container, I let my curiosity win out. "About what?"

"She can't eat that."

A pang of guilt hit me. "Has her morning sickness been bad? Maybe I could send over some ginger ale and crackers instead."

"Christ, it's not morning sickness, you idiot."

"Then what is it?" I crossed my arms.

He ran his hands through his hair, clearly warring with himself on whether or not to tell me. "I really shouldn't be telling you this."

"Liam, she's carrying my baby. I need to know if there's something wrong." Panic began to set in. What was going on?

Sighing, he gave in. "You have to understand. My brother broke her for sport. For no other reason than to know that he could."

I felt my rage simmering, my words clipped. "Spit. It. Out."

"She can barely eat solid food, and it's not because of the baby. It's because she's been anorexic for so long that her stomach rebels if she eats more than a few teaspoons worth of food. She's been sipping protein shakes to put on weight so that she doesn't lose *your* baby."

A red haze filled my vision. "What did he do to her?"

He grunted. "What didn't he do to her?"

"Liam—" I warned.

He ran a hand down his face. "He fed unflattering pictures of her to the least reputable gossip columns to make her think that she was fat. He wanted to see how far he could push her, to show that he could control her. And it worked."

"I could *kill* him." My hands dropped to clench the marble of the kitchen island.

"Yeah, well, get in line. I swear to God, if you fuck with her, I will come over here and kill you with my bare hands."

"You won't get an argument from me. Now, can you back off?"

"I don't like you," he spat.

Tell me something I don't already know, asshole.

"You don't have to like me. Just stay out of my way. Let me take care of my family."

Blowing out a breath, Liam looked skyward. "Fuck me. Your family. Just keep in mind that *your* family is fully intertwined with mine."

"You want to protect her. I get that. But at some point, you have to let her make some decisions for herself. Remember that she's your sister, not your child."

Eyes narrowing, he sneered, "I've seen the way you've always looked at her. She might be the only person alive who's never noticed. I'm not convinced you didn't pressure her."

I took a menacing step forward. Was Liam seriously implying that I took advantage of his sister? "Has she told you her side of the story? Because I can assure you, I've *never* been with a woman who didn't give her full consent. Multiple times, in fact."

"She used to lie to protect *him* all the time," he snarled.

I scoffed. "Well, I'm not him. She comes first. From now on."

He headed for the door, leaving the container of lasagna sitting on the counter, throwing over his shoulder, "Don't make promises that you can't keep."

The sound of the front door slamming echoed through the empty house. It was clear that Liam didn't want me around, but would he let Natalie make her own decisions?

Looks like I have my work cut out for me.

CHAPTER 8

Natalie

SIXTEEN WEEKS.

As much as I was in denial about this baby, it became more challenging by the day to ignore the reality of the life growing inside me. Thanks to the protein shakes, I'd put on fifteen pounds, had the tiniest baby bump, and little gummy bear—as I was calling it—was starting to flutter inside my belly. Thankfully, it was healthy and growing right on track, but that meant it was time to finally tell my kids.

There was no way I could handle this without support, so Liam and Amy made sure to be available for a fun breakfast for dinner Friday night going into the weekend. I'd hyped it up all week, so the kids were bursting with excitement when they got home from school for the weekend.

As a family, we spent a half hour mixing batter before putting it onto the griddle. All three giggled, deciding whether to add fruit, chocolate chips, or sprinkles as the batter bubbled. Amelia and Jameson took pride in being grown up enough to try their hand at flipping the pancakes. They groaned when they failed but cheered when they finally succeeded.

The kitchen was a total mess, but the kids were happier than I'd seen them in years. This was a rare glimpse into the life they deserved—the one they could've had if they hadn't drawn the short straw in the genetic lottery.

Plates piled high, we sat down, and I marveled at the family I'd created—Amy and Liam, my three children, and me. Through thick and thin, we always had each other's backs.

I managed to eat a whole pancake, albeit a small one, slowly making progress in eating solid food. Once I was done with mine, I took a sip of water and bit the bullet.

Tousling Beau's dark mop of curls, I began, "Thanksgiving is coming up, and I wanted to say how thankful I am for all of my kids. I am thankful for how helpful Amelia is every day. I am thankful for how hard Jameson works both in his academics and his athletics. I'm beyond thankful for how much Beau makes us laugh."

His giggles rang clear, and we all laughed in response.

I continued, "And I am the most thankful for how resilient and strong you've all been during the changes this year. I love you all so very much, and I think our love has room to grow."

Jameson's eyes lit up. "Are we getting a puppy?"

Beau screamed, "Yes! A puppy!"

Nervous laughter left my lips. "A puppy is a good idea, but maybe another time. How would we feel about another baby?"

Jameson's brow wrinkled in confusion. "A baby? But we already have Beau."

"I'm not a baby!" Beau protested.

"Beau may be our baby, but he's right. He's not a baby anymore," I responded.

Jameson tried again. "Is Aunt Amy having a baby?"

Amy began choking on the bite of food in her mouth, and Liam had to reach over to give her a pat on the back. Clearing her throat, she protested immediately, "No, Aunt Amy is *not* having a baby."

Amelia had been a silent observer this whole time. She was always like that, taking in a scene before deciding what to say. I'd named her after Amy, and she was so much like her namesake in that regard. Finally, she decided to speak. "Mom, are *you* having a baby?"

Managing a weak smile, I confirmed, "Yes, sweetheart."

Then I watched as fear entered her eyes. Her voice was shaky as she dared to ask, "Is Dad coming back?"

Oh, God. Of course that's where her mind would go. She was a child, and that seemed only logical as she and her brothers were all products of the union between her father and me.

Three sets of identical brown eyes stared at me in anticipation of the answer as I shook my head. "No, honey. Dad's not coming back." Watching as her tiny body relaxed, it broke my heart. She'd been through way too much in her short life. They all had. Taking a deep breath, I clarified, "This baby is going to have a different daddy."

Jameson asked, "Is he nice?"

I nodded. "He's very nice. I think you'll like him."

"Is he going to come and live with us?"

It was Liam's turn to choke before he sputtered, "Hell, no!"

"Liam . . ." I warned. Turning back to my children, I answered, "No, he's not going to live with us. But would it be all right if he came over sometime? Would you like to meet him?"

Jameson looked over to his sister—being so close in age, they were two halves of a whole. He always wanted her approval, so he asked, "Amelia?"

Amelia chewed her lip, thinking and processing, which was to be expected. Finally, she nodded. "All right."

One hurdle down, on to the next. "Now, this part is very important. We didn't like it very much when the camera people bothered you at school, right?" Three sets of heads shook in unison, so I went on, "Mommy having a new baby will bring them back. So, it's got to be our little secret. Okay?"

"Beau is gonna tell," Jameson complained.

I decided to pull out the big guns. "Beau, sweetie?" His brown eyes met mine. "Remember how you have to be *really* good for Santa to come?"

His eyes lit up. "Santa! I want presents!"

"Santa will definitely put you on his nice list if you don't tell *anyone* about Mommy's baby."

Eyes big, he nodded, his curls bouncing. "I won't tell."

Looking over to the other adults, I realized that our fate rested in the hands of a three-year-old. What could possibly go wrong?

"Girls' night in!" Hannah's voice carried down the hallway as she let herself in. Liam had taken the kids out for the night to have some fun after I'd dropped the baby news. Hannah was the last person I still needed to tell.

"In the kitchen!" Amy called out.

Hannah rounded the corner, a bottle of tequila in one hand, a bag of chips in the other. Setting them down on the island, she breathed out, "It's been too long."

Amy gave her a quick hug before joking, "Get to work on those drinks. It's been a long week at work."

Hannah bustled about the kitchen, grabbing the blender and various other ingredients for margaritas while asking, "Getting any closer to that promotion, Ames?"

Amy sighed, releasing her auburn hair from its low ponytail and shaking it out. "I think it could be a while yet."

"You'll get it. You were meant to be a badass boss lady."

Laughing, I grabbed a chip bowl and poured some salsa. Hannah wasn't wrong about that. Amy's first love was her career. Swearing off the possibility of a relationship after a bad interaction in college, she'd maintained that a man or kids would only slow her down. She loved my kids like they were her own, so she didn't seem to mind closing off that prospect for herself. Amy was fierce, strong, and independent—all the things that I wasn't.

The three of us couldn't be more different, but that's why we got along so well—we each brought something to the table. Hannah brought the craziness, Amy brought the common sense, and I brought the motherly caring and kindness.

Our looks were also completely different. Amy was taller than some men—standing at five-nine—with a curvy body, red hair, and green eyes. Hannah was the brunette, with bright blue eyes, standing at five-six, with an athletic build. I was the token blonde—at least now, anyway—with dark brown eyes, and was the shortest of the group, standing at five-four.

The familiar sounds of the blender filled the room, and I munched on a chip, savoring the salty flavor. Little gummy bear made its presence known, giving a little flip, reminding me that there was one more honorary aunt with whom I needed to share the news of their impending arrival.

I shifted on my stool before saying, "Hannah, can you make me a virgin?"

She joked, "Too late for that, Nat. Unless you finished the time machine?"

Laughing, I tried again. "No, I meant my drink."

Hannah looked at me, raising an eyebrow. "You on new meds?"

Pushing away from the island, I lifted my loose tunic top enough to show my tiny bump. Blue eyes went wide before she uttered a drawn out, "Nooooooooooooooo."

Letting my shirt fall back down, I shrugged. "Well, we all know it's not a food baby."

The wheels turned visibly in her head before she cautiously asked, "Is Leo—?"

Amy swiped her margarita glass off the island, leaning in, and ratting me out. "Jaxon."

"Shut up!" Hannah screamed. "When did it happen, where did it happen, how many times did it happen?"

I groaned. "I hate you both so much right now."

Then the lightbulb went off in Hannah's brain. "Oh my God! The opener. Was it before that? Did you already know? Is that why you skipped the barbeque? Does my *dad* already know? Is that why he's been in such a terrible mood?"

Running a mental checklist, I answered, "Yes, yes, yes, yes, and yes."

Hannah squealed, "Tell me everything! Is he as gorgeous below the belt as he is above it? I need details, woman!"

Amy chimed in, "Yes, do tell Nat."

My cheeks flamed. "I don't know how I'm supposed to have this conversation sober."

Hannah protested, "You *cannot* drop this bombshell and not give us the deets. It's only fair. He looks like a sex god. Is he a sex god?"

She wasn't going to let it go, so I grudgingly responded, "Well, he doled out orgasms like candy on Halloween. Does that count?"

"Oh my. Well done, Jaxon." Hannah pretended to fan herself.

Rubbing my belly, I repeated sarcastically, "Yeah, well done, Jaxon. A little too well done."

"I *told* you that he had a crush on you!"

Amy was grinning from ear to ear, asking, "Do you want to tell her, or should I?"

Hannah looked between us. "Tell me what?"

Shaking my head, Amy took that as a sign to continue, "Our sweet, innocent Natalie propositioned him."

Sizing me up, Hannah nodded approvingly. "Well, he is sex on a stick."

Amy called out, "That's exactly what I said!"

Reaching out her glass to clink Amy's, Hannah called out, "Cheers! Natalie, I swear your life is so much better than a soap opera."

Rolling my eyes, I responded, "I live to amuse you."

Taking a sip of her margarita, Hannah paused, then yelled out, "Oh! So, do you call Jaxon 'daddy' now?"

"Fuck my life." I placed my head down on the countertop.

Undeterred, she said, "I'm serious. Is he over here all the time now? Amy, please tell me he's over here, possibly shirtless. Because if so, I'm moving in. Immediately."

Propping my head up on my hands, I shut her down. "He hasn't been over here at all. I only told the kids yesterday. They need some time."

"So, you've been going over to his place, then? Is he shirtless over there?"

Amy smirked, "No, Nat's been over here, hiding."

Offended, I countered, "I'm not hiding!"

Nodding, she stated it like a fact. "Oh, you're hiding."

Hannah was having none of it. "What? Shouldn't he be rubbing your feet or something?"

Shrugging, I sighed. "It's not like we're a couple, Hannah. It was just the one time."

"Well, *damn,* Jaxon! That dude needs to step up his daddy game."

The man wasn't around to defend himself, so I felt the need to do it. "It's not that he doesn't want to. He said to let him know if I needed anything. I just haven't. It's awkward."

"Well, screw that!" I saw the mischievous gleam in her eyes seconds before she swiped my phone off the island.

"Give it back, Hannah!" I jumped off my stool.

Muttering to herself, she tested a few codes before jumping up, exclaiming, "Amelia's birthday—way too predictable." She went to work, typing, saying the words out loud as she went. "Hey Jaxon, the baby is really craving ice cream right now. Could you bring me some? Annnnnnnd send."

Staring at Hannah, trying to comprehend what she'd done, I heard Amy snickering from across the island. Turning on her, I accused, "Way to have my back, Ames."

Amy smiled. "Well, someone's got to do something to force you two into a room together. You can't have this baby and never talk about it. Hannah might be sneaky, but knowing Jaxon, his tires are squealing right now, running to buy out the closest store's entire stash of ice cream."

"Guys, this really isn't funny." I groaned.

My phone chimed, still firmly held in Hannah's grasp, and she lit up, proclaiming, "He's on his way!"

"I no longer have best friends," I claimed.

"That's fine. Amy and I will still have each other. Perks of a best-friend trio."

I glared at her while she made me my virgin margarita. She'd finished her first of the night and was already on to the second when the doorbell rang. We all knew who it was, and no one moved. The doorbell rang again, followed by a couple of knocks.

Shaking my head, I uttered, "Nope, nope, nope."

Amy drained her glass. "Would be a real shame if he thought something happened to you and called 911."

Shoving off my stool, I glared at her. "I named my first-born daughter after *you*. I'm strongly considering changing her name."

Halfway to the door, I heard Amy call out behind me, "You do what you've gotta do!"

Sending up a silent prayer that this wasn't going to be as awkward as I imagined, I took a breath and opened the door.

Damn, Amy was right. Jaxon was pacing.

Concern etching his face, he cautiously asked, "Are you all right?"

Sighing, mentally cursing my best friends for the millionth time that night, I nodded. "I'm fine. Come on in."

Closing the door behind him, he held up a brown paper bag. "I didn't know what kind you liked, so I got a bunch of different ones."

Without warning, Hannah appeared, snatching the bag from his hands, heading back toward the kitchen before throwing over her shoulder, "Thanks for the ice cream, Jaxon!" Then she turned, adding, "Oh, and congrats on the super sperm."

She's a dead woman.

Jaxon laughed. "Um, thanks?" When she was gone, his attention shifted to me. "Is *she* all right?"

"Oh, yeah, just drunk." Annoyance laced every word.

Jaxon flashed me that endearing crooked smile, and for the first time this evening, I took a moment to look at him. He was dressed casually, clearly having a night in himself before Hannah so rudely threw herself into the mix. Clad in black joggers, paired with a soft gray T-shirt capped with a moto jacket, it should be illegal for a man to look this good dressed down. Coming from a world where dressing down was frowned upon, it was refreshing and, honestly, a turn-on that he didn't feel the need to portray perfection.

Unsure of how long I'd been staring, his voice snapped me back to my senses when he asked, "Does she need a ride home? Coach would kill me if I let her drive like that."

"Don't worry. Girls' nights always involve a sleepover."

He nodded, and we descended back into silence. Shoving his hands into his pockets, he shifted on his feet while I nervously bit my lower lip.

Needing to break the silence, I explained, "I'm sorry about the ice cream. Hannah got ahold of my phone."

His chuckle, deep and low, caused warmth to flood my belly. "No problem. You know, if you actually *do* need anything . . ."

Sighing, I nodded. It wasn't going to be easy to let him in. Leo had been charming, luring me in, making me believe that he loved me. He'd never loved me. He'd loved the idea of controlling me, and I was too stupid to realize it before it was too late.

Now look at me—divorced at twenty-eight and knocked up by someone I didn't know very well. Crushing it at life. Yep, that's me.

Trying to throw out an olive branch, I offered, "Um, if you're around, I have an ultrasound next week."

"You'd let me come?" The hope coloring his words and shining in his whiskey-colored eyes had guilt swirling in my gut. I hadn't been fair to him in keeping my distance. I needed to do better.

"You're trying, so I'm trying. This isn't easy for me."

"Yeah," he breathed out, rubbing his jaw, which had the tiniest hint of black stubble.

The silence made its presence known once more until Hannah called from down the hallway, "Please tell me it wasn't this awkward when you guys fucked!"

My eyes slammed shut in embarrassment as my face flamed, and I groaned, "Oh. My. God."

The sound of Jaxon's hearty laughter shocked me out of my mortified state enough to open my eyes. I found myself gawking at him. Was he not at all embarrassed by Hannah's drunken outbursts? I was ready to crawl into a hole and die.

"Are. You. Laughing?" I asked in disbelief.

He smirked. "It was kinda funny. You have to be able to laugh at yourself sometimes."

"You and I are *not* compatible."

Then, Jaxon winked at me. He fucking *winked* at me. Just then, gummy bear started going wild.

I get it, gummy bear. He's adorable, but that's dangerous. We have to be careful.

Hannah was clearly over her limit because next, she yelled, "Take off your shirt!"

Spinning around, I screamed, "Jesus, Amy! Cut her off!"

Amy poked her head out from behind the wall of the kitchen. "Why would I cut her off when we're getting a show?"

"A show?" Amy pointed behind me, and my jaw dropped when I turned around. Jaxon had removed his jacket and was making a show of crossing his arms and pulling his shirt over his head.

Was it me, or was this happening in slow motion?

Jaxon's muscled torso rippled as he lifted his arms, and I had to stop myself from reaching out to trace the come-fuck-me lines that disappeared beneath the waistband of his pants. Why did he have to be so gorgeous? It wasn't fair. In a world that had demanded perfection of me, he achieved it so effortlessly.

Shirt in hand, arms outstretched, he asked, "Happy, Hannah?"

Not being able to tear my eyes away from his half-naked body, I heard her from behind me breathe out, "Damn, I gotta get me a hockey player. Well done, Natalie."

"Okay, time to go!" Without letting him get his shirt back on, I reached for the door and shoved him out. "Thanks for the ice cream."

His nipples hardened into rose-colored points when the cold air reached them, and I found myself thinking they looked sharp enough to cut glass, but he didn't flinch, holding my eyes. "You'll let me know about the appointment?"

"Yep. Night!" I slammed the door right in his face. Counting to three in my head, I took a deep breath and turned to face the traitors. There they stood, drinks still in hand, grinning from ear to ear. "Are you two *kidding* me?"

Hannah burst into giggles, stumbling her way to a living room chair and falling into it. "He actually took off his shirt!"

Amy began laughing. "You know, I did *not* see that coming. I think I really like him. He's fun."

"Not. Funny," I forced out through gritted teeth.

Hannah reclined, closing her eyes. How many drinks had she had? "Look on the bright side, Nat. You slept with that perfect specimen. I bet if you asked nicely, you could do it again."

Her breathing deepened, signaling she'd fallen asleep, so I turned to Amy. "Why are we friends with her again?" She had a smirk on her face, clearly weighing her words again. Unable to take it a moment longer, I snapped, "Spill it, Amy."

Taking a sip of her drink, she swallowed before replying, "I was thinking . . . If you hadn't become friends with Hannah all those years ago, you'd have never met Jaxon."

That stopped me in my tracks.

Amy was right. So many little things had to happen exactly right for me to end up in this situation. What if I'd never met Hannah? Would I be living in some strange alternate reality? I didn't like believing in fate—because that would mean I was meant for all the pain and suffering that came from a decade with Leo—but there were too many factors that combined perfectly to create this path.

Knowing Hannah.

Jaxon going to the Comets.

Moving in next door to Jaxon.

Jameson's ball.

The idea that this baby with Jaxon was somehow 'meant to be' was overwhelming. I allowed myself the tiniest feeling of hope that maybe, just maybe, this would end better than the doomsday scenario in my mind. Only time would tell.

CHAPTER 9

Jaxon

NATALIE WAS KEEPING ME at a distance. That was to be expected, considering she was struggling, dealing with invisible demons. Even knowing it wasn't my fault, it still stung because I cared about her, even if she didn't know. The other night when she'd texted asking for ice cream, I thought that was the opening I'd been hoping for—only to find out that her friends were drunk and having some fun.

It led to her inviting me to the ultrasound next week, so that was where I targeted my focus.

Buying the top-rated baby books online, I spent all of my spare time reading. I burned through them quickly, learning all that I could, not only about what was going on with Natalie and the pregnancy, but with my baby—*our* baby.

At just about seventeen weeks, our baby was the size of a turnip. You should have seen the weird stares I got in the grocery store for picking up and examining turnips.

I marveled at the fact that it took me weeks, sometimes months, to rehab from an injury sustained in the game. Yet our baby had grown all their major organs in that same amount of time.

Was Natalie beginning to feel those first flutters? And when they became more pronounced, would she ever feel comfortable letting me feel those movements?

I wanted to be there for her like my mom had suggested, but she wasn't letting me in. Maybe this ultrasound appointment could be the first step.

Texting earlier that day, I'd offered to drive her to the appointment, but she'd declined, replying it was better that we not be seen together. While I respected her wishes, it seemed unlikely that the pair of us would go unseen. At the very least, the ultrasound tech would notice, but I suppose they were bound by HIPPA laws. Either way, I told her I'd meet her there.

As I drove to the office, I noted it was on the opposite side of town. Did she do this on purpose, to be further from our community? What if something happened and she was too far away to get to her doctor quickly?

I'd never had to worry about anyone but myself, but now there were two other people I was responsible for. It was an uncomfortable new feeling, and I wasn't sure I liked it. I wanted to protect them both from everything and was finding that to be impossible. So much was out of my control right now.

Throwing on a ball cap and sunglasses to help disguise my identity, I entered the building, checking in at the front desk for Remington. The receptionist either had no idea who I was, or my disguise was sufficient enough, because she didn't spare me more than a glance. Standing from the desk, she opened the receiving door and motioned down the hallway, telling me a room number.

Finding my way to room number four, I knocked on the closed door before cracking it open, whispering, "Natalie?"

The room was dark, but I heard her soft voice. "I'm in here."

Slipping into the room, it was so dark I that was temporarily blinded. Removing my sunglasses, the room brightened somewhat, but it was still dim. Natalie was lying on what looked like a bed, and on the other side of her was a massive computer with lots of tubes and attachments.

I am in way over my head.

I must have been standing there for a while because she motioned to the chair next to the bed. "You can sit down if you want."

God, will it always be this awkward?

Sitting in the offered chair, I swallowed before asking cautiously, "How have you been feeling?"

Even in the darkness, her eyes seemed to stare into my soul. "Good. Better. Thank you for asking."

"That's good." Trying to lighten the mood, I offered, "I'm always available for a late-night ice cream run."

That earned me a light laugh, and my heart soared.

Natalie covered her face with her hands. "That was *so* embarrassing. I'm so sorry."

I couldn't help but chuckle in response. She was adorable when she was mortified. "It's fine. I'm used to Hannah by now."

"You'd think I would be too, but a few drinks made her extra bold."

The memory of my mini striptease brought a smile to my lips. I loved that I could shock her. Before I could say anything else, there was a knock on the door, and both of our heads turned to watch the ultrasound tech walk in.

If there were any weird vibes in the room, she pretended like she didn't pick up on them, her smile bright, tone chipper. "Hello! Are we excited to get a peek at baby today?"

Just like that, Natalie turned on her polished façade, smiling. "Yes, we are very excited."

The tech moved to sit at the machine on the other side, clicking through a bunch of screens and asking a variety of questions. Name, birthdate—*make a mental note of January 28th*—date of conception. Then she asked what number pregnancy this was for her.

"Fifth," Natalie answered.

Fifth?

I began using my fingers to count, trying to add that up. One was Amelia, two was Jameson, three was Beau, and four was this baby. Who was number five?

Natalie caught me counting on my fingers, quietly explaining, "I lost one. It's not a big deal."

How was that not a big deal? My own mother still mourned each one of her losses between me and my younger brother.

I wanted to know her, but she kept putting on a front, pretending she was strong. No one could possibly be that strong. She'd been to hell and back, and I'd barely scratched the surface of all that had happened to her. Each time she spoke, I learned it was worse than I could have ever imagined.

While I was stewing on that, the tech asked, "Are we interested in finding out the sex today? If baby will cooperate, of course."

Knowing full well that I was not in any way calling the shots when it came to this situation, I looked to Natalie in question. She looked back. "What do you want to do?"

Whoa, was not expecting that.

"Me?" I pointed a finger at my chest in shock.

She shrugged from her prone position. "I've never found out before. It wasn't allowed. This is your first baby, so you can decide. I'm fine either way, as long as it's healthy."

This was huge. She was letting me decide something for the first time. What did I want to do? I was *not* prepared to make this decision today.

Don't think. Trust your gut. It's gotten you this far.

"Yes, let's find out," I blurted.

Natalie smiled. "Okay." Then she turned to the tech. "I guess we are finding out."

The tech grinned. "Always so fun! Let's get a peek at this little one."

Natalie lifted her loose-fitting shirt, revealing a tiny bump right below her belly button. I couldn't help but stare. That was my baby in there. *Mine.* It was becoming more real with each passing day, but seeing it growing only cemented that fact. This was happening. I wasn't dreaming.

The tech squirted some gel on Natalie's exposed skin and turned on her machine, using the wand to glide through the gel. The TV screen on the wall opposite the bed came to life, and I was transfixed. On that screen was a black-and-white moving image of our baby. I could see their head, their arms, their legs.

It was a real person.

"Hey there, gummy bear," Natalie whispered beside me.

Tearing my gaze away from the screen, I asked, "Gummy bear?"

Even in the darkness, I could see her cheeks darken. "That's what I've been calling it. You know, because they kinda look like a gummy bear at the beginning?" When I didn't respond immediately, she quickly added, "I know it's stupid."

I didn't like that. Was she always so quick to backtrack? She'd done nothing wrong.

I whispered, just soft enough for her to hear, "It's not stupid."

Her eyes locked with mine for a split second before a whooshing sound filled the room. Looking to the screen, I could see a fluid motion right in the center of the baby's chest. Emotion clogged my voice as I gathered the courage to ask, "Is—is that—?"

"That's your baby's heartbeat," the tech answered.

There wasn't a name for the rush of emotions that hit me square in the chest. Seeing the life I'd created was one thing, but hearing that heartbeat? My world would never be the same, and I welcomed this new chapter with open arms.

"Wow," I breathed out.

I could hear the smile in Natalie's voice, "Pretty incredible, huh?"

All I could do was nod, my eyes glued to the screen. It was the most beautiful thing I'd ever seen. Watching awestruck, the screen filled with different body parts as the tech created lines to measure each perfect part.

"Is it healthy?" I dared to ask.

The tech kept moving around, but I heard her loud and clear when she said, "Yes, *she* is."

My gaze pulled away from the screen to stare at her in disbelief. "She?"

"She," the tech repeated. "You're going to have a little girl."

A girl.

My world shifted. The idea of a little girl with Natalie's chocolate eyes and my dark hair warmed something deep within me.

A girl.

Would she play pretend and have fake tea parties, or would she be a tomboy, more into sports than girly things? Either way, with crystal clarity, I could envision taking her out on the ice for the first time.

My excitement bubbled over, and without thinking, I reached over, grasping Natalie's hand, leaning over her, and placing a kiss on her forehead, saying out loud, "A girl!"

Natalie laughed—really laughed—in response. The same genuine laugh that drew me to her all those years ago, which had quickly become my favorite sound.

She squeezed my hand, asking, "Are you happy?"

Unable to hold back my own laughter, I squeezed back, relishing that she hadn't instantly pulled away. "So happy. I have *no* idea what to do with a girl, but I can't wait for her to wrap me around her little finger." Before I could stop myself, I added, "Just like her mother."

The tech was totally oblivious, clearly accustomed to scanning for real couples whose baby was a result of their love for each other. Natalie knew our relationship status—or lack thereof—and her eyes went wide. I was so caught up in the elation of finding out we were having a daughter that I'd accidentally shown my hand.

Deciding to be proactive before she had the chance to reject me, I slowly removed my hand from hers, asking, "Are *you* happy?"

Chewing her lip, she responded, "It's been a long time since I had a little girl. Amelia changed my world. I guess both of my girls are up to that task."

"We're all done here." The screen turned off, and the tech cleaned Natalie off with a towel before allowing her to lower her shirt. A few more clicks on the machine and a long strip printed out. Handing the strip to Natalie, the tech added, "Some pictures of your baby. Everything looks perfect. Congrats, you two. Take as much time as you need before you leave the room."

In an instant, she was gone, and we were left alone in the darkened room. Natalie sat up and threw her legs over the side of the bed. Out of reflex, I offered my hand to help her down, and thankfully, she took it. I wanted to place her in a protective bubble. The urge to protect her with everything I had was overwhelming—not just because she was carrying my baby.

Once standing, she looked down at the strip of pictures before looking back up at me, timid. "Would you like one?"

I nodded. "Yes, please."

Natalie glanced around the room. "I don't have any scissors on me. Maybe I can drop one off later?"

Taking a chance, I proposed, "Maybe we could meet at my house when we get back? If you don't have anything else going on, of course. It would be nice if we could talk for a bit. We haven't been able to do that much."

I watched her weigh the idea, but eventually, she agreed. "Okay."

"I'll go out first. See you there. Drive safely."

Leaving the office and getting behind the wheel of my SUV, all I could think about was how I would never let someone hurt my little girl the way her mother had been hurt. I would throw down my life before she suffered one ounce of pain.

My little girl.

Knock knock knock.

I'd been sitting—no, who was I kidding—I'd been pacing for the last hour, waiting for Natalie to join me. That was just long enough to realize she had the power to break me. I would forever pine for her, but what if she never wanted me back? It would kill me to stand idly by. Especially if—or when—she decided to date again. I'd have a front-row seat to every man she brought around *our* daughter, and I knew I'd hate every single one simply for the fact that I wasn't him.

Opening the door, I didn't have time to blink before she walked right in without an invitation.

Well, that's new.

Closing the door, I turned to find her pacing the room.

Something wasn't right. What changed in the last hour and a half since I'd left her at the doctor's office?

Treating her like a cornered animal, I kept my distance. "Natalie? Is everything all right?" Her eyes were wild, not focusing on anything. She was beginning to scare me. "Natalie, tell me what happened," I begged.

When her eyes finally focused on me, I could see how rapid her breathing had become. "I think someone was following me. At least until the gates."

Taking a moment to process that, I repeated, "Following you. Okay, who?"

She shook her head. "I don't know. Could be anyone."

I was trying to figure out if this was paranoia or a real threat. "Don't you have security? Can't they handle this?"

Good thing I didn't have carpeting in this part of my house because she'd have worn right through it. She was downright panicked, shaking her head. "No, the kids do. Liam does, too. I don't often go out without them, but even then, I'm not the one they're there to protect. I'm not worth it."

Did she genuinely think she was unworthy of protection? "Maybe it's time to think about hiring some for yourself."

Natalie got that spooked look, her eyes widening in panic. "No! We can't bring more people into this."

"This?"

Motioning her hand between us, she explained, "You, me, the baby."

I promised her we'd keep it quiet for as long as she needed, but it still hurt that she wanted to hide me. Even if I understood her reasoning—that her kids needed to come first—I couldn't help but have feelings about it.

"What do you want to do?"

Continuing to pace, she muttered to herself instead of to me, "I have to hide."

I felt the intense need to rein her in. The stress wasn't good for her or the baby. "Hide? Hide how?"

Startling, Natalie realized she wasn't alone. "Oh!" Her steps slowed. She was clearly working through whatever was going on in her mind. "I think I have to stay in my house from now on."

"Okay . . . What about doctor's appointments?" I asked.

Chewing on that for a minute, she mused, "Maybe I could hide in your trunk? No one is going to follow you."

She'd clearly lost all reason, so I reacted purely on instinct. "No, you can't hide in my trunk!"

Natalie flinched, and I instantly regretted raising my voice. I hadn't meant to, but thinking about the safety ramifications of her unrestrained, curled up in my trunk, drove fear into my heart. She wasn't making any sense. I needed her to slow down and think rationally.

Softening, I apologized. "I'm sorry, I didn't mean to yell. I was only thinking about how unsafe that would be for you, for our baby girl."

Her body relaxed a fraction. "Oh, right." She thought for a minute more, her breathing slowing gradually.

That's it, baby, you have to calm down.

"How about you sit in the backseat and scooch down while passing through the gates? Fully buckled," I offered.

Am I really entertaining this?

My more level-headed offer seemed to satisfy her, and she finally stopped pacing.

Thank God.

Natalie looked at me with those big brown eyes. "That could work."

With one more attempt to bring us back to sanity, I asked, "Are you seriously going to hide in your house, for what . . . Another five months?"

Deadly calm, she was determined. "I will do *anything* to protect my kids."

Fair enough.

Knowing one of those children was now mine, how could I argue with that? It was understandable that a parent would want to protect their child. Hell, I already knew I'd throw myself in front of moving traffic for my unborn daughter. But it was unacceptable that Natalie always came last, throwing on a brave front like it didn't matter.

It was now my job to put her first, and I'd spend every day showing her that she was worth it. Even if she never chose me back.

Fully up to the task, I begged her, "Natalie, *please* sit down. Let me get you something to drink."

Her mind was still racing. I could tell by her slow, dazed walk to the couch. Without hesitation, I practically ran into the kitchen, grabbing a bottle of water from the fridge before returning to where she sat. Sinking down beside her, she took the bottle I offered, drinking some before melting into the couch. The episode had clearly drained her.

Seeing the worry on my face, she patted my hand. "It's fine. I'm fine. It's not a big deal."

Not a big deal.

There were those words again. The same ones she'd used to brush off her miscarriage. I needed her to know I was here. She needed help shouldering her heavy load before it crushed her. I *wanted* to be here, to share in her burdens.

"Sometimes, it is a big deal," I whispered, grasping the hand that rested on top of mine. "You want to tell me what happened?"

Natalie knew exactly what I was asking and sighed. "Do you really want to know? It's in the past. I can't change it, and neither can you."

Knowing that I couldn't force her, I needed her to know that I cared. "We may not be able to change it, but that doesn't mean it wasn't a big deal. I can't even imagine what you went through."

Blowing out a breath, she replied, more to herself than to me, "Been through worse." She caught herself, quickly adding, "It's a long story."

"I've got time. For you." Leaning back on the couch, my body language indicated I was in no hurry.

Sighing, she finally gave in. "Well, I'm sure you've noticed Amelia and Jameson are very close in age. Ten months, to be exact." I knew they were close, but not quite that close, so I nodded, allowing her to continue, "We had our one girl and our one boy—the heir and, technically, the spare—so Leo decided we were done. It was convenient, for him at least. We'd 'knocked them out' quickly and could move on to more 'important' things."

To show I was listening and caring, for that matter, I asked, "And you were how old at that time?"

"Just turned twenty, not even legal to drink in my home country."

"That must have been hard."

Misunderstanding my words, she rushed, "Oh, no! Obviously, babies are demanding, but I wouldn't change them for the world."

Shaking my head, I clarified, "No. I meant having that decision made for you so young."

Nodding, her eyes drifted downward. "It was. They were a handful so close in age, but I cherished every minute with them. They still are my whole world. I figured that maybe he would change his mind down the road, but he never did. He—"

She paused, clearly uncomfortable, so I prompted, "It's okay if you don't want to tell me."

"He was sneaky and arrogant, confident that he could cheat the system in a way. Finding out when I had my periods from the maids, he would then strategically choose when to sleep with me based on that. His way of getting around using protection while still avoiding getting me pregnant. What he hadn't counted on was that because I was underweight, I'd started having longer stretches in between, which threw off his math."

Every muscle in my body tensed. I knew something terrible was coming, and through clenched teeth, I managed, "What happened?"

"That one was Beau. Leo was sure he *couldn't* be wrong, so it only made sense to blame me."

"That you'd tricked him?" I knew Natalie would never do that.

"No. That I'd cheated on him, and the baby wasn't his. He still insinuates that Beau isn't his because that would mean he'd made an error somewhere, which was impossible in his mind. He wasn't the best guy before, but everything got worse after that. So, when I found out I was pregnant again before Beau had even turned one, I was terrified of what he would do."

My fists clenched involuntarily. "Did he hit you?"

Natalie shook her head. "It never quite got to that point, but there was enough of a physical show—breaking and throwing things—that I feared at some point it would turn into physical abuse. Liam blew the whistle to their parents, letting them know all that was happening behind closed doors and that they needed to intervene. So, when Leo went out of town for business, their mom helped me pack up the kids, got me a jet, and told me they'd do whatever it took to protect their grandchildren. That meant coming home and not telling him about the baby." She sighed. "It didn't matter anyway. A couple of weeks after I got back here, to Connecticut, I lost it. I didn't even cry. I thought to myself, that's one more innocent life he can't get to now. I know that sounds terrible."

"I'm sorry." That was the only thing I could think to say, but it sounded flat. How could sorry ever be enough?

She smiled sadly. "Don't be. Without that angel baby, I wouldn't have gotten out. Who knows if I ever would have? They had a purpose, even if it wasn't to be here with me now."

Even after all the sadness she shared, I found myself smiling. "Everything happens for a reason."

Her eyes snapped to mine, and I could see a mix of emotions swirling in their brown depths—hope, fear, and something I couldn't quite name. Deciding to change the subject, focusing on the here and now, I asked, "What's next for baby girl?"

Placing a protective hand over her tiny belly, Natalie looked down. "Well, she can't stay *baby girl* forever, can she? Have you thought about names?"

I shook my head. "I didn't think it was my place."

Scoffing, she remarked, "Of course it's your place. She's your daughter, too, last that I checked."

"Were you thinking of any?" She'd caught me so off guard that I put it back on her.

Nodding, she began listing off names, "Eloise. Cecilia. Sophia. Charlotte."

"Charlie!" I called out without thinking.

Furrowing her brow, Natalie asked, "Charlie?"

"A nickname for Charlotte. I think that's the one I like best."

"Charlie. Charlie," she tested it on her tongue. "You know, none of my other kids have nicknames, wanting to break a little bit from the generation before them all having one. Might be fun. Charlotte it is—Charlie for short. What about a middle name? Charlotte came from my list, so it's only fair for you to suggest a name."

Girl names.

Think, Jaxon.

I'd been surrounded by men most of my life, except my mother. And my grandmother.

That's it!

Smiling softly, thinking of all the memories I had baking in the kitchen with my paternal grandmother on sunny and snowy days alike, I replied, "How about Rose? That was my grandma's name."

"Charlotte Rose Slate. Not half bad."

"*Slate?*" I hadn't been expecting that.

"She certainly can't be a Remington."

She made a good point.

My voice was clogged with emotion. "Thank you."

Natalie was only giving me one small piece, but it felt like she'd given me the world. That's when I knew that I could do this. If I kept showing up, being dependable, she'd keep giving me more pieces until I had the whole. I just had to be patient.

Natalie shrugged. "It's the least I can do, but I have something to ask of you."

"Anything."

"I told my kids not long ago, and they've had some time to process. If you want to be around more, we should probably tell them you're the father." Chewing on her lower lip, I could tell she was nervous.

"They don't know?"

"I'm taking it slow. They've been through a lot this year. I told them about the baby and that it would have a different dad. But haven't told them yet that it was you. They like you. I'm hoping they won't be terribly upset you're going to be their little sister's dad."

Mentally, I ran through my upcoming game schedule. "I am out of town this weekend, but I'll be back on Tuesday. I can let you know when I get home, and we can pick a day that works. How about that?"

"Sounds great." Natalie stood, and I scrambled to my feet as she headed for the door. "I better get home. Time to start working on my hermit skills."

Watching her walk away, I asked again, "Are you sure you want to do that?"

Throwing a thumbs-up over her shoulder, she called out, "Yep!" Opening the door, she left without another word.

It wasn't exactly healthy for her to essentially become a recluse, but I didn't have much say in the matter. At least I knew where to find her, but that likely meant Liam would always be around. Even knowing that he would be watching me like a hawk, it didn't matter. I had no intention of setting even one pinky toe out of line when it came to Natalie or her kids. My mind was made up that I would be there for all of them in any way they needed me.

They were mine to protect now.

CHAPTER 10

Natalie

TODAY'S THE DAY.

Today, Jaxon was coming over so we could finally tell my kids who the father of their baby sister was. They didn't know it was a baby sister yet, and I kept that to myself, hoping it might help soften the blow.

I wasn't sure how they would take it. They all had such vastly different personalities. Amelia was fiercely loyal and protective, so much like Liam. Jameson tended to be sensitive, whereas Beau was so carefree. He was untouched by all the darkness surrounding us before moving home. Grateful seemed almost too light a term to describe how I felt about him never knowing the monster *his* father was.

The doorbell rang, and a quick glance at my phone confirmed that Jaxon was outside. We'd discussed him arriving early so we could have a little time alone before the kids got home from school.

Opening the door, I felt flutters in my belly that were not from Charlie.

Jaxon was seemingly fresh from the shower. His hair, still damp around the edges, looked even darker than its usual midnight black, if that was even possible. Dark jeans hugged his thighs, his torso encased in a tight black henley. Damn, did this man ever *not* look incredible?

Down, girl. You're going to be dealing with him every day for the next eighteen years. Sex is what got you here. More is only going to complicate things further.

Chalking it up to pregnancy hormones, I shook it off, welcoming him in. "We've got about an hour before the kids get home. Want something to drink?"

Jaxon slid off his shoes at the door, answering, "Water is fine." As he followed me into the kitchen, he looked around. "This place is incredible. Are you sure we live in the same neighborhood? Your house must be at least twice the size of mine."

Laughing, I teased Jaxon, "Well, a whole family lives here, not just a bachelor. We need the room."

Feigning offense, he countered, "Hey! There will be room for Charlie at my place. It's not like I live in a shack."

"No, definitely not a shack. Shacks don't have pools." I winked, finding myself loosening up in his presence.

"I'd always wondered how you managed to have your entire support system living in this house without tripping over each other, but I get it now."

The house was massive. At 8,000 square feet, featuring seven bedrooms and seven and a half bathrooms, it was practically a fortress. I remember protesting that it was too large years ago when Liam had first pulled up to this house, but he'd insisted. It might be big, but it worked well for the six—soon to be seven—of us.

Grabbing a bottle of water and a diet cola out of the fridge, I mused, "I wouldn't have survived without Liam and Amy. They dropped everything to move in here with me, helping to take care of the kids when I couldn't.

Amy still works outside of the home, but Liam turned his life upside down for us. I don't deserve them."

Pushing the bottle of water across the island to him, I cracked open the can of diet cola. Almost instinctively, Jaxon blurted out, "Should you be drinking that?"

I felt the hair stand up on the back of my neck, reflexively yelling, "*Excuse me?*"

Regret instantly filled my body when I saw the look of shock on his face.

Throwing his hands up in defense, he backtracked, "Whoa. I'm sorry."

Rubbing my face, I sighed, trying hard to shake the shadow of Leo that had passed over me when he'd said that. "No, I'm sorry. It's not you. Being told what to do is a major trigger for me, and I lashed out without thinking. I shouldn't have yelled."

Compassion filled his handsome face without a trace of pity at my admission. "No, you're right. I shouldn't have acted so bossy. That stuff is basically poison on a normal day, but I've read about how some of the ingredients can be potentially dangerous to unborn babies."

He read the baby books? Who is he?

Leo had never bothered, had never cared enough. He'd told me it was my job as the mother to figure it all out. Everything inside of me was screaming that Jaxon was different, but that didn't mean I was ready to trust again. Apparently, I didn't have the best track record.

Finding my voice, I lowered my eyes, embarrassed. "And here I was, thinking you were trying to get me off the caffeine."

Nodding, he admitted, "Well, there's that too, but certainly less of an issue."

Guilt flooded my body. At least for now, I was the sole caregiver for our unborn daughter, and I owed it to him to take care of both myself and her.

Suddenly, the gravity of his words hit me. He was depending on me just as much as Charlotte right now.

Walking to the sink, tipping the can, I watched as the contents emptied down the drain. "You win. Water for me, too, I guess."

"It's not about winning or losing, Natalie," he said softly from behind, causing me to spin around to face him.

Wait, it's not?

My whole adult life had become a battlefield. *Everything* was about winning or losing. If I was being honest, I only knew what it was like to be on the losing end. I didn't know what to do with someone who didn't view every disagreement or argument as something to be won and then lorded over the other.

"What is it about?" I asked, genuinely curious.

Staring seemingly straight into my soul, he replied, "Taking care of you."

Breathe, Natalie.

Feeling the air rush back into my lungs, I couldn't find the words to respond to that. This was uncharted territory. I had no idea how to handle him. I was used to being controlled—trying desperately to survive—struggling to take care of myself and my children without help from my partner.

Maybe I'd been too badly burned by Leo, but alarms sounded in my brain, warning me that there was no way any man could be this good. Too good to be true was what he was, and I would forever be searching around the corner, waiting for the other shoe to drop and crush me as it had always done in the past.

Uncomfortable, nervous laughter left my lips. "Okay, moving on."

Nodding, Jaxon didn't press further, changing the subject easily. "Today I'm 'meeting' your kids, but do you think you could find some time to meet my parents? They'd like to meet you."

Jaxon was asking a lot, but not more than he was due. I was carrying their grandchild, even if every cell in my body screamed that I needed to preserve our little bubble.

"Can't they look me up on the internet?" Cringing, I thought better of my suggestion. "Maybe that's not the best idea."

"It doesn't have to be anything big. They're coming into town during the Christmas break and are planning to stay a little past that for some of my and Braxton's games. We could maybe have a simple dinner at my place. Just us."

"Just us," I repeated. "Who's Braxton?"

"Oh, he's my kid brother." He chuckled.

"You have a brother?" I was realizing there was so much I still didn't know about Jaxon.

"Yeah, he plays for Hartford State."

I did some mental math. Jaxon was in his late twenties but had a brother still in college. "So, he's a good bit younger than you? Must be nice having your brother living in the same city. Especially for your parents to visit."

"He's a freshman, a little over eight years younger than me. I left home when he was still a kid, so it's nice that he wanted to follow me here to New England. Getting the chance to see his games is great. Especially since I missed so much when he was growing up."

From the way he spoke about his brother, I could tell how much he loved his family. I had Amy and Liam—along with long-distance support from my in-laws—but it was nothing compared to what he described.

A real family.

A family my daughter now belonged to.

There was no option. I had to make this work for her.

Giving in, I agreed, "All right, a dinner after Christmas."

"What about your parents?" It was an innocent question, but I stiffened at the mention of the people who'd raised me.

Sure, let's open that can of worms.

"Nope." I hoped he could read that my one-word response meant I didn't want to talk about it.

No such luck.

Confused, he asked, "Nope?"

"Nope," I repeated. "I don't speak to my parents anymore. Ace and Amber are the closest things I have to parents."

"The fourth Moreau daughter," he said almost to himself.

"Yep, that's me."

"What happened?" Jaxon's voice dropped to barely above a whisper. He was beginning to realize that I walked away from people who'd hurt me in the past.

Gripping the countertop, I let out a heavy breath. "Oh, you know, same old story. My parents wanted the fame and power that came along with my marriage to Leo. When I pushed back, being only seventeen years old when he'd proposed, they wouldn't hear of it. They used guilt, declaring they'd given me everything and raised me as a debutante—therefore, my role was to be on the arm of a powerful man. My only value to them was what my marriage could gain them. Having worked tirelessly to build my dad's business, they were still outsiders regarding certain social circles. Becoming associated with royalty, even if only by marriage, was perceived as an opportunity to open those doors. Spoiler alert—the doors didn't open for them. All it did was wreck my life and ultimately cost them a daughter."

Jaxon silently stared at me, but it didn't bother me. It sounded like he had this perfect, loving family, and I simply didn't. It made sense that he couldn't comprehend all I'd been through, all the people who'd let me down. I was glad he would never know any of that hurt. He wasn't broken like I was.

"Jesus, Natalie," he breathed out. "I remember how happy you seemed when I first met you when Amelia was a baby. Were you ever truly happy? Or were you that good at hiding behind a smile?"

Poor guy. He looked like I'd just told him Santa wasn't real. I softened the blow a little. "Yeah, but only for a little while. When Amelia and Jameson were babies, they lit up my world. I know I'm jaded. I do. I've gotten used to being let down by almost everyone in my life, so I don't expect anything different."

When Jaxon rounded the island, my fight-or-flight response activated, but I wasn't sure which way it was going to go. He inched closer—so close I could smell the notes of bergamot and amber wafting off his skin—as he said, low, "I'll never let you down."

My chest tightened, and it became harder to breathe as my brain raced for something to say or do. The way Jaxon said those words sounded like a promise. Unfortunately for him, I was all too aware that promises could be broken, leaving me shattered along with them. I wanted to believe him, but I'd been burned too many times.

Thankfully, I was saved by the sound of the garage opening down the hallway, mere seconds before three sets of footsteps thundered through the door, headed right for us.

Instantly sobered, I pulled back from Jaxon quickly. "The kids are home."

I managed to put enough space between us before my two oldest children walked into the kitchen, searching for an after-school snack. The hormones snuck up on me, and looking at those two sweet faces, knowing all that I'd done—how I'd changed our lives—tears threatened to spill from my eyes.

Amelia immediately sensed something was off, her eyes going straight to Jaxon standing less than six feet from me. Looking between the two of us, she asked, "Mom?"

Plastering on my fake mom smile, the one I'd used countless times over the years to try and make everything seem okay, I deflected. "How was school?"

Jameson ignored the exchange, walking right up to Jaxon. "Hey, Jaxon! What are you doing here?"

Jaxon fist-bumped him. "Hey, bud."

Amelia narrowed her eyes at Jaxon. "Yeah, what *are* you doing here?"

She was in full-on protection mode. This would not be easy.

I quickly chastised her, "Amelia Faith! Don't be rude. Jaxon is a guest in our home. Is that how we greet our guests?"

Not softening her stare on him, she did as was expected of a proper princess, formally greeting him. "Hello, Jaxon Slate. Welcome to our home."

Lips pressed together, I had to hold back a snort. Oh boy, was she trouble.

There was the tiniest hint of sarcasm in her tone, as she continued staring at him like he was a bug she wanted to squash beneath her shoe. She suspected why he was here. That much was clear.

Breaking the tension, Beau bounded down the hall, spotting Jaxon, running to him, and calling out, "Hockey!"

I was *not* prepared for the tender way Jaxon dropped down to his knees to be at eye level with Beau, tousling his hair the same way I always did. "That's right, little man! I play hockey. How about if I bring some little sticks and nets the next time I come over, and we can all play together?" Then he locked eyes with me. "If that's all right with your mom, of course."

Beau's tiny face lit up. "Yes, please! Please, Mommy?"

Jameson chimed in, "That would be *so* cool! Can we, Mom?"

How could I say no to the joy on my boys' faces? Jaxon had no idea he'd just given me the most precious gift, seeing them so happy. Now, if only we could get Amelia there, I'd want for nothing else.

Tapping my chin, I pretended to think. "Well . . . As long as you promise not to break anything."

Both boys jumped up and down, chanting, "We promise! We promise!"

"All right, then."

Smiles lit up their faces, and my heart squeezed, knowing that Jaxon did this. *He* had put those smiles there. *He* had gotten down on their level and thought of something they'd like, making plans and promises. *He* was acting more like a father than their own, not caring that he barely knew them from passing interactions over the years.

Rising to his feet, looking me right in the eyes, he said, "It's a date then."

Is it hot in here?

The implication in his words was deep, and I felt heat rush to my face. No, it was my imagination. He couldn't want to date me. I carried too much baggage and was too damaged for someone like him. Every time I gave him a piece of my past, he'd stared at me in shock, almost unable to comprehend some of the horrors I'd experienced.

Jaxon was a good guy. If anything, he was trying to do the "right thing".

I didn't need to become an obligation, part of another forced relationship doomed to fail. Would he be here right now if not for Charlie? Definitely not. So much for a no-strings night. We were now tethered together for life.

Maybe I deserved more than being the convenient choice as the mother of his child. I couldn't put my kids through the wringer again if everything fell apart and they were already attached. There was no real basis for a relationship with Jaxon other than an accidental pregnancy. It was best to remain honest with myself and not forget that fact.

Amy entered the kitchen, dragging all the lunch boxes from the car and dropping them on the island. Sensing I needed a minute, she grabbed a quick snack for the kids and led them to the living room for some cartoons to unwind after a long day.

I mouthed, "Thank you," as she walked away.

Once I was sure they were all out of earshot, I looked at Jaxon, apologizing. "I'm sorry about Amelia. The last few years have been harder on her than the rest, and she's trying to protect me."

He'd put on a good show, but I could see now that she'd rattled him. Breathing a sigh, he smiled weakly. "I think if she knew my middle name, she'd have thrown that in there too." Glancing around to ensure we were still alone, he leaned in close enough to whisper, "She doesn't know how babies are made, does she?"

Caught off-guard, I nearly choked on my sip of water. Pulling back to look at him, sure my shock was visible, I shook my head violently—partly to clear it, partly in answer. "No. At least not that I know of, but she's almost ten, so I'm sure she'll want to know sooner rather than later. Pray that day is not today."

Shoving both hands into the pockets of his jeans, he added, "I had to ask because if she does, I'm in even bigger trouble. Liam is a tough act to follow, but I think she might have him beat."

"What do you mean, follow Liam?" For a second, I was confused, then the realization hit me. "Oh my God, what did he do?"

"He's only looking out for you." Jaxon shrugged.

Pointing a finger at him, I shook my head. "No. Don't you dare defend him. Sometimes, he needs to mind his own business. I'm a grown woman, not a child. He doesn't get a say in who I associate with."

Yes, Liam had taken good care of me these past few years, but he'd crossed a line going behind my back to threaten Jaxon. Anger clouded my vision.

Jaxon smirked. "Don't worry about it. I fully intend to prove him wrong. Amelia, too, if it comes to that."

I took a deep breath to calm my racing heart. "Guess we'd better go out there and get this over with."

Following me, we made our way into the living room. It was hands-down my favorite room in our house.

One wall featured floor-to-ceiling windows facing west, with a door that led to the deck overlooking the pool. The ceilings were high, and the room was open through the second story, with an upstairs hall-way visible along the upper wall opposite the windows. A sandstone fireplace stretched all the way up the central wall, with our flatscreen TV mounted above the mantle and built-in bookshelves on either side. Overstuffed couches were centered around a coffee table, with a chaise lounge flanking one side. It was homey and held so many memories of being cuddled up with my children, them making my worst days brighter.

The sun was beginning to set on this late fall afternoon, and the orangey glow casting the room from the wall of windows was strangely comforting. It was as if the universe knew I needed a calming atmosphere to get through this.

I can do this.

Amy caught my eye and left the room, leaving us to our task. Blissfully unaware, both boys sat munching on bowls of pretzels. Amelia's bowl sat untouched on the coffee table. Instead of watching the TV, she watched our every move until we sat down.

Not wasting any time, Amelia blurted out, "Is *he* the baby's dad?"

I glanced at Jaxon, who was silent, smartly allowing me to handle my children. He understood his role in this conversation was to be a prop in my explanation.

Turning back to my kids, Jameson had stopped eating. Clearly, Amelia's question interested him in our conversation, while Beau hadn't glanced away from the cartoons.

"Yes, he is," I confirmed.

"Well, that's just *great*," she spat out.

God, she is Liam's twin sometimes.

Instinctively, I reacted. "Hey! Who is the parent here?"

Amelia stared at me in shock. I wasn't often so assertive—in my life or with my children—but she didn't usually act like a moody teenager. Feeling like a failure for many reasons, I pushed through. "I know it's been challenging, but I want you to know that I'm here. I'm not going anywhere. You'll always have me. I love you all so much, just like I love your baby sister, even though she's not here with us yet."

Eyes as big as saucers, she asked, "Sister?"

Allowing myself a tiny smile, I confirmed, "Your baby sister, Charlotte. You were my first baby, but now you're my big, strong girl. I know that no matter who her dad is, you'll protect Charlie the same way you protect both your little brothers. Can I count on you?"

She looked down, and I could tell she had been hiding her emotions behind that brave, sarcastic front. Her voice was small, much more childlike, when she answered, "Yes, Mommy. I will always take care of you and the kids."

My heart was breaking, not only for the loss of her innocence but because I'd brought more hardship upon us. Blinking back the tears that threatened, I said softly, "Baby girl, look at me." Amelia obeyed, looking up, while Jameson sat beside her, watching, waiting to see how this played out—he never picked sides.

I spoke to my daughter. "I need to know that you're okay."

Looking between me and Jaxon—who was still silently watching this private family interaction—she finally asked, "What happens now?"

I made a sweeping hand motion. "This is new for *all* of us, but we have to work together. Our family is growing—changing—and it won't look the same as other families, but that's okay. We've always been different, with Aunt Amy and Uncle Liam living with us. Do you think we can make room in our big family to allow Jaxon in so he can be a good dad to your baby sister?"

Jameson chose to speak, effectively shattering me into a million pieces. "Dads should want to be with their kids."

Not the only one affected by his words, it seemed he got through to Amelia too. Hearing her sniffle, I battled to keep my own emotions in check, which was becoming increasingly more difficult by the minute.

She nodded to her brother. "You're right." Pausing, she then looked at me. "I'm sorry, Mom."

That was the final straw, and two hot, wet tears slipped down my face. She was apologizing to me? For what? For my actions bringing all our lives crashing down? She needed to know that none of this was her fault—that she didn't need to shoulder the burden of my failures.

Clearing my throat, I protested, "No, sweetheart, I should be sorry. I never wanted any of this for you. Sometimes, plans change, but how we change with them is what defines us. We're going to be all right. I promise."

Amelia turned to Jaxon without prompting. "I'm sorry, Jaxon. I was rude, and I know better than that. I'll try harder."

Holding my breath, I found myself awaiting his response. This was a heavy-duty situation for a single guy, but he stunned me when he addressed her. "Amelia, you don't need to apologize to me. I'm new here and still learning about a lot of things, especially how to be a dad. You seem like you know the ropes around here, so I'm hoping you'll help me learn how I can fit in."

"Do you love my baby sister?" It was a simple question with an automatic answer for most parents. But for my daughter, she was asking if Jaxon would provide something for her new sister that her own father hadn't offered to her.

Not skipping a beat, Jaxon smiled. "Of course I do. And I'm hoping you'll do me a favor, Amelia."

"Me?" His request caught her off guard.

"Yes, you. I'm gone a lot for work. I'd greatly appreciate it if you could help take care of your mom and baby sister when I can't be around. Do you think you can help with that?"

I could see that worried her. She knew he played hockey but didn't understand the practice, game, and travel aspects. Furrowing her brow, she glanced at me. "Gone like Dad was gone?"

Shaking my head, I eased her fears. "No, sweetie, not like that. Jaxon sometimes has work trips for a couple of days, a week or two, but then he comes back. It's only for little bits of time."

Reaffirming, Jaxon echoed, "I will *always* come back."

When she struggled to find the words—not used to trusting any man other than Liam—Jameson answered for her, "We can both help."

Smiling, Jaxon reached out his fist for a bump. "Thanks, Jameson. I know that I can trust the two of you."

Not knowing how much more any of us could handle today, I ended the conversation. "All right, guys. Time for reading and homework before dinner. Head up, and I'll be there soon to help and check things."

Before Amelia could leave with her little brothers, Jaxon had one more thing to say to my daughter. "I hope we can be friends. You can join us boys playing hockey anytime."

She stared at him. For how long, I wasn't sure. No matter what she said, he would be a part of our lives, but she assessed him before answering, "Okay. I'd like that too." Then, she ran up the stairs where her brothers had disappeared.

Once they were out of sight, Jaxon leaned back on the couch. "Wow. That was intense."

"Yeah." I sighed.

"Are you sure she's only nine?" he said in disbelief.

"Pretty sure." I laughed.

"I don't think I cared much about anything other than hockey at her age."

"Oh, only at that age?" I teased.

"Hey! I care about other things now," he protested.

"You and I were lucky growing up. We got to be kids. We didn't have to deal with half of what she's been through. I'm struggling with all of this, and I'm almost thirty. I can't imagine what it's like for them."

"I have no clue what I'm doing here, but you handled them so well. You're a pro." His tone was full of awe, like I'd done something incredible instead of making life harder for my children.

I chuckled. "You'll learn soon enough. Everyone thinks babies are a challenge, but the bigger they get, the more complex life becomes. Enjoy those early days when all they want is to be held and have their basic needs met. You won't get it back."

"I'm looking forward to it."

I laughed again. "That's what people who don't have kids say."

Smiling, he joked, "Oh, come on. Which one would you give back?" Pausing, he winced. "Maybe I don't want the answer to that. Probably mine."

Shoving his shoulder, I rolled my eyes. "Very funny."

"You know I'm kidding, but you wouldn't trade any of them. That much I know."

I sighed. "I wouldn't have survived if it wasn't for them. They gave me something to cling to—something to fight for—when I wanted nothing more than to give up. They're all a part of me, even Charlie, and I will continue to protect them with all I have. Nothing can change that."

"Charlie is a lucky girl. She's already so loved."

The tender way Jaxon talked about our baby girl was giving me those butterflies again. It was clear that he would be a good dad, but I prayed that once she was here, he would remain steadfast. I wasn't sure I could bear another child having to deal with the disappointment of feeling unwanted. Or worse, if he changed his mind about our verbal custody arrangement and my children were split up, creating two separate families.

Jaxon stood, breaking the moment. Before I could join him, he raised a hand, stopping me. "You sit. I'll let myself out."

Needing to tell him how much I appreciated him, I stopped him with a hand on his arm. "Thank you. Not only for sitting here while I had this talk with them, but for making them feel special, making plans for next time."

His lopsided grin was so genuine that my heart leapt. "They *are* special. I wasn't kidding. I'll be bringing sticks and nets next time. Prepare yourself."

Laughing lightly, I replied, "Can't wait."

Winking, he added, "Careful what you wish for."

Once he'd let himself out, I returned to the kitchen, where Amy casually sat on a stool at the island with her laptop. Pulling up my own stool, I teasingly accused, "Enjoy the show?"

Clicking away on her keyboard, she didn't look up. "No idea what you're talking about."

"Sure, you don't." I knew her better than that.

"But if I can say one thing?"

"There it is . . ."

She finally looked up, piercing me with her emerald gaze. "I think he's good for you. All of you."

"He's dangerous." I sighed.

Amy rolled her eyes. "He's a puppy."

"That's not what I meant. He's here now, making promises to me, to the kids. What happens when playing house isn't fun anymore? They won't survive it. I won't survive it."

Amy's tone grew serious. "Not all guys are bad guys, Natalie. I know it'll be hard to get past your hang-ups, but don't rule out the possibility that he might be the thing that finally puts your family back together."

Scoffing, I turned it around on her. "Oh, says the woman who has sworn off men after one bad experience of her own?"

Leveling me with a glare, she stated, "We aren't talking about me right now."

Grudgingly, I steered back to the conversation at hand. "I want more than a shotgun relationship. Don't I deserve more than that?"

"Of course, but do you really think he's here just for the baby?"

Throwing up my arms, I was frustrated that she was making me dig deeper into my feelings. "What else am I supposed to think? He didn't come looking for me after we slept together."

"Weren't you the one who insisted it was a one-time thing?" she countered.

"Yeah, but—"

"But what?" She cut me off. "I'm not suggesting you rush into anything. Just try to be open should anything develop. You deserve to be happy."

"All right, I'll keep an open mind." It was easier said than done.

Leaving her to her remaining work, I ventured upstairs to check on the kids and the progress they'd made on their homework.

No matter what Amy said, I had to be careful. There was too much at stake. I'd already made a steady stream of bad decisions that had brought us here. I couldn't afford to make another. *If* I ever let a man back into my life in a romantic capacity, I would need to be one hundred percent certain everyone was on board.

The kids were almost more of a factor in choosing another partner than my own feelings. Whoever that person was would have to love my kids, and they would have to love him. We were a package deal and came with a complicated past.

I wasn't sure there was a man alive up to the task.

CHAPTER 11

Jaxon

DING DONG.

The mystery guest list kept growing each time I'd opened the door, this time to Amy on the other side. Amy seemed to be the most rational and patient of Natalie's friends. I wasn't sure I could handle it if Hannah appeared on my doorstep.

Snowflakes fell slowly behind her as November had turned into December. She stood there, sizing me up. "Jaxon."

"Amy."

"Are you going to let me in?" she asked.

"Depends. Are you here to berate me like Liam?" I eyed her warily.

She smiled. "Actually, I'm here to help you."

Intrigued, I stepped aside so she could enter, holding out my arms to take her coat as she slipped off her boots. Motioning her forward into the house, she headed for the kitchen rather than opting for the comfort of the living room.

Once she reached the island, she leaned a hip against it, tucking a strand of auburn hair behind one ear. "First things first. Do you love her?"

Rational and direct, I decided that I definitely liked Amy.

Rubbing my jaw, I mused, "I think, on some level, I always have. I know that sounds crazy, but there's always been something about her that's drawn me in."

She nodded. "It's not crazy. Next, you understand that she's a package deal, correct?"

"Her kids are amazing." A smile touched my lips, picturing Natalie's kids.

Seemingly satisfied, she said, "Good. Now, you need a little bit of a history lesson." When I remained silent, she continued, "Without going into details, you need to know the *asshole's* motto was 'a scared Natalie is a controlled Natalie,' and he implemented it almost daily. He didn't love her. He loved controlling her."

My hands curled into fists, and I clenched my jaw, forcing out, "If I ever see that bastard again . . ."

Amy waved her hand, cutting me off. "I didn't come here to tell you about *him*, just how it comes into play. What you really need to know is that Nat is a hopeless romantic."

"A romantic," I repeated. What did that have to do with anything?

"When we were growing up, she was always curled up with a romance novel. She never cared that they usually followed a predictable storyline. What she loved the most about them was that they always had a happy ending. She never tires of watching the same rom-coms over and over, having memorized every line, unable to stop from crying happy tears at the end. I may never understand it myself, but it's how she's wired."

"But she never got her happy ending," I finished for her.

"See, I knew you were smart." Amy smiled.

"What do you suggest I do? She keeps me at arm's length."

Amy smirked. She was up to something. "Well, I'm certainly *not* going to tell you that this entire month should look like something out of an overly cheesy romantic Christmas movie."

Cluing into what she was doing, I stated, "Noted."

"And I'm definitely *not* going to leave a key to the house right here on your kitchen island on my way back home." Reaching into her pocket, the key she placed down clinked against the marble.

Mission accepted.

Done with the conversation, Amy headed for the door, grabbing her coat and shoes before she looked back, her tone serious. "One last thing. Don't fuck it up."

She was gone, and I was stunned. Not only had she given me a literal key, but the figurative key to unlocking Natalie. Maybe this was the opportunity I was waiting for.

Smiling to myself, I knew exactly what I was going to do and hoped that everything else would fall into place.

After a week on the road, I was more than ready to implement my plan to win over Natalie *and* her kids. Armed with bags of supplies, I used the key Amy had given me to enter Natalie's house, praying that that part of the equation didn't backfire. I knew I had some time to set things up before the kids got home from school with Amy, but Liam was a wildcard. Not to mention how Natalie might react to me having a key to her house without her knowledge.

Those thoughts were gone the second I opened the door and heard loud Christmas music filling the house. Grinning, I slipped into the kitchen, setting the bags down on the counter next to the large stainless steel fridge. There were more items in the car, but I'd grab those later.

The music came from the living room, so I headed toward the arched entryway the kitchen shared with that room. Peeking around the wall, I froze in my tracks.

Natalie was singing along with the music at the top of her lungs while placing ornaments on the giant tree that took up a large chunk of the room. Instead of alerting her to my presence, I leaned against the wall, enjoying the private show she was unaware she was putting on. Smiling to myself, she seemed like that happy, almost carefree girl I had known a long time ago.

She's still in there somewhere.

Biting back a groan, I fully drank her in. With her back to me, I had the perfect view of her curved backside, generously hugged in what looked like the softest gray fuzzy shorts. Momentarily, I was mesmerized by the sway of her hips, before trailing my view down the few inches of exposed skin to a pair of thigh-high pale pink cable knit stockings covering the rest of her legs.

Holy shit. Is that a crop top?

A good four inches of skin showed above the waistband of her shorts. You couldn't tell she was pregnant from this angle, but I felt a rush of possession knowing my baby was growing inside her. An oversized, cream, cropped sweater hung off one shoulder, and her hair was pulled up in a loose bun atop her head, showing off the delicate curve of her neck, framed by loose blonde tendrils.

I loved seeing this comfortable, more relaxed version of Natalie. I only wished she didn't feel the need to hide this side of herself.

As she bent down to grab another ornament, I became hyper-aware that she was standing on a step stool, a good eighteen inches off the ground. One wrong sway . . .

My body reacted before my brain could fully process the thought, moving forward automatically. Hands gripping her waist, I gently pulled her against me before setting her down on solid ground.

Her surprised scream didn't register until she turned around, eyes wide in shock as she batted at my chest, yelling, "Jaxon! What the hell are you doing?"

The heat from her exposed waist seeped into my hands, and awareness dawned. I was still holding her. Was I that starved for her that the mere touch of her skin was enough for my brain to short-circuit?

Beneath my palm, I felt a push, then what felt like a roll.

Now, it was my turn to be shocked. "Was—was that . . .?"

Natalie softened, choosing to remain in my arms instead of putting distance between us. "Yeah, she does that."

"There's a person in there," I whispered, amazed.

Laughing lightly, she glanced down to her belly between us, which was growing with each passing day. "I know." Looking back at me, she asked more calmly, "Jaxon, what are you doing here? And what made you think it was a good idea to grab me like that? I could have fallen."

Stunned, I blinked. She thought *I* was the one who was going to cause her to fall?

"That's exactly why I grabbed you. Let me help put up the higher ornaments, and you can tell me where you'd like them. But please, *please*, stay off the step stool or any ladder. You nearly gave me a heart attack."

My concern got through to her, and she nodded in agreement before asking, "How did you get in here?"

"Amy gave me a key." I held back a sheepish grin.

Natalie shook her head. "Of course she did."

"I like her," I declared.

"Yeah, well, she likes you too, but that doesn't mean you can walk into my house without my knowledge. What if I had been in the shower?"

Pausing, the mental image of her in the shower stole my attention away from our conversation.

Water cascading down her creamy skin, every inch exposed. Her hands rubbing soap over every curve of her body.

"Oh my God, forget I said *that*," she said, stepping out of my grasp, clearly imagining where my mind had gone.

Unable to hold back, I teased, "Too late. I mean, if you want to take a shower right now, I can hold down the fort. I've got work to do."

Face turning pink, Natalie shook her head. "No, I've got to finish the tree." Pausing for a minute as my words registered, she asked, "What do you mean you have work to do? Here?"

"I've got some time to help with the tree." I pretended to check my watch. "But then, I have to get some baking done."

"What baking? Is something wrong with your kitchen?" Her forehead wrinkled in confusion.

This was it. Time to let her know I was the real deal. "I brought some stuff to make cookies and a gingerbread house for the kids to decorate when they get home."

She stared at me in disbelief. While it hurt to know that no one had taken care of this woman and her children, I was determined for them to get a fresh start. With me.

"Why would you do that?" I could see her pulse pounding where her throat met her chest.

"What? You don't like cookies?" I tried to bring some levity to the situation. This was clearly a big deal for her.

"Of course I like cookies. Why do you want to make cookies with my kids?"

Time to go for broke.

"Because that's what families do at the holidays."

"Families," she repeated, bewildered.

Giving her an out, not wanting to make her too uncomfortable, I added, "We may be more of a blended family, but a family all the same. I can go if you want. It was just an idea I thought might be fun for the kids."

Natalie took a deep breath. "All right. You help me with the tree, and then I can help you in the kitchen."

My foot was literally in the door. Time for some of that movie magic. Motioning to the tree, I directed, "You hand me the ornaments, and I'll put them exactly where you'd like them."

We approached the tree, easily ten feet tall in the open space. Glancing around, I wondered where Liam was and why he wasn't helping her. Did he know she was up on step stools at five months pregnant? A shudder ran through my body, imagining what could have happened if she'd fallen.

Picking up on my physical distress, Natalie asked, "Are you cold?"

"No, I'm fine." I waved her off.

Relief flooded her face. "Okay, good, because I'm like an oven. I'm not sure I could have offered to let you turn up the heat."

Scanning her again, my gaze lingered on the areas of bare skin that were visible on her body. It made sense now why she wasn't wearing more on an early winter's day.

We worked together for the better part of an hour, getting all the remaining ornaments onto the tree before taking some time to add a few final touches to the room, such as stockings and decorations. Once she was satisfied, we made our way into the kitchen.

I still couldn't get over this house, and I had only been in a handful of rooms. The living room alone felt like it was bigger than my whole house. Then, there was this kitchen. It would be any chef's dream. Not only was it equipped with massive state-of-the-art stainless steel appliances, but the grey and white marble island at its center was as large as a twin-sized bed. Stools were lined up on one side, providing a casual eating option, but there was also a full-sized kitchen table next to bay windows overlooking the backyard.

Another reason I hadn't gone overboard when buying my house was that I hadn't grown up with money. My parents owned a house on a small lake back in Minnesota, but it was cozy. They probably could have afforded a bigger house if it weren't for my massive hockey bills, so it felt wrong to flaunt my money when it came to making my first home purchase. I'd offered to upgrade my parents a few years into my career, but they were too proud to accept, even when I'd argued it was only fair to pay them back for all they'd spent getting me to where I was today.

Unlike many of my teammates, I didn't own a second summer home where I'd grown up. Now, with Charlie coming, I would never consider leaving for the offseason. Hartford would be my daughter's home, and therefore, I was here permanently. Thank God for my non-trade clause—there was no possibility of being traded to another team in the league without my express permission.

Oblivious to my train of thought, Natalie eyed the four brown shopping bags on the counter. "How many cookies are you planning to make? The kids might help for a while, but they'll lose interest, leaving you to finish. That's just my experience, so prepare yourself."

Rounding the island, I began emptying items from the bags. "It's not about finishing the cookies."

Confusion filled her beautiful face. "It's not?"

"I don't care if any of the cookies make it into the oven. I only want the kids to have fun."

A full minute passed as she stared at me before asking, "Where did you come from?"

"Next door."

Unable to keep from smiling, I knew she wasn't asking where I'd physically come from, but I was trying to play it cool. The plan was working. She was starting to realize I wasn't just here for Charlie.

Natalie shook her head. "All right, funny guy. Where do we start?"

"I want to get the gingerbread pieces baked before they get home from school. That way, when they get bored of baking, they can ice and decorate the houses."

Her jaw dropped. "You're making the gingerbread house from *scratch*?"

"You say that like it's a bad thing. That's how my mom always did it." I shrugged.

"Your mom sounds amazing," she breathed out.

I grinned, thinking of my mom and the memories we'd made during the holidays. "She's the best. I never realized the importance of keeping these traditions alive, but I'm glad I'm getting the chance."

Giving her the time to absorb that I was claiming her children—giving them *my* family traditions to cherish and pass on—I made my way around the kitchen, looking for the tools to begin baking.

Stand mixer, check.

Bowls, check.

Measuring cups, check.

Once everything was organized on the island, I rolled up my sleeves and got to work.

Natalie was tasked with measuring out all the ingredients while I took care of mixing and getting the dough prepped, shaped, and put into the oven. Turning from the closed oven, I found Natalie trying to clean up after us.

Not on my watch.

"You sit for a while. I've got clean-up." She continued to bustle around the kitchen, so I tried a different tactic. "Natalie. If you don't stop cleaning right now, I'll lift your ass onto this counter and make a real mess."

My words achieved their desired effect, stunning her enough that she froze, her mouth dropping open slightly. I took a moment to picture myself softly biting on her lush lower lip. Stalking to where she stood, I caged her in, an arm on either side of her gripping the edges of the marble countertop. Our heads were so close that her breath fanned my face as she peered up at me from beneath her eyelashes.

Pressing further, I closed the gap between our bodies. "Once I got you up onto this cool marble, I would remove these tiny shorts with my teeth. The sexy-as-hell stockings can stay on. Then, I would spread you wide and feast on you until you were begging me to let you come on my tongue."

Her eyes never left mine, but a gasp escaped past her parted lips.

"You still want to keep cleaning?" I challenged.

Swallowing, I watched her eyes as she weighed her options. A small thrill of victory ran through me that she was even considering letting me eat her out in the middle of her kitchen, with minutes to spare before we were interrupted by the thundering of tiny footsteps. She might deny it, but she still wanted me.

Finally, Natalie shook her head, whispering, "You can clean."

I'd rather be worshiping her with my hands and mouth, but I stepped back, smug. "That's a good girl. Sit. Let me take care of things."

Pulling back, I was thankful for the jeans that were partially containing my raging hard-on as I headed toward the sink to cool off. Busying my hands, washing and drying all the items we'd used to make the dough, I tried desperately to think of anything other than the mental image of what I wanted to do to her on the kitchen counter.

Down, boy, we're playing the long game.

The oven timer buzzed, and I pulled out the perfectly baked gingerbread shapes—walls, roofs, and gingerbread people. Smiling to myself, I was excited to see how surprised the kids would be. All of this felt right. I might be getting a crash course in Parenting 101, but I knew Charlie would reap the benefits of the time I spent with her older siblings before she made her arrival. She deserved a whole family. They all did.

As I moved the pieces over to the cooling rack, I heard the garage door opening, quickly followed by those telltale footsteps resounding down the back hallway. Smiling, I remembered the days of coming home to my mom baking in the kitchen. I was carefree; my only duty was to be a child. It was time to give that luxury I'd taken for granted to these children.

Jameson burst into the kitchen first. "What smells so good in here?" Then, he spotted me. "Jaxon! You're back!"

The blond little boy had quickly become my ally, and I was grateful to him. "I thought maybe you guys would like to make some cookies with me."

Amelia joined us, not quite giving me the same cold treatment as my last visit but still remaining cautious, as she asked, "What kind of cookies?"

Assuming that, like her mother, she didn't like to be told what to do, I had already planned on making this a more open-ended activity.

Smiling, I asked, "What kind do you like, Amelia?"

Wide-eyed, she looked to her mom, and they shared a glance.

That's right, ladies. With me, you have a choice.

The very picture of her mother, Amelia identically chewed her bottom lip when she was unsure how to respond. It almost seemed as if Amelia thought this was a trap, signaling that I had my work cut out for me. A family activity of baking cookies wouldn't be enough to fix all the emotional wounds that had left deep scars behind.

Amy walked in holding Beau's hand, taking in the scene before her, and jumping right on board. "Ooooh! Looks like Christmas in here! What are we making?"

Deferring to the nine-year-old gatekeeper once more, I answered, "Well, it depends on what Miss Amelia chooses. Her favorite cookie is up next."

Amy didn't skip a beat. "Oh, well, in that case, it must be sugar cookies. With icing, of course. Isn't that right, Amelia?" Then, she walked behind the family, flashing me a quick thumbs-up gesture on her way out of the room.

Turning back to the girl in question, I asked, "Are we going with classic drop cookies, or do you think we should use cookie cutters?"

Warming slightly, her smile was shy. "Cookie cutters."

"Cookie cutters it is." I grinned at her. "Will you help me?"

Amelia nodded as Beau chimed in, "I want to help! I love cookies!"

Beau was so innocent, clearly untouched by the past that haunted the rest of his family. Immediately, I jumped on his enthusiasm. "Let me get you a chair, little man. You can help me pour ingredients." Turning to his siblings and his mother, I said, "I need a few more volunteers. Someone to mix, someone to roll the dough, and someone to cut out the shapes."

Jameson jumped to volunteer. "I want to cut out the shapes!"

"Ladies?"

Amelia finally took the leap, offering, "I can mix."

"Perfect! I think that leaves your mom to roll the dough. If she's up for it, that is," I said.

With all three of her children actively involved, Natalie didn't hesitate. "I'm in."

Getting to work, all three kids pulled up chairs to reach the height of the massive island, spreading out to their stations. Beau chatted eagerly as I measured the ingredients in cups for him to pour into large and small bowls before combining our wet and dry mixtures. Once completed, we handed the largest bowl to Amelia to mix before making icing—one for the cookies and another for the gingerbread house.

Beau was done—his attention span being the shortest of the three—so I sent him off to play while the rest of us continued. Walking over to Amelia's station, she was nearly there, so I offered, "Can I help?"

Big brown eyes, so much like her mother's, locked on mine, and she nodded, relinquishing the big wooden spoon. A few quick stirs, and it was the perfect consistency. Wanting to keep her included, I split the dough, remarking, "It looks like we have enough to need two rollers. Amelia, if you can give your mom some extra help rolling, you can be the one to lick the spoon."

Natalie instantly intervened. "Oh no. No one is licking the spoon. It's not safe. There are raw eggs in there."

Glancing at the spoon I held in my hand, then back to her, I teased, "Aw, come on, that's no fun. I've licked the spoon my whole life and lived to tell the tale."

Not backing down, she held my stare. "Not happening."

"Your mom's the boss," I acquiesced with a smile. "I guess I'll just have to think of some other incentive for you, Amelia."

Amelia went to a drawer and pulled out a second rolling pin. "I don't need anything to help Mom."

Jameson had already moved on to assembling the pieces of the gingerbread house, cementing them together with icing while he waited, calling out, "Hurry up. I want to cut out the cookies!"

Throwing down some flour, I laid out one larger and one smaller ball of dough for the ladies of the house to begin rolling until they were flat. While it was pleasant working in the kitchen, it needed something more to achieve that *family* feel I aimed to create. The dough was getting thinner and broader with each pass of the pins on the marble, and thinking back to my own family kitchen, inspiration struck.

Knowing it was a gamble, I reached a finger into the flour and used it to put a dot right in the middle of Amelia's nose. Caught completely by surprise, she turned to me, eyes huge, mouth open in a perfect little O.

That's when the most beautiful sound filled the room—Natalie's unfiltered laughter.

Amelia's head whipped to look at her mom behind her, laughing in a way I hadn't seen in almost a decade. If I hadn't heard it in that long, Amelia was likely too young to remember it.

Natalie prompted her daughter, "I think it's only fair you get him back."

Mischief entered Amelia's eyes, and she reached into the flour herself, gathering a good amount before rubbing a bit more than a finger dot on my nose. When I laughed, her face lit up, her own laughter spilling out, and for the first time in a long time, she resembled a carefree child. It made her look younger, less like a tiny adult.

"Oh, game on." Grabbing more flour, I smudged some on her cheeks.

Mock outrage filled her face, and she went for more, gathering a handful and throwing it. Ducking the main hit, flour rained down above.

Natalie began backing away from our mess, but I rounded Amelia, heading her way. "Oh, no. You're not getting away."

A squeal escaped her mouth as I pulled her into a bear hug from behind, shaking my head so that flour rained down onto her hair and shoulders. Allowing her to turn in my arms, the smile on her face was so genuine that my heart ached. The woman I'd fallen hopelessly in love with over the years was slowly coming back to me.

Reaching up, I smudged her nose with flour, whispering, "You've got a little something right there." I motioned to my own nose.

Eyes sparkling, she reached up, wiping at her nose, only managing to spread the flour further. "Did I get it?"

Shaking my head, I wanted nothing more than to kiss her right now. Radiating happiness, she'd never looked more gorgeous, but I reminded myself to be patient. She wasn't ready yet.

Giggles and motion caught my eye, and I turned in time to see Amelia pull a sneak attack on Jameson with more flour. The idea of finishing the cookies was forgotten as a flour war raged in the kitchen.

The mess didn't matter. I knew I would clean it later, as this day had gone even better than I'd planned. This was what I'd wanted—to bring love and laughter into this house. To let these children be children and return to being taken care of by adults.

This was only the beginning.

CHAPTER 12

Natalie

CHRISTMAS WAS DAYS AWAY, but it wasn't the holiday magic that was putting smiles on my kids' faces—it was Jaxon. Coming into our lives like a whirlwind, it was becoming clear he was the key to freeing the older kids from the chains imposed upon them by a life with their own father.

Not wanting to rock the boat on this newfound happiness, I silently prayed that Leo would stay gone.

Amy was firmly on Team Jaxon along with Hannah, but Liam was insistent that he remain the only man taking care of us.

I didn't know which side I was on. With Liam, we knew what to expect. He was loyal, dependable, and, above all, predictable. On the other hand, Jaxon made the kids so happy that my heart was close to bursting. Almost desperately, I wanted them to like him because he would be a permanent fixture in their lives as a result of their baby sister. He fit, that was for sure, but I wanted him to want me for more than the surprise of Charlie's impending arrival.

A shiver ran through my body thinking about the picture he'd painted with his words in the kitchen while making cookies. Growing up, I'd been a good girl, learning about sex from all the romance novels I'd devoured. But my favorite historical genre had not prepared me for the mouth on him—both literally and figuratively.

Did people really talk like that? My extremely limited experience said no, but Jaxon had shocked me into thinking there was this whole other world out there. One where people told each other exactly what they wanted, and it wasn't only about a man seeking his own pleasure. He turned me on with only his words, and I already knew he could back up those words with action.

Upon further reflection, he seemed like a better match for Hannah than for me—she was the outrageous one without a filter, she had more experience, and she knew what men wanted.

I had no clue what I was doing, and everything felt awkward.

That was another reason why I was still wary of letting him get too close to me. How many women did you have to sleep with to get that good at sex? I knew I hadn't been with anyone else, but how many women had he slept with since we'd conceived Charlie? I wasn't wholly convinced he wasn't still sleeping around. As a single man, I couldn't judge him for what he did while away from us. I only knew that I didn't want to be a number in the likely endless stream of women coming in and out of his life.

I couldn't deny that things were just *easy* with him. He had this knack for getting me to let my guard down, and his rapport with the kids seemed effortless. It would be so *easy* to fall into him. He was gorgeous and seemingly perfect—as Amy and Hannah often liked to point out. I'd learned the hard way that if something seemed too good to be true, it usually was.

Sitting in the glow of the Christmas tree, ordering a few last-minute presents for the kids, Amy walked in, joining me on the couch, breathing out, "Damn."

Looking over in question, she was staring at her phone, so I took the bait. Amy was careful about her words, and there was no doubt she wanted me to ask what she was looking at. "Damn, what?"

"That man looks good with a baby." Her poker face was shit, and she was trying hard to contain her smile but failing miserably.

That left no question that the man she was referring to was Jaxon. Sighing, I held out my hand. "All right, hand it over."

Dropping the phone into my hand, I peeked at the image on the screen. There he was, a red Santa hat on his head, holding a baby. It appeared to be from the annual Comets trip to the local children's hospital. The team went to spread cheer and bring gifts to those who were sick and stuck there for the holiday. The picture simultaneously warmed and broke my heart—knowing how much these visits meant to the children and their families, but that there were babies so tiny in the hospital at Christmas.

Before I knew it, I was crying.

Amy was instantly pulling me into her embrace. "Oh, Nat. I'm sorry. That's not quite the reaction I was going for."

Sniffling into her shoulder, my response was muffled. "Damn hormones."

Her laugh vibrated through us both, and she pulled back. "He hasn't been around for a couple of weeks, and I thought we needed a Jaxon fix. I'm sorry if I overstepped."

Furiously wiping the tears from my cheeks, I shook my head. "No, it wasn't even about Jaxon. I started thinking about the sick babies." The tears rose again, and I cursed in frustration. "Dammit!"

Understanding dawned on Amy's face. "Aw, Natalie. Your babies are all whole and well, right here under this roof. We will give them the best damn Christmas they've ever had."

I nodded. She knew my emotions had a deeper root cause. Jameson had been a preemie, arriving seven weeks early. He had been due shortly after Amelia's first birthday but surprised us all, arriving unexpectedly and quickly. The image of his tiny body hooked up to all the wires and tubes had been conjured up in my mind thinking about the kids in the hospital Jaxon went to visit.

Those two months in the NICU had nearly broken me. If he hadn't made it, I wasn't sure I would have either. Leo had been convinced I'd done something wrong and that the male heir might not make it because of me. Even if I'd physically survived the unthinkable, it was apparent that Leo would have made sure I never mentally did. Not that I'd fared much better when he'd thrived and had grown into a perfect, strong little boy.

That was the turning point in our marriage. Leo went from accusing me of failing to carry Jameson to term to being jealous that I gave him so much attention. I now know I'd been fighting a losing battle—if I hadn't cared as much for our frail baby boy as I did, Leo would have called me a neglectful mother. Jameson's early arrival gave him the perfect excuse to flip the switch from the charming, caring husband and father I'd thought he was, into the controlling, emotionally abusive man I'd discovered beneath that polished façade.

Shaking off the bad memories, I handed Amy her phone. "You're right."

"Sooooo," she continued. "Is he invited to the Christmas festivities?"

"Yes, Mom." I rolled my eyes.

Amy smirked. "The kids certainly like him."

"I know." I took a deep breath. "It's a good thing, I know that, but I still worry they will get too attached. Eventually, something is going to wreck this. I can't handle the thought of another father figure walking out on them."

"You know, there are millions of *happy* families out there. Something doesn't always have to go wrong. There are *good* men out there. Has Jaxon given you any reason not to trust him? Have you seen any red flags?"

"Does being too perfect count as a red flag?" I knew I was grasping at straws. I wanted to believe her that Jaxon was the real deal, but I wasn't sure if I'd ever be able to battle past my demons.

Would Leo's shadow ruin any chance at happiness that ever came my way?

Christmas Eve had always been my favorite day of the holiday season. Watching the kids open presents on Christmas morning was magical, but the excitement on Christmas Eve was infectious. Lists to Santa had been "sent" weeks ago, and all day there was chatter amongst the kids guessing which items they might receive. There was a charged energy in the air that was unparalleled.

Jaxon set up camp in the kitchen, making batch after batch of cookies—this time, without a flour fight. Amy and Hannah were sipping cranberry cocktails while I had the mocktail version. Charlotte seemingly loved all the sugar I had been consuming throughout the day because she was especially active. I smiled as my hand rested on my belly, thinking that next year, she would likely be crawling around, and we'd have to protect her and the tree from each other.

Then there was Liam, literally pouting in the corner. He knew if he wanted to avoid Jaxon, he'd miss out on most of the holiday, so he made his choice but was visibly unhappy about it.

We ordered pizza for dinner, content to keep the day casual and cozy. Liam started a fire in the fireplace, and we made hot chocolate, relaxing as we watched a classic cartoon Christmas movie before the kids headed to bed. My heart began to swell when Beau curled right into Jaxon's side on the couch. Jaxon cuddled him like it was the most natural thing in the world.

It was our family tradition to open matching holiday pajamas to wear on Christmas Eve. They'd been wrapped under the tree for weeks, so when the movie ended, the kids knew the drill, finding the packages with their names on them.

Amelia made sure to hand out the wrapped boxes to the adults. Amy, Hannah, Liam, and I started this tradition of matching them when we'd moved back home, trying to create new memories to cover up the bad ones.

Everyone in the family had their box, but Amelia returned to the tree, producing one more and handing it to Jaxon.

He flashed that ridiculously charming, crooked smile at her, asking, "Is this for me?"

She nodded shyly. "Everyone in the family wears the same pajamas for Christmas. You're part of our family now, right?"

"Yes, I am," he said without a moment of hesitation. "Thank you, Amelia. It means a lot that you would include me."

Jameson jumped in, "You're staying tonight like Aunt Hannah, right Jaxon?"

Jaxon looked at me, unsure. "That's really up to your mom. I can come back for you to open presents first thing in the morning."

Beau sleepily leaned against Jaxon, his words drowsy. "Stay, Jaxon. Read me a story."

Who was I to say no to these children, who were so desperate for affection from a man in their lives?

I nodded. "Of course, Jaxon can stay." Looking at him, I explained, "Hannah already has the guest room, so unfortunately, the best I can offer is the couch."

Jameson panicked. "Not the couch! Santa won't come if there's someone down here!"

Quick to soothe him, Jaxon stepped in. "Well, we can't have that."

Hannah came to the rescue. "I have an idea."

"Can't wait to hear this," Liam grumbled.

"Hush, grouch," she snapped at him. "How about I bunk with Amy tonight, and Jaxon can have the guest room? That way, no one will scare Santa away."

"Works for me," Amy agreed.

They were obviously working together, but I let it slide. "Guess that's settled. Now, let's open these pajamas and get up to bed before Santa skips our house."

Everyone opened the boxes containing this year's pajamas in a flurry of flying wrapping paper. Leaving the mess behind, Amelia and Jameson placed a plate of milk and cookies for Santa before hurrying up the stairs to get ready for bed. Beau was struggling to keep his eyes open, so Jaxon helped him open his box.

Standing, I walked over to their couch, reaching down to pick up Beau, but Jaxon stopped me. "I can take him. Just point me in the right direction."

I wasn't going to argue. Beau was getting heavier by the day as he transitioned from toddler to kid. Grabbing their pajamas and mine, I led him up the stairs, stopping first in Beau's room. Jaxon laid him down on his bed, fully clothed, eyes drooping.

Sitting down next to his tiny body, I began to strip off his clothes and change him into his pajamas as I handed Jaxon his box. "Go change. The guest room is across the walkway over the living room. It's the door on the left."

Jaxon left the room, and I could hear Amy with Amelia and Jameson down the hallway in the bathroom brushing their teeth. Beau was dead weight as I finished getting him changed before removing the covers and tucking him in.

Leaning down to kiss his forehead, I whispered, "Goodnight, baby. Merry Christmas."

As I pulled away, he whimpered, rousing from his semi-conscious state. "Story, Jaxon."

"Oh, honey. It's okay. You'll see Jaxon in the morning," I soothed him.

"No. Story," he mumbled.

From behind me, I heard the rich timbre of Jaxon's voice roll over me. "I'm here, little man."

Looking over, I couldn't help but smile as I took in the muscular man before me, clad in plaid reindeer pajamas—the mixture of ridiculous and adorable was almost too much to handle. He held his hand out to me, so I took it and used the leverage to stand from the bottom bunk.

I glanced over my shoulder at Beau, then back to Jaxon, whispering, "He's almost out. It's fine."

Squeezing my hand, Jaxon stared right into my eyes as he whispered back, "I made a promise."

Nodding, I walked over to the bookshelf in the corner, grabbing Beau's favorite book, and handing it to Jaxon. He took it, motioning to the door. "Go. I've got him."

Walking out, I could hear the hushed tones as he began reading the familiar words, and I smiled to myself. He was quickly becoming a part of this family, just as Amelia had so cautiously declared downstairs.

After tucking in Amelia and Jameson, I changed into my matching pajamas before heading back down to the living room.

Everyone else was ready to play their part in making the Santa magic happen, but we all knew we had to be sure all the little people were sound asleep, lest we be discovered as elves. That meant another round of hot chocolate for me, a round of eggnog for everyone else, and my favorite holiday romantic comedy. Yes, it was cheesy, but it wasn't officially Christmas until we watched it.

As the opening scene played on screen, I turned to the ladies. "The pajamas? Really?"

Amy shrugged. "Amelia asked me to make it happen. What was I supposed to do? Say no?"

Liam grumbled, "Yes."

Nudging him, I acknowledged that she had a point. "She actually asked you to get them for Jaxon?"

Amy took a sip of her eggnog. "He's made quite the impression on the kids. But that begs the more important question. Has he made the same impression on you?"

Not having an answer to that question, I fell into the movie. By the time we'd made it to the famous dance scene through the Prime Minister's house, I realized that Jaxon hadn't come back. That book wasn't very long, and Beau was minutes away from passing out when I left them.

Leaving the comfort of the couch and the movie, I padded back up the stairs to the open doorway of Beau's room.

Leaning against the doorframe, I couldn't help but smile at the scene before me. Jaxon was asleep alongside Beau, with the book draped across his midsection.

It struck me that this must be what it was like to have a partner—someone to share the load of parenting. Sure, I had Liam and Amy, but more often than not, I felt like a burden. What was developing with Jaxon felt different, but in a good way.

Time seemingly stood still, so I was completely unaware of how long I'd been standing there, staring at them, when I heard Hannah behind me. "Well, *damn*. Good thing you're already pregnant, or that would do it."

Oh, Hannah.

Turning, I found both Amy and Hannah craning their necks to see into the room around me.

I bit back a grin. "All right, ladies, show's over. I'm going to wake him up. You two go check on the older kids. Make sure the coast is clear, and we can get to work."

As they made their way down the hall to the other bedrooms, I finally entered Beau's dimmed room. Sitting down on the edge of the bed, I put a hand on Jaxon's ankle and shook gently, causing him to stir slightly, but then his breathing deepened again. Shaking him again, I whispered, "Hey, sleepy head."

Those devastatingly gorgeous whiskey-colored eyes opened slowly, but when they focused on me, he startled, sitting up suddenly. "What happened?"

Throwing a finger first to my lips, then at a still-sleeping Beau, I whispered loudly, "Shhhhh."

Realizing where he was, Jaxon relaxed again but slowly edged off the bed. "Sorry, I fell asleep."

"I noticed." I couldn't help but smile as he rubbed his eyes, trying to wake up more fully. His dark hair was sticking up from where it was pressed against the pillow, and if it weren't for the stubble lining his jaw, he'd have resembled an oversized sleepy toddler.

Walking together out of the room, I softly latched the door as Jaxon asked, "How long was I out?"

Leading him back downstairs, I decided to tease him for falling asleep on the job. "Well, we have about an hour before the kids get up."

Panic filled his voice as he trailed behind me. "What? Why didn't you wake me sooner?" Reaching the bottom of the steps, I couldn't keep the giggles from escaping when I turned around to face him. One look, and he knew I was messing with him.

"You make it so easy," I teased.

Raising a brow, he smirked. "Oh, so that's how it's going to be?"

Shrugging, I returned to the living room, where Hannah and Amy had already started bringing up the gifts we'd wrapped over the last few weeks for the kids. Some from Santa, some from each of us, some from their grandparents overseas.

Jaxon leapt into action, joining them in the trek up and down with armloads of presents.

Once everything was in one place, I surveyed the massive pile, remarking, "I think we may have gone overboard this year."

Liam countered, "You say that every year."

He was right. I did. On some level, I was trying to compensate for their absent father. I knew that a mountain of toys wasn't enough to patch that hole in their hearts, but it didn't stop me from trying.

Beginning the herculean task of sorting the substantial heap, Jaxon excused himself. "I need to run next door and get my gifts. I didn't expect to stay tonight, or I'd have brought them earlier."

Hannah couldn't resist. "Please, tell me you're coming back dressed as a sexy Santa?"

I bit my lip. The image of Jaxon, half-naked, wearing a Santa hat, was enough to send my overly sensitive hormones into overdrive. Come to think of it, I probably wouldn't say no to Jaxon gift-wrapped beneath the tree.

Completely obviously, he taunted Hannah right back. "You know, Hannah, one of these days, that mouth of yours is going to get you into real trouble."

"I'm counting on it. Do you happen to know any muscular athletes who might want to punish me for such an offense?" Hannah was over-the-top, and she knew it, causing Jaxon to chuckle on his way toward the front door.

Hearing the door click, I turned on her with a warning tone. "Hannah . . ."

"You're not fooling me. You totally were picturing him doing a Santa strip tease." Hannah was smug, taking a sip of her eggnog.

"No, I wasn't." Denial was the official party line. If I even hinted that I was picturing Jaxon in more of a sexual capacity, both Hannah and Amy would be all over the chance to tell me to "get mine".

"I've known you for half your life, lady. You can't fool me. He's hot, amazing with the kids, and you're already pregnant—with his baby, I might add. Why not jump his bones? He will be sleeping here, next door to your room. When are you going to have easy access like this again?"

So much for denial. Would it be that easy? Just sneak into his room, slip under the covers, and then . . .

No.

What was wrong with me? My kids were in the house. It didn't matter that he was sexy as sin, accessible, and openly reciprocated the sexual attraction I felt. If I needed to get off that desperately, there was a drawer full of handy helpers right next to my bed that could get the job done.

Amy added, "She has a point. Thank God you two are isolated in your own wing, with everyone else on the other end of the house. I don't want to hear anything." She pretended to plug her ears to emphasize her point.

Liam groaned. "I do *not* want to hear any of this. Can we please focus on Christmas?"

Hannah, done with Liam's bad attitude, threw out, "Maybe *you* need to get laid, Liam."

As if suspended in time, the room seemingly stood still. Hannah was always bold, but she'd never directly come at Liam before. Frozen, all three of us stared at him as his permanent scowl slowly turned into what could only be called a smile on any other person, but it was something we'd never seen on Liam.

Hannah leaned over, whispering, "Natalie, I'm scared. His teeth are showing."

Eyes still stuck on Liam, I whispered back, "Well, you poked the bear. Whatever happens next, you're on your own."

"Some friend you are." She scoffed.

Liam leaned forward, enjoying drawing out the dramatic suspense he'd created. "Are you offering, Hannah?"

Stunned, we sat there as Liam burst into laughter. Liam didn't make jokes. Ever. Just another sign that the world was currently upside down, and we were all along for the ride.

Hannah grabbed a throw pillow off the couch, chucking it at his head, declaring, "In your dreams."

The tension now broken, we got back to work setting up the perfect Christmas morning scene. I was on my hands and knees, grabbing presents and organizing them into stacks—making sure everything looked aesthetically pleasing—when Jaxon returned from next door. Amy left my side to help him with whatever he'd brought. She reentered the room with another armful of presents to add to the growing mass, and Jaxon sat down in a clear space with a large brown box.

Peeking over occasionally, I noticed he'd gotten the box open and laid a bunch of red pipes and white netting in all directions.

My curiosity eventually got the better of me. "What have you got there?"

Not looking up from whatever he was assembling, he replied, "Hockey net."

"Hockey net?"

"Yeah, I promised the kids we would play mini sticks when I first came over. I've got sticks and balls for them, too. Among other things."

Jaxon still hadn't looked up, but I was staring at him, my mouth hanging open slightly in shock. This was the second time tonight he'd mentioned promises and then taken action to keep them. Empty promises had filled my life for so long that seeing them fulfilled was alien to me. That dangerous hope began to rise once more inside my chest.

Maybe Amy was right. Maybe Jaxon truly was a good man. I prayed that was the case because, with each passing day, he was slowly wearing down my defenses.

My phone was dinging on the coffee table, jarring me from my thoughts, but I knew that specific tone. Ignoring it, I went back to work.

When I was almost done with the seemingly endless sorting and stacking, Jaxon asked, "Whose phone is that?"

Relaxing against the lower half of the couch, not ready to work my way off the floor just yet, I sighed. "It's mine. Ignore it."

"It seems important," he commented as his brow furrowed.

I waved him off. "It's not, really. It's the alert that, somewhere, my name was mentioned in the media."

Looking at the rest of the adults in the room, he cautiously responded, "That seems . . . healthy."

Liam, breaking his freeze out of Jaxon, replied, "Yeah, it's not."

Glaring at my big brother in annoyance, I snapped at him, "Not helpful."

Jaxon wasn't deterred. "What could they possibly be saying about you? As far as I can tell, you've been holed up here for over a month. I was with you the one time you went out, and you were hiding in my backseat."

I'd ignored it because it was Christmas, not wanting whatever it was to ruin the holiday. The story would still be out there in the universe days from now. Obviously, Jaxon wasn't willing to drop it, so I motioned to the phone. "Be my guest."

He was hesitant but stood to reach the phone, sitting on the couch next to where I leaned. Silence descended upon the room as everyone waited while he read. It could be anything. I'd seen—and read—it all by now. Usually lies, but sometimes with a hint of truth—enough to cause a direct blow to my sense of self-worth.

Clearing his throat, Jaxon seemed hesitant. "Um, I don't know what to think about this."

Not even bothering to look back, I held out my hand as he relinquished the phone. Scanning the text, the headlines read: *Princess Natalie Remington Disappears from the Spotlight. Checks into Rehab Facility, Location Unknown.*

In the grand scheme of things, this was minor. I'd survived worse.

Placing the phone back on the coffee table, I declared, "It's not that bad. We can work with this." Amy and Hannah leapt to the phone, eager to learn what I deemed not-world-ending. Right away, they nodded, agreeing it wasn't terrible.

Poor Jaxon was exasperated. "You'd rather have the world thinking you're in rehab than having them learn you're pregnant with my baby?"

Oh, boy. He's taking this personally.

I gave Amy *the look,* and the room cleared.

Finding my way off the floor, I sat on the couch next to Jaxon. Taking his hand in mine, my thumb lingered on his wrist where I could feel his pulse racing. Guilt flooded me for bringing him into my mess and creating stress he shouldn't have to deal with.

Reverting to the only way I knew to deal with a man, I tried to please him and flip the situation to make it more about him than me. "I'm trying to protect you."

Feeling him stiffen next to me, I realized instantly that I'd miscalculated. His voice was clipped when he finally responded, "I don't need you to protect me."

"I'm sorry," I said on reflex.

The words seemed to startle him, and he relaxed slightly. "Why are *you* sorry?"

"You're mad." I bit my lip. I didn't know how to read him, and it made me nervous.

"I'm not mad. I'm just . . . frustrated." He ran a hand through his dark hair. "Help me understand because I'm really struggling. How is this story better than the truth?"

"I can see how you would think people believing I'm in rehab is bad. But if the tabloids place me elsewhere, they won't be looking for me here. It draws public attention away from home, away from the kids."

Thinking on it for a minute, he pulled me toward him, and I let him, curling into his side. Running his hand up and down my arm, I felt him lean his head onto mine, whispering, "I'm sorry I made this about me."

God, laying in his arms was so damn comfortable. I felt myself say words in response, but the soft glow of the fire, combined with the warmth radiating off the man holding me close, had my eyelids drooping. I'd be the first to admit that I was tired. Tired physically—sure, it was late—but also mentally tired of carrying the weight of the world on my shoulders. Now, here was this man, who was so good with my kids, who wanted to take care of all of us, and part of me really wanted to let him.

That was my last thought before I drifted off to sleep in his arms.

CHAPTER 13

Jaxon

I LOVE YOU.

Those were the words I'd dared to whisper out loud after carrying a sleeping Natalie upstairs and tucking her into bed. I knew she couldn't hear me. She wasn't ready to hear it, but I was ready to say it.

Unknowingly, she'd given me the ultimate Christmas gift—allowing me to hold her tonight as she fell asleep in my arms. I didn't need anything else.

Once I was sure she was settled, I went back downstairs to finish constructing the net for the kids before heading to bed myself.

Feeling as if I'd only closed my eyes for a minute, I was jostled awake by Beau bouncing on my bed, yelling, "Wake up, Jaxon! Santa came!"

Rubbing the sleep from my eyes, I teased the little boy, who was bursting with excitement. "You didn't peek, did you?"

A sheepish grin crossed his face. "I only looked! I didn't open anything."

"I won't tell," I promised. A quick glance to the open doorway told me there were no other lights on inside the house. "Is anyone else awake, little man?"

"No." He continued to bounce up and down on my bed.

Finally daring to check the time on my phone, I rubbed a hand hard over my face. It was only 5:30 AM. I'd gotten about four hours of sleep and was determined to make sure Natalie got as much rest as possible.

I stood, holding my arms out to him. "All right, little man. Let's go back to your room and play for a little bit until everyone else wakes up."

Without hesitation, Beau jumped into my arms, and I held his small body close. He was in that weird stage—almost too big to be a toddler, yet too small to be classified as a kid—and I found myself wishing that I could bottle his innocence. Trust was something he gave freely, and I strove to remain worthy of that trust.

All three of Natalie's kids had found their way into my heart, just like their mother, and I would do anything to protect them. They were my family now.

The world faded away as we sat on the floor in Beau's room, playing with cars, constructing train tracks, and stacking blocks.

Eventually, natural sunlight filtered through the windows, and I glanced up to find Natalie leaning against the doorjamb. Looking adorable in the silly pajamas—her long blonde hair piled high atop her head, half of her face slightly reddened from sleep—I knew without question that she was the woman I wanted to spend the rest of my life with.

Smiling at the thought, I acknowledged her presence, uttering softly, "Merry Christmas."

Beau noticed her standing there, jumping up and running to hug her legs. "Merry Christmas, Mommy!"

Her brilliant smile stole my breath away as she looked down at Beau, hugging him close. "Merry Christmas, sweetheart." Looking over his head, she trained that smile on me. "Can I get you some coffee? Maybe an energy drink? You know that you could have sent him down to my room. I'm sorry he woke you."

Beau ran down the hall to wake his siblings. Standing and making my way to the doorway where she stood, I utilized her oft-used phrase, "It's not a big deal." Stalking closer, I dropped my voice an octave. "If you're going to be sleep-deprived, I'd rather it be because I kept you up all night screaming my name."

Natalie looked up, tugging on her lower lip with her teeth, causing me to bite back a groan. That lip had been taunting me for weeks, begging to become my own personal chew toy. Before she could respond, the thundering herd of footsteps was headed our way.

Leaning in close to her ear, I whispered, "To be continued."

Her breath hitched, but she quickly transitioned into mom mode—gathering up the kids so they could go down and see what awaited them beneath the tree.

Hanging back, I observed them. I wanted this. I wanted to have these intimate moments with Natalie and then to seamlessly switch to focusing on the kids. I'd never expected that this would be the life I craved, but sometimes, life knew better what you needed.

Heading for the stairs, following behind, I knew the exact moment they saw the fully assembled net with three mini sticks resting on top. Voices floated up to the second story, Jameson first, "Whoa! This is *so* cool!"

Then, Amelia, "There's a stick for me too?"

Finally, Beau said, "Hockey! I wanna play!"

Making my way into the living room, three sets of eyes were on me. Their smiling faces made the long night worth every minute spent fighting with the netting.

Jameson turned to Natalie, begging, "Can we play, Mom?"

She looked at the massive pile of presents next to and under the tree. "You don't want to open your gifts from Santa first?"

"No way! Can we play?"

"Well, if it's all right with Jaxon." She shrugged as a small smile crept onto her lips.

He grabbed one of the sticks. "Please, Jaxon?"

Holding up a finger, I stopped him. "I've got one more thing, so you're ready for the full mini-sticks experience. Then, I'll help you move it down the hallway so you can play."

Natalie turned to me. "There's more?"

Winking, I replied, "I'm nothing if not thorough."

There's that blush I love.

Stepping over different piles of gifts, I grabbed four wrapped boxes, handing one to each of the kids, and then one to Natalie.

She stared up at me, then lowered her eyes, whispering, "I didn't get you a gift."

Sitting down beside her, I tipped her chin up with my hand until her brown eyes met mine. Then, I took my other hand and rested it on her belly, smiling. "Charlie is the greatest gift you could have ever given me."

Her hand found its way to covering mine, and for a moment, it was as if we were the only two people in the world.

I forgot where we were until Amelia asked, "Can we open them?"

Natalie pulled her hand away quickly, and I followed suit, although more reluctantly. Turning to Amelia, I gestured to their boxes. "Yes, open them. Then, it's game on!"

Paper went flying as they tore into the packages. Jameson got his open first, pulling out the child-sized version of my navy blue and gray Comets jersey. The other two finally got theirs open, revealing their own jerseys, each with my number twenty-three and the name Slate stitched across the back.

They all stared at me in awe, so I urged them, "Put them on. You have to look the part if you want to play hockey."

Jameson threw his on first, then looked to Natalie. "Are you going to open yours, Mom?"

Peering down at the box in her lap, she slowly unwrapped it. Taking the top off the box, she froze, realizing I'd also gotten her a jersey with my name and number on it. Her silence triggered my sweat response. Had I gone too far? The subtle undertone was that I was laying claim on all of them—branding them with my name—but maybe that was too much too soon.

All she managed was, "Oh."

Playing it cool, I asked, "Wrong size? I guessed. I can take it back and exchange it for another."

"It's not that." Her eyes were still downcast, refusing to look up at me.

Hannah's voice cut in, making her presence known. "Nat already has yours."

After a quick glance at Hannah, I turned my attention back to Natalie. "You do?"

Her throat bobbed as she swallowed. "Uh-huh."

The mental image of her already wearing my name in the stands was overwhelming. That was the point of getting her my jersey, but to know that she'd been doing it all along filled me with a sense of possession. She was always meant to be mine.

Hannah grabbed the net and moved it into the open hallway for the kids to play. Natalie excused herself to grab a cup of tea from the kitchen, and Amy rounded the couch to occupy the space Natalie had left empty beside me.

Nodding, she indicated down the hallway where the kids were giggling, playing the sport I'd devoted my entire life to. "I think you stole the show."

Watching the kids play, realizing they were becoming my entire world, I smiled. "I want them all to be happy."

Amy gave me a playful nudge. "And that's why I like you. Keep it up. I've got your back."

Nudging her back, I couldn't tear my gaze away from the happy kids. Genetics be damned, this was *my* family. I wasn't about to let anything or *anyone* hurt them ever again.

"Congrats on the All-Pro Game selection, man." Cal sat next to me in the locker room after I returned from the shower.

Shrugging it off, I replied, "It's nice the fans want to see me there, but I'd much rather have the mini break."

"Aw, come on. You love the attention," my best friend teased.

I'd much rather have the attention of a certain blonde that weekend, but I couldn't tell him that. Keeping this huge part of my life from my best friends was more difficult than I'd expected. I desperately wanted to tell them. They'd probably give me shit for not telling them sooner, but they'd be happy for me. They knew Natalie was the dream—even if a seemingly impossible one. Now, it was reality, and I was so close to letting her know how much I cared about her. Breaking the promise I'd made to keep things quiet could cost me everything, so I kept the truth locked away from my best friends.

Cal joked, "You could always turn it down and come to Mexico with the boys."

Mexico was our "place". The single guys on the team had been going together since before I was a rookie. In the years I wasn't selected for the All-Pro Game, there had never been a question of my attendance. We'd had some wild trips down there, but I couldn't tell Cal that I wouldn't be going this year even if I didn't have the game. The road trips to the other side of the country were already further away than I could stand to be from Natalie right now. I wasn't going to travel that far away on purpose, and for what? To drink and wheel women? The only woman I wanted was right here in Hartford. My bachelor life was dead, and there was no need for a funeral. I was happy with the direction my life was headed.

Laughing, I gave him a playful punch to the arm. "Nah, it's my job to give back to the fans who voted me into the game. It is a good opportunity to face time with the kids and keep growing the American youth game."

Cal grinned. "That's why they love you, you selfless bastard. We'll miss you while we are hanging poolside."

Standing, ready to head home, I threw back, "I'm sure you'll have a drink for me."

"I plan on having so many drinks that I won't remember my name, let alone yours." A mischievous gleam entered his Arctic blue eyes.

"Sounds about right," I mused.

Cal changed the subject. "You free tonight? Some of the guys were thinking of meeting up for a poker night."

I shook my head. "Sorry, can't tonight. My parents are coming over for dinner."

"Shannon and Michael are in town? Give your mom a hug for me."

The hockey community was a gigantic family. Everyone looked out for each other, and that included our parents, who treated each teammate like one of their own. Cal loved my parents as much as I loved his. We were lucky that so many people had our backs.

"They'll be at the game tomorrow night," I replied. "I'll make sure you can give her a hug yourself."

"Deal. Your mom is the best."

Smiling to myself, I headed out of the locker room toward the player parking lot. My mom *was* the best. Tonight, Natalie was coming over to meet my parents. Mom had insisted on a home-cooked meal for the evening when I'd suggested that we order in. Her motto was that you show love for your family by cooking for them, so I allowed her to take over. It hadn't escaped my notice that Natalie was eating more these days, her body continuing to fill out, and she'd never looked more incredible. Mom was going to love her—she'd been a mix of anxious and excited all week. Dad, on the other hand, had been warned to be on his best behavior.

Tonight was going to be a huge step for us, and I needed it to go well.

CHAPTER 14

Natalie

THE MAGICAL HIGH CREATED by Jaxon for Christmas was still lingering in the air as the holiday break ended and the kids went back to school. Jaxon texted over the weekend, bringing me back down to Earth, asking if I was free for dinner with his parents before they returned to Minnesota.

He'd painted this perfect picture of family for my kids, drawing on his own experience growing up in a functioning, loving household. I wasn't sure I fit into that kind of life. My upbringing hadn't been exactly warm, and my marriage certainly wasn't. I strove to provide better for my kids, but it wasn't as effortless as Jaxon had made it seem.

Spending over an hour getting ready, trying multiple outfits, determined to make a great first impression, I'd eventually settled on a simple look of black leggings paired with a tunic top. Styling my hair in loose, long waves, I allowed makeup to highlight my features for the first time in months.

I desperately wanted them to like me. Charlotte was their granddaughter, and I wanted her to have the loving family Jaxon brought to the table. Familiar doubt crept into my mind that I wasn't good enough. Jaxon's life—and theirs by extension—was forever changed because I couldn't control myself one summer night. How could they possibly like me?

Putting on shoes was where I hit a snag. Everything on my body was expanding, and that included my feet. Sitting on the mudroom bench, I tried in vain to force my feet into my trusty fur-lined boots, to no avail. Next, I tried my black flats but couldn't feel my toes with how far forward they pressed into the unyielding leather. Checking the weather report, the temperature was in the low 30s, but there wasn't any snow on the ground.

Fuck it.

Giving up, I threw on my black flip-flops, rationalizing that I was only going next door and could drive rather than walk to protect my feet from frostbite. Just add showing up in inappropriate footwear to the list of judgments I would probably receive this evening.

Making a mental note to order new shoes, I headed out.

Driving to Jaxon's house took less than a minute, but I sat in his driveway, gathering the courage to go inside. Placing a hand on my belly, I knew I couldn't take anything back now. Charlie was coming whether I was ready or not.

For some reason, Jaxon's parents were the most daunting of all the people I'd faced since finding out I was pregnant. Maybe it was because I was a parent myself—I could put myself in their shoes if it were my son. Jaxon wasn't your ordinary boy next door. He was a world-famous athlete who made a lot of money, and I could only imagine his parents thinking I'd trapped him.

Unable to sit in the car all night unnoticed, I shook off the doubts and scenarios running through my mind, turned off the car, and got out. Heart beating out of my chest, I rang the doorbell and waited for whoever might happen to open it. A breath rushed out when that person was Jaxon, relief washing over me. He provided a calming presence I hadn't realized until this moment. It sure didn't hurt that he was easy on the eyes, clad in dark wash jeans and a navy blue button-up.

Smiling, he took my hand, ushering me in and out of the cold. That smile faded as he took my coat and noticed I was slipping off my flip-flops. Wasting no time in chastising me, he asked in disbelief, "Where are your shoes? It's January in New England!"

I was momentarily embarrassed but then remembered he was partly to blame for my inability to fit into any weather-appropriate shoes. Avoiding his gaze, I whispered, "I couldn't get my feet into any of my closed-toe shoes. It's not a big deal. I only walked twenty steps from the car to your door."

Guilt flooded his handsome face as he ran a hand through his dark hair. "I'm sorry, I didn't realize." A smile touched his lips as he scanned me from head to toe. "You look beautiful."

My self-image had been so damaged that I didn't know how to take compliments. I'd been torn down so often that it was hard to believe anyone could find anything good about my appearance and vocalize it. Feeling my face heat up, I looked away, busying myself with hanging up my purse with my coat.

Jaxon grabbed my hand with one of his, then took the other and cupped my face. Melting into his touch, allowing him to force my gaze up, he stroked my cheek with his thumb before whispering, "I wish you could see yourself the way that I see you."

My lips parted, and his eyes dropped to them. I could tell he wanted to kiss me. Hell, I wanted him to kiss me. His words and actions these past few months were wearing down my defenses. It was only a matter of time before I gave in to this man who had captivated not only me, but my children.

Noises from the kitchen broke our trance, and Jaxon glanced over his shoulder. When he turned back, he leaned in close, brushing a quick kiss against my cheek before asking, "Are you ready for this?"

Nodding as he pulled away, I'd already accepted my fate. "Time is running out. Now or never, I guess."

Hand still in mine, he led me towards the living room. "Just be yourself. They'll love you."

Love was perhaps too strong of a word. Very few people in my life truly loved me, and most of them lived next door. I wasn't even sure my own parents felt that way about me. Why should his?

My brain told me to put on my big-girl panties and meet this challenge head-on, but my body betrayed me—my feet dragging as we ventured further into Jaxon's house.

A woman with short brown hair laced with silver stands, and a face featuring noticeable laugh lines in her early fifties emerged from the kitchen. Her face lit up with a warm smile, and she clapped her hands together, exclaiming, "Oh! Well, aren't you pretty! I can see why Jaxon is so smitten."

"*Mom.*" Jaxon shifted next to me, clearly embarrassed. That was new. He was always so confident and self-assured. It was nice to see that he wasn't completely perfect. He was human, just like the rest of us.

Looking back toward the kitchen, his mom called over her shoulder, "Michael, get in here! She's here!" Then she rushed toward us, pulling me into a hug, completely catching me off guard, gushing, "We are so glad that you're here!"

This was not at all what I'd been expecting. Still mid-hug, my shock must have been visible when I looked at Jaxon, who simply shrugged before telling his mom, "Let her breathe, Mom."

A tall man, also early fifties, came into the room, his hair beginning to gray, giving him a salt-and-pepper look. More intimidating than Jaxon's mom, he made his way to the group, placing a chaste kiss on my cheek before pulling back. "Lovely to meet you."

Jaxon tensed slightly; the movement barely caught out of the corner of my eye. Not knowing where to start, I introduced myself. "I'm Natalie. It's so nice to meet you both."

His mom threw a hand to her chest. "How rude of me! I was just so excited to meet you that I forgot my manners. I'm Shannon, and this is Michael. And, of course, you know our Jaxon."

We all laughed, which helped break the ice. Shannon was so kind that I felt comfortable joking in response. "The name rings a bell."

Jaxon placed his hand on the small of my back. "Why don't we sit down before dinner?"

Shannon's eyes sparkled as she concurred, "Oh, yes! Let's get you off your feet." His parents sat on one couch together, so he led me to the other, taking a spot by my side. That's when Shannon noticed my bare feet, not skipping a beat, immediately instructing Jaxon, "Goodness dear, go and get her a pair of socks!"

My jaw dropped as I watched Jaxon jump up and race up the stairs. Shannon reached over and grabbed my hand. "You'll have to forgive him. He's only had to take care of himself for so long."

Still trying to process how quickly he'd jumped into action at his mother's command, I found my voice. "Oh, it's no trouble. I apologize. I couldn't get any of my winter shoes on. I should have thought ahead to bring a pair of socks for inside the house."

She was sympathetic in her response. "Nonsense, we'll get you all taken care of."

Jaxon appeared back at my side with socks—two pairs, in fact. One was thick and fuzzy, another low-cut like the ones he currently wore. I reached for the low-cut pair but couldn't get my hands on them as he knelt before me, placing them on my expanded feet. It hadn't escaped my notice that he was initiating physical contact more frequently, but surprisingly, I didn't mind it so much. He was affectionate—which was certainly something I hadn't experienced in my sole prior relationship—and I was finding that I liked it. It was calming—comforting, even.

Jaxon looked up, smiling before me. "Better?"

Nodding, I found myself at a loss for words. Was I swooning over him touching my ankles right now? What century was this, where that innocent contact was enough to cause my stomach to somersault? The gesture seemed incredibly intimate, especially in front of his parents.

Rising, he joined me back on the couch as his mom asked, "So, Jaxon tells us you're originally from Hartford?"

Turning my head in her direction, she was still smiling. I looked down, checking to make sure that my bump was still there—that I hadn't imagined the reason I found myself sitting here inside Jaxon Slate's home, meeting his parents. Charlie chose that moment to give me a little roll, a reminder that she was not a figment of my imagination.

I must have gotten lost in my thoughts because I heard Jaxon prompt, "Natalie?"

Snapping back to reality, I took a moment to try and remember the question. "Oh! Yes, I grew up a couple of neighborhoods over from where we are now."

Shannon smiled. "What a small world! It must be such a comfort to be near home."

Were we honestly sitting here ignoring the elephant, or more accurately, the beached whale in the room? This was a refreshing change of pace for me, so I wasn't about to rock the boat. If they wanted small talk, that's what they'd get from me.

Nodding, I answered, "You don't realize how much you miss home until you leave."

Shannon smiled softly. "Jaxon mentioned that you'd left home when you were young, just like him. It's nice that you have that in common." Quickly, she changed topics. "Tell me about your little ones."

I was beginning to get whiplash, but asking about the kids disarmed me. "My oldest is Amelia, and she's nine. Then there's Jameson, who is eight currently but will be nine in March. They're my Irish twins, ten months apart."

"Oh, goodness!" she exclaimed. "You are brave. My boys are over eight years apart. I can't even imagine two babies so close together."

I was used to that kind of reaction when people learned how close in age my oldest two children were. "Wasn't exactly how I'd planned it, but I wouldn't change it for the world. Then there's my baby, Beau, who is three and a half." Pausing for a moment, my hand dropped to my belly. "Was my baby, I guess now."

Shannon jumped on that opening. "I can't tell you how excited I am for a little girl. I'd always prayed for a little girl, but it wasn't the path laid out for me." Gazing fondly at Jaxon, she added, "But I do love my boys. They're both good men."

I peeked at Jaxon beside me, saying softly, "I'm starting to see that."

He took my hand, squeezing it lightly before adding to the conversation himself. "I have no idea what to do with a little girl, but I'm excited to learn. Spending time with Amelia has given me a glimpse, but she's a bit older, so I'm sure it'll be different."

Unable to contain my smile, I recognized how hard he was trying. I'd have to be blind not to see that, so I squeezed his hand back. "It won't be much different from the bond that you seem to have with Beau. He thinks you've hung the moon, and I'm sure Charlie will too."

There was a tenderness in his eyes. "Beau is really special."

Oh no, the hormones took hold once again, and I was on the verge of crying. All because of how much he cared about my sweet baby boy. It washed over me all at once, the realization that he was going to be an incredible father to Charlie. Unable to look away, I was oblivious to the tear that slipped down my cheek until Jaxon reached up with a thumb to wipe it away.

Sensing my distress, he leaned in close. "Hey, are you okay?"

Nodding, blinking furiously as more tears spilled from my eyes and a lump formed in my throat, my words were shaky. "I was just thinking how lucky Charlie is."

Taking both hands, cupping my cheeks, he held my gaze. "No, Natalie. I'm the lucky one. You've given me everything I've always wanted and never thought that I could have."

Damn him. What is he doing to me?

My lower lip trembled, so I bit it hard, tasting blood as I tried to hold back the sob that threatened to break free, but it was useless. My conditioning had taught me that crying was a sign of weakness, so I cursed myself for making a fool of myself in front of his parents, having just barely met them. My vision was blurry from the tears I couldn't stop, but instead of the expected look of pity on Jaxon's face, there was something else etched on his face—a softness.

"Baby, come here." He pulled me into his arms, and the dam fully broke. I'd held everything in for so long, trying to keep it together for my kids, and now here was this man. He gave himself freely to me and my kids, never looking for anything in return. It was such a stark contrast from everything I'd ever known about relationships that I didn't know how to process it—hence, my current meltdown.

Consistently steadfast, he rubbed my back soothingly. "I won't let anything hurt you. You're safe."

Safe.

That word startled me enough to pull back and look at him. It hadn't been a part of my vocabulary since I'd been a child. Searching his face, there was only concern in his eyes—concern for me. Suddenly, I started to think that maybe I was the one who wasn't good enough for him, instead of him creating a potential threat to my family's delicate balance. He was whole and confident—things I wasn't sure I'd ever be again. I wasn't sure I could forgive myself if I pulled him into my messy life.

Wiping furiously at my eyes, my default kicked in. "I'm sorry."

"Nat, look at me." Compelled to obey, I dropped my hands from my face. He'd never called me Nat before, only Natalie. "You are human. You're allowed to have emotions. You shouldn't have to apologize for that. *I* don't need you to ever apologize for that."

Realizing we had an audience, I looked around at the now empty room, feeling my cheeks heat, embarrassed. "Your parents must think I'm insane."

Jaxon chuckled. "You didn't hear it from me, but I grew up with that woman in the kitchen, and she's been known to have her own moments of emotion. You have nothing to worry about."

Mulling that over, it was so different from all that I knew. My mother was the typical high-society wife. She'd always made sure to fall apart in private to maintain her façade of perfection. Leo had mocked me as weak anytime I'd become emotional—even in private—so I'd eventually hidden my true feelings, even from him.

Was what Jaxon told me how healthy people viewed emotions? Were there people out there who were unafraid of being their authentic selves? It seemed strange and frightening to be vulnerable in front of others.

Standing, he held his hand to me. "Come on, let's eat."

Taking his hand, I allowed him to help me up from the couch. Hiding behind him as we entered the kitchen, his mom was bustling about, putting the final touches on dinner, while his dad was setting the table for the four of us.

Jaxon cleared his throat, and his mom looked over to us, dashing over to pull me into a hug.

When she pulled back, my default was to apologize. It was too deeply ingrained into the fabric of who I was to this point. "You'll both have to excuse me. I don't know what came over me back there."

Shannon brushed it off. "Oh, sweetie, it's fine. Life is messy sometimes. There's beauty to be found in the imperfections."

Before I could fall apart again, Jaxon interjected, "All right, let's eat before the food gets cold."

Our meal was pleasant, reverting back to small talk. I enjoyed hearing Shannon and Michael talk about their home in Minnesota on the lake and the stories they shared about Jaxon and his younger brother growing up. It was easy to see how Jaxon became such a good man—he had good parents as role models.

Before they left for the evening, Shannon gathered me into one more tight hug. Smiling, she smoothed the hair away from my face. "We are family now. You call me if you need anything, even to vent about my son. I mean it." Glancing down to my belly, she added, "And you take care of yourself and that sweet baby girl. We can't wait to meet her."

Family.

It had been so long since I'd had a family outside of the one I'd created. Could it be that easy to be adopted into Jaxon's by virtue of being Charlotte's mother? I thanked her for cooking dinner, and she brushed it off, saying it was what she loved to do. Leading Michael out, they said goodbye. It was easy to see that Jaxon's dad was a man of few words simply because his wife was so dynamic. It was refreshing to see a strong woman unencumbered by a man's ego.

Jaxon closed the door, then closed the distance between us. "I think my mom likes you."

"I think I really like her too." The admission was easy.

"Do you have some time before you have to head home?" He motioned to the living room, a silent invitation to stay longer.

"Yeah, the kids should already be in bed." Truthfully, I was enjoying the calm at Jaxon's house and would have been reluctant to leave even if he hadn't asked me to stay.

"Care for some dessert? I think I might have some ice cream."

A laugh bubbled up from my chest. "Never going to let me live that down, are you?"

Leaning in, his eyes were full of mischief. "Not until you learn that your every wish is my command. You say jump, and I will always ask how high."

Taking in a shaky breath, I tried to project confidence. "Well, in that case, I would like some ice cream." Licking my lips, I added, "Please."

Those whiskey-colored eyes of his flared, and I watched as his breathing became ragged. A thrill shot through me, knowing I could use that same power with words he'd wielded on me so many times.

Feeling emboldened, I left him standing there, making my way to the living room, knowing full well he was watching as I walked away.

Sitting on the couch, I looked back over my shoulder to find him still standing there, fists clenched at his sides. Noticing the bulge in his pants, I bit my lower lip. There was a sense of satisfaction in knowing I did that to him.

"Ice cream?" I batted my eyelashes at him innocently.

That seemed to jolt him back to reality, and he blinked before finally striding toward the kitchen. "Right. Ice cream."

Jaxon came back into the room with three pints of ice cream and two spoons. Watching me eye the pints, he shrugged. "I'm a heathen." Placing them on the coffee table before me, he asked, "Which one would you like?"

Surveying the options, I grabbed the middle pint of cookie dough and then took a spoon out of his hand. Observing as I ate a spoonful, he teased, "Of course, you would choose that one."

My hand froze, a second spoonful halfway to my mouth. "Oh, did you want it? You can have it. I'll pick a different one."

Sitting next to me, he dipped his spoon into the pint before asking, "Wanna share?"

Letting him take the burden of the freezing cold pint, we sat side by side, eating the cookie dough ice cream together. We'd made it halfway through when I decided I'd had enough, licking my spoon clean before placing it on the coffee table. Jaxon mirrored my actions, placing the container on the coffee table.

Leaning back on the couch, he put an arm around my waist, and I allowed him to pull me close so my head could lay on his chest. His other hand came up to rest on my belly. This was all so foreign to me. Leo had been disgusted by my pregnant body, going out of his way not to touch me. With Jaxon, it almost seemed like a magnetic pull, his hands were always finding their way onto my body.

Looking down to where his hand rested atop our daughter, my insecurities got the better of me, and I found myself asking, "Are you sure you don't feel trapped?"

"Trapped? No." The vibrations of his words through his chest under my head were strangely soothing.

I pulled back slightly, just enough to look up at him. "You can tell me the truth."

His eyes stared into my soul. "Natalie. I've never lied to you, and I don't intend to start now. I don't feel trapped, especially not by you. We used a condom. Sometimes, they don't work."

"That's how I was trapped." The words were out of my mouth before I realized it, and I sat up, slapping a hand over my big mouth.

Oh my God, did I just say that?

For a second, Jaxon was confused. "What are you talking about?" When I didn't respond, he began working through it in his mind, and his eyes widened. "The unopened box of condoms?"

Closing my eyes, I nodded. When I opened them again, there was an anger in Jaxon's eyes—something I'd never seen before from him. Teeth clenched, he managed to ask, "What did he *do?*"

Scooching to the other end of the couch to put some space between us, I attempted to brush it off. "It doesn't matter anymore."

"Natalie. . ." There was a tone of warning in his voice. He wasn't going to drop this.

I sighed, swallowing, before I began, "Amelia was the result of my ex poking pinholes in condoms." I watched the anger in his eyes turn to pure, unfiltered rage, but I continued anyway, feeling compelled to confide in him. "I had no idea for years. I'd always assumed there was a failure rate on condoms because there is, as we both know. But that wasn't it. One night, something small set him off, and he made a point of establishing that I knew he was always in control. He told me he'd poked the holes through the wrapper so that I wouldn't know. I'd been apprehensive about marrying him and was still talking about going to college. I was only eighteen at the time. The idea of me not being constantly under his thumb—meeting new people and becoming independent—scared him. So, he found a way to get me pregnant without my knowledge, so I'd abandon that idea, and it would be harder for me to leave him."

Staring at me, I watched as he tried to process how fucked up my life had been behind the scenes. I couldn't blame him for struggling to grapple with the idea that a husband would do that to his wife. My body involuntarily shuddered at the thought of how Leo had sneered when he'd dropped that bomb on me.

When Jaxon finally spoke, his voice was calmer than I expected but laced with hurt. "You thought I would do that to you?"

He was referring to when I'd requested an unopened box of condoms the night that Charlie had been conceived—not that it had mattered much in the end. Shaking my head, I closed the distance between us, resting a hand on his thigh. "No, but I'm so messed up from all he's done to me. I was already being completely reckless, so some small part of me needed to make sure I was looking out for myself. It took too long for me to realize I can only count on myself."

His hands went to his head, and he began to grip and pull on his hair, breathing through his nose loudly—each exhale a sharp punctuation to his anger. He was struggling. I'd never seen him so close to losing his temper like this. Every ounce of his effort was going into not exploding. I knew I needed to diffuse the situation. Now.

Knowing nothing could be done to change the past, I tried gently to pull his arms down. He let me, and I turned his head so that he was looking directly at me. "You can't fix this, Jaxon. I know it's hard for you to let it go. I'm not sorry for Amelia, even if it was shady as hell how she came to me."

Deadly calm, the anger still in his eyes, he breathed out, "I want to *kill* him."

That was when it hit me that Jaxon might honestly be the white knight he'd projected to be this whole time. Knowing how badly I was hurt in the past was killing him. He wanted to take Leo head-on, and I couldn't let that happen. His base instincts compelled him to protect me, but now it was my turn to protect him. There was only one thing I could think of that would calm him down and get him to move past this.

"Jaxon, he doesn't belong here with us," I whispered.

Never breaking eye contact, I stood up from the couch. Panic filled his face for a split second before I put one knee on either side of his lap, straddling him. His breathing became uneven, and I felt my heart racing, beating so loudly that it roared in my ears. I knew he'd wanted this for months, and I was kidding myself if I didn't admit that we were always going to end up here.

Maybe not like this, but it was inevitable.

Looking down at him from my vantage point, I ran my hands through his black hair, closing my eyes as I relished the feel of its softness. Slowly, I leaned down, peppering kisses along his clean-shaven jaw as he held stock still, not daring to move. Pulling back for a second, I bit my lower lip before releasing it and lowering my lips to his. He groaned, opening for me and kissing me back with a desperation that had heat pooling between my thighs instantly.

I was ready to get lost in this man.

CHAPTER 15

Jaxon

AM I DREAMING?

Natalie was in my lap, kissing me like she hadn't just told me something so horrific that I couldn't even wrap my mind around it. My anger melted, replaced with desire, causing my dick to swell as her hot center pressed down on me. Even separated by several layers of clothing, I could feel her heat and wanted nothing more than to sink into it once more.

No, I *needed* it.

I'd been paralyzed as I'd watched her take control, afraid that if I made a movement, she might realize what she was doing and run as she'd done in the past. Tasting her again threw my senses into overdrive. She was every bit as incredible as she'd been the first time.

Finally daring to put my hands on her, I ran them up her sides until I reached the nape of her neck, grabbing a fistful of her long blonde hair. Keeping one hand in her hair, I used the other to trail down her throat—her skin was as soft as I remembered—until I reached a breast. Groaning against her mouth, I loved her breasts' new fullness as they overflowed my hand. Her hips ground down hard over mine as I ran my thumb over where I knew her nipple was hidden beneath her clothes. Ripping her mouth away from mine, she arched into my touch, moaning.

Goddamn, she's even more responsive than before.

Fingers digging into my shoulders to steady herself, she returned to my mouth, attacking hungrily. Meeting her stroke for stroke, I tangled my tongue with hers in a silent fight for dominance. I felt cool air on my heated skin as she worked the buttons on my shirt. Once she had it completely undone, her hands reached down to skim over my chest, down to my abs, my muscles contracting with every touch of her small hands.

Natalie's mouth followed the path of her hands down my torso. Closing my eyes, I savored the feel of her wet lips on my bare skin. "Baby, you have no idea what you do to me."

Feeling her fingers graze the waistband of my jeans, my eyes snapped open to find she'd moved onto her knees before me. A cocky grin crossed her lips, and she stroked me over the thick denim. "I think I have some idea."

Transfixed, I watched as she undid the button on my jeans, slowly pulling the zipper down. Flashing her eyes to mine, I could see how much she was enjoying her power over me. I was afraid to move—afraid to breathe—as she tugged at the waistband, lowering them just enough to reach inside my boxer briefs and free my cock.

Unable to stop myself, I hissed as she slowly ran her thumb over the head before gripping my shaft and giving a single pump over its length. Eyes locked on mine, she lowered her head and took the tip into her mouth, giving a strong pull. I almost came from the sight of her mouth on my dick, let alone the feel of it. Never breaking eye contact, she went deeper, taking long, slow drags up and down, teasing the tip with her tongue every time she came back up.

My fingers itched to grab her hair and set the pace, but I knew that would scare her. She was coming to me freely, and I wasn't going to ruin that, even if it killed me to let her be in control. She felt so good that I had to close my eyes, throwing my head back and gritting my teeth in an effort not to come in her mouth. Maybe she sensed my need for mercy because she released me suddenly.

Taking a jagged breath, I dared to look at her, excited for my turn to tease her. Natalie was still kneeling on the ground before me, but something wasn't right. Her hands gripped my knees, head hanging down, as she took in slow, deep breaths.

"Nat—" I began, but she held up a finger, silencing me. Before I could blink, she was on her feet, running from the room. Stuffing myself back into my pants, I ran after her, my shirt still undone, billowing with my quick movements. A quick scan showed her shoes by the door, so I knew she was still in the house somewhere.

My heart was racing. Where had she gone and why?

That's when I heard a noise from the bathroom down the hall. My blood ran cold, and I was terrified that something was wrong with the baby and she needed my help. Running, I burst through the door, not bothering to knock. Guilt flooded me when I found her hunched over the toilet, losing the contents of her stomach.

Instinctively, I went to her side, moving her hair away from her face. To my surprise, she flinched at my touch, wiping her mouth on her sleeve and backing away from me until her back hit the wall. I froze when I saw her eyes were full of fear.

Was she scared of me? Had I done something without realizing it?

Curling into a ball against the wall, she whispered, "I'm so sorry."

My feet were glued to the spot. As much as I wanted to go to her, she was frightened, and I didn't want to make it worse. Before I could find the words, she started to cry, her rambling filling the silence. "I tried; I really did. I just couldn't. I know it's a requirement. Please don't be mad."

A requirement?

I wasn't one to have a temper, but I wanted to punch a wall right now—or anything where I could picture her ex's face being pummeled by my fists. I'd hated him since the moment I'd laid eyes on him all those years ago, but only because he'd found the girl of my dreams first. Then, I'd hated him for throwing away the family I'd coveted my entire adult life. Now that I knew probably only half of what he'd done to her, I wanted to make him pay.

Natalie was curled up on my bathroom floor, bawling, apologizing to me, afraid of me for not being able to complete a blowjob because of *him.* I was just beginning to realize the depth of his mental abuse. Amy and Liam warned me, but their words were nothing compared to witnessing firsthand how deeply affected Natalie still was.

Would there ever come a time when he wasn't the voice in the back of her mind, controlling her life even in his absence? I wasn't so sure.

"Baby, I'm not mad." Natalie stared up at me with those big doe eyes, glassy with tears, mascara running down her cheeks. The sight of her broke my heart. Slowly, I put my hands up and made my way to where she was on the floor, kneeling next to her. Gathering her to my chest, I whispered, "You're safe. I've got you."

She collapsed against me, sobs racking her body as I held her. It was clear she didn't need more from me in this moment other than to be there, solid and steadfast. I vowed that if I ever saw Leo again, I would tear him limb from limb. It scared me to think that if he could do this to her, what he might've done to those innocent children I had grown to love. I couldn't bear the thought of him hurting any of them, but I would spend the rest of my life making sure he never got close enough again.

Eventually, she ran out of tears, and her body went limp against mine, physically spent from the emotional toll of the episode. Lifting her from the floor, I carried her up the stairs, tucking her into bed in the guest room. If there was one thing I knew for sure, it was that I couldn't allow the kids to see her like this.

I was rattled, and I was a grown man.

Quickly, I texted Amy to let her know that Natalie had suffered an emotional breakdown and I was going to keep an eye on her for the night. She responded saying that she'd be right over to check on her. I didn't argue. Amy knew more about this than I likely ever would.

I left the bedroom door slightly ajar in case she called out for me and headed downstairs just in time to hear Amy's knock.

Letting her in, she took one look at my tense body before asking, "Was it meeting your parents?"

I gave a quick shake of my head before I forced out, "Leo."

Amy grimaced. "Are you okay?"

Rubbing my jaw, desperately trying to shake it off, I was failing miserably as I kept picturing her on the bathroom floor. "Not really."

She nodded sympathetically. "I'd be more concerned if you were fine. Even if she told you some of the lesser evils he inflicted upon her, I would tell you right now to walk if you weren't this shaken."

"How did he get away with it? How did nobody stop him?"

"He's a powerful, public figure." She sighed. "Combine that with the fact he kept most of his abuse behind closed doors or even behind her back. She was so afraid that she distanced herself from those closest to her. She didn't want anyone else to become a target, so she tried to shoulder it all herself."

Pacing, my mind raced. "Tell me what to do. I can't think straight and don't want to do the wrong thing. She needs me right now, and I can't risk doing something that will scare her or push her away."

Calmly, she sized me up. "You need a release. It's the only way you can reset and get your head level. Get in your car, close all the doors, turn up the radio, and let it out. Take a pillow if you think that'll help. Don't come back inside until you've expelled every ounce of the anger you feel right now from your body. You can't help her in the state you're in."

Warring with myself, I debated the rational choice of taking care of myself so that I could better take care of Natalie versus the physical impulse to not leave her side after what had just happened.

Amy, sensing my distress, placed a hand on my arm. "Go. Trust me. I will look after her until you get back. Take all the time you need."

I knew on a subconscious level that she was right. She'd been around this long enough to know better than me how to cope with these emotions. My protective instincts were in overdrive, but I nodded, turning on my heel and heading for the garage.

Jumping into my cold SUV, I let the temperature shock me a bit. I needed to snap out of this fast to get back to Natalie. Turning on the accessory power, I blasted the music and gripped the steering wheel until my knuckles turned white. Then, I let out a roar so loud it raised above the volume of the radio, and I kept going until my voice was hoarse as the tension slowly drained from my body.

Depleted from the exertion, I rested my head against the steering wheel until my breathing steadied before exiting the car and reentering the house. Amy was sitting in the living room, and when she saw me, she stood. "She's fast asleep."

Relief washed over me that she hadn't needed me while I selfishly took care of myself. "I've got her tonight."

Patting me on the shoulder, Amy headed for the door. "That was never in doubt. Make sure she knows I've got the kids handled when she wakes up."

Nodding, I was glad to have an ally in Amy. There was a comfort in knowing that when I couldn't be there, Natalie had someone who would prioritize her and protect her if needed. Once she let herself out, I returned to the guest bedroom where I'd left Natalie. Hearing her deep breathing calmed me further, and I made my way to the recliner in the corner. Pulling the leg rest into position, I settled in for a night of keeping vigil over the one person who had become the most precious to me.

The All-Pro Game was the perfect distraction from all that was happening at home. The Comets were on a four-game losing streak, and my head hadn't been right since the night Natalie came over for dinner with my parents. This weekend gave me the ability to compartmentalize for a bit, and the screaming crowds of young fans invigorated me.

I made a point to sign as many pieces of memorabilia and clothing as possible on the red carpet. The smiles on the faces of the kids reminded me that while I loved the game, it was for the fans. They were the ones who made my career possible. If no one wanted to watch the games, I wouldn't be able to play and get paid to do so.

The night before brought the All-Pro Skills Tournament, where we were asked to compete in different skill challenges against our peers from other teams in the league—things like fastest skater, hardest shot, accuracy, goalie shootouts, and more. It was more fun than the game the following day because we could hang out on the ice with no helmets, enjoying ourselves while catching up with players from the other teams.

This year, I focused on how many participating players had their kids down at ice level for the challenges. Some were old enough to be on skates themselves, others were hanging out on the benches, and even a few babies were held in the arms of their player dads. Family was the focus, and it humanized us to the fans. We were just like them—husbands and fathers. I smiled to myself, thinking of someday bringing Charlie and the older kids to an event like this or even something as simple as having them come up to the glass during a regular season game's warmup.

As much as I loved connecting with fans, I was ready to get home after a weekend away. Each road trip became harder and harder—the pull to be back with my new family grew stronger with each passing day.

Natalie's birthday was coming up, and I was already formulating a plan. She always put herself last, and I was determined that it was finally time for her to see that someone could put her first. I needed her to know that I would cherish her and treat her the way she had always deserved.

CHAPTER 16

Natalie

BIRTHDAYS HAD BECOME JUST another day while under Leo's thumb in Belleston. Most years, I'd spent the day working, out at engagements—the emphasis from him was that my only remaining purpose was to serve others. Wanting something for myself made me selfish. In a complete contradiction, however, he'd always made sure to have lavish birthday parties, where I'd been required to stand smiling by his side, fawning over the man who was the villain in my living nightmare.

Since returning home, I'd made it my personal mission to ensure the kids had over-the-top birthdays so they always knew how much I loved them and how special they were. Despite my protests, Amy, Hannah, and Liam made a big deal of my birthday every year. I absolutely didn't feel like celebrating this year, but they couldn't be dissuaded.

They'd adjusted their plans a bit from years past since I wasn't leaving the house outside of doctor's appointments, but they were still hell-bent on celebrating. Balloons were everywhere inside the house, and as per tradition, Amy and Hannah had taken the day off work to be with me.

The only one missing was Liam.

On occasions when Jaxon had come over to the house recently, Liam had made sure to keep his distance, and I could admit, it stung. It felt like he was trying to make me choose between the two of them. He'd been my rock for so long, and I didn't want to lose him over this. Charlie deserved her father. How could Liam not see that? Did he expect to step into that role for her, too? He'd become my best friend—my protector over the years—and I missed him. Especially today.

Determined to fix whatever was going on between us, I made my way down to his suite of rooms in the basement.

When we'd moved here, he'd transitioned to more of a background role with his charitable pursuits, which meant hours in front of a computer, organizing and coordinating from afar. The six-hour time difference meant that some days, he was on a completely different schedule than the rest of us—forced to take video calls with those on the ground in Belleston in the middle of the night on the East Coast.

Finding him in his office, I knocked on the open door. Looking up from his work, Liam stood when he realized I was the one at his door. "What's wrong?"

Walking in, I stopped him with a dismissive wave of my hand. "Is that where we are right now? The only reason I could have for coming down here is if something is wrong? When are you going to stop punishing me?"

Sinking back into the desk chair, he sighed. "I'm not punishing you, Nat."

Coming further into the room, I rounded the corner of his desk and came to lean on the edge of it. "Sure feels like I'm being punished. You're hiding down here most days. I miss my big brother."

Leaning back in the chair, he ran a hand through his dark hair. "It's hard for me to see you with him."

I crossed my arms over my chest. "Is it just him? Or would it be like this with any man coming into our lives? Am I expected to remain single forever? Is that what you want?" I didn't come down here to berate him, but my hurt feelings got the better of me, and the words flowed from my mouth without warning.

"The Natalie I knew six months ago was excited about the prospect of finally becoming independent and standing on her own two feet," he argued.

This was not going the way I'd hoped. Anger churned in my belly. "Circumstances change. People change."

"I don't trust him," Liam snapped. "How can you be sure he didn't use the same trick as Leo? Any fool with eyes could see the way he's been leering at you for years. Who's to say that he wouldn't capitalize on a once-in-a-lifetime opportunity to have you for his own?"

My temper flared, and I lashed out, "Do you think so little of me? That I'd choose to be with someone simply because they'd knocked me up?" Liam reached for me, but I moved out of range. Backing away to put more distance between us, I could see the regret on his face. He hadn't meant for me to take it as a personal attack, but it was too late. "Maybe you're the fool if you can't see that he's been here, not just for me, but for the kids. Where the fuck *have* you been? Huh? Sulking? Worried that I don't need *you* as much anymore? Get over yourself. This isn't about you."

He stood, taking a step toward me. "Nat, that's not what I meant."

I didn't want to hear his hollow apologies. "You're just like your brother, trying to control what I do and don't do. And you know what? I'm sick of it. Fuck you, Liam."

Turning on my heel, I fled the basement. How *dare* he? First off, Leo and Jaxon were on complete opposite ends of the spectrum. Jaxon spent months proving he was nothing but kind, caring, and considerate. Second off, he'd gotten up before dawn with Beau on Christmas morning. How many single men would jump into fatherhood like that with kids who weren't theirs? If he was only looking for a way to get back into my pants, he was really committing. Most importantly, he'd made promises and kept them without fail.

By the time I reached the main floor, I was shaking with rage, and angry tears were flowing freely down my face. Why was I made to feel guilty for letting a good man take care of me? Didn't I deserve that after all I'd been through?

I was done allowing the Remington men to control *my* life. It was my turn to call the shots. Sure, I might be turning twenty-nine today, but better late than never, right?

I made it as far as the kitchen before I ran into Hannah and Amy setting up brunch. Hannah knew I'd gone down to try and make amends with Liam, so when she saw my face, she threw her hands on her hips. "Let me guess. He's a bullheaded man."

Collapsing onto an island stool, I wiped away my tears, but the anger still simmered beneath the surface. "What does he want from me? He talks about me wanting to be independent without a man, yet he wants me to be dependent on him alone. He can't have it both ways."

Amy tried to be the voice of reason. "Liam is a natural-born protector. He already feels like a failure that he couldn't protect you from his own brother, and now he's terrified he'll fail again. He cares about you but sometimes has a backward way of showing it."

"You need to do what's best for you and the kids," Hannah added.

I put my head down on the cool marble. "I don't want to have to choose between the father of my daughter and my big brother. It's not fair."

"He's not going to make you choose," Amy declared with confidence.

I lifted my head. "He *hates* Jaxon."

"He hates what Jaxon represents. If you let Jaxon take over the role as your protector, he won't know where he fits in your life."

"What if I don't want a protector? What if I want a partner? Liam can't fill that role." I sighed.

Hannah was giddy. "Does that mean you want Jaxon?"

"I don't know." I groaned. "He says the right things, does the right things, but is that enough?"

"Speaking of the right things . . ." Hannah moved aside, revealing a giant bouquet of roses.

"The balloons weren't enough?"

Hannah's grin grew. "Not from us." Reaching into the mass of red roses, she plucked out a card and extended an arm over the island to hand it to me.

The card read: *Happy Birthday, Natalie. I would be honored if you'd join me for dinner tonight at my house at 9 PM.*

Laying it on the island once I was done reading, the girls pounced on it. Hannah jumped up and down. "You *have* to go!"

Not convinced, I debated, "I don't know. I'm sure you two have the day all planned out, plus the kids will want to celebrate after school."

Amy was already two steps ahead, as always. "We can knock out all we have planned before nine. The kids only care about cake and will be in bed by then anyway. This is doable. The only question is, do you want to go?"

"I haven't seen him in weeks. I was afraid I'd scared him off after the dinner with his parents. That wasn't my finest moment."

Hannah brushed it off. "The Comets were out of town for weeks, then he had the All-Pro Game."

"I know. I just really embarrassed myself that night." Heat flooded my cheeks thinking about it now.

Amy added, "I saw him that night—he wasn't scared. He was pissed. And it wasn't at you. Honestly, what are you afraid of?"

Making a frustrated noise, I responded, "There's an attraction there. I can't pretend there's not. He *says* things that shock me and turn me on all at the same time, but he can have any woman he wants. I just happen to be the one carrying his baby. What if he doesn't really want *me*? What if it's convenient because I'm the mother of his child? Boom, instant family. It's easier to try to build something with me than attempting to split custody as co-parents. I've already been in a one-sided relationship. I can't do it again."

Amy scoffed. "You come with baggage, and I don't mean that in a bad way. What man would find it *easier* to take you on with three additional kids?"

"He is incredible with the kids, and they do love him. I don't know what to do." I groaned.

"Go to dinner." She made it sound so simple. "What's the worst that could happen? You eat a free meal? Doesn't sound that bad to me."

Cringing, I thought back to how quickly things had turned the last time I'd just *gone over for dinner*. Making one final attempt at an excuse to stay home—where I was safe from myself—I rubbed my belly. "I don't have anything to wear. I have a feeling this isn't a come-in-your-sweats kind of dinner."

Hannah and Amy shared a look, instantly showing their hand that there had been collusion. Of course there was—they'd been on Team Jaxon since day one. Smiling, knowing that my friends would always have my back, I gave in. "All right, you win. Did you happen to buy me new shoes too? Because Jaxon was not a super fan of the flip-flops in the dead of winter."

Amy smirked. "What kind of friends would we be if we let you lose your toes to frostbite?"

"At least tell me you exercised some discretion in choosing an outfit." Sending a pointed glance at Hannah, I added, "I don't need things hanging out at almost seven months pregnant."

Hannah pretended to be offended, throwing a hand to her chest. "I would *never*!"

I gave her a wry smile. "Yeah, sure. Don't think I've forgotten the giant box of lingerie you presented me with at my bridal shower when we were still in high school."

"If I thought you could fit in any of those, I'd suggest you bring one tonight," she retorted.

"Hannah!"

She shrugged. "Tell me to my face you don't want to jump his bones, and I'll drop it." Unfortunately, my silence was a dead giveaway. She gasped, accusing, "Oh my God, did you already jump his bones? And you didn't tell us? I thought we were friends!"

"Not exactly." I blushed at the embarrassing memory.

"What does that even mean?" she asked. "Was it one of those 'just the tip' kinda things?"

I buried my face in my hands, releasing a muffled scream of frustration into them.

Amy jumped in, "I think we need more details to determine if, in fact, you did or did not jump his bones."

I sighed. "I don't want to talk about it."

Hannah was like a dog with a bone. "No, you can't give us a breadcrumb like that and not give us the whole story."

If she wanted the truth, fine. "What do you want me to say? That because of the pregnancy, I triggered my overly sensitive gag reflex on his dick and ended up running from the room to puke in the toilet? Then, I had a freaking nervous breakdown and he had to pick up the pieces? Are you happy now?"

They stared at me in stunned silence. Then, Hannah started to laugh so hard she had to clutch her sides. Amy couldn't help the infectiousness of Hannah's belly laughs, and soon, she was in a fit of giggles too.

Hannah forced out, "Can't. Breathe."

Rolling my eyes, annoyance colored my words. "So glad my train wreck of a life amuses you both."

Amy began to come down from her laughter. "I'm sure that made quite the impression."

I thought back to that embarrassing night and how I'd revealed more to him about how fucked up my life had been with Leo. He should be running for the hills. I wouldn't blame him if he did. I was completely aware that I was more than most men could handle, even if I didn't come with the extra kids. He'd taken it in stride when I'd been terrified that he would think I was a tease who couldn't finish the job. Taking care of me, he'd watched over me while I'd slept off the hysterical episode that had debilitated me.

Thoughtfully, I responded, "I think his response was more telling than anything."

Hannah calmed down but still clutched her side. "Let me guess, white knight Jaxon made everything all right."

"Ugh, why does he have to be so good? Why couldn't he be some asshole who wanted nothing to do with us? He's unapologetically walked into our lives and shaken them up. Just not the way I thought he would."

Amy was ever the voice of reason. "Maybe your life needed a little shaking up. You haven't been living. You've been trying to survive."

She was right. I knew she was. Jaxon had an effect on me, and I constantly found myself spilling all the horrors of my past to him—which, in a way, was cathartic. Maybe I'd needed someone good and kind from the outside to come along so that I could divest myself of all those deep, dark secrets that lived inside my head—someone who didn't already know my sad story, who wanted nothing more than to listen without judgment. Jaxon had become that person. I'd felt compelled to share more with him because it made me feel lighter. Starting to find myself again with his help, I relied on his understanding presence.

Something about tonight felt special, and not because it was my birthday. There was a shift happening. I could feel it. My guard lowered more with every interaction, and if I knew Jaxon even a little, he would pull out all the stops.

Maybe it was finally time to stop fighting it. He'd continued to pursue me, even when I'd given him every reason to flee.

Perhaps he was the real deal after all.

CHAPTER 17

Natalie

THE HOURS WERE TICKING down on my twenty-ninth birthday, but I found myself on Jaxon's doorstep a few minutes before 9 PM. The girls had set me up with a timeless long-sleeved black wrap dress that hit at the knee and some new black ballet flats—a size larger than my usual. A shimmery silver wrap shielded me from the cold.

Knocking on the door, I shivered, but not because of the frigid winter temperature. I knew what waited on the other side of that door had the potential to become my future. Holding my breath, I stood in anticipation for what seemed like an eternity before Jaxon finally opened the door, and my heart stopped. He was handsome on a good day, but the man who stood in the open doorway could only be described as devastatingly gorgeous.

Blinking to make sure I wasn't dreaming, I drank in the view he provided. Clad in a black suit with the jacket open revealing a white button-up featuring an open collar, it gave him a formal yet relaxed look. Clean-shaven, his short black hair was perfectly styled, a stark contrast to the carefree look he'd portrayed these past few months.

He took my breath away.

Jaxon reached out as I watched, frozen to the spot, wondering if this would be when I finally woke up. Touching the bottom edge of my hair, he smiled, remarking, "This is new."

Reaching up to where his hand was, I snapped back to reality, realizing what he was talking about. Amy had helped me dye my hair back to its natural color, which was almost as black as Jaxon's. She'd also cut it so that now it barely brushed my shoulders, curled as it was tonight. Taking my hand, he pulled me out of the cold, closing the door behind us.

Finally finding my voice, I explained, keeping it light, "I didn't feel like hiding in your backseat anymore. I figure with a pair of sunglasses and the new hair, no one will recognize me."

He smirked. "Maybe your next job could be working undercover for the government."

"Not a half-bad idea. I do have some experience working with foreign dignitaries," I teased back.

Changing from joking to serious, he stated, "I think it looks great. If possible, you look even more beautiful."

I wasn't sure there would ever come a day when I could take those compliments without blushing, but the more he said them, the more I began to believe them. Rounding behind me, he eased the shawl from my shoulders, whispering in my ear, "Happy Birthday, Natalie."

Unable to keep myself from smiling, I looked back at him. "Thank you."

Allowing me the time to slip off my shoes, he took my hand, leading me into his dining room. I'd never been inside this room before, and tonight it was dimmed, lit by candles on the table, featuring two silver trays laid out waiting for us to sit. Holding out a chair for me, I sat before he rounded to the opposite side of the table.

Smiling back at me, Jaxon lifted the tops of the trays, revealing the plates beneath, before sitting himself. The meal set before us consisted of crab cakes with remoulade and steamed vegetables—my favorite. There was no way he came up with this meal on his own, but I wasn't mad. My friends wanted the best for me and thought that was Jaxon.

Maybe they were right if he went to such great lengths to make this day special for me.

"Had a little help, did you?" I teased him.

He chuckled. "Just a little."

"It looks amazing, thank you."

He popped a bottle of sparkling cider for us, and we ate quietly. I made a mental note to ask where he'd gotten the food because the crab cake was hands down the best I'd ever had. A tiny moan had escaped my lips when I'd first tasted it, eliciting a smirk from Jaxon across the table and then my resulting blush.

After we finished dinner, he led me to the kitchen, where a small naked iced cake sat on the center island, garnished with a few candied cherries. Lighting a single candle in the center, Jaxon stood by my side, whispering low in my ear, "Make a wish."

Closing my eyes, I took a deep breath in preparation.

I want all my children to be happy, whole, and loved.

Blowing out the breath, the candle's flame died, smoke billowing in a thin stream toward the ceiling. My wish might have been considered cheating a little bit because they were almost there. Jaxon had helped so much to fill the hole created by being practically abandoned and emotionally abused by their father. He'd given himself selflessly to them, asking for nothing in return.

Jaxon cut two slices of cake, suggesting we eat in the living room more comfortably. Taking the plate containing my slice from him, I followed him to the oversized leather couch that was starting to hold more than a little history for us. Sitting slightly apart, I took a bite of cake, letting the flavors of the light almond cake with cherry filling dance across my tongue.

Watching as I took that first bite, waiting until I finished, he admitted, "I hope you don't mind that I had a little help with this as well."

"So, was tonight your idea? Or did Hannah and Amy put you up to it? Seems like they touched every part of it." I took another bite of cake. It was too delicious to wait for his response.

Still not touching his slice of cake yet, he smiled, showing off his straight white teeth, a total contradiction to the hockey player stereotype of missing teeth. "I wanted tonight to be perfect for you. Who better to help me with all your favorites than your best friends?"

"Sure doesn't hurt that they're on Team Jaxon." Sarcasm entered my tone.

"Team Jaxon?" His eyebrows climbed higher on his forehead.

Did I say that out loud?

Taking another bite of cake, trying to cover my slip of the tongue, my words muffled by my full mouth. "Nothing."

He didn't buy it but let it slide, changing the subject. "So, when did you go blonde?"

Setting my plate down on the coffee table, I swallowed the bite of cake in my mouth. "I think it was when I was seventeen? It seemed like a fun idea at the time when Leo suggested that it would make us more aesthetically pleasing as a couple. The joke was on him when Amelia came out with jet-black hair and ruined the image he'd hoped for of a perfectly blond family."

Jaxon smirked. "I remember thinking that when I first met you. Amelia seemed like she didn't belong. I know now that she's got your exact coloring. She's as beautiful as her mother."

My lips twisted in thought. "Beauty will only get you so far in life. I'd rather she be confident. That's not something that can be manufactured."

"She certainly wasn't afraid to give me a piece of her mind a couple of months ago. You don't have to worry about her."

"I wish I could be a better role model for her in that regard. Thankfully, she has Hannah and Amy to look up to." Thinking about it, I amended, "Well, maybe just Amy. Hannah is a little too confident."

That made him laugh. "Yeah, Hannah's something special, that's for sure."

I found myself smiling as well. "Amelia's named after Amy. I remember thinking that I wanted my daughter to be like her. Maybe if I'd been more like her, I wouldn't have been so easily manipulated."

"I'm sure you did the best you could." Jaxon's tone softened, sympathetic.

Exhaling deeply, I replied, "I wish I could believe that. I fell so easily into the trap. Enticing a perfectionist to be more perfect? It was so easy to be fooled. I did everything he suggested, essentially becoming a living doll. The blonde hair was only the start. Then came the laser eye correction, the veneers, injectable fillers in my face, and even the suggestion of plastic surgeries like a tummy tuck and a breast lift. I was living under the illusion that perfection was enough to make everything better. Newsflash—it wasn't. I never got there, and life only got harder."

Sliding closer to me on the couch, Jaxon tucked my newly shortened hair behind one ear. "The problem wasn't with you. The first time I saw you, I fell under your spell. I have to confess that I silently prayed you were a player's nanny, and it ripped my heart out when I realized you were already taken. I was never the same after that day."

Brushing off his words, I countered cynically, "I'm sure there have been plenty of women since then."

"There have been," he admitted truthfully. "But none of them were you. I couldn't stand to be with blondes because the only blonde I wanted was you."

Letting that sink in, I asked, "So everyone was right? Saying you've always had a crush on me?"

He dropped his gaze, timid. "I wasn't the best at hiding it. I think you may have been the only person who never noticed. I'm sure if you had, you would have avoided me. Maybe you should have. I've turned your life upside down."

"But-but you barely knew me," I breathed out in disbelief.

Warm brown eyes met mine. "Everything I found out about you made me want to learn more. Getting to know you these past few months, you've proven to be even better than how I'd built you up in my mind. You may not think you're perfect, but I know you're perfect for me."

The air grew thick as I grappled with his words. "Me? Why, when you can have anyone?"

Leaning in close, Jaxon cupped my cheek with his warm palm. "Natalie, it's always been you. Since I was eighteen, no other woman has ever come close. There hasn't been a woman since you, and there won't be ever again. You've ruined me for other women, now that I know the reality blows the fantasy out of the water. You're it for me, and I'll wait for you as long as it takes. I'm not going anywhere. I'm in love with you."

Suddenly, the world faded away, and all I could see was Jaxon—finally able to truly see him for the first time. There were no games, hidden agendas, lies, or attempts at control. He'd bent over backward to fit into my complicated life simply because he cared about me. *Me.* Now here he was, baring his soul, telling me there weren't any other women, and he was willing to wait until I was ready, continuing to put me first.

Undoubtedly, this was the ultimate defining moment in my life. I'd either choose to live in the past—letting those demons haunt me forever—or I'd move forward and begin to live again. It didn't take much time to realize that I couldn't waste this opportunity to try to build a life, a family, with this man who gave me every reason to believe that he loved me as much as he'd just proclaimed.

I'm not going anywhere. His words were stuck in my brain. He'd seen me at my absolute worst and had been nothing but kind and understanding. If he hadn't run by now, the odds were good that he wasn't going to.

With no idea how long I'd been sitting there processing his words, I closed my eyes, inhaling deeply the scent of him—letting it invade my senses with how close we were. Feeling the feather-light touch of his thumb on my lower lip, I dared to open my eyes, gasping at the intensity of Jaxon's stare.

Coming closer, his lips hovered over mine, and my eyes fluttered closed again as I heard him whisper, "Tell me you don't want this."

Finally taking something for myself, I sank my hands into his hair and pulled his mouth down to mine, eliciting a groan from deep within his chest. Allowing me to take charge of the kiss for a few seconds, I felt when the shift happened as he tugged on my lower lip with his teeth. His mouth then consumed me, taking total control of the kiss, our tongues battling as I tugged at the lapels on his suit jacket in a desperate attempt to bring our bodies closer.

My pulse throbbed between my legs. I'd never felt a need like this before—like if I didn't have him, I might combust. A whimper escaped my lips as he left my mouth, kissing a path along my jaw before he nipped at my earlobe, sending shockwaves through my body.

Gasping, I arched into his body. "I need you, Jaxon."

Growling into my neck, he moved lower to my collarbone, setting little fires everywhere his mouth touched. Cool air caressed my heated skin as he pulled away, I panicked, thinking maybe he had changed his mind. Forcing my eyes open, I found him looking up at me with an intense fire blazing in his whiskey brown eyes.

Taking one finger, he toyed with the tie of my wrap dress resting under my breasts, a question in his eyes.

Nodding, expecting him to make quick work of my dress, he teased me, pulling on the tie inch by inch, his eyes never leaving mine. Needing physical contact, I ran my hand back into his hair, tugging lightly, silently urging him to stop playing with me. Smirking and giving in to my demands, he pulled harder, freeing the knot holding the dress together, exposing me to his gaze, and allowing the room's cool air to rush over my heated skin.

Every instinct screamed at me to cover myself. I knew I didn't look like the same woman he'd seen laid bare before him months ago. Everything was bigger, fuller than it had been before. That also extended to my now swollen belly, which could no longer be ignored.

Instead of being turned off by my temporary figure, Jaxon's eyes flared as he surveyed the sight before him. He ran a single finger down my body, beginning at my collarbone, tracing the swell of my enlarged breasts along the outline of the black lace bra Hannah and Amy had provided along with the dress, running it down over the bump containing our daughter, only stopping when he reached the edge of my matching black lace panties.

Voice low and rough, he breathed out, "Gorgeous."

The conviction in his declaration awoke a confidence in myself that had laid dormant all these years. Shoving the sleeves of the dress down my arms, I reached behind my back, unhooking the clasp of my bra, allowing my heavy breasts to bounce free. Jaxon wasted no time, testing their new weight with both hands, closing his eyes and groaning as I responded with a moan of my own, arching into his light touch, silently begging for more.

At my urging, he lowered his head to one breast, teasing the overly sensitized nub with his teeth before sucking it deep into his mouth. A gasp flew past my lips, the pulsing between my thighs growing more insistent with each passing minute. Shifting my hips, looking for relief, he continued his assault, his other hand caressing the side of my belly. Giving one last strong pull before a light flick of his tongue, he moved his attention to the opposite breast.

Once he'd had his fill, he moved down the couch to the floor, getting on his knees before me. Gripping my hips, he pulled me toward him so I was in a semi-reclined position, my ass right on the edge of the couch. Hooking his thumbs into the waistband of the black lace panties resting low on my hips, he tugged them down my legs before dropping them on the ground.

Fully naked now, laid open before him, there was something so erotic about him still being fully dressed while I was entirely exposed.

Jaxon just stared, causing me to squirm under his gaze. Needing something—anything—and not wanting to wait any longer, I reached up and started to roll a nipple between my thumb and forefinger. Closing my eyes, I savored the pleasure flowing through my body.

"You're killing me, Natalie," he groaned.

"Then fucking touch me, Jaxon," I practically begged.

Hearing the noise he made low in the back of his throat, I smiled, knowing he was similarly affected by our connection. My body was a live wire at this point, so I jumped when he gently laid his hands on the inside of my thighs. Forcing my eyes open, I found his head only inches from where I needed him the most.

Allowing one hand to wander closer to my throbbing pussy, he ran one finger through the slickness he found there, groaning, "Baby, you're so wet for me."

Hips bucking uncontrollably into his touch, I was on edge, needing this more than I needed to breathe. "Please, Jaxon."

Head dipping lower, I could feel his breath against my heated flesh as he inhaled deeply. "I've dreamt of this every single day, wondering if I'd imagined how incredible you tasted right here." His tongue snaked out for a quick flick on my clit, and I couldn't contain the squeal that escaped my lips. "God, you're more delicious than I remember. I could worship you like this every day." He punctuated his words with flicks of his tongue. "Just. Like. This."

Shamelessly, I rode his face—as he took his time with long, slow strokes—trying to urge him to move faster, chasing my release. Jaxon pulled back enough to teasingly chastise my efforts. "Patience, baby. It'll be worth it, I promise." His lips were still so close that his words vibrated against my sensitive flesh, and I moaned, my hips lifting involuntarily.

Jaxon licked circles around my clit, close enough to drive me wild, but not close enough to bring me the release I so desperately craved. A light sheen of sweat coated my body as I strained against his touch. Eyes clenched shut, focused on the pleasure coursing through my body, I felt him lift my thighs onto his shoulders as he finally put his tongue where I needed it, pressing down as I bucked against him.

"More, Jaxon," I pleaded, the throbbing almost reaching the point of pain.

Tingling everywhere, I felt my legs begin to shake uncontrollably, tightening around his head situated between my thighs. I was wound so tight—right on the edge—that when he took two fingers, thrusting them inside me and redoubling the efforts of his tongue, I shattered.

Arching my back, I screamed out, clutching the couch cushions at my side as wave after wave of pleasure rolled through me while Jaxon continued to use his tongue, drawing out my orgasm.

Only when I fell limp against the couch did Jaxon kiss a path back up my body until he reached my mouth, kissing me deeply, allowing me to taste myself on his tongue.

Sighing against my mouth, I felt the smile on his lips. "I love watching you fall apart. The way your skin flushes, how responsive you are, not holding anything back."

Eyes still closed, trying to slow my erratic breathing, I whispered, "Only for you."

Feeling him still next to me, I dared to open my eyes after that admission. The look in his eyes was primal, bordering on dangerous, but I wasn't scared. Not of him.

A corner of his lips turned up, and he stroked my cheek with a thumb. "Never doubt that you come first with me. Always. I will never take my own pleasure before I've seen to yours." His other hand grabbed mine and brought it to the bulge in his suit pants. "Do you feel that? Pleasuring you makes me so hard that I struggle not to come in my pants like a teenager."

Gripping his length through his pants, I marveled at the idea that he could be this hard, this desperate for me, and still see to my needs first. Jaxon made me feel cherished, special, and above all, loved. A calm settled over me, being with him like this, even completely nude. Suddenly, I knew this was exactly where I belonged.

Giving his cock a little squeeze, I heard him hiss. Finding the strength to stand on shaky legs, I left him sitting on the couch as I headed for the stairs, putting a little extra sway in my step, feeling sexy for the first time in my life. Reaching the stairs, I peered over my shoulder, asking, "You coming?"

Jaxon blinked, then swallowed, still glued to his seat on the couch. "What?"

Smiling, I took three steps up, calling back, "I'm going upstairs. If you're not up here in five minutes, I'll just have to finish the job myself." I'd never been so bold, but I liked teasing him, eliciting a response.

I reached the top of the staircase before I heard Jaxon bounding up the steps, hot on my heels. Wrapping his arms around my belly, pulling my back against his front, he growled in my ear, "My little vixen."

A shiver racked my body at his rough tone. Leaning into his embrace, I turned my head to look back at him. "Took you long enough."

His laugh vibrated through his chest into my own before he nipped at the sensitive spot where my neck met my shoulder, causing me to involuntarily arch against him. I felt the erection insistent beneath his fly, pressing against my bare ass.

Turning in his arms, I shoved his suit jacket off. "You're wearing too many clothes. Strip for me."

Stepping backward, he let me slip from his grasp as I carefully backed down the hallway toward his master bedroom. Like a lion stalking its prey, he matched me step for step, slowly undoing the buttons of his white shirt before working on his belt. Kicking off his shoes, he continued to follow me, undoing the button at the top of his pants before lowering the zipper, letting the fabric pool at his ankles before stepping out of them. Now, he stood before me clad only in an open shirt and his black boxer briefs, which were doing nothing to hide the proof of his arousal.

Crossing the threshold of the bedroom, I gripped the sides of his open shirt, pulling him to me, kissing him, rekindling the fire he'd stoked within me downstairs. Turning him around, I shoved him into a sitting position on the edge of the bed, remaining standing before him. With him sitting like this, he had no height advantage, and I stepped into his arms, feeling his warm skin against mine.

Pushing the shirt off his shoulders, I ran my hands over every inch of exposed skin on his chest and abdomen. Biting my lip, I admired all the muscles he'd likely spent years developing. Jaxon allowed me free reign to explore his body until my fingers reached the waistband of his underwear. When his hand lightly circled my wrist, I looked up in question.

He groaned. "Natalie . . ."

"I want to touch you." My words were barely above a whisper.

Swallowing, his Adam's apple bobbing, he clarified, "I need you to know that there are no requirements with me. You are free to do as much or as little as you choose. My love for you doesn't hinge on which sexual acts you are comfortable performing."

Pulling lightly against his grasp, he released the loose hold on my wrist, not stopping me when I went back to where I'd begun. Reaching inside the waistband, I freed his waiting cock and gripped the warm length in my hand. In a counter move, Jaxon reached up to tease my nipple with his teeth, and I gripped even harder in response, throwing my head back on a moan.

The moisture was gathering between my legs again as I rocked against his muscular body while continuing to stroke up and down along his length, using my thumb to circle the tip. He was thrusting into my hand, and I enjoyed having total command over him.

Instantly, I decided to take charge this time. I got a small thrill thinking that I could be in control.

Pulling back, I shoved his chest lightly. Jaxon got the message and leaned back against the bed. Shoving his boxer briefs down his legs, he kicked them off, moving further back onto the bed. His eyes were shadowed with lust, and I watched his chest heave, breathing heavily, as I crawled onto the bed to where he lay.

Straddling his prone form, I gripped the base of his dick and let it slide through my slickness, moaning as it made contact with my still-sensitive clit. Jaxon's hands gripped my thighs, letting me take what I needed. Lining the head up against my entrance, a shadow of doubt crossed Jaxon's face.

"Are you sure? I don't want to hurt you." His words were strained, but I knew he would stop if I asked him to.

My response was wordless as I sank down onto his length, slowly letting my body adjust to his size until I was fully seated atop him. Giving a roll of my hips, I threw my head back, letting the sensation of having him fill me roll over my body.

Feeling Jaxon's hands move from my thighs to my hips, I rocked against him again until I heard a groan slip from his lips. "Jesus, Nat. Baby, you're so tight. You feel amazing."

Leaning forward slightly, I rested my hands on his chest and slowly moved my hips up and down, savoring the feel of him for myself and teasing him at the same time. Jaxon allowed me to set the pace—to use his body for my own pleasure—but I could tell when his control began to slip. His grip tightened, holding my hips still as he pumped into me from below, the angle perfect for his cock to graze my clit with every stroke.

My fingers dug into his pecks, getting closer and closer to that peak as his body threatened to throw me over. It was almost too much, the friction delicious and overwhelming at the same time.

"Jaxon, I can't . . . It's too much."

Jaxon only increased his pace, grunting with the effort, forcing out the words, "Yes, you can. Come for me, baby. I've got you."

His words only heightened the sensation, and my body coiled tighter and tighter until it snapped, and it felt like I stopped breathing, seeing stars behind my eyes as my world came apart. Jaxon's grip grew almost painful as he pumped harder before I felt the groan of release ripped from his throat, and he thrust a few more times, emptying himself into me.

Collapsing on top of him, he carefully rolled my body, tucking me into his side. For a time, we just lay there, allowing our breathing to even out.

Running hands along his smooth chest, I boldly asked, "Is it always like that?"

I needed to know. My limited experience said no, but maybe it had more to do with the man's skill set than the chemistry between a couple.

Capturing my hand with his own, Jaxon turned to look into my eyes. "No. I'm not going to pretend that I haven't enjoyed my fair share of sex, but there's never been a connection like this. Nothing has ever come close to how I feel when I'm with you."

He'd never lied to me and had claimed he never would, so how could I not believe him? There was no denying that what we shared was special, even if it wasn't the most conventional start to a relationship.

No matter how we'd come together, I knew one thing for certain—my life would never be the same again.

CHAPTER 18

Jaxon

I WAS ADDICTED TO Natalie. There was no other way to describe it. When she was near, I couldn't keep my hands off her, and when we were apart, the craving for her was so intense that it was difficult to think straight.

We fell into a steady routine, with me spending every spare moment I had at her house—playing the father role to her kids—and at night, we found new ways to drive each other wild with pleasure.

Unable to slake my thirst for her, I soaked up every minute in her presence, whether at family dinners, game nights, or during those private moments when it was just us. Being with her was enough. This was the dream—this was our family—and Charlotte would only make our world complete.

Well, almost.

Knowing she was my forever, I'd made a pit stop while on a road trip to New York, picking out an elegant yet understated diamond ring for my girl.

My girl.

Having pictured the dream for so long, it took time for it to sink in that Natalie had truly become mine. The ring was secured at home in my safe, waiting for the timing to be perfect to ask her to be my wife. She wasn't ready yet. Moving too fast would only scare her, but we were making leaps in the right direction.

Making sure to tell her that I loved her every chance I got, I knew I could wait for her. There was no set time frame. I'd promised myself a long time ago that I was playing the long game, and so far, it was working. Having waited this long—never dreaming she could be mine—I could wait a little longer.

Valentine's Day was coming up. There was a Comets game that night, and the team was leaving for a week-long road trip the following day, so we decided to celebrate early with the kids. The push for the playoffs was on, so my schedule was getting crazier, and I only had one free night that week before I left.

Arriving that evening, I was mobbed by the trio of tiny Remingtons I'd come to love.

Beau hugged my legs. "Jaxon!"

Amelia's eyes widened when she saw the roses in my arms. "Oh! Mom is going to love those!"

Jameson offered to take bags from my arms, then asked excitedly, "Will you help us with our valentines tonight?"

Handing him a bag to lighten my load, I answered without hesitation, "Of course, I'll help. Let me get dinner started, and then we can get to work."

Walking into the kitchen, I brushed a quick kiss on Natalie's lips before emptying my arms. Grabbing the bouquet of red and white roses from the pile, I handed them to her. "For my best lady."

Taking them, she smiled, lighting up my world. "Thank you. They're beautiful."

"Not as beautiful as you." I winked. I loved watching the resulting blush any time I complimented her.

Natalie busied herself, finding a vase for her flowers. Once they were settled, I plucked a single red rose from the bouquet. Turning around, getting down on one knee, I held it out to Amelia. "For my best girl."

Amelia stared at the flower I held. "For me?"

Leaning in to brush a kiss on her cheek, I pushed the rose into her hand. "Every girl should get flowers on Valentine's Day. No exceptions."

Her cheeks turned a beautiful shade of pink, and it struck me how much she was like her mother. I decided at that moment to shower her with compliments as she grew up, so she'd know exactly how precious she was. She deserved to know her worth so that, hopefully, she would never allow a man to take advantage of her.

Grabbing a tall glass from the cupboard, I filled it halfway with water, inviting Amelia to place her single rose inside. Starting to unpack all the bags I'd brought, I sorted it all on the island—food for dinner, sparkling cider, and four heart-shaped boxes of chocolates.

Jameson took inventory of the massive haul, exclaiming, "Chocolate!"

Natalie chided, "Not before dinner. Go make sure all your homework is done, then play with your brother."

They all ran off, and I was finally alone with the woman I loved. Pulling her close, I took advantage, claiming a deeper kiss from her mouth. She sighed against me, and I felt blood pool in my groin. Breaking the kiss, I leaned my forehead against hers. "Happy Valentine's Day, love."

Natalie's eyes sparkled. She'd been coming alive before my very eyes these past few weeks, and I had to pinch myself. How had I gotten this lucky?

Reaching up, she toyed with my hair, which I loved. Tilting her head up to look up at me, she remarked, "You know, I really liked your hair longer when you were younger."

That was *not* what I was expecting, and I pulled back, surprised, before feeling a corner of my lips quirk up. "Were you checking me out?"

"I'm always checking you out, babe." She winked, causing my budding erection to swell into a full-blown hard-on. Her newfound confidence was sexy as hell.

Laughing, I stole another kiss. "You are just full of surprises. I love this side of you. Playful Natalie might just be my favorite."

"Then I'll have to make sure she comes out to play more often." She licked her lips, signaling she was getting turned on too.

"Don't tease me," I warned. "I can't ravish you in the kitchen while the kids are home."

That blush was back, and she deflected, looking at the ingredients I'd picked up for dinner. "So, what do we have here?"

Rearranging the items, I said, "Well, I thought we'd go for comfort and elegance. I was thinking mac and cheese, which the kids will love, and I've got a couple of filets for us."

Natalie fake pouted, her heart-shaped lips pushing together. "What if I want the mac?"

"Baby, with me, you can have whatever you want. You know that." I nipped that protruding lower lip of hers.

She moaned as I released it slowly from my teeth before saying breathlessly, "Just kidding. The filet sounds amazing."

I smirked. "That's what I thought. Now, be a good girl and get off your feet while your man cooks for you."

Moving behind me, she gave my ass a quick grab, teasing me once more on her way out of the kitchen. "Your wish is my command."

"Temptress," I called after her.

Looking over her shoulder, she couldn't resist one last taunt. "Maybe later."

God, that woman. My love for her grew by the day—hell, it grew every time she opened her mouth.

Once she was gone, I snuck a peek to ensure she was relaxing before getting to work on dinner. I could spend the rest of my life doing this, coming home to her after a long day or a long road trip, cooking for her and the kids. I could picture our life together with vivid clarity but forced myself to remember to take things one day at a time.

Amelia helped me set the table, and Beau wanted to be helpful, so I let him stir the mac and cheese. It was heartwarming to realize I could give them the same experiences I'd had growing up. Cooking in the kitchen as a family had been a weekly occurrence in the Slate house when I was a kid. My childhood was full of good memories, and it felt incredible knowing that I was changing the narrative for these children.

Dinner was a noisy affair, as always, with the kids talking over each other and laughter filling the air. I marveled at how quickly the shift had happened—going from my family being my hockey brothers to these children and their mother. Deep in my soul, I knew I didn't want it any other way.

After clearing the dishes, I presented each child with their chocolates in a heart-shaped box. Natalie let them choose two pieces each to eat before we started on their valentines and receptacle boxes to take to school for the exchange. Amelia and Jameson dragged out large boxes of craft supplies and three shoe boxes, setting up in the middle of the living room.

The older kids had a list of names to address valentines for their classmates, but Beau was only tasked with writing his name on each card. It was quiet for the first time that evening as they all concentrated on writing. Once that was accomplished, the flurry of activity was back.

Amelia was independently working while Jameson buddied up with me, asking for my help in building his box to his liking. Natalie stuck with Beau, whose demands were simple. Jameson and I spent an hour building his box into a robot with heart-shaped eyes and a big rectangular hole for a mouth to accept the cards meant for him.

This was all so simple, but it meant the world for this to be my life.

The thought crossed my mind that I wanted to take them home to Minnesota this summer in the off-season. The kids would love the lake, whether it was simply swimming or going out on the boat.

This right here was my future. The best was yet to come.

CHAPTER 19

Natalie

JAXON AND I WERE living in this perfect little bubble of happiness, and I finally began to believe that I was worthy of his love. The kids were thriving, and Charlotte was growing healthy and right on track. Liam and I still weren't speaking, but I pushed that to the back of my mind most days. I couldn't turn down the chance to give my kids a functioning family in favor of his ego.

Even with the strained relationship with my brother, I felt free for the first time in my life. I'd turned off the press alerts on my phone, felt comfortable in my own body—despite its rapid expansion in growing Charlie—and I was truly loved by a good man who put me and my kids first.

Just as I let my guard down, the bubble burst.

On Valentine's Day, the kids went off to school, and shortly after lunch, the doorbell rang.

Amy was working from home and decided to answer it so that I didn't have to get up. Joking on her way to the door, she called back, "I bet it's something else from Jaxon."

Curled up reading on the couch, the hairs on the back of my neck raised when I heard the hostile tone in her voice from down the hallway. "What are *you* doing here?"

Amy was kind to everyone, minus one person—the person who still haunted my nightmares. Putting down my book, I sent up a silent prayer.

Please, don't be him. Please, don't be him.

All hope fled my body when I heard the booming footsteps and that familiar voice striking fear into my heart. "I have every right to see *my* children, Amy."

Leo came into view as I stood. Sizing me up with his cool, calculating stare, he made me squirm—he'd always had the ability to strip me down with only a look, making me feel like less for simply existing.

Finally, he let out a dark laugh, sending a shudder down my spine. "Well, well, well, what do we have here? I thought the rehab story would have been enough to smoke you out, but now it makes sense why you've been hiding." Clicking his tongue, he added, "Naughty, naughty Natalie."

Amy must have run to warn Liam in the basement because suddenly, he burst into view, followed by Amy. The tension radiating off Liam was palpable as he asked through clenched teeth, "What are you doing here?"

Completely ignoring his brother, Leo asked me, "I know for sure that this one isn't mine. What unsuspecting fool did you trick this time, Natalie?" He gestured to my growing belly as his lips curled in disgust.

Trying to use some of my newfound confidence, I stared him down. Mentally, I was shaking in my boots. "None of your damn business."

Pretending to be offended, a sinister smile formed on his lips. "Ooh, the cat has claws. That's new and, might I add, doesn't suit you. I much prefer you docile."

Pushing his words about how meek I'd been in the past to the back of my mind, I pressed, "How did you get past the security gates, Leo?"

"That was easy. Need I remind you who purchased this house?" The smug look on his face was one I knew all too well. Leo was arrogant to a fault.

Liam came closer to stand beside me. "That would be me."

Leo's face darkened. "That's right. Little brother, always trying to be the better man. Not the more important one, but a valiant effort, nonetheless. Regardless, when your last name is on the deed to the house, it's quite easy to make it past the front gates."

Liam's hands formed fists at his side, but he remained rooted to the spot. "I'll ask again, *brother*. What are you doing here?"

"That should be obvious, I would think." Leo inspected his fingernails as if bored with the conversation. "I'm here to see my children, my *heirs*. Where are they?"

Liam continued to fight the fight for me, even though we weren't on speaking terms, answering, "Not here. Ever heard of a little thing called school? It's barely noon on a Friday."

Undeterred, Leo countered, "That's fine. I'll wait."

"Not here, you won't." Liam took a threatening step forward.

Taking a calming breath, I intervened, "Leo, I think the best thing would be for you to come back tomorrow. They are usually cranky after school and won't be in the best mood for you to interact with them. You'd want them compliant, wouldn't you?"

He took the bait, nodding. "You know what, that would be ideal. I hope they haven't become ungrateful brats like their mother."

Liam took one more step forward, growling, "Out. Now."

Leo smirked. "I'll go, but I'll be back bright and early tomorrow. Make sure they're ready for me." Turning on his heel, he left as suddenly as he'd appeared, but my world had shifted on its axis.

Collapsing onto the couch, I barely breathed out, "Oh my God."

Liam sat beside me, vowing, "I won't let him hurt them."

Shoving him in the shoulder hard, my fear turned to anger. "Now, you want to help me? You've been so worried about protecting me from Jaxon that you forgot all about the monster lurking in the shadows. Do you feel better now? Because I sure as hell don't."

Pulling me into a tight hug, I struggled against him for a second but gave up the fight when he whispered, "I'm sorry. You're right. I made a mistake."

Liam loosened the hug, and I pulled back, accusing, "You made a *big* mistake."

His blue eyes were filled with regret. "Forgive me? I was only trying to do right by you, even if it was slightly misguided in hindsight."

"You actually think you can protect them from him?" My body shook, fear gripping my heart thinking about what Leo would do if he got his hands on my kids.

"Nat, just remember that legally he can't take them. We made sure of that. Tomorrow, we will make sure everyone stays here. It's safest if they stay under this roof, with supervision. You and I both know that I could take him if it came down to a physical threat."

If there was one thing I knew about Leo, it was that he didn't fight fair. If he wanted my children, he would take them. In his mind, he was above the law and would have no qualms about sending his own brother to jail for assault if challenged physically. Nothing would stand in his way.

My mind was racing. "Why now? He's wanted nothing to do with them for years."

Liam sighed. "Why does he do anything? My guess is that he wants to remind you he's always there. He gets off on fear."

My lip trembled as I found myself on the verge of tears. "What am I going to tell the kids? Amelia doesn't trust him, and Beau doesn't know him. Jameson . . . Oh God, Jameson will be the most confused. I know you haven't been around to see it, but we've fallen into a good groove. They're happy and well-adjusted, and it's all because of Jaxon. He's helped us become more of a family than we've been in years. No offense."

Liam shrugged. "As much as I've tried to step in as their father, they know I never can be. Someday, I knew you'd move on. I just never expected it to be so quickly."

"You and me both," I said under my breath.

"It's my problem to deal with. I can't let it tear apart our relationship anymore." He pulled me into another hug, and I sank into his embrace.

"So, you're done being a jerk?" I challenged.

His heavy exhale could be felt where my head rested against his chest. "I'm not ready to jump on the Team Jaxon bandwagon, but I will always be on Team Natalie. Always."

A small smile crept onto my lips. It was good to have my big brother back. "I guess I'll take what I can get. Now, what are we going to do about Leo tomorrow?"

Liam didn't hesitate. "First things first. I will call the front gate and ensure they know he's only a visitor. No more sneak attacks. We will have a warning next time."

Nodding, I felt my body reverting to that familiar state of numbness, trying to protect myself. If I couldn't feel, he couldn't hurt me. "Whatever you think is best."

"No." His voice held a tone of authority.

Snapping back to my senses, I looked up at him. "No?"

"No," he repeated. "You're not going to shut down on me. You're going to fight. *We* are going to fight. Do you understand me?"

He was right. The same old Natalie that Leo knew was not going to get the job done. Mentally manning our battle stations, we created our plan of attack—what to tell the kids, how to deal with Leo, and contingencies in case things went south.

Leo returned early on Saturday morning. We'd prepped the kids the best we could for his arrival, but I wasn't sure it would ever be enough. Liam and Amy chaperoned the visit in the living room because I couldn't bear to do it. If I was going to stay strong, I needed to keep a clear head. That was impossible when I was near Leo for too long. He'd spent years honing his skills in breaking me down. It was his favorite pastime.

Sitting on a stool in the kitchen, I listened intently for any signs of trouble or distress from the kids. Time seemed to slow down as I sat there, praying the whole time that he would leave and never return. Tense and frozen in place, my back and legs began to ache, needing to stretch and move.

Easing off the stool, I bumped into a solid body. In my state of hyperawareness, my body's startle reflex activated, and I jumped back screaming. Heart beating so hard that I thought it would burst right out of my chest, I barely heard the surprised voice from behind. "Whoa, Nat. It's just me. Didn't you hear me come in?"

My mind recognized it was Jaxon, but my body was flooded with adrenaline from the surprise, not knowing he was there. Placing my head down on the cool marble of the island, I leaned over, breathing deeply, fixated on the effort to calm myself.

Feeling him touch my back again, I flinched involuntarily, causing him to withdraw like he'd been burned. I felt guilty when I heard the hurt in his tone. "Baby, you're scaring me."

After a few more deep breaths, I managed to straighten. Jaxon's eyes were wide, scanning my body, searching for signs of physical damage, but I knew he wouldn't find any. It was all emotional.

Reaching out to take his hand in reassurance, I explained, "I'm sorry, I didn't hear you come in, and you scared the hell out of me. I thought you were heading out of town today."

Concern was still etched on his handsome face. "Natalie, we talked about this. The plan was to come over after practice before I had to head out to check on you." He cupped my belly with both hands. "To check on Charlie. Are you sure everything is all right? You're acting strange."

Vaguely, I remembered a conversation about him stopping by before his trip, but Leo's reemergence eclipsed everything. As if on cue, I heard Amelia yelling at the top of her lungs, "That's not my name!"

Cringing, I closed my eyes for a split second before Jameson screamed, "Leave my sister alone!"

Involuntarily, my hand went to the countertop, gripping tightly, needing something to ground myself before opening my eyes. Before I knew what was happening, Jaxon had bolted toward my audibly agitated children.

Hurrying after him, I called out after him in a panic, "Jaxon, don't!"

Ignoring my plea, he didn't stop until he'd reached the scene playing out before us. Leo was in Amelia's face, trying to cajole her, as Jameson tried in vain to pull him away. "Don't you want a nice L nickname like the rest of your family? Lia is such a pretty name."

Skidding to a halt beside Jaxon, that's when I realized Leo's hands were on Amelia as she twisted away from her father, screaming in his face, "No!"

Something ugly flashed in Leo's eyes. It wasn't often that someone dared to defy him, and I feared for my daughter.

Jaxon's tone was calm, but there was a steel edge to it—I could tell he was wound tight. "Amelia, honey. Are you okay?"

Relief flooded my daughter's face, and she rushed to Jaxon, throwing her arms around him, trusting him to protect her. Jameson ran to me, and I held him close. Beau was crying in Liam's arms, but when he saw us, he tried to leap from his uncle's arms to get to us. Liam set him down to avoid dropping him in his struggle, and he ran to me as I scooped him up in my arms.

Looking at the father he didn't know, Beau pointed, accusing, "He's a bad man."

Out of the mouths of babes.

Leo sneered at us, at how we stood together, united like the family we had become over the past few months. "Isn't this sweet? A picture-perfect little family." Before I could blink, he'd pulled out his cell and snapped a picture of us huddled together.

"Guess I shouldn't be surprised." He gestured to Beau in my arms, addressing Jaxon, "Is he yours, too?"

Liam warned, "Leopold . . ."

Leo mocked him, "William . . ."

They were using full names, underscoring the threats just below the surface. Leo turned back to me, dismissing his brother. "The timeline adds up perfectly with those fall hockey parties you insisted on coming home for. His coloring is spot on, too."

To avoid scaring the children, Jaxon kept his tone even. "I should be so lucky. Beau is an incredible little boy, but you'd know that if you'd spent any time with him."

That seemed to spur Leo on. "Maybe I should remind you that, without a doubt, that is *my* daughter clinging to your leg."

"She may be biologically yours, but you're no father," Jaxon spat back.

My body began to shake in response to the stress and tension it had been under for the past twenty-four hours. It wouldn't be long before my legs gave out. Knowing my body's limits, I recognized its need to sit down but couldn't afford to show any signs of weakness in front of Leo.

Leaning slightly toward him, I whispered to Jaxon, "Take Beau."

Without a word, Jaxon reached over, pulling Beau into his arms. Beau buried his tiny face into Jaxon's neck.

Jameson could feel my shaking, and he looked up. "Mama?" I couldn't remember the last time he'd called me that instead of Mom, which spoke to how scared he was.

Trying desperately to hide it, my voice shook with the same fear. "Leo, I think it's time for you to leave. You came to spend time with the children, but as you can see, they're not interested."

Leo narrowed his eyes. "You think I'm going to leave them here with you so you can keep poisoning them against me? They're my GOD-DAMN KIDS!" It never ceased to amaze me how he could go from calm to furious in a split second.

Mentally cursing myself for flinching, I tried again. "Legally, I have full custody. Do I need to call the cops?"

That wicked smile curled on his lips—the one that signaled something truly sinister was about to happen. Leo reached into his pocket, waving his phone. "I'll leave, but remember, this isn't over. A little push of a button and this picture goes to the press, and you'll be ruined in the court of public opinion. No judge would allow you to keep them after that. Would serve you right for not being able to keep your legs closed."

Liam stepped forward with murder in his eyes, and just when I thought he might hit Leo, he grabbed the phone from his hand, smashing it on the ground. "Leave. Now."

Backing away from his brother, he put his hands up. "Fine. I'll leave." Heading for the door, he paused a step before passing me. "Don't think this is over, Natalie. I'll be back for what's mine."

Standing stock still, I tried to keep all emotion from my face—anything that would feed into him. He continued past, and I looked at my children, huddled against Jaxon and me. Amelia had silent tears streaming down her face, and Jameson's vise-like grip on my leg grew painful.

I'd grown accustomed to Leo terrorizing me, but it was unacceptable for my children to live in fear, with the looming threat of their father coming back to take them away from everything they knew, including me.

Leo's footsteps were loud on the hardwood floors as he headed toward the door, with Liam shadowing him to make sure he left. The sound of the door slamming echoed throughout the house. Knowing he was gone, my body finally gave out, and I descended into darkness.

CHAPTER 20

Jaxon

THE BANG OF THE door slamming shut sent my world into chaos.

Beau was still held in my left arm when Natalie began to sway to my right. In the blink of an eye, her body slumped, and I stuck my arm out quickly to loop under her armpit, managing to pull her limp form toward my body.

That was a close call. Too close.

My quick actions barely prevented her from hitting the floor. I sent up a silent prayer of thanks to the game of hockey for my lightning-quick reflexes and impeccable hand-eye coordination honed over the years during my intensive training.

Having been so focused on catching Natalie, I'd been deaf to the kids' panic and screaming around me until I had her safely in my arms. Suddenly, their cries reached me, with Beau's being the loudest and most insistent, right next to my ear.

Jameson's eyes were filled with tears as he tugged at his mother's limp arm. "Mom, wake up!"

Amelia implored me, "Help her, Jaxon!"

Struggling to hold both Beau and Natalie, I looked over my shoulder, calling for help, "Liam!"

Within seconds, Beau was lifted out of my grasp, and I was finally able to get both arms around Natalie's body. Lowering her to the ground, I cradled her head in my lap. Smoothing the dark hair away from her face, I begged, "Baby, please wake up."

Amy knelt beside me, and that's when I realized she'd been the one to take Beau from me as I saw him clinging to her neck. She touched my arm. "She'll be okay. Just stay calm."

Looking at her like she'd lost her mind, I retorted, "Stay calm? I just watched the woman I love get terrorized in her own damn home, and now she's unconscious! We need to call 911."

From behind, I heard Liam's voice saying, "Absolutely not. That's out of the question."

Turning my head, I narrowed my eyes at him as he stood there with arms crossed over his massive chest. "You're kidding, right?"

Liam held firm. "Nat tends to do this. Her body can't handle extreme amounts of stress and shuts down. She'll be fine. Let's get her upstairs."

"She'll be fine," I repeated the words. "She's pregnant, for God's sake, Liam! She needs to get checked out!"

"Get her upstairs, and I'll make a call. She'd never forgive us if we called for an ambulance."

My anger was simmering right beneath the surface. Leo had gotten it started, but his brother was the one who had it threatening to boil over.

"You talked a big game about being enough to protect her," I accused. "Looks like you're knocking that out of the park." I couldn't keep the sarcasm from my tone.

A muscle in his jaw twitched as he stared me down with those intense blue eyes. "Don't you have a plane to catch?"

Shit.

I'd completely forgotten in the commotion that I'd only stopped by to say goodbye before the Comets headed west for a week. Never in my life had I felt this torn between my career and my personal life. Rationally, I knew I had an obligation and needed to go, but looking at the woman I held in my arms and her upset children, my heart begged me to stay.

Amelia's voice cut through the fog. "Jaxon, you're not leaving, are you?"

Looking over at her chocolate brown eyes that matched her mother's closed ones, the decision became crystal clear. "No, sweetheart. I'm not leaving."

The relief that filled her face centered me. I was exactly where I *needed* to be right now. Natalie stirred in my arms, reminding me that we needed to move her. Scooping her up, I headed toward the back stairs that would take me straight to her bedroom, whispering, "It's all right. I've got you."

Reaching her bedroom, I laid her down and tucked her in. Placing a soft kiss on her forehead, I walked to the hallway to make the calls necessary to be able to stay. Closing the door but not latching it in case Natalie needed me, I met a waiting Amy in the hall.

Sighing, I ran a hand through my hair. "Amy, talk to me. What the hell happened? How did he get in here?"

Amy looked at me with empathy shining in her green eyes. "He showed up yesterday and got past the gates using the last name on the deed to the house."

Yesterday.

Natalie hadn't trusted me enough to let me know he was back.

Pushing down the hurt, I asked Amy, "And you let him come back?"

"Nobody *lets* Leo do anything." She scoffed.

"Entitled asshole," I muttered under my breath.

"Sums it up."

"I've got to make a call, tie up some loose ends. Can you keep an eye on her?" I knew I could trust Amy to look after Natalie in the same way I would.

"Of course." She nodded. "Liam called in a favor, and we've got a doctor coming over to check her out."

"Good," I ran a shaky hand over my face.

The tightness in my chest loosened a fraction, but I wouldn't be able to breathe easy until both Natalie and Charlie checked out all right. So help me God, if that man did something to harm either one of them. . .

I'd wanted to take Leo out the minute I saw his hands on Amelia, but I knew that wasn't what any of them needed. They'd been through enough, and beating the shit out of their father in front of them would only make them afraid of me instead of him.

Walking down the main upstairs hallway, I paused at the top of the massive curved foyer staircase, taking a seat on the top step. Pulling my phone out of my back pocket, I cringed when I saw all the missed messages and phone calls from not only my coaches but half of my teammates, wondering where I was.

There was only one person I knew I could call. Scrolling through my phone, I reached Coach's name and hit dial. One ring in, Coach's voice filled the speaker. "You'd better be calling to tell me you're pulling up to the airport, Jaxon. The plane leaves in fifteen minutes."

Closing my eyes, I forced myself to say the words, "I'm not going to make it, Coach."

"Why the hell not?" his voice boomed through the phone.

"Leo showed up."

His sharp intake of air was audible. "Shit."

"Yeah." I sighed.

"Everyone all right?" Concern colored Coach's words.

I swallowed past the lump in my throat. "The kids are rattled. Natalie passed out, and she's still unconscious."

"Fuck," he breathed out.

Rubbing my free hand down my face, I said, "I have to stay tonight. I can catch a plane out first thing tomorrow and still make it in time for pre-game practice."

"Of course. Call Amber if you need anything, and I mean anything. Do you hear me?"

"Yes, sir," I replied.

"Take care of our girl."

"Not as easy as it sounds." I blew out a heavy breath.

"I know, son. I'll see you tomorrow."

Hanging up, I finally took a moment to let the events of the afternoon wash over me. Everything had happened so quickly that I hadn't had time to process it. Leo was back, threatening Natalie over custody of the kids, and she was so stressed out that her body could barely handle it.

My gut reaction was to try and fix everything, but I was learning there was so much about this situation that was beyond my control. I hated this feeling.

Behind me, Amy's voice called out, "Jaxon?"

Wound so tight, I jumped at the sound of her voice. Taking a calming breath, I stood, facing her. "Is she all right?"

"She's awake and asking for you."

Hurrying down the hallway, I slowed my steps before reaching the bedroom door, pushing it open gently to the view of Natalie on her side in bed, awake.

Thank God.

Striding to the side of the bed, I sat on the edge, rubbing a soothing hand up and down her arm. "Hey, baby. How are you feeling?"

Her weak attempt at a smile nearly broke my heart. "A little woozy, but I'll be fine."

"Just rest. Liam called a doctor to check on you and Charlie."

Reaching up, she gently tugged on the tie I still wore, having been dressed in my suit, minus the jacket, ready to head straight to the airport when I'd stopped by this afternoon. "You have to go. The team is counting on you."

I shook my head. "I already called Coach. I'm not going tonight. I'll charter a plane for the morning."

Natalie sighed. "You have to go. People will be wondering where you are."

I felt my temper flare. "I don't give a damn what anyone else thinks."

"Hockey is your life," she tried again.

"Hockey is my *job*, Natalie. There's a big difference. Hockey is temporary. What we have right here is more important. It always will be."

Her eyes were bright and shiny, and I watched as tears welled up, threatening to fall. I knew she had major trust issues, so I had no problem reaffirming time and time again just how much she meant to me. Nothing was more important. Nothing ever would be.

Blinking a few more times, her voice was thick when she asked, "How are the kids?"

I tucked a strand of hair behind her ear. "They're scared. Worried about you more than anything else."

"I *hate* him."

The vise grip inside my chest tightened again, and I nodded. "I know, baby. I do too."

"He's going to try to take the kids," she whispered, voice trembling.

"Listen to me, Natalie." I waited until her eyes met mine before continuing, "The only way he's getting the kids out of this house is over my dead body. I mean that literally—I will die fighting before I let anyone take the kids."

A corner of her lips quirked up. "I think you could take him."

She was joking. That was a good sign, so I teased back, "You *think*?"

A light laugh fell from her lips. "All right, all right. I know you could take him."

"That's my girl." I bent down to place a kiss on her forehead.

There was a knock on the door, and I turned to find Liam standing there.

My free hand clenched into a fist. I was furious that he'd let his brother come in here and do this to Natalie, to the kids. He'd been so confident months ago, going on and on about how he could protect her, that she didn't need me. How had he sat idly by while Leo had gotten close enough to put his hands on Amelia?

"What do you want?" My tone was lethal. I didn't care what he thought of me anymore.

Challenging me right back, he snapped, "You wanted a doctor, didn't you?"

I growled, "We wouldn't need one if you hadn't let him into this house."

Natalie's hand reached up to my neck, rubbing up and down in an effort to soothe my temper. "It's okay, Jaxon. He's trying to help."

Frowning, I kept my glare on Liam. "Yeah, he's helpful, all right."

Liam pushed the door wider, revealing a middle-aged man with salt-and-pepper hair. The man entered the room, carrying a large black bag, holding his hand out to me. "I'm Dr. Collier."

Nodding, I shook his hand. "Jaxon."

Releasing my hand, he moved to the head of the bed. "And you must be Natalie."

"Nice to meet you." Natalie's smile was stronger than it had been only a few minutes ago. That was promising.

I stood to allow Dr. Collier easier access to Natalie while I rounded the bottom of the bed, coming to the other side and sitting against the headboard, taking her hand in mine.

Setting his black bag down on her nightstand, he addressed Natalie once more. "I heard you had a little fainting spell earlier. How are you feeling now?"

Natalie rolled onto her back, scooching to sit up against the pillows piled along the headboard. "Better. I was woozy a little bit ago, but it's easing."

"That's good. Do I have your permission to examine you?"

She nodded in response. "Yes, that's fine."

"Wonderful." He pulled out a blood pressure cuff and a stethoscope from his black bag. "How many weeks along are you?"

"30 weeks," she replied.

"No other complications during the pregnancy?"

"No." She shook her head as he wrapped the cuff around her arm, pumping the bulb and listening to her pulse.

Letting the bulb deflate, he noted, "A little high, but nothing too worrisome. Now, I'll check on the little one."

Pulling out a handheld doppler similar to the one I'd seen used during the numerous doctor's appointments I'd accompanied Natalie to in the past few months, he had her lift her shirt. Protectively, I reached out with my free hand to touch her bare belly and was rewarded with a little push back from our daughter.

Natalie squeezed my hand and smiled. "See? She's just fine."

Dr. Collier squirted a little gel on her exposed skin, then turned on the doppler, reaching it out to press on her belly. Charlie's heartbeat filled the room, and I breathed out a sigh of relief. What if I hadn't been here today?

What if we'd left for the road trip yesterday? What would have happened to my family? Someone must have been looking out for us today that I was standing right next to Natalie when she collapsed.

"Sounds good to me." Dr. Collier removed the doppler from Natalie's belly and wiped the gel away with a towel. "I'll put a call in to your OB this evening and recommend a non-stress test to be on the safe side. Make sure to take it easy for the rest of the day."

"Done. Thank you, Doctor," I replied, reaching across the bed to shake his hand one more time in gratitude before he left. Sagging against the headboard in relief that Natalie and Charlie were all right after the day's events, I closed my eyes, exhaling deeply.

"Hey, we're okay." Natalie's words had me taking another deep breath before I forced myself to look at her.

"What if you weren't?" I cupped her cheek.

"But we are."

Leaning over to brush a light kiss on her lips, I whispered, "I love you. Do you know that?"

Feeling her smile against my lips, she whispered back, "I know."

"Good. Now, you listen to the doctor and rest tonight. I will take care of everything else. I don't want you stressed out about anything else. Understood?"

Giving me a mock salute as I pulled back, she smiled. "Yes, sir."

"That's my good girl."

Making my way downstairs, I made a mental checklist of what I needed to do to protect my family while I was gone. Apparently, living in a gated community wasn't enough anymore. Hiring permanent security was the only answer, but Natalie would kill me if she knew, so they'd need to be inconspicuous.

First, I needed to check on the kids and ensure they knew they were safe. Rounding the bottom of the back staircase into the living room, I found Amelia sitting with Amy. She looked up at me with those big brown eyes. "Is my mom okay?"

Sitting on the other side of her, I pulled her into a hug, stroking her hair. "She's fine. After dinner, I'm sure she'd love to have you sit with her for a while. Maybe read her a story? You think you can do that?"

Pulling back, she nodded. "I know just the book."

"I knew you would." I smiled at the girl I'd grown to love as my own.

Jameson timidly entered the room, asking, "Are you staying tonight, Jaxon?"

Patting the spot on the couch beside me, I invited him to join us. "Do you think I should, buddy?"

"I think Mom would like it." He nodded thoughtfully.

"Just Mom?" I questioned.

"I'd like it, too," he admitted, lowering his eyes.

Pulling him into a side hug, I confirmed, "I'm not going anywhere, buddy. If you need me, I'm here. Always."

Jameson sniffled. "That's good. Thanks, Jaxon."

Needing to do something to take their mind off the terrible afternoon they'd had, I asked, "What do we think about pizza for dinner? Maybe an impromptu game night with Aunt Amy? I bet if we called her, Aunt Hannah would love to come too."

Jameson's voice brightened. "I love pizza!"

Chuckling, I tousled his short blond curls. "I had a feeling. Can I tell you a secret?"

He looked up at me with a genuine smile, nodding enthusiastically. "Yes! I'm the best at keeping secrets!"

Leaning in close, I cupped a hand next to his ear, making a show of whispering a big secret, before uttering in a low voice, "I love pizza, too."

Jameson pulled back, accusing, "That's not a secret!"

"Of course it is!" I protested. "If Coach knew I was having pizza the night before a game, I'd be in big trouble. So, promise me that you won't tell."

He made a motion of zipping his lips and throwing away a key, causing me to laugh, feeling lighter than I had all day. This was what I needed in my life. Never once had I mourned the loss of my bachelor life, and it was easy to see why. My world had narrowed to focus on the people living in this house, and they were more than enough to fulfill me. When I had bad days, this was where I wanted to be. A smile from Natalie or one of her kids was enough to snap me out of any bad mood or shake off any loss.

The rest of the evening was spent diverting the kids' focus. Hannah came over with fixings to make ice cream sundaes after our pizza dinner. We broke out the board games at the kitchen table once it had been cleared and spent hours playing games, laughing, and teasing each other. After a few games, Amelia excused herself to read with her mom.

Eventually, Beau curled up in my lap, and I felt his breathing slow, his body slacken. The weight of his tiny body against mine had the same effect as a weighted blanket—it was pure comfort. His soft snores were music to my ears.

When Jameson began to yawn, we ended the game night and got ready for bed.

Amy walked over to my chair, arms ready to take Beau, but I wasn't prepared to let him go. As far as he knew, a stranger had walked into his house that day, causing his mom and siblings to be upset. I wanted to make sure he knew that I would always protect them. I tightened my hold on his tiny body.

Amy reached out again. "Jaxon, he's safe. They all are."

That was finally enough to convince me to relinquish my hold on him. I shivered at the loss of his warm body against mine. Immediately, I regretted handing him over, but thankfully, Jameson distracted me, asking, "Will you take me to bed, Jaxon?"

There weren't words to express how incredible it felt that this family didn't always need me, but they seemed to always *want* me. They had a choice, and they chose me. The feeling was mutual, and I hoped that my actions today had shown Natalie the level of my commitment.

Standing, I reached out to Jameson. "Let's go, buddy."

Walking upstairs, we picked out pajamas and got his teeth brushed. Jameson's room was decorated to reflect his older age. While Beau's walls were covered in trains, Jameson's had a baseball theme. I knew he played the sport, but I was determined to bring him over to the dark side and hoped that someday, he'd ask me to help him change this theme to a hockey one.

Tucking him into bed, I sat on the edge. "Goodnight, buddy. I'll be gone in the morning, but I'm here tonight if you need me for anything at all."

Looking up at me, his eyes drooping, he smiled as sleep began to pull at him. "I wish you were my dad, Jaxon."

The words tugged at my heartstrings, and I fought the urge not to get emotional in front of this little boy who'd already been through so much—not only today, but during the entirety of his short life.

Swallowing, I leaned down to hug him, whispering, "Me too, buddy."

As if his earlier statement wasn't enough, he whispered back, "I love you."

Pulling back, I cleared my throat, trying to dislodge the lump formed there, as I responded, "I love you too, buddy. I'll see you when I get back in a week. Make sure you help take care of your mom, okay?"

Jameson nodded, and I watched as his eyes slowly drifted closed.

Standing, I crossed the room, latching the door silently behind me. Walking down the hallway, I checked on Beau, who was still sound asleep, albeit now in his own bed, before heading toward Natalie's bedroom. The door was cracked open, so I pushed it open slowly in case she was asleep.

Natalie still sat up in bed, reading her own book, as Amelia was laid out beside her, asleep, with an open book across her chest. The room gave off an air of softness, just like its owner—it was soothing. A sage accent wall behind the quilted cream headboard of the bed was the perfect complement to the color scheme of pink and beige. It was feminine; it was all Natalie.

Natalie smiled when she saw me standing in the doorway, observing her. "Hey."

Smiling, I crossed the room to sit on the edge of the bed. "Hey, yourself. How are you feeling?"

"All better," she replied, her tone light as if we hadn't just been through the day from Hell.

"Good, the boys are both in bed."

Natalie nodded in the direction of Amelia passed out beside her. "You think you have it in you for one more?"

"Nah," I smirked. When she looked at me confused, I offered, "She can stay here with you. I'll make up the guest room for myself."

"You don't have to do that," she protested.

Patting her leg, I agreed, "I know I don't have to, but I'm happy to do it. Amelia needs you tonight, and I don't want her to wake up alone. Today was enough to give me nightmares. I can't even imagine what it's done to her."

She chewed on her bottom lip. "I'm sorry you had to see that today."

I gaped at her. "Are you kidding? I have spent all day thanking God I was here today." A shudder ran through my body. "I can't stop thinking about what would have happened to you or any of the kids if I hadn't been."

Natalie reached out and grabbed my hand. "You're a good man, Jaxon."

What she didn't realize was that I viewed this as my family, my responsibility. The thought of any one of them hurt or scared was like a knife to my heart. An incident like the one that occurred today could *never* happen again. My entire future was in this house, even if most of them didn't know it yet.

Leaning over, I quickly kissed Natalie's lips. "I'll be gone before you wake in the morning, but I'll make sure to call you when I land. Take it easy this week, and don't think for one minute that Amy won't tell me if you don't."

Natalie lifted her eyes skyward but smiled. "Traitor."

"I prefer the term ally," I corrected her.

"Whatever you say."

"Well, I say get some rest. I'll see you in a week."

"Yes, Dad," she teased.

Another quick kiss to her forehead, and I stood, heading out of her room. I knew I wouldn't rest easy the entire time I was out west. God help anyone who got in my way until I got back home.

Sweat ran into my eyes. My heartbeat thundered in my ears, but I felt no pain as my fists continued to connect with the face of Trey Carr of the Denver Glaciers. It was almost as if I was having an out-of-body experience, watching as I lost all control, taking out all the aggression I felt toward Leo on my opponent. I tasted blood but couldn't feel any of Trey's blows from his counterattack. My body was numb to everything except the rage that had been simmering over the past twenty-four hours.

I'd been wound tight going into the game, so it hadn't taken much to set me off. A hard hit into the boards was all it took, and Trey had been the unfortunate one who'd laid the hit. Forgetting the game on the ice, I'd charged at him, knocking his helmet off in a single blow to the head.

Fighting had always been a part of the game, but I normally kept my nose clean. I was more level-headed than most of my teammates. Sure, I would always jump to the defense of my goalie but never was one to instigate. That was until Leo had walked in and scared the hell out of my woman.

As I knocked Trey to the ground, I felt arms pulling me off him, but I struggled against them, even knowing that was when the fight had to end. The referees trying to restrain me warned that if I didn't settle down and make my way to the box to serve my five minutes for the fighting penalty, they'd assess me with a ten-minute major on top of it. I told them where they could shove their major, not caring that it sealed my fate.

Fifteen minutes in the box did nothing to cool my temper. I kept seeing the terrified faces of my family and was filled with the overwhelming urge to tear someone's head off. The first whistle after my penalty had expired, I was allowed out of the box during the stoppage, and Coach screamed my name, calling me to the bench.

Skating to a hard stop at the bench, I looked up at my mentor. His face was hard-set as he glared at me. "I know you have some shit you need to work out, but not out here. Get your ass to the locker room. You're done for the night."

Knowing better than to argue with Coach—even if I was looking to pick a fight tonight—I accepted his command. Opening the bench door, I headed down the tunnel to the visiting team's locker room, throwing open the door and slamming down my stick and helmet.

My heart was hammering against my ribcage as sweat dripped from my hair and down my neck. I needed to cool down in more ways than one.

Untying and removing my skates, I didn't bother taking off any of my gear before getting into a freezing cold shower. I'd apologize to the equipment crew later for the soaking-wet gear they had to pack to fly to San Francisco tonight before our next game.

Unsure of how long I spent under the cold water, I made my way back to the locker room, shucking my wet gear and toweling off before dressing in my suit. A few dots of crimson dripped on my gray suit pants, and I cursed, my temper flaring again. "Fuck."

Grabbing a smaller towel, I held it to my face, unsure exactly where the blood was coming from and not really caring. As the team came in for the second intermission, I allowed the medical staff to lead me into a separate room to assess my facial injury. Three stitches to the bridge of my nose later, I was released back into the locker room, which the team had already vacated to play the third period without me.

The only thing I knew that would center me was Natalie's voice, knowing she was safe. But checking my watch, I found it was already 10 PM in Denver, which meant it was midnight back home. Not wanting to wake her but needing something to soothe the rage still coursing through my veins, I shamelessly trolled the internet for old clips of speeches she'd given during engagements back when she was a working royal. Slowly, my muscles loosened, and the red haze around my vision cleared. This woman was my focus, and I was determined to make sure she always would be.

Hearing the heavy footsteps coming down the hall of my teammates, I stuffed my phone into my pocket. From the lighthearted nature of the first ones to enter the locker room, I surmised that we had won.

Eventually, everyone was in the room, beginning to undress, as Coach addressed the room. "Good effort out there tonight, boys," he began.

"No thanks to someone." I swung my head around to look for who made that snarky remark, clearly aimed at me. Of course, it was Levi Nixon, our resident hotshot rookie. I'd never liked his cocky attitude on the ice, and I sure as hell didn't like him throwing shots my way in the locker room.

Standing, I challenged, "Why don't you say that to my face, rookie? Maybe I can rearrange your face like I did Carr's."

Coach shouted, "Enough! Fighting is a part of the game, but we leave it on the ice. In this room, we are a team. You have a lot to learn, Nixon."

Grumbling, Levi backed down. No one crossed Coach if you wanted to keep playing. It was a silent rule, similar to the one about his daughters being off-limits. I was smug, remembering how well I'd followed that one, but I couldn't find it within myself to be sorry.

"As I was saying," Coach began again. "We did a good job of controlling the play and taking advantage when we had opportunities. Take a few minutes before I let the media in for interviews, then it's ninety minutes until asses are in seats on the bus."

Coach turned on his heel and left the locker room with the rest of the coaches, likely submitting to his interview first in the hallway. I knew that after being kicked out of the game by my coach, combined with the fight and major penalty, I'd be a target tonight for the pack of traveling reporters.

Cal, to my right, remarked, "You were in rare form tonight."

Digging my heels in, I responded, "Carr was asking for it."

He shook his head. "You were like a man possessed. I was worried you were going to kill him with your bare hands. Want to talk about it?"

"No." I leveled a glare in his direction.

Throwing up his hands, he backed off. "Fine, but if you need to blow off some steam, I know a club in San Fran . . ."

I snapped at him, "Aren't you tired of that shit yet? Fucking anything with legs? Being nothing more than a story they can tell their friends?"

Cal kept his cool. "So, I'll take that as a no."

"Stop asking. I'm done with that life."

"Noted." He finally backed down. Hopefully, I'd made my point.

The doors opened, and the media filed in, picking and choosing which player to interview for their specific news outlet back in Hartford. I wasn't in any mood to talk to anyone right now but knew it would stir more shit, and I'd be fined if I refused. Putting my head down, I got through it with simple answers, not wanting to explain why I'd acted so out of character.

The only place I wanted to be right now was home.

Chapter 21

Natalie

HEARING THE DOOR OPEN and close put a smile on my face. Jaxon was home. Charlie gave a little roll, indicating that she was just as relieved that her daddy was home after a week on the road.

Standing in the kitchen, I waited for him to find me and was pleasantly surprised when he came up from behind, leaning in low to nuzzle the side of my neck.

Melting into him, I whispered, "I missed you."

Sighing behind me, his hands came around the sides of my belly. "Not more than I missed you."

Arching into his touch, I loved the scratch of the stubble he'd grown while on the road against the sensitive skin of my neck. Turning in his embrace, Jaxon used that opportunity to get down on his knees, kissing my belly before looking up. "How's our girl?"

Running my hands through his hair, I smiled at the tenderness in his voice. "She checked out just fine."

Closing his eyes, he whispered, "Thank God." Standing, he scanned my face, noting, "You look tired. Have you been having trouble sleeping?"

I shrugged it off. "It's fine, just having trouble getting comfortable these days with Miss Charlie jumping around on my bladder. I'm sure I'll sleep better tonight, knowing you're home."

"You and me both." Changing topics, he asked, "How are the kids? There wasn't any more trouble while I was gone?"

"No, just the opposite, actually."

He tilted his head. "How so?"

I explained, "Liam called his parents, and they doubled down in their support of me and the kids. They'll make sure that Leo doesn't even attempt to come back and take them from me."

"That's great." Relief flooded his face.

"My mother-in-law even called to check on me, and I told her about Charlie. In fact, she was so thrilled for me that she sent all those boxes you probably tripped over in the hallway. Knowing that I'd gotten rid of everything after Beau, she sent all kinds of baby gear, clothes, you name it."

Jaxon frowned, repeating, "Mother-in-law."

Unsure of what he was getting at, I stated, "Well, I guess not legally anymore, but I owe her my life, the kids' lives."

Making a conscious effort not to dwell too much on my old life, I looked up at his handsome face, reaching up to trace a soft outline below the stitches along the bridge of his nose. "At what point did this seem like a bad idea?"

Jaxon smirked. "Who said it was a bad idea? I'm not sorry."

I rolled my eyes playfully. "Yeah, it sure didn't seem like you were, sitting in the box for extra minutes and then having Ace throw you out of the game."

He grimaced. "You saw that?"

"Even if I hadn't, it's been all over the news."

"The kids didn't see, did they?" Panic filled his voice.

"No," I reassured him.

Jaxon blew out a breath. "Good. I just—"

I could tell he was struggling with what had happened before he'd left as I'd watched him beat the living shit out of Trey Carr on live television. Cupping his face, I stood on my tiptoes to kiss his lips, whispering, "It's over. I'm fine, Charlie's fine, the kids are fine." One more kiss and I went all in, or at least as far as I could allow myself. "I'm yours."

Growling, he took my mouth as his hands pulled my body flush with his. There was a desperation to this kiss, unlike anything I'd ever known—like if he didn't consume me right now, he might die. Groaning into his mouth as his tongue swept inside mine, I clung to him, my legs shaking like they might give out if I didn't use his body for support.

As he pulled back, I whimpered, wanting more. His eyes were glazed over with lust, but he took my hands in his, taking two steps back before scanning me from head to toe. "Goddamn, Natalie. What are you *wearing*?"

Sparing a glance down, I realized I was sporting a black one-piece bodysuit that hugged my body like a second skin. Feeling beautiful just as I was, thanks to this man who currently devoured me with his eyes, I answered innocently, batting my eyelashes. "Clothes?"

Shaking his head, I bit my lower lip when a lock of dark hair fell across his forehead. "No. Clothes leave something to the imagination." Coming close again, he leaned down to whisper in my ear, "I can see *everything*."

My nipples hardened against the spandex holding everything in place in response to his words. Gently, Jaxon nipped my earlobe before trailing his mouth down my neck, licking the outline of the scoop neck on the bodysuit, where my breasts rose as a result of my ragged breathing. With hands on either side of my body, he began trailing them up my sides, beginning at my hips and moving upward until his fingers grazed the edges of my breasts, causing a shiver to run the length of my body.

Standing at his full height, his stare was intense enough that I already felt naked. "Good thing you're not leaving the house right now because I'd have to fight every man who dared to look at you wearing this. This is only for me." Tilting my face up with a hand under my chin, he asked, "Do you understand me, Natalie? You are mine."

Mouth suddenly dry, words escaped me at his possessive tone. I swallowed before managing a nod.

Looking around the kitchen, he asked, "Kids at school?" I nodded. "Amy and Liam home?" Shaking my head, I barely heard him groan out, "Good. I don't think I can wait. I need you now."

The breath froze in my lungs. Breathless, I asked, "Now?"

"Now," Jaxon confirmed. His eyes—dark and dangerous—locked with mine seconds before his mouth descended with a renewed hunger. I was lost, drowning in this kiss, until I felt his hand tweak my nipple. I tore my mouth from his, gasping at the shock of pleasure that shot through my body.

Hungrily, Jaxon gazed down at his hands on my body, growling, "You're wearing too much."

"I thought I wasn't wearing enough," I taunted.

That earned me another nipple tweak, causing me to squeal. "Jaxon!"

Those whiskey eyes flared. "That's right, baby, scream my name. Remember who you belong to."

Slowly, he peeled the straps of the bodysuit off my shoulders, pulling the top down enough that my breasts could burst free, spilling into his waiting hands.

Groaning, he palmed them, asking, "No bra?" Shaking my head in response and biting my lip, his eyes darkened. "Nothing underneath?" When I didn't answer, that gave him all the confirmation he needed, and he growled against my mouth, "Naughty girl."

Feeling wicked and looking to level the playing field, I held his stare, reaching down, gripping his rock-hard cock through his joggers. Satisfaction coursed through me as his eyes slid shut, and he hissed, "Fuck, Natalie."

Taunting him with his own words, I smiled as I squeezed his length in my hand. "Remember who *you* belong to."

Any illusion of turning the tables vanished when his eyes snapped open, and I saw the hunger he didn't bother to hide. Mine widened in response—knowing I'd just unleashed him—as a shiver ran through my body at the thought of him taking total control.

My sweet, kind, caring Jaxon was about to devour me, and I'd never wanted anything more in my life.

"Now, you've done it," he growled.

My brain processed the sensation of cool air flowing over my body before it heard what sounded like fabric ripping. Blinded by lust, it took a second to realize what had happened. Looking down at my naked body, then back to the wolfish gleam in Jaxon's eyes, it finally dawned on me. He'd torn the bodysuit right off my body.

Holy shit. That was hot.

Gripping his face in my hands, my voice was breathy. "Where the hell has this Jaxon been hiding?"

His voice grew husky. "Not hiding. Just been waiting for you my whole damn life."

Those were the last words I heard before his mouth descended upon mine, my arms looping around his neck. Ferocious was too tame a word to describe how he ravaged my mouth, his tongue claiming every inch. When he reached between my legs, they threatened to buckle—I was riding the edge of release already.

Reaching down, Jaxon's hands slid over my ass around to the back of my thighs before lifting me onto the kitchen island, the cool marble a sharp contrast to my overheated skin.

Regardless of my height advantage in this position, he continued to dominate my body. Sucking one peaked and aching nipple into his mouth, a hand moved along the inside my thigh, teasing its way until it reached my core. His fingers spread around my body's natural lubrication before focusing solely on my throbbing clit. A few quick passes of his thumb, combined with his relentless assault on my breasts, and I could barely breathe.

"More," I demanded.

Switching to attend to my other breast, Jaxon shoved two fingers inside me as his thumb rubbed tighter circles, increasing with intensity and pressure. My back bowed, holding his head to my breast as tremors racked my body, desperately seeking release. Curling his fingers inside me, he massaged my G-spot, and my soul left my body. My orgasm crested so suddenly that a scream ripped from my throat, bouncing off the kitchen walls. I clutched at Jaxon, needing an anchor to ride out the storm he'd stirred within my body.

I barely had time to recover from the earth-shattering climax before Jaxon thrust into me in one smooth motion. The sensation was so overwhelming that I screamed out again, torn between needing it to stop or wanting it to last forever. My thighs trembled uncontrollably, but my arms finally loosened enough to pull back and look at the only man to ever put me first.

Jaxon's eyes were on me as he started to pump into me, slowly at first, balancing me on the edge of the countertop. Leaning back so that I was lying across the island, propped up on my elbows, I realized he was still fully dressed as he claimed my body again and again. Each slow thrust was a torturous graze against my clit, overly sensitive and throbbing from my earlier orgasm.

Spying the tendons straining in his neck, I knew he was holding back, and I couldn't take much more, so I egged him on, "Fuck me, Jaxon."

Stilling for a moment, Jaxon stared down at me before he grinned, gripping my hips tighter, and letting loose, just as I'd demanded. His thrusts grew punishing, each one harder than the one before. Watching him was erotic, especially when he looked down to where our bodies were joined, licking his lips seconds before he began to grunt, trying to hold off his orgasm, waiting for me to come again.

Deciding to give him a much-needed assist, I lowered my back flush with the kitchen island. Reaching down, I barely grazed my clit before jumping slightly, finding it almost too sensitive.

I can do this. Or die of pleasure trying.

Gritting my teeth against the intense sensation, I delved back in, determined to make quick work of aiding my second orgasm because I wasn't going to last much longer like this. Barely hearing Jaxon groan through my lust-hazed hearing, I rubbed quick, tight circles over the slippery nub.

It was Jaxon's words that threw me over as he repeated over and over, "You're mine."

Pleasure shot through me again, this time stealing my breath, bringing tears to my eyes with its intensity. The edges of my vision darkened—this climax so powerful that I teetered on the line of consciousness. Jaxon's thrusts became erratic, pounding a few more times before a guttural groan signaled his release.

Air finally entered my lungs again as he slowed his rhythm, coming down from his own powerful orgasm.

Jaxon squeezed my full hips. "Do you have any idea what you do to me?"

My breathing was still erratic as I tried to force my lungs to fill with air, but I smiled, closing my eyes, teasing him by tensing my inner walls against him. "I have some idea."

His reaction did not disappoint—a groan was ripped from his throat. "Nothing else exists when I'm with you."

My vision began to clear, and I stared up at him. Nothing but love was shining in his eyes, and I felt my heart squeeze.

He'd become the rock I'd always dreamed having of growing up. I knew he'd be there if I called him for anything. Hannah had tested that theory months ago, but it still rang true today. Hell, he'd beaten the living daylights out of an innocent man on the ice just thinking about Leo causing us any harm. He was selfless above all, giving himself freely, asking for nothing in return. Most importantly, he'd become the father my children had always deserved.

Unable to deny it any longer, I dared to utter those most sacred words out loud, whispering, "I love you."

Sitting up in his arms, both of us groaned as he slipped out of me, and he whispered, "Fuck."

Biting my lip, I teased, "We already did that."

Shaking his head as if to clear it, Jaxon tried again to form a coherent thought. "I'm sorry, I think I'm imagining things. What did you just say?"

"We already did that?" I knew what he wanted to hear, but I enjoyed playing with him.

The last time I'd said those words to a man, they hadn't been returned. This time around, he'd said them first, and I knew from both his words and his actions that Jaxon had meant them every single time. We fit together, body and mind. He brought a sense of peace and comfort to my life that I'd never known before.

"No, smartass," he teased while giving a playful swat to my behind. "Before that."

"Fuck me, Jaxon?" I batted my eyelashes.

Groaning in frustration, he tried again. "After that."

"I love you?"

His eyes flared. "That."

Reaching up into his hair, I pulled his mouth to mine, emphasizing each word between kisses. "I. Love. You. Jaxon."

CHAPTER 22

Jaxon

SHE LOVES ME.

I thought touching, hell, even just seeing Natalie would be the best part of my day. I'd been so very wrong, but in the best possible way. The woman I'd loved my entire adult life—if I was being completely honest—and the mother of my child, had just told me that she loved me back.

This was hands down the best day of my life, but I knew it would only hold that place for a short time. There were so many amazing days ahead that would claim that top spot. The day Natalie agreed to marry me, the day she walked down the aisle and took my name, and most likely, the best of them all, the day our daughter was born.

Discreetly tucking myself back into my pants, I kissed her deeply, taking the time to make her breathless again before pulling back. "God, do I love you."

Natalie was still completely naked while I was fully dressed, but I wasn't sure how long that would last. Just looking at her flushed and bare had my cock stirring again.

Glancing down at the ripped fabric she'd claimed was clothing where it lay discarded on the floor, I smirked. "Sorry."

Following my gaze, she glanced back with a wry look. "No, you're not."

"No, I'm not," I admitted. "I'll buy you a new one, but I can't guarantee it won't meet the same fate."

"If I knew it was going to provoke that kind of reaction, I'd have worn it sooner," she teased with a smile.

"If I recall correctly, I offered to take you on this kitchen island once before."

Cheeks turning pink, her eyes held mine. "I remember."

Nipping her bottom lip with my teeth, I replied, "I'm glad you changed your mind."

"I also remember you making mention of the shower. Or did I mention that one?" she mused.

Groaning against her mouth, I was back to fully hard again. She was intoxicating, and her newfound boldness was enough to throw me over the edge. Our kitchen coupling had been frantic, primal. I'd *needed* her in that moment. This next one, I could take my time and tease her, just as she was teasing me now.

Nuzzling into her neck, I gave a light bite where it connected to her shoulder, eliciting a sharp inhale from her soft, sweet mouth before moving up next to her ear. "The shower was all you, baby."

"I'm all sweaty," she whined, a smile evident in her voice.

"Then we'd better get you all cleaned up."

Natalie's laughter was infectious, and I found myself laughing too. Each day, I fell more in love with her. It almost didn't seem possible to love her more.

Allowing me to ease her off the island, she reached up, rubbing a hand against my cheek, remarking, "I like the stubble. Feels amazing against my skin."

"Well, in that case." I leaned down again to rub my face into the soft, sensitive skin of her neck, relishing the sound of the moan pulled from deep within her throat.

Pushing against my chest, she warned, "Keep doing that, and we won't make it up to the shower."

"Oh, we'll make it to the shower. I don't care if it's round two or round seven," I declared.

Natalie's eyes widened. "Round *seven*?"

"When it comes to you, baby, I could go all day."

Taking a step back, she shook her head. "No, that's just something men say to stroke their egos."

Stalking her, matching her retreat step for step, I teased, "You sure that you want to test that theory?"

She took a shaky breath, unsure. "No?"

"Is that a question or an answer?" I crept closer. "I'm not sure if you've noticed, but I'm a competitor. I play to win. If you say yes, I'll take it as a personal mission to conquer that challenge."

"You're making an awful lot of promises for a man who is still wearing all his clothes," she taunted, a smirk gracing her lips.

Lunging for her in response, she squealed, twisting away from where I reached for her. "It's all fun and games until you're screaming while riding my tongue."

All laughter faded, and she froze, mouth dropping open in shock at my brazen words, but she quickly recovered, countering, "We're going to have to make sure to wash that dirty mouth out with soap while we're in there."

"My mouth is at your command."

Natalie headed toward the back staircase, tapping her wrist, pretending she was wearing a watch. "Time to get to work, Mr. Slate. I don't have all day."

God, hearing her find her voice and tease me was even more of a turn-on than her luscious body.

I pretended to give her a head start, calling out, "When I get to ten, I'm coming up there! One . . . Two . . . Ten!"

Laughter floated down the stairs as I took them two at a time, catching up to her in the bedroom and pulling her into my arms once more.

Natalie pouted. "That wasn't fair!"

Bending down to one of her heaving breasts, I said against her flesh, "Who said anything about playing fair?" The nipple barely an inch from my mouth puckered, anticipating my attention. Done talking, I pulled it deep within my mouth, first sucking hard, then teasing the bud with my teeth.

"Shower, Jaxon," she breathed out.

Reaching down, I ran a hand between her legs. Groaning, I found her ready for me, murmuring against her breast, "Who needs a shower when you're already wet?"

A moan ripped from her throat, so breathy that my cock began to throb. As much as I wanted to tease her, my resolve to go slowly was waning.

She was right. We needed to head to the shower. Taking her mouth once more, I savored the taste of her. She always had that slight hint of mint, but I'd never seen her chewing gum.

Feeling her hands lifting the hem of my T-shirt, I pulled back, raising my arms so she could remove it. She dropped it behind her back before running both hands down my outstretched arms and over my chest, skimming the muscles of my abs, which bunched and contracted against her featherlight touch.

Tracing my Adonis belt with her fingers, she licked her lips, then flashed her eyes to mine. "You know, when you did that mini strip tease for Hannah, I dreamt about *this* for weeks. Damn, your body is gorgeous. It's not fair."

Remembering that night well, I'd been going for maximum shock value, and it would seem that it had worked. I grinned down at her. "I knew you were checking me out."

Rolling her eyes but still smiling, Natalie moved toward the master bathroom. Hearing the water running in the shower, I joined her as promised. Crossing the threshold into the bathroom, I paused in the doorway, leaning against the wall as I drank in the sight of her.

Natalie was in full view behind the glass wall of the shower, hands running through her now wet hair. I could have watched her all day, wet and naked, but heat fogged up the glass, obscuring her from my view.

Hooking my thumbs into my joggers, I removed both those and my boxer briefs in a single motion, kicking off my socks as I made my way to her slick, warm, waiting body.

Joining her under the warm spray of water from overhead, I slid my hands over her ass, gliding until I gripped her hips, groaning at their new fullness. Natalie looked up at me before running her hands through my hair, slicking it away from my forehead.

Taking her mouth with mine, I loved the feel of the warm water cascading between our bodies. Reaching between us, she grabbed my dick possessively, gliding her hand up and down its length effortlessly, the water aiding her smooth movements.

Pulling back from our kiss, she smirked up at me. "This what you had in mind?"

Blinded by the lust-induced haze caused by the ministrations of her hand, I tried to focus on what I'd planned for us once we'd made it up here. Currently, all the blood from my brain was rushing to where she was currently stroking me. As amazing as her wet, warm hand felt, I knew the real thing was better.

Forcing her back against the cool marble wall, I growled, "Not even close."

Gripping her wrist, I pried her fingers loose reluctantly. Taking both her wrists in one hand, I pinned them above her head while keeping my body mere inches from hers. Natalie squirmed, arching, trying to gain contact with my body now that I'd taken away her hands. Keeping my body just out of reach of hers, she moaned, her legs shifting restlessly.

"You want me to touch you, baby?" I crooned.

"Please," she whimpered.

"What my baby wants, my baby gets." Releasing her hands, I dropped to my knees and threw one of her legs over my shoulder in one fluid motion. Her hips jutted forward, trying to make contact where I knew she was aching. Wanting to drive her wild before I devoured my afternoon snack, I rubbed my stubble against the inside of her thigh.

"Oh, God." Her moan was muffled by the rush of water echoing off the shower walls.

Her reaction spurred me on, and I lowered to her anchored leg at knee level, slowly inching my way up, peppering kisses, and rubbing my face against her soft, slick flesh. Feeling her legs begin to shake, I gripped her hips to keep her upright seconds before I dove into her with a long slow stroke of my tongue.

Natalie trembled in my arms, and I knew she was putty in my hands. Pulling back to peer up at her, I gave her a choice. "Fast or slow?"

Her closed eyes popped open suddenly to meet mine. "Excuse me?"

Tightening my grip on her hips, I asked again, "Do you want me to make you come fast or slow, baby?"

Watching her swallow, debating her options, she took a shaky breath before answering, "Fast."

Growling, I resumed my position between her thighs, taking her clit inside my mouth and sucking on it while giving it little flicks with my tongue. I heard her call out, her body tensing moments before it began thrusting against me. Natalie gripped my hair, bucking wildly as she came all over my mouth. Easing her down with long, slow licks, her hips rocked forward each time my tongue passed over her sensitive little nub.

Standing to my full height, I drank her in—flushed face, eyes closed, and breasts rising and falling rapidly with her labored breathing. She'd never looked more beautiful, fully sated as she was right now.

No one else would lay eyes on her this vulnerable ever again. This was my Natalie. *Mine.*

"You still with me?" I asked, using my thumbs to caress her cheekbones.

Nodding, she licked her lips, still forcing out short breaths. "Uh-huh."

"Good, because I'm not done with you yet."

Natalie's eyes snapped open, panicked. "No. I can't take any more."

Drawing her lower lip between my teeth, I gave it a gentle tug, causing her to moan, throwing her head back as I released it. "I think you've got one more in you."

She shook her head weakly. "You're going to kill me, Jaxon."

"You wanted the full shower experience, didn't you?" I teased.

"Jaxon," she groaned.

Leaning in to nuzzle her neck, I asked against her soft flesh, "Is that a 'Fuck me, Jaxon'? Or a 'Fuck off, Jaxon'?" She only moaned in response, so I pulled back to make eye contact, prompting, "Use your words, Natalie."

Closing her eyes tight, she whispered, "Fuck me, Jaxon."

"Excellent choice."

A shaky laugh left Natalie's lips as she opened her eyes again, and I tugged her further into the giant shower toward the marble bench. Positioning myself behind her as she faced the bench, I commanded, "Kneel."

Glancing behind me, she obeyed, placing her knees onto the bench and facing the wall. Taking her hands, I positioned them—palms flat against the marbled wall before her. Using my knee, I forced her legs further apart, coming flush behind her, reaching around to cup one breast.

Natalie arched into my touch as I bent slightly at the knees, entering her from behind, groaning into her neck. "Say the words again, Natalie," I demanded, deep inside her.

Looking back, her eyelids heavy, pupils dilated, a corner of her lip twitched up. "I love you."

Pulling almost fully out, I slammed home hard, causing her to scream. "Say it again."

That minx clenched her pussy around my cock in response, causing my free hand to slam against the wall next to hers, gritting my teeth against the intense pleasure it sent through my body.

Jaw clenched, I forced out, "Again."

Whimpering, she said it once more, "I love you."

"Fuck, I love you," I forced out, slamming into her over and over. Her screams punctuated each thrust, this angle proving almost too much for her to handle. Pulling her body flush with mine, I continued my onslaught until her head fell back against my shoulder. Her body shuddered in release before I finally allowed myself to give in to the orgasm I'd been holding at bay since I'd stuck my head between her thighs. Two more strong pumps into her screaming body, and I exploded inside her tight pussy, biting her shoulder to muffle the sound as my knees nearly buckled beneath me with the force of my climax.

This woman was going to be the death of me, but I would die a happy man.

Our bodies still connected, I held her as our breathing slowed enough for Natalie to force out, "Did you *bite* me?"

Licking the mark I'd left behind, I smiled. "Maybe."

Turning her head to look back at me, she was incredulous. "*Maybe?*"

My laughter echoed off the shower walls before I teased, "Don't girls dig that whole vampire thing?"

Reaching up, she traced the teeth marks with her finger. "You're terrible."

"And you're all dirty. Come on, let's clean you up."

Pulling out of her warm body, I helped her down from her perch on the bench.

She turned and sized me up warily. "That better not mean something else. I'm pretty sure my life flashed before my eyes on that last one."

"That only means I'm doing something right." I winked.

Shaking her head, she walked toward the warm spray from the showerhead. Taking a seat on the bench, I merely watched as she soaped up her body. I marveled that this woman had given herself over entirely to my care, body and soul. I'd promised her we were done—for now at least—so staying five feet away while she was still naked was for her own protection. I was already contemplating taking her again. I would never get enough of her.

Only once Natalie had stepped out, wrapping her body in a fluffy white towel, did I allow myself to venture forth, giving myself a quick wash with her flowery soap. I smiled to myself with the knowledge that I would be smelling like her for the rest of the day.

Closing my eyes, I let the water cascade over my body, replaying the morning's events in my mind.

What a welcome home.

Sitting on the living room floor—assembling what seemed like the tenth item of baby gear contained within the boxes in the front hallway—I heard the telltale sounds of the kids returning home from school. Door bursting open, overlapping voices, door slamming closed, then running. I'd missed them, so I'd made sure fresh cookies were waiting for them in the kitchen.

Natalie could be heard greeting them in the kitchen and handing out cookies, mere moments before they burst into the living room.

It was Jameson's voice I heard first. "Jaxon! You're back!"

Pushing off the ground to sit on the couch, I took in his smiling face, grateful that Leo's visit didn't appear to have any lingering effects. Reaching out a fist for him to bump, I responded, "Good to see you too, buddy."

Beau crawled right up next to me on the couch, reaching up to grab the sides of my face in his chubby toddler hands before touching my nose. "You got a boo boo?"

He made it sound simple when it was so complex, but I was grateful for his innocence. Nodding, I confirmed, "Yeah, little man."

Leaning in, he placed a sloppy kiss on the bridge of my nose, declaring, "All better now, Jaxon!"

"Thanks." I couldn't help but chuckle.

Amelia surveyed the mess I'd made in the living room, remarking, "Grandmama went a little crazy." Seeming so much older than her almost ten years, my only wish was that I would be able to take over the burden of caring for her mom so that she would feel comfortable enough to go back to being a kid.

"I'm sure she loves all of you very much, and it's hard to be so far away." My words were genuine. Not knowing the woman personally, I was forever indebted to her for not only helping to get Natalie out of a bad marriage, but for stepping in to help her keep her kids now that there was a threat from her own son. I knew from experience how difficult it was to be apart from this particular family, and I could only imagine how much their grandparents missed them.

Natalie came in from the kitchen, holding a cup of tea in her hands, stopping behind the couch.

Jameson looked over to her. "Did you ask him yet, Mom?"

Feeling my eyebrows draw together, I looked between them. "Ask me what?"

Natalie shifted on her feet, blushing. Damn, she was adorable when she was nervous. "Well, um, the kids and I were wondering if, maybe . . ."

"Maybe what, Natalie?"

Jameson jumped in, "We want you to move in! Please, say yes!"

Did he say move in? Like, as in, live here? Turning to Natalie, I asked, "Whose idea was this?"

Amelia didn't let her answer, volunteering, "We are a family. You take care of us and Mom, so you should be here with us."

Natalie clarified, "The kids called a family meeting, and we all agreed it would make us happy if you moved in. But . . ." She pointedly looked at each kid before continuing, "We also discussed that it was okay for you to say no since you do live just next door."

Of course I wanted to be here with them. They were constantly on my mind, and I missed them desperately when I wasn't around. However, there was still one factor to consider. "What does Uncle Liam think about this?"

"Uncle Liam wasn't consulted," came a voice from behind us. Almost as if the mention of his name was enough to summon his presence, there stood Liam, scowling as per usual. "But it would appear I've been outvoted."

"Liam . . ." Natalie warned.

"I don't want to cause any problems. As you said, I live next door and can come over any time you need or want me," I offered, standing to face both Natalie and Liam.

Natalie leveled Liam with a glare before responding, "Liam can hide in his basement cave if he doesn't like it. Or maybe go back to Belleston if his attitude doesn't improve."

The last thing I needed was to drive a wedge between them, leaving Natalie to resent me later. "Like Amelia said, we are a family, but I'm not going to tear apart the family you already have. With how much I'm gone, you need Liam here. I'm a big enough man to admit that."

Liam grumbled something under his breath, and Natalie addressed him again. "I thought *someone* apologized last week and said they were Team Natalie." Tapping her chin in feigned thought, she mused, "Now, who was that again?"

Deciding to let them hash this out, I watched their exchange.

Liam sighed. "That was me."

A smile graced her lips, and she knew she had him, going in for the kill. "Are you really gonna let Jaxon be the better man? Can your ego handle that?"

"It's not about ego, Natalie," he declared.

Natalie rolled her eyes. "Of course it is. Jaxon can admit that we need you around, but you can't admit that maybe we also need him around?"

"It's not the same," Liam countered.

"You're right. It's not the same. You're my big brother, and your role is very different from Jaxon's in our lives. Your vision has been clouded by your need to protect me, but he's been good for us. You're not being replaced. We still need you, but our lives are changing, and we need to adapt."

The scowl never left Liam's face—I couldn't recall a time I'd seen the man genuinely smile—but he nodded, gruffly responding, "Fine. He can move in."

"And you'll be civil to Jaxon?" Natalie pressed.

Liam crossed his arms. "Well, we're not going to sit around braiding each other's hair if that's what you mean."

"Liam . . ."

"As long as you're happy and the kids are happy, I'll do my best not to cause any problems," he grumbled.

"Good." Natalie turned to me. "Now that that's settled, what do you say?"

Looking at her kids' three pairs of brown eyes trained on me, I asked, "Are you sure you want me here *all* the time?"

"Yes!" came the chorus of small voices.

Smiling, I responded, "Well, then how could I say no?"

"You can't!" Jameson claimed proudly.

"Then I guess it's settled, buddy."

He pumped a fist into the air, shouting, "Yes!"

Beau jumped up onto the couch and then into my arms, giggling. Liam had left the room, but I looked to Natalie. "Are we really doing this?"

The smile she gave me stole my breath from my lungs as she leaned in close enough to whisper, "Well, I do sleep better when you're around, so it's purely selfish of me."

Smirking, I retorted, "Oh, I see. I'm just your personal body pillow. Got it." She laughed, and my heart squeezed in my chest at the sound, so I added with a mock salute, "Ready for duty."

Stealing a quick kiss from my lips, she pulled back. "See? I knew I liked you."

The rest of the afternoon and evening were spent building more baby gear with Jameson's help while Natalie and Amelia sorted the baby clothes, got them organized, and started to wash the smallest ones. Beau played with his wooden trains on the table while we worked.

It was domestic bliss at its finest. It was everything that was missing in my life, and I hadn't even realized it.

CHAPTER 23

Natalie

"Girls' night in!" The familiar words from Hannah brought a smile to my lips. Our monthly tradition was still going strong after years of friendship, although slightly modified now that I wasn't drinking and currently the size of an elephant.

On tonight's agenda was a movie marathon consisting of some of my favorite rom-coms. We were all aware that this might be our last one before Charlotte joined our girl gang as an honorary junior member.

The fireplace was roaring, keeping us warm as we weathered likely the last winter snowstorm, seeing as it was nearly the end of March. School had already been called off for the kids the following day, so they would be staying up too late with whatever shenanigans Jaxon had cooked up for them. He was always thinking of new activities to keep them occupied indoors while the weather was still bad. I knew he was itching for the weather to turn so they could have outdoor fun.

I'd been concerned about Jaxon moving in—potentially disrupting the cadence we'd developed since moving back to Hartford—but as always, he'd proved to be an overachiever. His transition from daily visitation to cohabitation had been seamless. A month in, it was as if he'd lived with us forever. Liam had loosened up a tad, at least managing to make family dinners and game nights, so long as Amy was there to act as a buffer.

Feet propped up as I rested on the chaise lounge, I snuggled into my blanket while we decided which movie to watch first. The debate was currently whether to go with one that featured an enemies-to-lovers theme or one with a second chance romance.

"I vote for the second chance romance. There are two gorgeous men to drool over in that one, not just one." Hannah declared.

Amy wasn't having it. "Nope, if I'm forced to watch this lovey-dovey crap, at least I can watch them attempt to kill each other first. Minimal mushiness."

After almost fifteen years, I was accustomed to their differing viewpoints and knew there was no changing either of their minds regarding their perception of love, so I stated, "You know we are going to watch both, right?"

That did nothing to settle the dispute, and they began talking over each other, trying to explain why their choice was the better for our first viewing.

Jaxon walked in, carrying two bowls of popcorn, handing me one with a light kiss on the cheek, then placing the other on the coffee table for the girls to share.

Hannah stopped arguing when she noticed Jaxon, dressed in plaid flannel pajama pants and a fitted white T-shirt. "Hey there, Jaxon."

Nodding, he acknowledged her. "Hey, Hannah."

"Great game last night."

"Thanks, it was a team effort." You'd never know this man was one of the most talented players in the league. Humble didn't begin to describe him.

"Settle something for us?" she asked.

"Sure."

"If you had to choose, would you go with a movie where the main characters hate each other before falling in love or one where it's more of a second chance at love?"

Jaxon had zero hesitation, answering, "Oh, hands down, enemies-to-lovers. It's usually comedy gold."

Hannah groaned. "You're no help."

Amy reached out to high-five him. "I like you more and more by the day."

Jaxon turned his attention back to me. "You couldn't break the tie?"

Shrugging, I explained, "There was no point. We're going to watch them both, and I don't need one of them pretending to be mad at me for half the night."

Understanding, Jaxon shot me a sultry look, the one he reserved especially for the bedroom. "I'll get the real answer of which one you would have chosen later. I have my ways."

Blushing, I changed the subject. "What are you up to with the kids tonight?"

"We've got a fort set up in Jameson's room. It'll have to do until we get the treehouse built this spring."

That had been Jaxon's birthday gift to Jameson a few weeks back—plans for a treehouse in the backyard. He had earned major brownie points with that one. They couldn't wait for the crew to come and begin construction.

"Well, have fun. Don't keep them up too late."

"You got it." Turning to Hannah and Amy, he added, "Same goes for you two. Don't keep her up too late. She barely gets enough sleep as it is."

"And who's fault is that?" I countered.

Dropping one more kiss to my lips, he chuckled. "Guilty. And not even a little bit sorry."

Jaxon headed up the main stairs toward the kids' bedrooms, and I could feel Hannah's eyes boring into the back of my head. Mildly annoyed, I asked, "What?"

Hannah pretended to act innocent when she was anything but. "Oh, I don't know. Just over here wondering what Jaxon's doing over here in his pajamas while we're having our girls' night."

Amy took a sip of tonight's signature cocktail, a creamy mint chocolate concoction. "Oh, didn't you hear? He lives here now."

Hannah's mouth dropped open, seconds before she shrieked, "*What?*"

"For a month," Amy added, smirking. She had always enjoyed riling Hannah up.

"A *month*? What's next? You get married and don't tell me?"

"Don't be so dramatic, Hannah." Annoyance filled my tone.

Hannah shook her head, holding up her hand. "No, I'm not being dramatic. This is a major life change. Plus, I have to live vicariously through you. You can't be holding out on me at this point. Shacking up and procreating with a hockey player? Where do I sign up?"

"You know your dad will never let that happen," I argued.

There was a wicked gleam in her eye. "Doesn't mean I can't keep trying. Eventually, I'll break one of them."

"Can't wait to see Ace have a stroke when you do."

Hannah huffed. "It's his own fault. You can't raise three daughters around the game and then tell them they can't date one. It's like he's daring me to do it. I want it even more because it's *forbidden*."

"Allison and Chrissy didn't seem to have an issue finding non-hockey players," I countered.

"Yeah, well, my sisters are boring. Their husbands are also boring. I've been around long enough to know those hockey players know how to *fuck*." She stood up, thrusting her hips for effect.

"Hannah!" Heat crept up my cheeks.

"Oh, so you're saying Jaxon's a lousy lay?" she challenged, taking a seat.

Looking around wildly to make sure none of the kids, Jaxon, or God forbid, Liam were within earshot, I lowered my voice before rushing out, "I didn't say that."

"So, then you're confirming what I already know. It's like those muscles give them magical sex powers. And don't even get me started on their protective instincts. They protect what's theirs." Hannah made a show of fake fanning herself.

She had a point. Being with Jaxon often separated my soul from my body, and he had beaten Trey Carr almost to the point of unconsciousness thinking about Leo being a danger to our family. But I couldn't enable her. I knew how Ace felt about his daughters—and me, by extension—being dated by the players in his locker room.

Trying to cool her jets, I offered, "What Jaxon and I have is more than sexual."

Amy grabbed a handful of popcorn, enjoying the show, as Hannah accused, "You wouldn't even have the emotional relationship with Jaxon if it weren't for the sexual one."

Damn her.

I couldn't argue with that point. Knowing deep down that I would never have fallen in love with Jaxon if I hadn't accidentally gotten pregnant didn't make me feel all warm and fuzzy inside. Those old insecurities began to rear their ugly head, but I pushed them back down. Who cared how we found our way to each other? What we found as a result was real.

"Look," I began. "What we have may be unconventional, but there's one thing I do know. When Leo showed up—" Both Hannah and Amy made a move to cross themselves to ward off the evil, and I laughed, the mood sufficiently lightened. "I realized how different they are. When Jaxon stood up to him and told him he'd be lucky to be the kids' father, I knew. He was the one. My life may have taken a really fucked up path to bring us together, but we finally found each other. I'm ready to be done with all the bullshit."

Hannah softened. "I'm happy for you, Nat. I really am. But is it so wrong to want what you have? Maybe minus the knocked-up part. I'm all set over here."

"No, it's not wrong. I'm only pointing out that there are millions of men out there outside of the twenty-four currently rostered on the Comets—only ten of which are available at present. I'm sure out of those millions, you can find one that knows what they're doing in bed."

"Haven't found one yet," she grumbled. Amy snorted, causing Hannah to turn her focus on her. "Oh, don't get me started with you."

Amy put her hands up in defense. "Hey, I'm not interested. That's my choice."

"You can't let one bad experience ruin the rest of your life. I should know." I offered.

"That's for me to decide. I'm happy with my life," Amy declared.

Hannah and I shared a look. Amy'd had a bad experience in college that had shaped how she viewed relationships—sexual or otherwise—with men from that point on. It was a long story, and one for another day.

Yawning, I covered my mouth before returning to the task at hand. "Are we watching movies or what?"

"Fine, but I know you would have chosen the second chance romance," Hannah accused, narrowing her eyes.

"Start the movie, Hannah."

She was right. Once upon a time, it had been my favorite trope, probably because I'd longed for a do-over. Now that I was living it, I didn't need to see it played out on screen quite so desperately. My ex was far behind me in the rear-view mirror, and I was more than ready to move on with my handsome new hero.

I'd finally found what I'd been searching for since I was thirteen and had picked up my first romance novel—my happily ever after.

It was about damn time.

CHAPTER 24

Jaxon

MARCH TURNED INTO APRIL, which meant only one thing in the hockey world—playoffs.

The entire season led to this point, and all eyes were on the Comets. When I'd been drafted number one overall almost ten years ago, there had been an expectation that I would be the cornerstone needed to get the team back on track, headed toward winning a championship. Getting that top pick in the draft meant that your team did poorly the previous year, so everyone knew it would be a process that took time to build back up.

But here we were, ten years later, and we'd come close, but never close enough. A professional hockey championship was one of the most challenging championships to win in sports, requiring sixteen wins to claim it. Sometimes it seemed fucking impossible, yet, somehow, every year, one team managed to win it. That team just hadn't been us.

This year, we were at the top of the division and second overall in the conference, so we'd secured home-ice advantage for now and hopefully going forward, but it would depend on how the other series turned out.

You could feel the energy inside the locker room as we inched closer and closer to the date circled on the calendar as the first official day of the playoffs.

That wasn't the only date circled on my calendar. April also brought Charlie's due date, and I'd be lying if I said I wasn't on edge.

I wasn't afraid to become a father—I'd grown into that role with my daughter's older siblings—but I was terrified that something would happen while I was traveling with the team. What if I wasn't there when Natalie needed me the most? The thought paralyzed me, so I shook it off, putting positive thoughts into the universe. I *would* be there.

Training was rigorous as we barreled quickly toward Game 1 of the first round against the Indianapolis Speed. Team meetings, workouts, on-ice practices, medical evaluations by the training staff, and film review filled our days. All of this kept me away from home more than I liked, but it was temporary. As long as I made it home in time to tuck the kids into bed and spend a few hours with Natalie, I could manage the grind over the next *hopefully* two months.

The day before Game 1, Coach took it easier on us, knowing we needed a slight rest before the gauntlet laid before us. We all knew the next two months would be Hell. Our bodies would be pushed to the brink, and we'd lose guys to injury along the way. Our mental mindset would be just as important as our physical stamina.

Getting stretched out and massaged after practice, Cal was laid out on the table next to mine. Even though this was supposed to help ease the tension in my body, my mind was racing between my current personal life and my responsibilities to the team, so it was counterproductive. I'd never been wound so tight.

Drawing me from my thoughts was Cal's voice. "Hey, Jaxon?"

Turning my head to look at him as the therapist worked on my thighs, I responded, "What's up?" Cal paused for a minute, almost unsure, so I prompted, "Spit it out, man."

Clearing his throat, he spoke. "I only wanted to make sure everything was all right with you. Aside from the fight, you haven't been acting like yourself. I get you're done with the nightlife, and that's cool, but you won't even go out to dinner with us anymore on the road. You shut yourself in your room. I'm worried about you."

A pang of guilt hit me—this was one of my best friends, and he was in the dark about the biggest part of my life. He thought something was wrong with me because he was right—I hadn't been going out. I'd been video chatting with Natalie and the kids in my room because *they* were my priority now. Charlie would be here sooner rather than later, and I knew the time was coming when I wouldn't have to keep her existence a secret any longer.

Praying he would forgive me when he found out the real reason why I'd been distant, I went with a blanket excuse. "Sorry, brother. Been dealing with some family stuff."

Concern filled his face, and I felt even worse about my lie of omission. "Aw, shit. I'm sorry. I had no idea. Is it Braxton? Your parents? Anything you need, I'm here."

"No, really, it's no big deal. Don't worry about it."

Cal's face was full of doubt. He wasn't buying it entirely, but dropped it. "Well, the offer stands. I mean it—anything you need."

"Thanks, man. I appreciate it."

We finished our rub-downs in silence, but the guilt still nagged at me. How much longer would Natalie insist we keep our daughter and our relationship a secret? Until Charlie was born? Until the season was over? I didn't want to push her because I knew she'd been through Hell, but I wanted the world to know she was mine. I didn't give a damn what anyone else thought of us—they were our lives, not theirs. Knowing I'd promised her as much time as she needed, I just had to wait. She'd have to be ready eventually, right? It wasn't like we would send Charlie off to kindergarten having had no contact with the outside world.

Throwing on a newly printed Comets playoffs shirt marked with the year and my number, I sat down at my locker to prepare for the final film session of the day before I could go home to my family. Cal plopped down next to me, also getting ready to spend our afternoon game planning how best to beat Indy.

Grabbing my phone from my locker to check if I had any messages, my heart stopped when I saw multiple bubbles on my lock screen indicating text messages.

Natalie: *Feeling a little bit off. Amy's going to take me in to get checked out. Probably nothing to worry about.*

Amy: *Hey. Don't panic, but you should probably meet us over at Hartford General. They're admitting Natalie.*

Cursing, I noticed the difference between time stamps on their messages. Natalie's was three hours ago, and Amy's was two. Anything could have happened in that amount of time. My heart pounded in my chest as I threw on my sneakers, grabbed my keys, and sprinted out of the locker room.

Behind me, I heard Cal mutter, "Yeah, definitely no big deal."

Charlotte Rose Slate was born at 5:23 AM on April 12th, and my world was forever changed. The whole experience had been raw and real, terrifying and exhilarating, all at the same time. I could honestly say I'd never felt more alive.

She was perfect.

Our Charlie girl was a raven-haired beauty, just like her mother and sister. I took great care to count each of her ten fingers and toes. She weighed in at a touch over seven pounds and felt feather-light in my arms.

Then, there was Natalie.

God, she was incredible. She was so strong, and the realization instantly struck me that I would never be able to repay her for giving me this most precious gift.

Looking at her now, my heart was bursting with love for this woman. Her skin was shiny, still coated in a thin sheen of sweat. Her dark hair was pulled up into something that had at one time resembled a bun but now had multiple pieces falling out in a chaotic mess. She'd never looked more beautiful.

Natalie had demanded that I go with Charlie for her vital checks while the doctors fixed her up. Now that they were done, I made my way back over to the side of her hospital bed, carrying our daughter. I had whiplash from how noisy and animated this room had been barely half an hour ago to how calm it was now.

Charlie was asleep in my arms, but I couldn't tear my gaze away from her perfect little face. I marveled at my beautiful daughter, whispering, afraid to wake her, "Did we really make this?"

Natalie laughed lightly, and I let my favorite sound wash over me. "Well, your contribution was certainly more fun than mine, but yes."

If she was joking, that meant she must be feeling well, so I relaxed a bit, teasing her back, "So, what you're saying is . . . It's like that class project where one partner does most of the work, and the other one cashes in on the A?"

"Nailed it."

Gently placing Charlie in her mother's arms, I bent down to brush a quick kiss on her lips. "Thank you."

Still in a playful mood, she smiled. "Eh, it's not like I had anything better going on today." Staring down at our sweet girl, she added, "You know, I think she looks a little bit like you."

"No, she's way too beautiful," I protested.

Peering up at me, she countered, "Are you saying you're not a beautiful man? I recall ordering top-shelf hunky superstar athlete genes. I may have to return this package."

Laughing—loving how light and free she was, knowing I'd brought her out of her shell—I acquiesced, "Well, we can't have that, but I think she has hints of both Amelia and Beau."

Smiling that brilliant smile, she nodded. "I'll allow it." Unable to hide the yawn that came upon me suddenly, sympathy filled her warm brown eyes. "You should go home and sleep. You've been up all night and have a big game tonight."

This woman. She was just as sleep-deprived as I was, and undoubtedly physically exhausted, but she was worried about me. I, on the other hand, had barely thought about what lay beyond this hospital room since entering it yesterday afternoon. She was trying to take care of me when I should be taking care of her.

"I'm not leaving."

Hearing the determination in my voice, she frowned, chiding, "Jaxon. You *have* to go to the game tonight. You're not the first nor the last Comets player to have a baby during the season."

"I'll go to the game, but I'm not going home to sleep while the two of you are here alone."

Natalie tried to reason with me. "I'm going to sleep, so there's no point in you staying. Go home. Rest. I'll be right here when you get back after the game."

"I can sleep here while you sleep." She wasn't going to win this battle.

"That's not a great idea, Jaxon. If you stay here, nurses will be coming in and out every hour to check on me. If you go home, you can get a solid seven hours and be more than ready to play."

"I said no, Natalie." I kept my voice calm, knowing that if I raised my voice, she would feel like I was trying to control her. I didn't want to trigger her on such a happy day.

There was something in her eyes that I couldn't quite nail down—almost like she wanted me to stay but also wanted me to leave. I'd promised myself I would be the dependable, caring partner she hadn't had before, but I could tell she didn't know how to respond to that in certain situations. Regardless, I wasn't going anywhere until I absolutely had to.

Sighing, she shrugged. "Don't think I won't say, 'I told you so.'"

Reaching out, I touched a hand to the foot that had escaped the blankets surrounding Charlie's tiny body. "It's a deal."

Gathering up blankets and pillows left on the reclining chair by the nursing staff, I began building a nest for myself. My six-foot frame would be a squeeze in this chair, but my discomfort was nothing compared to what Natalie had endured bringing our daughter into the world.

As I drifted off to sleep, having been awake for twenty-four hours straight, I heard her mutter, "Stubborn man."

I will always be stubborn when it comes to putting you first. Accept it.

CHAPTER 25

Natalie

"Knock knock! Aunt Amy's here!" Amy's voice floated through the doorway as she entered the hospital room mid-afternoon, arms bursting with gift bags and balloons.

"You know we will be home tomorrow. You didn't need to bring all this here." I gestured to the items she carried.

Dropping everything on the long bench couch situated along the large window, she came over to hug me. "Don't you dare try to take this from me. This is my first time visiting my best friend in the hospital after she's had a baby. Let me enjoy it." Looking around the room, she asked, "Where is my new honorary niece? I mean, rumor has it this one isn't named after me, so I don't know why I bothered to come all the way down here."

"I fully expect your firstborn to be named after me, just so you know."

Amy threw me a look. "Well, then. The joke's on you, lady. No babies happening over here. Ever."

"Maybe someday you'll change your mind."

Shaking her head, she was adamant. "Nope. You can keep popping them out and satisfying my baby fix. Then eventually, your kids will get older and have kids, and I can play grandma with them. See? I've thought this plan out."

Knowing better than to argue this point, I conceded, "All right. Aunt Amy for life."

"Don't you forget it. Now, where is that baby?"

"They took her to do tests in the nursery," I explained.

"You finally scare Jaxon away?"

Rolling my eyes, I couldn't help but laugh. "He wouldn't let her out of his sight. So, I'm sure he's down the hall watching through the glass of the nursery window."

"As Hannah would say, protective instincts." Taking a step back, she surveyed me from head to toe. "How are you feeling?"

"Tired, sore, the usual."

Almost as if on cue, Jaxon's voice filtered in from the doorway. "You haven't been messing around and not taking your pain meds on schedule, have you? They don't hand out medals for suffering in silence."

"Speak of the devil." A smile crept onto my face. Jaxon had not only been overprotective of Charlie, but me as well. Having a partner who cared so much about my well-being made me feel cherished. I didn't deserve him.

Amy saw the bassinet he was pushing and left my side. "I've been waiting for you!" Reaching inside, she scooped up Charlotte, cooing, "Well, hello, beautiful."

"Hey, Amy." Jaxon chuckled.

Amy responded, not even sparing him a glance, "You're not the star today. This sweet baby girl is."

Moving the bassinet on wheels to the corner of the room, he admitted, "Fair enough. She is a showstopper."

Swaying from side to side with Charlie in her arms, she remarked, "You know, I couldn't properly judge your handiwork until just now, Jaxon, but

I have to say, I was right. This is one gorgeous baby. Even if she isn't named after me."

Jaxon glanced toward the mountain of bags and balloons, asking, "Jeez, Amy, did you buy out the entire gift shop?"

She nodded to a single brown bag in the bunch. "There might be a little something in there for you."

Plucking the brown bag off the bench, his eyes widened. "You brought me food?"

"Figured if I was tagging you out, it was the least I could do."

Opening the container, he found a mountain of pasta and grilled chicken—his usual pre-game carb and protein combo. Sinking into the recliner, he sniffed deeply, whispering, "You're a Godsend, Amy."

"Yes, I know, I'm an amazing friend. Had lots of years of practice. Now, eat up so you can go win a game and dedicate it to Charlie."

"Yes, ma'am."

One thing I'd learned living with a professional hockey player was how much they ate. They burned so many calories that they even ate during intermissions at the games. Combine that with the water weight lost due to significant sweating, and they dropped anywhere between five and ten pounds during a game. Talk about a high-intensity workout.

Jaxon sat down in the recliner, practically inhaling the giant container of food.

Checking the wall clock, it was nearing four o'clock, and I knew the game tonight was at seven. Jaxon was almost done with his massive meal, so I prodded softly, "Babe, you have to go."

Exhaling, he stood, throwing out the takeout food container. "I know." Stopping in front of Amy, he took Charlie into his arms, placing a kiss on her head. "Daddy's got to go to work, but I'll be back later. Be good for Mommy."

Handing her back to Amy, he came over to my bed, leaning down to kiss me, lingering for a moment as I sighed into his mouth. Pulling back slightly, he leaned his forehead against mine, breathing, "I wish I didn't have to go."

My heart went out to him. It did. I knew what it was like to have to leave your babies behind, and it had broken my heart every single time. It felt like a piece of you was missing—a phantom limb you could feel but couldn't see.

"It's only for a few hours, and you can make it up to me by changing all the diapers when you get back."

That loosened him up a bit, and Jaxon forced out a laugh. "Deal. I love you."

"I love you too. Now, go win. There will be one extra Comets fan pulling for you tonight. Make her proud."

Rising to his full height, Jaxon gave Charlie one more soft kiss before forcing his feet to carry him out of the room. Watching as he left, a piece of my heart felt like it was leaving with him. Jarring me out of my thoughts was the soft cry coming from Charlie, held in Amy's arms.

Smiling, I remarked, "You forget how tiny their cries are when they're this little."

Amy laughed. "Oh yeah, she's got nothing on Beau's eardrum-bursting screams."

"She's probably hungry."

The moment Charlie was placed in my arms, she immediately began rooting, trying to nurse.

Amy shook her head. "Girl knows what she wants. Dad got fed, so she got jealous and wanted next dibs. Then, we'll make sure to feed Mom." She winked at me.

Amy was the best friend I could have ever asked for. She looked out for me even when I got in my own damn way, including when it came to letting Jaxon into our lives. No doubt I owed her everything, and I feared I'd never be able to repay her for all that she'd done for me and my kids.

Showered, fed, and feeling more like myself than I had in months, Amy and I settled in for the start of the Comets' playoff game while Charlie snoozed away.

The pre-game commentary was in full swing when a knock sounded on the door. Expecting another nurse check, I was startled when a girl in her early twenties wearing a Comets-branded polo shirt entered the room. Immediately, panic pierced my heart that, somehow, the organization had found out about Charlie and her connection to their star player.

Smiling, she introduced herself. "Hi, I'm Madison, and I'm with the Connecticut Comets Foundation."

Amy, having sensed my panic, took the lead. "And how may we help you, Madison?"

That's when I realized there was a package in her hands. She explained, "In celebration of the first round of the playoffs, the Connecticut Comets Foundation has sent over some gear for our littlest hockey fans here in the maternity ward."

"Well, look at that. Charlie made it just in time. We were getting ready to watch the game ourselves." Amy smiled at the girl.

Walking to my bedside, Madison handed me the package containing a Comets-branded blanket and a tiny onesie that read: *Tiniest Comets Fan*.

Finally finding my voice now that I knew the threat to our anonymity was imagined, I smiled, touching the items. "Thank you."

The girl clearly enjoyed her job, smiling ear to ear. "It's my pleasure. Enjoy the game! Congrats on your new addition."

Amy walked over, looking over the items. "Well, how about that? Too bad you're not on social media, or we would have to post her with all her new gear. Although, something is missing."

Feeling my brow scrunch up in confusion, I asked, "What's missing?"

Walking over to the bags on the bench, she plucked one out. "A little something from Amber and Hannah."

Taking the bag from her hands, I discarded the tissue paper, pulling out a teeny tiny Comets jersey with Jaxon's twenty-three on the back—the nameplate reading Daddy instead of Slate. Having spent over a decade attending Comets games, I'd seen all the players' kids wearing similar jerseys. Picturing them against the glass pre-game, excited to see their dads and making special memories, brought tears to my eyes. Charlie was going to have everything I'd always wanted for my children—a loving father and a place where she belonged. Charlie was already a part of the Comets community at barely twelve-hours old.

The game started, and I watched as the man I loved took the ice with his teammates. I would never tire of watching his powerful strides, incredible stick-handling skills, or almost uncanny ability to know exactly where his teammates were at all times—even when they were behind him. But something was off tonight, and looking toward the sleeping baby in the bassinet, I had a sneaking suspicion of why.

He was making careless mistakes that cost us, allowing Indianapolis to score a goal early, setting us behind. By the end of the second, we were still losing, and the team seemed disjointed. Their star being out of whack caused a ripple effect, putting the entire team out of sync.

My phone buzzed on the rolling tray table, and I picked it up to check the incoming message.

Hannah: *Your boy's looking like shit out there tonight. What did you do to him? Keep him up all night having a baby or something?*

Natalie: *Something like that. Stubborn ass wouldn't go home to take a nap.*

Hannah: *Guess it's a good thing it's a best-of-seven series.*

Natalie: *Thanks for the jersey for Charlie.*

Hannah: *It's a rite of passage for any hockey kid. Can't wait to take her to her first game!*

As if she could sense that we were talking about her, Charlie began to stir, whimpering. I stood to pick her up, shushing her gently while bouncing her a little so that her eyes began to drift shut once again. Holding her in my arms, a feeling of peace flowed through my body. She and her daddy were the missing puzzle pieces in my life. They made it complete.

Hearing the noises of the game coming from the wall-mounted TV, I smiled. Hannah was right. Charlie was a hockey kid now, and I knew if Jaxon had his way, the older kids would be as well.

The only step that remained was conquering my fears about going public with my relationship with Jaxon and the daughter we'd kept completely secret. Now that she was here, I knew this bubble we'd created couldn't last forever, but a part of me wished it could.

We were so happy. I didn't want to risk anything changing that.

CHAPTER 26

Jaxon

DESPITE DROPPING GAME 1 to Indianapolis the day Charlie had been born, we'd rallied back to win four straight games, clinching the best-of-seven series against the Speed and earning a few days of rest while waiting for our next opponent to be decided.

I'd spent those extra days getting to know my daughter. Currently, my favorite place was the reclining rocker in her room, while I rocked her to sleep against my chest.

My heart was so full it was close to bursting. This was the family I'd always imagined but never thought I could have. I was the luckiest man alive.

Our second-round opponents turned out to be the New Orleans Gators, and we maintained home ice for the series, which meant almost another whole week before we had to hit the road again. We split the two games played in Hartford, so we headed to New Orleans with the series tied at one apiece for Game 3.

Cal had been distant since the day I'd run out of the locker room to be by Natalie's side. He was my best friend, and I was struggling, knowing

I'd hurt him by closing myself off. There was an idea I'd had as I'd rocked Charlie to sleep right before we'd left on this four-day road trip. It was firmly in a gray area regarding the promise I'd made to Natalie, but I couldn't alienate my best friend any longer.

Coach gave us the day off between Games 3 and 4, so we had a free day in New Orleans. Heading to Cal's room after breakfast, I knocked on the door.

After a few minutes, Cal opened the door but hesitated when he saw me on the other side, pulling on the back of his neck. "Uh, hey, man."

Yeah, this was uncomfortable. We'd always had an easy relationship, and I knew it was my fault that things were strained. Shoving both hands into the pockets of my jeans, I rocked back on my heels. "Hey. You got some free time this afternoon?"

Cal looked wary, and I couldn't blame him. I'd been short with him more than once since my life had been completely turned upside down. "I don't know . . ."

Extending the olive branch, I offered, "I know things have been weird for a while between us, and I can't tell you exactly what's been going on. I'd like for you to come somewhere with me this afternoon. It might give you a little insight into what's been going on with me, but I need you to promise me something first."

His face held traces of intrigue mixed with apprehension. "What?"

"That you observe and don't ask any questions."

Blowing out a breath, Cal looked toward the ceiling. "Fine. Just let me know what time, and I'll meet you in the lobby."

"Let's say noon. Thanks, man."

"Whatever." He closed the door right in my face.

I deserved that. I'd been a lousy friend, but I was trying now. I just needed him to meet me halfway.

A few minutes before noon, I ventured down to the hotel lobby.

Word always got around about which hotel we used in various cities, and it was crawling with Comets fans. Stopping here and there, I signed autographs and took a few selfies with those who had traveled the distance to see us play.

In addition to fans, there were always the puck bunnies—the girls who made it their life's mission to sleep with a hockey player. It made getting laid easy when you wanted to, but that life had lost its appeal for me long before Natalie came knocking at my front door.

Of course, when I spotted Cal, he was cuddled up with a bunny at the bar.

Walking over, I tried to ignore the way her hand moved up his thigh possessively. Were they always this brazen, and I'd simply ignored it? It was noon in a crowded hotel lobby, for crying out loud. There were kids around.

Walking up to the pair, I cleared my throat, causing the brunette perched on the barstool next to Cal to look me up and down before her eyes widened in recognition. "Aren't you Jaxon Slate?" Her voice contained a southern accent so sugary sweet it made my teeth ache from just listening to it.

Having been raised to be polite, I nodded. "Yes, I am."

Looking back to Cal, she smirked. "You know, I've always wanted to have a threesome with a pair of teammates."

Fixing her with a hard glare, my tone was cold. "Not interested."

Completely unphased, she continued, "Well, that's all right, sugar. I'm sure we could find another to join us."

Ignoring her, I asked Cal, "You ready to go?"

Pushing off the stool, he stood. "Yeah."

The bunny pouted, tugging his hand. "Are you sure you have to go?"

Turning so she wouldn't see my exaggerated eye roll, I heard Cal reply, "Yeah, but I'll be back later."

Walking toward the exit, Cal joked, "Thank God you said no to her. I did *not* want to cross swords with you, man."

I caught myself laughing. Now, *that* was my best friend. "I missed you."

Clapping me on the back as we made our way out of the lobby to meet the car I'd called, he responded, "I've missed you too, brother."

Half an hour later, we were dropped off on the far side of town at our destination. Cal looked up at the neon sign outside a simple brick building before turning to me, slightly shocked. "A tattoo parlor? I thought you were too strait-laced for this kinda thing."

Shrugging, I headed for the door. "I've changed."

"No kidding," he muttered under his breath. I knew he didn't only mean the idea of me getting a tattoo.

A bell above the door signaled our arrival to those working inside, and a heavily tatted woman greeted us. "Can I help you?"

Taking in all the various tattoo art options on the wall, I answered, "Yeah, I called earlier. Appointment for Slate?"

She nodded. "Yeah, you sent over a pic."

"I did. Are you able to do that?"

"We can. Mike over there will be your artist today." Eyeing my clean-cut look, only slightly marred by my three weeks of playoff beard growth, she asked, "First time?"

Glancing at Cal, I asked, "Is it that obvious?"

Cal laughed. "Dude, you're a walking billboard for the all-American boy."

"Yeah, well, not all of us are crazy enough to get our junk pierced," I shot back.

Raising an eyebrow, he smirked. "Don't knock it 'til you try it."

Shaking my head, I laughed. "Never gonna happen. A tattoo is enough."

Seriously, he asked, "You can tell me—is this like an early mid-life crisis?"

"What did I say about questions?"

"Fine. No questions." He sighed.

The tatted girl offered, "Just remember, the fleshier the spot, the less it'll hurt."

"Thanks. I'll keep that in mind," I replied.

Cal leaned in close to whisper, "Please tell me I'm not going to have to stare at your ass for hours."

Groaning—but inwardly glad we were working back toward our old, comfortable rapport—I shook my head. "Unfortunately for you, no."

The guy identified as Mike earlier called over to us that he was ready, and I headed for his chair, removing my shirt. Cal waggled his eyebrows suggestively, so I threw the shirt at his head, eliciting a snicker.

As I took a seat, Mike introduced himself. "Hey, I'm Mike."

Reaching my hand out to him, I replied, "Jaxon."

Mike shook my hand, continuing, "I've got your stencil ready. You wanted it on your chest, correct?"

Tapping my right pec, I confirmed, "Right here."

Cal uttered, "Bold move, man. Front and center." Giving him a look, he threw his hands up. "What? It was a statement, not a question."

"Keep your mouth shut, and you might learn something."

Mike cleaned my right pec before applying some petroleum jelly. Then, he took a piece of what looked like transfer paper with my chosen design and placed it face down. When he pulled it back, the design was fully displayed, ready to be inked.

Mike asked, "Does it look good? Placement and sizing?"

Handing me a mirror, I checked it both in the mirror and by glancing down at my chest. Turning to Cal, I asked, "What do you think? Look good?"

Cal's eyes widened as he took in the design. I'd sent over a scan of Charlie's footprints from the hospital, and they replicated them for my tattoo, adding her full name of Charlotte in the script underneath. It was simple yet meaningful. A piece of my baby girl near my heart, with me wherever I went, especially when I was on the road.

"Holy shit," Cal whispered.

"I'm sorry I wasn't able to say anything, and I still technically can't. This is the most I can give you."

"Family stuff," he said, still stunned.

"Family stuff," I confirmed.

Remorse filled Cal's face. "Aw, shit. I'm sorry, man. I was a real dick to you. If I'd known what was going on . . ."

"But you couldn't have. It's . . . complicated."

Cal quickly transitioned from remorse to panic. "Oh, shit. Did you get a bunny in trouble? Are you being extorted?" Then he caught himself. "Damn, no questions. Sorry."

"No, it's nothing like that."

"Phew," he blew out, visibly relieved.

"Hopefully, soon I can let you know more, but for now, my hands are tied."

"Understood, man. This is *huge*." He held his massive hands wide for emphasis.

"You have *no* idea." I chuckled.

Mike asked if I was ready to get started, and I nodded. Having played hockey my whole life and sustaining several major injuries over the years, I'd developed a high pain tolerance. The prick of the needle inserting ink under my skin was a mere annoyance.

Cal and I spent the time chatting about random stuff. I'd been distant and busy the entire season—not without good reason—but I was glad we were getting our relationship back on track.

We might be on separate paths in our personal lives, but we were teammates for life. That was a bond that could never be broken.

CHAPTER 27

Natalie

THE FIRST SIX WEEKS of Charlie's life were a blur. I'd forgotten how exhausting newborns could be, and I was never more grateful for the help that Liam and Amy provided, caring for the older kids.

Regardless of how tired I was, my heart was so full of love. Everyone was entranced by Charlie. She became the focus of our lives. The kids loved her, Amy and Liam adored her, and Jaxon, oh, she had Jaxon wrapped around her tiny little finger. Watching him with her was the highlight of my day. Able to experience the joy of new parenthood through his eyes, his love for her drove my love for him to new heights.

The playoff run was taxing on us all. Jaxon was far busier than he'd been most of the season, and we were all fully invested. The kids' bedtime evolved from a strict time of 8:30 PM to whenever the second period was over. I'd never been more stressed out while watching hockey in my life. Knowing how badly they wanted to win, I wanted it for them too. Some games, I was barely able to breathe.

Round two with New Orleans had gone to six games, but the Comets pulled off the series win. That brought them head-to-head with the Atlanta Aviators, the only team with a better record than the Comets in our conference, thus causing us to lose our home-ice advantage for the series.

The Conference Finals was a big deal. The Comets were four wins away from playing for the league championship. This was everything Jaxon had been working for his entire life, and I knew how important it was not just for him, but for his teammates, the Moreau family, and the city of Hartford.

This series with Atlanta seemed to hinge on who had the home ice for each game. Atlanta won the first two at home, putting the Comets into a two-game hole and leaving no room for error if they wanted to advance to the next round. The Comets rallied back to win the next two games on their home ice, tying the series at two apiece. Atlanta took Game 5 at home, so Game 6 in Hartford became do-or-die. If they lost, the dream was over for the Comets—at least, until next season. If they won, they would force a Game 7 in Atlanta, where it would be winner-take-all.

While Jaxon was upstairs getting ready to leave for the game, the kids had returned home from school. As soon as they'd dropped their gear, they'd run upstairs to change into the Comets jerseys Jaxon had gotten them for Christmas. Amelia and Jameson knew the importance of tonight's game, but Beau simply loved jumping up and down during games screaming, "Go, Daddy! Go hockey! Score!"

When we'd brought Charlie home, explaining to my almost four-year-old son that Jaxon was her daddy, Beau immediately began referring to him as Daddy. Jaxon never faltered, leaning into it, being there for the little boy who didn't know his own father. It was a blessing, to be honest. Jaxon was a better father to my kids than the man who biologically held that title.

The three of them were gathered together on the couch, clad in their Comets jerseys, when Jaxon made it downstairs, looking handsome as ever in a navy blue suit and matching tie. A smile broke out on his face when he saw the kids, exclaiming, "Well, if it isn't my biggest fans! You guys look great!"

Jameson's bond with Jaxon had grown significantly since the day Leo had shown up, and he whined, "I wish we could go."

Jaxon's eyes flashed up to mine, and my heart twisted. I knew he wanted us there, but I wasn't ready yet. The backlash of going public would totally eclipse the Comets and had the potential to be an unnecessary distraction for everyone.

Jaxon was a good man, and he covered for me, fist-bumping Jameson. "I know, buddy, but it's a school night. I'm sure there will be lots of games next season when you can all come." He was incredible. He didn't just shoulder the load, but he often carried it for me. We were all so blessed to have him in our lives.

Amelia hugged him. "Score a goal for me."

Laughing, Jaxon hugged her back, dropping a kiss to the top of her head. "I'll try, sweetheart, but I can't make any promises. It's not quite as easy as it looks."

Beau jumped up and down on the couch, yelling, "Catch me, Daddy!"

This was a game they played, where Beau jumped up and down while Jaxon reached out to grab him mid-jump. Jaxon obliged, grabbing him, and Beau's sweet giggles filled the room. Jaxon swung him around before pulling him close to blow raspberries into his neck, causing him to squeal even louder.

Setting him down on the ground, he told him, "Be good for Mommy, okay?"

Beau bobbed his head up and down in response. Jaxon made his way over to me, and I smoothed my hands over the lapels of his suit jacket. "Looking good, Mr. Slate."

That crooked smile of his, when trained on me, made the temperature in the room jump ten degrees. "Good luck kiss?"

Teasing him, I asked, "Do you really need luck? Isn't it more about skill?"

Lowering his head to mine, he whispered against my mouth, "A little luck never hurts." Then his lips were on mine, and I melted into him. We were so focused on hockey and Charlie that there hadn't been much time for us. There was something to be said for the non-physical intimacy we shared, but honestly, the physical part was hot enough to burn down the world most days.

Pushing against his chest, I broke the kiss, looking up into his eyes. "Go get 'em, big guy."

Winking, he responded, "Yes, ma'am."

Jaxon went to the bassinet where Charlie was sleeping, and I smiled as he squatted to kiss her head. He'd called me ma'am the first time we'd met. Never in my wildest dreams could I imagine that this was where we would be ten years later. He was everything I'd always wanted and had been under my nose this whole time. I may not have been available, but by some miracle, he was there, ready and waiting at the exact moment I'd needed him most.

If he wanted to believe in luck, maybe I was the lucky one.

My heart was about to explode, my breathing shallow after witnessing the Comets win in overtime to force a Game 7 in the Conference Finals of the playoffs. The stakes were at an all-time high as overtime was sudden death—the first to score a goal won. Nothing beat the adrenaline rush of celebrating a win as the puck hit the back of the net versus watching the clock tick down. Seeing the bench clear to celebrate always gave me goosebumps.

Charlie had thankfully slept through the high-stress extra time but was now beginning to whimper, ready for a late-night feeding before going down for the night. I took a few deep breaths to settle my heart rate before picking her up out of the swing and sitting down to nurse.

Maybe she'd been Jaxon's lucky charm tonight. Dressing her in her custom Comets jersey, I'd sent a pic to him about an hour before puck drop. He'd given the picture a love reaction, indicating that he'd seen it before taking the ice tonight. Jaxon had played an incredible game, netting two assists and the tying goal that had forced overtime.

Amy settled on the couch beside me and breathed out, "I still can't believe they pulled that off."

Nervous laughter escaped my lips. "I'm going to sleep well tonight."

We relaxed into companionable silence as the screen shifted from the commentators' final thoughts on the game to the post-game locker room interviews. My breath caught as the giant screen filled with an image of Jaxon—freshly showered with damp hair, shirtless. Usually, he was still in his skintight base layer for these types of interviews.

If I had to choose, he would always be shirtless. The other girls could eat their hearts out. He was all mine.

Amy's voice brought me out of my possessive haze, and I caught her pointing at the screen from my peripheral vision. "What is that?"

Turning to her instead of where she pointed, I asked, "What is what?" When she hesitated a moment too long, I felt the hairs on the back of my neck rise. Something was wrong, I could sense it.

I asked more insistently, "What, Amy?"

"On his chest."

Snapping my head toward the screen, that's when I saw it. What looked like baby footprints were tattooed on his chest, and something too small to see was written underneath.

I shook my head. No, it couldn't be.

Amy kept her voice calm. "Did you know about that?"

Gesturing to the baby beginning to fall asleep as she fed, I snapped at her, annoyed, "I've been a little busy, Ames."

Then the words being said reached me from the TV. That one female reporter who was always a little too flirty in the locker room asked him, "Can we ask about the tattoo?"

The camera zoomed in, and now there was no denying it. It was an exact copy of Charlie's footprints, with her name written in script right below. I froze, startling Charlie to stop eating and cry. I bounced her, shushing her, mentally on the edge of my seat, waiting to hear what his response would be.

My heart stopped when he smiled, addressing the aggressive reporter. "It's for my daughter."

Not realizing I'd been holding my breath until my vision began to blacken at the edges, I breathed out, "Oh my God."

Amy reached over. "Give me the baby."

I didn't even feel her take Charlie into her own arms as I stared at the screen, numb once again. How could he sit there, smiling, when he'd just sent my world crashing down? He'd promised we could move at my pace, going public with the news of our daughter only when I was ready. What other promises had he broken?

My mind was reeling. Only eight hours ago, we were all here, happier than we'd ever been, a family. Now, everything had changed.

The truth hit me that I was right from the start—*I* was the only one who could be counted on to put my family first.

It was up to me, and me alone, to protect my children. I was such a fool. I'd trusted him against my better judgment. I'd known better, but he'd charmed me into letting my guard down long enough to fall in love with him. Hell, I still loved him, but none of that mattered now. My focus reverted to my main objective—protecting my kids.

Jaxon was stronger than me, both mentally and physically. I knew deep down he would never lay his hands on me, but he wouldn't willingly walk away from what we'd built together these past few months. If given the chance, Jaxon would sweet talk me into seeing that this wasn't the end of the world. Of course, he would—it wasn't for him. I had much more at stake.

He'd *seen* how rattled I'd been at the mere threat of exposure from Leo months ago, and now he was the one to do it.

There was only one way left to protect my family. I had to push him away. I already knew it would shatter my heart, but my children were worth it.

Sitting in the living room, a single lamp lit next to my chair, I heard when Jaxon walked in less than an hour later. I wouldn't have heard him if I hadn't been waiting up. He'd had plenty of practice coming in quietly after games.

Silent and still, I didn't say a word as I heard him climb the stairs, assuming I was in bed. It didn't take long for him to realize I wasn't in there with a sleeping Charlie.

Coming down the back steps toward where I sat, I heard him whisper, "Nat? Is that you down there?"

I remained silent. I was still processing his blatant betrayal, but time was up. Watching as his feet hit the landing of the stairs, I closed my eyes for a second, taking a deep breath. They snapped open when I heard him say softly, "Hey, there you are."

The sight of Jaxon, clad in his navy suit pants and white button-up shirt open at the neck, broke my heart all over again. My heart hurt with the knowledge that no matter how much I loved him, it wasn't enough, and I would have to break his heart to get him to walk away.

There was no doubt in my mind I would mourn the life I could've had with this seemingly dependable man for the rest of my life.

Slowly, I stood on unsteady legs.

You can do this. Just think about the kids.

Hardening my heart, I calmly accused, "How could you?"

Understanding dawned in Jaxon's eyes, and he tried to come closer, but I put up my hands, effectively stopping him in his tracks. Running a hand through his dark hair, he began to explain, "Nat . . . I—"

I cut him off, "How could you be so careless? You *promised* me that we would go at my pace. Go public only when *I* was ready."

He emitted a sigh. "I'm sorry. We have to leave tomorrow, and taking a shower before the press meant I could get home sooner. I just wanted to be home with you."

Don't cry. Don't cry.

"You couldn't even warn me that you had our daughter's name and footprints tattooed on your chest?"

"I wanted a piece of her with me wherever I went. You know how often I travel."

A tiny piece of my heart melted, but then I threw up the protective walls around it, remembering the consequences his actions would have for my family. My voice was small as I whispered, "You've ruined everything."

Jaxon shoved his hands into his pockets. I knew he wanted to reach out for me—to pull me close into his strong embrace—but held himself in check, respecting the boundary I'd set. It was almost enough for me to falter. I'd never known a man to exhibit restraint like this.

Then he spoke, "It'll be all right. No one needs to know right now that you're her mother." The way he brushed it off hardened my resolve.

A scoff slipped past my lips. "How can you be so naïve? They know her first name, thanks to you. Anyone with a computer can pull up her birth record with both of our names attached!"

He froze. "I didn't even think about that."

"That's because you weren't thinking!"

Remorse filled Jaxon's face. "Baby, I made a mistake."

"One that will cost us everything."

Taking a step forward, he held out a hand to me. "We can figure this out. Let's go upstairs, get a good night's sleep, and then in the morning, we can make a plan on how to get ahead of this. You're tired."

Jaw clenched, I forced out, "Don't treat me like a child. This isn't going to magically disappear in the morning."

Dropping his outstretched hand, Jaxon sighed. "You're twisting my words."

"I don't think I am. I think you knew exactly what you were doing tonight."

"What are you talking about, Natalie? I messed up. I said I was sorry. I'm here, willing and ready to find a solution."

"Really? Finding a solution was getting a tattoo that practically broadcasts our daughter's existence to the world and then hiding it from me?"

"I wasn't hiding anything." God, the way he'd said that, he truly believed it.

I crossed my arms. "Then why didn't you tell me about it? It's not like a cut or a bruise you forgot about. You went out and had that done with intent. Then you didn't tell me, knowing full well I wouldn't see it because we're not having sex at the moment."

His jaw twitched, but he kept his tone calm, rational. "I live here, Natalie. I shower here. I change here. At any point in time, you could have seen it. I'm actually more surprised that you didn't notice it."

"Don't try to turn this around on me." Running both hands through his hair, I could tell he was frustrated that I was talking him in circles. Frustration was the first step. Now, I needed to push him to anger. Going in for the kill, I leveled him with a glare, my voice steady. "I think you did it on purpose."

"Did what on purpose?"

"Exposed our private life."

"Come on, Natalie. I told you. I wasn't thinking. It was an honest mistake." Exasperation filled his voice.

"No. You couldn't wait a few more weeks. You had to be the center of attention," I sneered.

"What are you talking about? I've kept this quiet from the start. I didn't even tell my own brother. Doesn't that tell you how highly I value your wishes?" My heart twisted as he pleaded his case.

I shook my head. "No, your actions tonight show me that you wanted absolute control over when and how the world found out about Charlie. About us."

"Natalie, we love each other."

"It's not enough." It was a miracle I'd kept my voice from shaking.

His control was beginning to fray, and I was pushing him toward the breaking point, exactly as I'd intended. Jaxon paused for a minute before he fired back, "Maybe I was a little tired of being your dirty little secret. Why are you so ashamed to be with me?"

There it is.

"I have four children now, and it's my job to protect them! Now, everyone will think I'm a whore who can't keep her legs closed when it comes to a fat bank account. All anyone will see is a woman who gets her claws into a rich and famous man so she can cash in on child support. The first time could be brushed off, but the second is where it becomes viewed as a pattern."

Jaxon threw his arms wide. "So, what, are we supposed to keep our relationship—our *daughter*—a secret forever? At some point, the truth was going to come out. I hate to break it to you, Natalie, because you've been holed up here for months, but nobody cares. Why should you?"

The words hit me, and I flinched as if I'd been physically struck. He didn't know me at all. He'd seen and heard about the physical and mental toll that living with every move being monitored and criticized had taken on me. I was living with PTSD from past storylines. God, how could I have been so stupid?

This is what you wanted. You pushed him too far. You knew there'd be consequences.

It didn't matter that I could see the shock on his face after he'd uttered those words—they cracked my heart wide open.

Jaxon rubbed his dark beard. "I didn't—"

Not letting him finish, I cut him off, my voice deadly calm. "Get out."

Jaxon shook his head. "No. We need to talk this out. Please, Nat."

"I said get out of my house. Now."

Watching the shift happen behind his whiskey eyes, even in the dim lighting, I knew I'd hurt him deeply.

Guess that makes two of us. Welcome to the party.

"This was always how it was going to end, wasn't it?" he accused. "With you pushing me away. Is this how you did it with Leo?"

Within an instant, I switched from soul-crushing sadness to pure rage. But instead of lashing out, I tilted my head, calling out, "Liam!"

Jaxon put his hands up. "No, I'll go. You can call off your guard dog."

Feeling the need to drive home the finality of my demand, I added, "Leave your keys."

He paused halfway to the door, turning to face me. "What about my daughter? Or was this your plan all along? You had the parental rights termination papers ready to sign months ago, but I promised I'd never take her from you. Maybe I should have been the one worried about having her taken from me. You do have a track record, after all."

Leveling him with a glare, I forced out through clenched teeth, "How long have you been holding onto that? All this time spent getting me to trust you when you never trusted me. You can reach out to Amy or Liam about Charlie. You and I are done, but I won't keep you from our daughter so long as you want to be a part of her life."

As he turned and walked the rest of the way to the door, I heard as he muttered under his breath, "Unbelievable."

The sound of his keys hitting the front hallway table before the door clicked closed shattered me. Even with my legs feeling like jelly, I made my way over and turned the deadbolt. Placing my back against the door, hugging my arms to my body, I slid down until my butt hit the floor. The tears burning behind my eyes for hours finally broke free, my body shaking as uncontrollable sobs racked my body.

I'd purposely pushed him too far, but it crushed me that he hadn't fought harder to stay. He'd walked away easily enough that I knew he wouldn't come back. That was the moment I knew with certainty that I would never recover from this loss.

There would always be a Jaxon-sized hole in my heart.

Chapter 28

Jaxon

"Fuck!" I shouted as soon as I opened the door to my dark, empty house.

I fucking *knew* she was going to find a way to push me away, but I'd been so blinded by our love that I'd ignored that nagging thought every time it had popped into my mind. Never could I have predicted she would push me past my breaking point to get me to say things I didn't mean. Words I knew I couldn't take back now echoed in my brain.

I hate to break it to you, Natalie, because you've been holed up here for months, but nobody cares.

Had I actually said that? I'd been frustrated, and she'd twisted my words around so I couldn't get my point across—that I'd messed up, and I was sorry. Then I saw my life flash before my eyes when she'd told me to leave and not return. Fear blinded me at the thought of losing Charlie, and I'd snapped, comparing our relationship to the one she'd had with her ex.

She'd pushed me, but I was the one who broke.

Nothing could mask the anger I had with myself. I was fooling myself if I didn't know that getting this tattoo would get me into trouble. I just had no idea how much it would cost me. A moment of carelessness, and my life went up in flames faster than I could blink.

I wasn't thinking when I'd showered before the press entered the locker room.

I wasn't thinking when I didn't throw a shirt over my bare chest.

I wasn't thinking when I'd assumed that a vague response about the tat being for my daughter couldn't be traced back to Natalie.

No matter her response, this was my fault. I mentally retraced my steps, from talking about my daughter, to not wearing a shirt, to not telling Natalie about the tattoo, to finally, the conclusion that getting the tattoo was the biggest mistake of them all. If I had waited, none of this would have happened. No tattoo, and I'd be next door right now, my family still intact.

"Fuck!" I yelled out again, this time acting on my anger and punching the wall, my fist going right through the drywall, leaving a gaping hole. My right fist throbbed, the knuckles scraped and bleeding lightly when I pulled it back out of the hole in the wall. The rational part of my brain told me that I needed to ice it—so it didn't swell and impair my ability to play in Game 7—but the emotional side said fuck it. I wanted to feel the pain of blowing up my life.

Walking into the kitchen, I poured a tall glass of scotch, which only served to remind me of Natalie and that fateful day that she'd shown up on my doorstep. Throwing it back, I let the liquor burn my throat before going to bed, praying I would wake up to find that this night had just been a bad dream.

My legs and lungs burned as I pushed myself to the limit, shift after shift on the ice. My body was there, running on autopilot, but my heart wasn't in the game. If we lost the game, the worst that would happen was that the season would be over.

I'd already lost everything that mattered to me. This was nothing in comparison.

Barely functional, going through the motions—relying purely on muscle memory—everyone could tell. Cal yelled from the defense's side of the bench, "Jaxon! You gotta help out on the backcheck, man. I'm not always gonna be able to save your ass if you keep getting stripped like that."

In my current mental state, I didn't trust myself not to say something I would regret to my teammate and best friend, so I just nodded. Coach leaned in to talk low to my ear, "You need a break?"

"No." My voice was devoid of all emotion.

That wasn't enough for Coach. "Fine, but if you continue to be a liability out there, I'm going to bench you."

"Whatever."

For the first time in my career, I didn't care. I didn't care if I sat the rest of the game. I didn't care if we lost. I didn't care if this was the last game of my career. Hockey no longer defined who I was. It was a job and nothing more. If it were gone tomorrow, I would replace it with another job.

What I couldn't replace in my life was Natalie.

"Slate's line out on the ice!" I heard Coach shout from behind me.

Hopping the boards, I went out with Benji on my right and Levi on my left. Catching the puck on my stick, I skated hard toward the Atlanta goalie before taking a bad angle shot that went wide, ricocheting hard off the boards, creating a rush going the other way. Before I knew it, the puck was in the back of our net. Our goaltender, Reed, slammed his goalie stick against the post, breaking it in half, punctuating his frustration.

Levi bumped me hard. "Hey, hotshot. I was wide fucking open."

"Fuck off, rookie." I skated back to the bench, where a red-faced Coach waited for me.

Here we go.

"Slate! You're done!" he screamed.

Like I cared anymore. Without a word, I sat down on the bench, watching the rest of the third period play out. The final score was Atlanta Aviators 1, Connecticut Comets 0. My mistake leading to a goal the other way was the only goal in the entire game. I felt nothing as I watched the Atlanta bench clear to celebrate with their goalie as the buzzer sounded.

Tradition dictated that every playoff series ended with a handshake line between the teams at center ice—the ultimate show of sportsmanship. Taking my place at the front of the line as the team's captain, I congratulated those on the other side, receiving words of encouragement from veterans on the opposing team in return. When a young player for Atlanta thanked me for the assist, I remained expressionless, letting the jab slide.

Cal skated in line behind me, and when I didn't respond, he nudged me. "What the hell is wrong with you, man? You were on fire last game, but today it's like you fucking hate the game and are just collecting a paycheck."

"I don't want to talk about it," I barked back. Sensing the tone, he dropped it.

Either everyone was pissed at me for my costly mistake, or I was giving off major don't-fuck-with-me vibes, because not a single teammate bothered to talk to me for the rest of the night, including on our three-hour flight back to Hartford.

This was the new theme of my life, apparently. I fuck up, and everyone hates me for it. Might as well get used to being alone.

Despite landing at 2 AM, sleep eluded me when I got home. I just sat in my living room, staring out the window toward Natalie's house, waiting for daybreak. As soon as the sun peeked above the eastern horizon, I grabbed my phone.

Jaxon: *I'm home. I'd like to see my daughter today.*

Holding my breath, I prayed that Natalie wouldn't punish me by withholding our daughter, regardless of what she'd said the night she'd kicked me out. She was angry with me—correction, she was downright pissed with me—so there was no telling what she might do.

I wanted to believe that she wasn't so mad that she'd keep me from Charlie, but there was some truth behind the words she'd provoked from my mouth that night—she had cut and run in the middle of the night with her kids once before.

Gripping my phone tightly in my hand, I felt the sweat gathering on the back of my neck the longer I waited for a response from Amy.

Were they even still next door?

Had they left, knowing I was out of town?

Was my daughter gone forever?

My phone finally buzzed, and the words blurred as I tried to read them with how badly my hand was shaking.

Amy: She's eating right now. I can bring her over in a bit. You around all day?

Jaxon: You haven't heard? I'm out of a job til September.

Amy: Sorry, we didn't watch.

That crushing blow cemented where we stood. She was so done with me that she hadn't even watched my game. Just like that, she'd completely cut me out of her life. Was I going to be co-parenting Charlie with Amy as a proxy for Natalie for the next eighteen years?

You did this to yourself. Now, you suffer.

While I sat and waited for an audience with my daughter, I realized she wasn't the only one I'd missed desperately these past seventy-two hours. I'd missed Amelia's sweet smile, Jameson's excitement, and Beau's giggles.

Above all, I'd missed their mother. She'd lit up my life during these past few months when she'd truly been mine.

Having had a taste of life at Natalie's side and then losing it was worse than never knowing what it was like at all.

Hearing the light knock on the door, I ran to open it. Eager to hold my daughter after a hellish three days, I was *not* expecting to see Liam on the other side of the door. At least he had a stroller, indicating he'd brought Charlie with him.

Holding open the door, I allowed him entry as he rolled the stroller past the threshold. Closing the door behind him, I muttered, "I was expecting Amy."

Parking the stroller, he looked over his shoulder. "Yeah, well, you and I need to talk."

Sarcasm colored my words. "Oh, goodie." Brushing past where he stood in my entryway, I reached into the stroller and pulled Charlie close to my chest, bouncing her in my arms. Holding her soft weight was like a balm for my battered soul, but my heart was still just as broken.

"I love you, sweet girl," I whispered against the top of her head.

Liam eyed the hole I'd left in the wall, one corner of his mouth quirking up. "Redecorating?"

"Something like that." Walking further into the house, I made my way to the couch, ready to make up for lost time with Charlie. Not sparing another glance at Liam, I added, "I'm not really in the mood for a lecture, so if that's what you're here for, I'm not interested."

He followed me into the living room, sitting in the armchair, assessing me. "You look like shit."

"Jesus, Liam. What do you want? To gloat? Because if that's the case, you can see yourself out. I just want to sit here and hold the only piece of Natalie I have left."

"You try reaching out to her?"

I scoffed. "She made it clear when she kicked me out that she was done with me. I'm not a glutton for punishment."

Pausing for a minute, Liam replied, "You're an idiot."

"Excuse me?"

"I said you're an idiot."

Annoyed now, I snapped, "I'm not deaf. I heard what you said. I'm just wondering if you'd care to elaborate on that?"

"Do you think you're going to win her back by sitting over here licking your wounds?"

I glared at him. "What else am I supposed to do? She told me to leave and not come back. She didn't care what I had to say. I made a huge mistake and don't have a leg to stand on."

"Looking at you and having been with her these past three days, she's just as miserable as you are."

My heart squeezed, a tiny seed of hope taking root deep inside. "She's miserable?"

Leaning forward on his knees, Liam was direct. "Look, I've never been your biggest fan, but part of that falls on me. I viewed you as a threat because it was always my job to play the role of Natalie's protector. When you showed up, it was hard to swallow that I was becoming more of a background character in her life. After some internal reflection, I realized that she would never need me the same way she needs you. I was merely a placeholder."

Huffing, I countered, "Well, looks like you got what you wanted. She doesn't want me."

"Shut up and let me finish." Liam looked skyward before continuing, "I've seen what you bring to the table. You made her happy. The Natalie I knew from long ago was suddenly back in my life. She was present for her kids. She started taking care of herself again, and she was glowing. You have no idea how much I've missed the sound of her laughter. You did that."

Looking down at Charlie in my arms, I smiled. "Her laughter is the first thing that drew me to her. I heard that sound, and I had to know where it was coming from. Then I saw her, and her smile sealed the deal."

Liam continued, "Beyond that, she began to stand on her own two feet, finding an inner strength that none of us knew she possessed. You made her a stronger person. Leo tore her down, but you built her up."

"I've loved watching her find herself." A small smile crept onto my face, even through the gut-wrenching pain.

"The bottom line, Jaxon, is that I thought my brother broke her with his manipulation and emotional abuse tactics, but what you did was worse. You shattered her heart."

Way to twist the knife, Liam.

"You love her." It was a statement, not a question.

My eyes snapped to his. "You know I do. I always have."

"Then you have to show her."

Frustrated, I blew out a breath. "How? She won't even talk to me."

"Talking to her is useless right now. You didn't ruin this with your words, did you?"

Rubbing the spot on my chest where the tattoo that ruined everything was permanently situated under my shirt, I shook my head. "No."

"Natalie has been fed so many lies over the years that words are meaningless. Actions will always trump words with her."

"Actions," I repeated.

"She's withdrawn to try and protect herself. She says it's for the kids, but she was hurt so badly by my jackass brother that she's afraid it will happen again."

"So, she's pushing me away. With good reason. I did fuck up," I admitted.

"Yeah, you did, but you've been a persistent motherfucker throughout all of this, so don't tell me you're just going to let her go now."

Trying to think of something—anything—I could *do* to show her how much I loved her, I remembered what Amy had told me when she'd come here wanting to help me win Natalie over.

Nat is a hopeless romantic.

What would one of her fictional male characters do if they'd mucked things up this badly?

That's when it hit me.

"I need to make a grand gesture."

Liam sat back in his chair. "See? I knew you were smarter than you looked."

A grand gesture.

What could I possibly do to *show* Natalie that I was sorry—that I'd meant every promise I'd made—but simply was human and had made a mistake? What was she most afraid of?

Clear as day, I could picture her here, on this couch, with parental termination papers in an envelope, ready for me to sign. How she was shaking in the kitchen just thinking about someone seeing her in my house when my food had been delivered.

She wasn't afraid of people knowing about us being together. She was scared of losing her kids.

I knew exactly what I needed to do.

CHAPTER 29

Natalie

ONE WEEK. THE WORST week of my life, and I'd had some pretty bad ones over the years.

For seven days, I'd sat and nursed my broken heart.

As soon as I'd sent the kids to school each day, I'd crawled into bed and cried—the same routine every day—making sure to be up and about by the time they got home. They'd lost Jaxon in their daily life and couldn't afford to lose me, too.

Watching as Liam and Amy took turns taking Charlie next door for time with her father, I'd forced exactly what I hadn't wanted—two separate families. It had become a necessary sacrifice to shield them all.

If it was the right thing to do, why didn't I feel better about it?

Barely functioning, I was a hollow shell. Physically present, my mind was elsewhere, replaying the events of the night I'd kicked Jaxon out of my life for good. Liam tried in vain to get me to eat—even if just for Charlie.

I hardly cared that my milk was drying up. Resorting to pumping so she could spend time with her father, each session produced less.

Her father.

God, I finally thought I'd found the perfect man to give my kids a real family. And what did I go and do? Shove him out the door.

Each day I questioned if I'd made the right choice. Especially when Beau cried, begging to go next door to see his daddy, not understanding why Charlie could go but he couldn't.

I could see the questions in Amy's eyes as I struggled, but she didn't push. She knew my history well enough to know that I could be stubborn when protecting myself and the kids.

What if I said I was sorry?

No.

I'd forced Jaxon to say things he couldn't take back and I couldn't un-hear. It didn't matter if I was sorry for pushing him—he'd said them. They were there in the back of his mind, ready to be fired off when provoked.

That also didn't change the fact that he'd stayed away.

The words he'd said countless times haunted me in my loneliness.

I'll always come back.

Another empty promise, it would seem. The Comets were eliminated from the playoffs less than forty-eight hours after I'd kicked him out. Jaxon was done playing for the next few months and right next door. He had let me down, just like almost everyone else in my life.

Leaving Leo had given me strength, but pushing Jaxon away had crip-pled me. A huge piece of my heart was missing. He'd taken it with him when he'd walked out that door. I finally understood what it was supposed to feel like when you ended a relationship. It hurt like hell.

Hearing the doorbell, I held my breath. Could it be Jaxon? Had he final-ly come back like he promised he always would? Shaking in anticipation, I sat in the living room while Charlie was sleeping in the swing nearby.

Amy's voice called down the front hallway, "Nat, you have a visitor."

My voice trembled. "I'm in the living room."

Amy walked into the living room, where I sat, and my heart fractured yet another degree when, instead of Jaxon, it was his mother who walked in behind her. Blinking back the disappointed tears that threatened to spill over, I stood, acknowledging her. "Mrs. Slate."

Waving a hand, she responded, "Mrs. Slate is my mother-in-law. It's Shannon, sweetie."

I nodded. "Shannon. Of course. If you're looking for Jaxon, I'm afraid he's not here." God, it hurt to say his name out loud.

Walking forward slowly, Shannon made her way closer to me. Amy glanced at me, gauging if I was okay, and when I nodded in response, she left us alone.

Minding my manners, I gestured toward the couch. "Would you care to sit, Shannon? Can I get you something to drink?"

She took a seat on the couch. "Nothing for me." Patting the spot beside her, she invited, "Join me."

Well, this is awkward.

Sinking back down onto the couch beside her, I wrung my hands. What did you say to the mother of the man whose heart you'd broken? What did she want from me? Had he sent her?

Clearing her throat, Shannon began, "I heard that you and Jaxon had a little disagreement."

Unable to stop the scoff that slipped from my mouth, I muttered, "Is that what he's calling it?"

"Not in so many words. Actually, he told me it was none of my business," she replied.

"With all due respect, Shannon, I don't want to talk about it either. It's a personal matter."

Smiling, she took my hand. "Of course. I didn't come here for him. I came here for you."

The shock of that knocked my world off kilter.

She was here for me?

She was *Jaxon's* mom, not mine.

I was just some woman he'd knocked up and who had then stomped on his heart. Trying to find the words, all I managed was, "Um . . ."

Squeezing my hand, she continued, "I'm here for you. If you need someone to watch Charlie while you take a nap, I'm here. If you need me to whip up a week's worth of dinners so that you don't have to worry about it, consider it done."

There had to be a catch. There's always a catch.

"But why?" I asked, stunned.

Shannon didn't hesitate. "Above all, I'm a mom, and moms take care of their families. No matter what happens between you and Jaxon, you and Charlie are my family now. You will fall under my protection as a mom for as long as I'm living. Nothing can change that."

A mom.

She wanted to be my mom.

I'd become a mom so young myself.

I was the one who had always taken care of everyone else.

I'd put my children's well-being before my own wants and needs.

Shannon was showing me unconditional love—something I'd never known from my own parents. I'd been a pawn in their social games, and here was Jaxon's mom, taking me in, even after I'd broken her son's heart. The weight of that hit me like a ton of bricks, and I couldn't contain the whimper that broke free before tears flooded my eyes.

Gathering me in her arms, Shannon held me close, stroking my hair the way a mom would to comfort their child. The same way I'd comforted my own children over the years.

This was what I'd needed for the last ten years. I'd needed a mom, someone to look out for me with no agenda of their own, who was happy if I was happy. Ready and waiting on the sidelines for when they were needed.

When I had no more tears left, I pulled back, wiping at my swollen, red eyes. "I'm sorry."

She looked at me with understanding, handing me a tissue. "Sweetie, there's nothing to be sorry about. Life is complicated. There are no right answers. You do the best that you can in the moment and hope for the best."

Doubt crept into my mind. "What if I've made a mistake?"

"You want my advice?"

"Desperately," I begged.

"As someone who's been married for thirty-five years, let me offer you this. No relationship is without its ups and downs. There are days when I want to strangle Michael, and he feels the same about me. You find a way to work through it because you love each other."

"We crossed a line. I'm not sure it can be uncrossed."

"Well, if that's the case, you find a way to move forward. Even if that's separately. You have to do what makes *you* happy and no one else."

"You're really here for me? No matter what?" I asked in disbelief.

"Absolutely. Even moms need a mom sometimes." She tucked a strand of hair behind my ear.

"Thank you, Shannon. It means more to me than you will ever know."

"Of course, us girls have to stick together," she said with a wink.

Shannon spent some time cuddling Charlie while I took a shower, and then she made dinner for us before she left. When she was gone, I took some time to reflect on our interaction this afternoon. Shannon was self-less, putting my well-being first, even if that meant I wasn't with her son.

Maybe that was the silver lining. I'd given up Jaxon, but I gained a mom. Something small to comfort me after I'd gone and blown up my life.

It had been two weeks.

Two weeks, and I was still living in this self-inflicted purgatory without Jaxon in my life. The reality was sinking in that maybe this was what the rest of my life would feel like, and the sooner I picked myself back up off the ground, the better it would be for all of us.

But I wasn't ready to do that yet, fully prepared to stew in my misery a while longer.

Knock knock.

Liam had taken Charlie next door, Amy was at work, and the kids were at school, so there was no one else home to answer the door. Padding barefoot to the door, still in my pajamas, I no longer cared what anyone might think of my unkempt appearance.

The irony of that was not lost on me. I'd lost the man I loved because I'd cared more about what others thought of me, and now that he was gone, it didn't matter.

I opened the door, and my heart stopped. Almost as if I'd dreamed him into reality, there stood Jaxon.

He came back.

No.

Don't get your hopes up.

Don't you dare.

I was so weary from the past two weeks that I leaned against the doorframe, taking my time soaking in the gorgeous man before me. His face was clean-shaven for the first time since before Charlie was born, and I'd forgotten how truly handsome his face was. Wearing a plain white T-shirt and khaki shorts, he looked so good, his body filling out his clothes so well, that it took little to no imagination to see how sculpted he was underneath.

It was difficult to believe that only two weeks ago, I'd been able to call him mine. He would probably still be mine if I wasn't so damn stubborn. But he was here now. That had to mean something, right? I'd learned long ago that hope was a useless emotion, so I shoved it down deep when it began to rise within me.

My voice sounded strangled, even to my own ears. "What do you want, Jaxon?"

Unable to read the emotion in his eyes, it was as if the weeks apart had killed the connection we'd once had. Jaxon shoved one hand into his pocket, asking, "Can I come in?"

God, there was nothing I wanted more, but I was still so hurt. I hugged myself tight against the fresh wave of pain, shaking my head. "I don't think that's a good idea."

"All right." He nodded, bringing forth a manilla envelope. "I needed to give this to you. It's important."

Hesitating, I reached out to take it. Opening the metal clasp and pulling out the papers inside, bile rose in my throat as I read the header—*Child Custody Agreement for Charlotte Rose Slate.*

I had no words.

If losing Jaxon had broken me, losing Charlie—the one thing he'd *promised* he would never do—would kill me. Looking up at him, I tried to say the words but kept opening my mouth and closing it, never fully forming the thought I wanted to convey.

That's when I realized he was here. Alone.

Pushing past him, I ran out onto the circular driveway, regardless of my lack of footwear. I scanned left and right before whipping around, accusing him, "Where is she?" Then panic set in. "Where *is* she?!"

Jaxon was calm. Of course, he was. He'd fooled me all over again. He reached an arm out to me, but I backed away. His tone was soft. "Nat, let's go in the house."

Shaking my head, my mind raced with the possibilities. "No! You tell me where my daughter is. Right. Now!"

"She's asleep. Next door. With Liam."

My eyes went wide. "With *Liam*!"

"She's safe."

"If you think you can just waltz over here after having stolen my daughter from me, you've got another thing coming. I'll spend every single penny I have fighting you in court."

Jaxon looked at me with a confused look before insisting, "Natalie. Read. The. Papers."

"I don't need to read them! I've got identical copies in triplicate in my safe!" I screamed.

"You can add these to those."

This was beginning to feel like an out-of-body experience, and my voice jumped a few octaves. "Are you out of your fucking mind? There's no way I'll accept this as is!" He began to chuckle, and I saw red. "Are you *laughing*?"

Putting his hands up, Jaxon tried again. "I'm just saying, you might want to read the papers before you go silent-dog-whistle on me. Merely a suggestion."

Narrowing my eyes in distrust, I glared at him, but something deep down forced me to pull the papers all the way out of the envelope. I scanned the legal jargon, and that's when I saw it—*Full legal custody shall be awarded to the mother, Natalie Remington.*

I read it over three times, making sure I wasn't imagining those words.

My eyes burned with unshed tears, and I begged them not to fall. No, I would not cry in front of him as I grieved the loss for my daughter. She'd be just like her older siblings without a full-time dad. He'd given up on her, the same way he'd given up on us. Not that I'd give him much of a choice. I would have to be enough for her, for all of them.

Nodding, my eyes were cast downward, not trusting my emotions if I looked at him directly. "I understand."

Jaxon tipped my chin up carefully so that I was staring right into his gorgeous brown eyes. "Do you?"

"Yes. You tried the dad thing, but it wasn't for you. That's okay. It's better to make a clean break now before she remembers you."

He cocked his head. "I'm not going anywhere."

"Then why—why did you do this?"

He smiled. "Nat, I made a promise to you. That I'd *never* take her from you. I keep my promises. Always. I want to be a part of Charlie's life, but you will always have the power to set the terms. I trust you. I've seen how you'd put your own life on the line for your kids. How could I not want that for our daughter?"

One word stood out among the rest. "You trust me? After everything?"

Jaxon pulled me into his arms, gently at first. When I didn't immediately draw back, he tightened his hold. My mind raced, but I was frozen to the spot. In such close proximity, I could smell his intoxicating scent. The one I'd found myself shamelessly sniffing from Charlie's clothes when she came home from his house each day.

Feeling his hand on my cheek, I closed my eyes, leaning into his touch as he whispered, "I will always trust you."

Opening my eyes, I searched Jaxon's. Shining through them was hope—the one thing I'd tamped down inside of myself for years. I would always have emotional scars, but he'd been patient with me and helped heal the wounds they'd stemmed from.

Living without him for two weeks, they'd been the worst couple of weeks of my entire life. Worst-case scenario, I knew I could live without him. I would survive, but I'd never truly be living the way I had been when he was by my side.

I swallowed, my voice thick with emotion. "I'm sorry you lost the game."

His other hand joined the first, both now cupping my face. "Don't you get it? I don't care about the game."

"You don't? But you love it."

"Baby, I love *you* more. You, and Charlie, Amelia, Jameson, and Beau. All five of you are my world. I choose you. Every time."

Testing the words on my tongue, I asked, "You choose me?"

Jaxon smiled. "I knew the first time I saw you that my world was forever changed. I remember thinking I would do just about anything to see your smile, hear your laugh. You were real when so much of my world was artificial. Back then, I only knew what you'd shared on the surface. But now that I know what's underneath? I want all of you. I want to raise Charlie together with her older siblings. I want to be there for all of you every single day if you'll let me. I want all of you forever."

I stared at him, repeating breathlessly, "Forever."

"I've had some time these past few weeks to reflect on our relationship. Not only this past year, but the past ten years we've known each other. I used to curse the timing. That I'd met you too late, and it could have been me in your life if I had been just a year or two earlier. I know now that I wasn't enough for you back then. I was this eighteen-year-old kid—yes, kid—who barely could take care of himself and had a one-track mind focused on hockey. I wish I could erase all the pain you've suffered, but I needed that time to become the man you truly deserved. There was a reason I'd never dated seriously or entertained the idea of settling down. I was always waiting for you. It didn't matter that you were unavailable. No one could compare to the standard for women you'd created in my mind. And then, one day, the universe rewarded my patience when a little boy threw his ball over my fence. Someone was looking out for me that day because you fell into my lap and gave me everything I'd always wanted but never thought I could have. There's only one more thing left to do."

Jaxon stepped back, reaching into his pocket before pulling out a velvet box. Knowing where this was headed, I yelled, "Stop!"

He looked like a kicked puppy, but he did stop, nodding. "All right."

Reaching for him, I clarified, "No! I mean, you can't do it like this. Look at me!"

Scanning me from head to toe, his smile was genuine. "You've never looked more beautiful."

I blushed, gesturing to my appearance. "I'm outside barefoot, in my pajamas, smelling like baby spit-up." A hand went to my unwashed hair, thrown into a bun. "I can't even remember the last time I took a shower. This can't be how this happens." Looking down, I added, "I'm not even wearing a bra!"

"I've noticed." He smirked, his gaze lowering to my nipples, visible through the thin fabric.

"*Not* funny."

Letting him pull me back into his arms, I melted into the embrace I'd craved while we were apart. "Baby, I love you just like this. This is you, the real you. The you that no one out there gets to see but me. We did everything backwards, but I wouldn't change any of it. I don't care where we are, if no one knows or everyone knows. If you want me to put it in skywriting or sign an NDA, either way is fine. All I want is you."

"Are you sure?" A hot tear rolled down my cheek.

Jaxon wiped it away with his thumb. "I love you, Natalie. Something deep inside my soul knew the day we met that you were my future. I just didn't understand then how that would ever be possible. Even if it took twenty years to find our way together, you were always worth the wait."

"Jaxon." His name was a whisper on my lips. I didn't know how to tell him how much he meant to me, so I decided to show him.

I ran my fingers into his hair, which he'd started wearing longer again, simply because I'd mentioned I had liked it. Jaxon closed his eyes at the contact. Raising up on my toes, I pulled his mouth down to mine. He sighed into my mouth, and I took advantage, teasing into his mouth, tasting as his arms tightened around me, pouring all the tenderness of his words into this kiss—the promise of unconditional love combined with the knowledge that he'd fought for me, for us.

This was my second chance, and I knew I had to grab hold with both hands.

Gently, I broke the kiss, and with my eyes still closed, I felt him drop his forehead to mine. Taking that ultimate leap of faith, I uttered a single word, "Yes."

Jaxon's head left mine, and I glanced up to find hope shining in his eyes. They searched mine. "Yes?"

"Yes," I repeated, smiling so hard my cheeks hurt.

Picking me up around the waist, Jaxon spun us around. Wrapping my arms around his neck, I hugged him close to me. After all these years lost, I finally knew where I belonged—here, with this man, in the place I called home.

The road had been full of pain and heartbreak, but if this was where it had led me, I wouldn't change a thing.

He set me down as I laughed, finally free of those invisible chains that had kept me prisoner for far too long. I cupped his face with my hands. "You came back."

Jaxon kissed me long and slow before breaking away. "Of course, I came back. I will *always* come back. That's the deal. You're stuck with me now."

Those words hit me, and I couldn't hold back a moment longer. I buried my head in his chest and let the tears flow. He was steadfast, as always, stroking my hair and murmuring soothing words as I wept, wetness soaking his T-shirt. These tears were washing away the past, leaving me free to pursue my future.

This was how it was supposed to be. I'd finally found real love with a man who loved all my children as his own. Nothing was too big to overcome. It would take some getting used to, being truly loved for who I was, but it was time to be happy. To give my children the loving family they deserved.

Maybe this fallen princess had finally gotten her happily ever after.

Epilogue

Jaxon

Four Months Later

The roar of the crowd was deafening. There was nothing that could compare to the excitement that came with a Comets home opener.

Taking the ice before the home crowd for warmups, their excitement was contagious. Going through my warmup routine, I made stops for kids with signs asking to play rock, paper, scissors for a puck or even requesting a selfie. I'd always been a sucker for our youngest fans.

The most important stop along my way was at the curved glass in the corner, the open space behind it, empty of seats where the players' families stood.

For the first time in my career, my family was waiting there for me.

Amelia and Jameson stood shoulder to shoulder, smiling wide as I made my way over, flipping each a practice puck over the glass. Beau stood on a chair to see over the boards, bouncing up and down, banging on the glass to get my attention until I gave him a fist bump through the glass. Next to them, holding my daughter—carrying my name beyond where it was stitched on the back of the jersey she wore—was the girl of my dreams.

Natalie Slate. My wife.

Natalie beamed back at me, holding Charlie up to the glass. Tiny noise-canceling headphones protected Charlie's ears from the crowd noises. When she saw me, her pudgy hands reached out toward me, and I waved as she smiled at me.

This moment was better than I could have ever imagined.

The start of the season usually meant that our lives were about to become busier than ever when it came to games and travel. But compared to the whirlwind of the past few months, it would be a refreshingly slower pace.

After coming clean to my best friends and teammates, Natalie and I got married in July in an intimate ceremony at the lake behind my parents' house in Minnesota. Since no one had put two and two together about our relationship after the tattoo debacle, we'd decided to go public with our wedding photos.

Now, I wasn't one to brag and say, "I told you so," but the news of our relationship, our marriage, and even our daughter, was surprisingly well-received by the public. As it turned out, it's not quite as gratifying to tear down happy people, and that's exactly what we were. The city of Hartford ate it up, loving that the hometown princess married their favorite hockey hero.

Natalie's inner radiance had been on full display since we'd shared our lives publicly, and the sky hadn't come crashing down. She was free in a way I'd never seen, and I was so proud of the progress she'd made in coming out of her shell. She'd even returned to wearing her hair blonde—her choice, for the first time. It's more of a honey color instead of champagne this time around, and it suited her. She could dye it purple for all I cared, and I would still love her with every cell in my body.

It only took eleven years, but I'd finally found my way to scoring the princess, and we'd built an incredible family together.

There was only one thing left to do. Win a championship with my family by my side.

The quest began tonight, and I was ready to put up a hell of a fight.

As Liam had once said—I was a persistent motherfucker.

For a bonus scene from Natalie and Jaxon's wedding, you can find it under the Bonus Scenes tab at https://sienatrapbooks.com/

The saga of the Remington Royals continues with Liam and Amy's story in *Playing Pretend with the Prince*

Acknowledgements

To my husband, for being my biggest supporter, telling me that I should write a book and persisting in that belief for ten years before I finally sat down and did it. Thank you for reading every word I continue to write, making funny growling sounds and making me laugh.

To my children, for being excited to see my book listings and telling anyone who asks what I write that it's for "adults only".

To my parents, who have had my back since Day 1, supporting me in every career venture until I finally found the one that is my true passion. Dad, thanks for stepping in as tech support. Mom, thank you for fostering my love for reading, especially in the romance genre.

To Katie, my friend and editor, thank you for scanning every line meticulously, for being only a text away to work out how a sentence or idea should work until it makes sense from a reader's point of view.

To Nina, my proofreader, thank you for being the punctuation police because that is *so* not my strong suit, and for supporting my work, helping build me up, and pushing me to keep moving forward.

To my Vipers hockey moms, thank you for being my biggest cheer-leaders, giggling over plotlines at our kid-free lunches.

To my readers, thank you for taking a chance on my story. Hearing from you how my stories impact you individually makes this all worthwhile.

About the Author

Siena is originally from Pittsburgh, Pennsylvania, where a love of sports is bred into a girl's DNA. Her love of romance novels came early as well. She would often accompany her romance reviewer mom to book lover's and romance writer's conventions, where she sat in on workshops and met numerous best-selling authors. It wasn't long before she was filling notebooks with her own stories, which often starred herself and a certain real-life prince.

As luck would have it, she met and married a handsome athlete instead. After several temporary residencies in multiple states and Germany, they finally settled in Michigan, the land where youth hockey reigns supreme.

Her stories no longer feature herself, but draw from her past experiences as an educator, businesswoman, fashion consultant, and world traveler when creating her strong heroines. "Oh yes," she says with a wink and a smile, "There are bits of me in all of them." Now she spends her days writing happily ever afters for fictional characters and her evenings at the local hockey arenas cheering for her three children.

Siena loves to hear from her readers, you can email her at: siena.trap.books@gmail.com

More Books By Siena Trap

Remington Royals Series

Scoring the Princess
Playing Pretend with the Prince
Feuding with the Fashion Princess

Connecticut Comets (Hockey) Series

Coming in 2024
Bagging the Blueliner
(Cal's story)
Surprise for the Sniper
(Benji's story)
Second-Rate Superstar
(Braxton's story)

Made in the USA
Columbia, SC
06 November 2024

45421243R00221